Rayda Jacobs

SACHS STREET

Kwela Books

Cover picture © Gadidja Majiet
Cover design by Nazli Jacobs
Book design by Nazli Jacobs
Set in Palatino
Printed and bound by NBD
Drukkery Street, Goodwood, Western Cape
First edition, first printing 2001

ISBN 0-7957-0105-5

ACKNOWLEDGEMENTS

Always, even in a book of fiction, or perhaps especially in a book of fiction, there are people who sail in and out of your life and contribute to the telling of a tale.

My thanks go first to Fawzia Taliep, for her wonderful stories of life in Sachs Street in the 1950s. To her sister, Gadidja, for lunch and more stories, and also for the use of the photograph of her daughter, Wasefa Majiet, for the cover. To my publisher, Annari van der Merwe, for her honesty regarding my work. To Irene, who knows who she is, and who sorted through the debris. To my children Zaida and Faramarz, for understanding their mother's writing fix, and always being supportive.

There is also the inspiring work of other authors from which I have taken generously: *The Complete Fairy Tales of the Brothers Grimm*, translated by Jack Zipes, first published in 1812 and 1815. *Emotional Intelligence: Why it can matter more than I.Q.*, Daniel Goleman, Bloomsbury Publishing, London, 1996. *The Mysterious Stranger and Other Stories*, Mark Twain, Harper & Brothers, New York, 1916.

Last, and with great fondness, a special thanks to the ragpicker in the rusty old bucket, and to the real Ulf, who tells me that some stories need never end.

Rayda Jacobs
JUNE 2001

I remember the wind on the day my great-grandmother arrived in Bo-Kaap in 1955. I was eight years old, playing high 'n low with Fatima and Kulsum Gamieldien in the street, skipping without my shoes on, when the black car took the turn into Sachs. When a car turned into our little street, it was almost always for us or our next-door neighbours, the Gamieldiens. All three of us stopped playing as it came to a halt in front of our house. A delicate woman with eggshell skin and grey eyes stepped out with a cane, the south-easter lifting her skirts to her waist, exposing thin little legs and cream underclothes, the wind beating my sausage curls about my face in a plaster of grease. The man who'd driven the car looked at a piece of paper in his hand. He didn't seem familiar with the neighbourhood or this wind, or he would've known to hold on to her to keep her from blowing down the slope. Just then my mother came out of the house. She was tall for a woman, with a strength about her that told you to stay out of her way. She came down the step of the stoep and kissed the woman. I was too far away to hear what was said, but my mother knew her, I thought, and had expected the visit. I heard the name Solly blown across the wind, but couldn't be sure.

The man shook my mother's hand. They spoke for a few minutes, then the man carried a box and two cases into the house, pressed something into the woman's hand, kissed her, and left.

I separated from my friends and came to stand at my mother's side.

"This is your other oemie, your great-grandmother, from Paarl. Oemie's coming to stay with us," my mother said.

I raised myself up on my toes to make myself tall to kiss her so she didn't have to lean down. But I didn't like the name oemie for her. This unusual-looking woman didn't look at all like an oemie, which was a Bo-Kaap word for grandmother, or like the oemie who was my father's mother and wore a doek on her head and black stuff under her eyes, and covered herself from head to toe. This was a white person. Anyone could see that. There was no doek on her flaming red hair which had patches of silver at the temples, no tasbieh in her hand on which you recited the name of God thirty-three times, no smell of rose water about her clothes. And even though she walked with a cane and took out a little tin which she held to her nose, sniffed at, and blinked, there was a stringiness about her that made her different from all the oemies I knew. The oemies I knew were mostly round ladies in cloaks who stayed home all day looking after grandchildren. This great-grand-mother had a delicate beauty, and a pair of eyes that looked right into your heart and spied all your secrets. She didn't look at all like the Chiappini and Pepper Street oemies of Bo-Kaap.

I waited for her to open her mouth. I could tell right away by the way people spoke what they were. Bo-Kaap people spoke mostly Afrikaans, but didn't sound like the Afrikaners you heard on the radio. In our house we also spoke English. My mother bought us *School Friend* and *Girl's Crystal* on Friday nights, and we never would've dreamed of reading a book or comic in Afrikaans.

My great-grandmother took my mother's arm, and stepped onto the stoep.

"'n Pragtage huisie," she said.

My heart sank at the common way she said pretty little house. She didn't say pragtig; she said pragtag. She wasn't a real Afrika-ner, I thought.

I followed them into the house. My friends were waiting for me at the gate, but I didn't go out to play again. All afternoon, I sat with my back against the low, three-foot wall on the edge of the stoep and listened to the two women talk. Playing han'eklippe with five stones, I didn't look up. To look up was to draw attention to myself and be dismissed. I didn't want to be sent off. I wanted to hear the family secrets. I had a greedy curiosity to know things, an inquisitiveness that often landed me in trouble, and at that moment, my one interest was this grand old lady sitting on our stoep.

The first thing I noticed about people was their hair. My own hair I was horribly ashamed of. *Die blas enetjie met die kroes hare* – the brown one with the kinky hair – someone had said once to distinguish me from my fairer sister. My mother had overheard and told the woman never to come to her house again. I don't know which upset her most: that I was called brown, or blush as some people liked to refer to me, or that I had this embarrassing hair. My hair was climate-controlled. A little humidity, and it swelled like baked bread. A little drizzle, and it grew legs. A little wind, and it reshaped itself about my head. And where we lived, on the hip of the hill, with the docks to your left, the mountains to your right, the city at your knees, you had the smell of the sea, the whip of the south-easter, and the mist rolling down the peak. I was a living barometer of where I lived. You only had to look at me to know the weather conditions in Bo-Kaap. But if my sister Murida had the looks and the hair, I saw that I had my great-grandmother's grey eyes.

Still, the big questions were who she was and where she'd been all my life and sprung from so suddenly. I had never heard of her, never knew we had family in Paarl. I didn't even know where Paarl was. And the man who'd brought her was also a complete mystery.

Sitting out of the wind, conscious of her every flutter and tick, I felt in my heart that the two of us would be friends. She didn't seem to be like my father's mother who frightened me with the rules of religion. I was extremely frightened of God. I didn't even know if this great-grandmother had a God, or believed in one, or whether she herself wasn't scared of what God might do to her for not wearing a scarf. She knew things, I thought, more things than my mother or my father's mother. Perhaps she even knew of a way to fix my hair. But what was I to call her? Not oemie, I de-

9

cided. I thought of my friend Alison on Pepper Street. Alison's grandmother, Maybeline, lived with them. Alison called her Granny May.

So on I sat with my back to the wall, playing with my stones, and listened to the two women talk. My mother had just told how my father had gone out to the café for cigarettes three years ago, and had never returned. I was tired of the story, and had seen my father a few times since when he visited us and came with a woman in the car. The woman was always dropped off on Wale Street at the entrance to the Gardens before he picked us up so my mother wouldn't see her in the car, then dropped off there again before he returned us. In the car my father would ask Murida to sit on the nice aunty's lap. Murida would climb up right away and talk all kinds of nonsense. Not me. Not on the aunty's lap, and not on his. I would never climb on any man's lap. And I hated my father. He'd never once tied my laces or washed my face or read me a story or paid any attention to me. The only thing I really remember was the hair of the different women he brought along; straight, brown or straw-coloured with kiss-me curls and ponytails. Even then I knew they weren't women like my mother or me.

"… that's what you get for marrying the son of a slave … I should've known better."

My ears pricked up. I didn't know this great-grandmother, but somehow felt it was the wrong thing for my mother to say. I was right. My great-grandmother's head turned from where she'd been watching children play hide 'n seek on the hill.

"My grandmother's mother was a slave woman," she said gently. "The man who raised my grandmother was also a slave. Not the blood father – he was an Afrikaner – but the one who put clothes on her back and shoes on her feet." She dabbed at her lips with the corner of a handkerchief, and I caught a whiff of eau de cologne. "So don't say slave as if you have nails in your mouth, Ateeka. Every Mohammedan born here has a slave in his background. You too."

I felt the sting of her words in my own heart. And the information was too much to take in. I knew a little about slaves. The teacher had taken the class to the Castle to show us the fort Jan van Riebeeck had built when he arrived three hundred years ago. Did my great-grandmother mean that we were from these people who arrived in our country in chains and rags with no shoes on their feet?

"I didn't mean it that way, Oemie. What I meant was –"

"I know what you meant," my great-grandmother said. "There're others in the family who don't want to know their beginnings. Don't you be one of them."

My mother was dark, but turned the colour of a mulberry. She was embarrassed, and in front of me. I waited to hear what she would say, expecting at any moment to be told to go and play, but she fidgeted with her skirt and sat silent. Then my great-grandmother started to talk about her family.

"Solly's a good son, and took care of me these last years after your grandfather died. Still, it's hard living with a child who can't face what he is. His father was white. That didn't make him so. Your mother and he didn't have the same father. Your mother's father raised him. He was black, but he had a heart of gold."

I couldn't believe what I heard. Two husbands, one of them a white man. I felt sure now that I would be told to scram.

My great-grandmother blew her nose in a small handkerchief. "Olive asked me to stay, you know. I didn't tell you that when I asked Solly to write the letter. But three years was enough after your grandfather died. I was lonely, and was going to get a woman to come and stay with me in the house. I only moved in with Solly because he wanted me to. Olive didn't have any problems with me. At least I didn't give her any. There was an understanding."

"What was the understanding?" my mother asked.

My great-grandmother bobbed her head a little as if she was having trouble getting the words out. "Well, no one really said it in so many words, but I didn't talk about religion, and she pretended I was one of them."

"One of them? A'oenzoebillah," my mother said in disbelief. "But how could anyone live like that, not say anything to one's own children? Couldn't people tell from where aunty Olive and uncle Solly lived what they were?"

"The farm's out of the way – not in a white area and not in a coloured area, so you can't be sure. But of course, people know these things. They're not stupid. You only have to look at Olive's nose and hair to know she's a baster. You get Griquas also with white skin and blue eyes; they're not white. They're evidence of the master's devilry. But this one wants to believe she's white. To the visitors who came there, I was Solly's mother. No one knows him as Suleiman. And your grandfather was never mentioned, and was never invited to the house when he was alive. He was a good man, and looked after Solly like his own since he was seven years old. Solly never really took to him. I blame myself for how things turned out."

"It's not Oemie's fault," my mother said.

My grandmother continued. "That's why I agreed to go to Paarl when Solly asked me. I thought – well, I thought I could change things. I thought if I stayed there with them in the house, that I might make a difference. Of course, you can't change anything. After a while, I missed the old way, my people. No one visited me. In my room, I had my muslah and my tasbieh. In the dining room there was a picture of Jesus with a bleeding heart and a shiny halo. On Sundays Solly drives his family to church. He doesn't go in, but he takes them." She bobbed her head, as if holding a private conversation in her head. "A bird can't make a home with a fish, my girl. There's no common ground."

My mother's expression told me that the information was more than she'd expected to hear. "Could I ask Oemie a personal question? I know it's not my business, but how could Oemie allow such a thing? For Uncle Solly to marry Olive?"

My great-grandmother took out her snuff box, and peered into it. "I didn't *allow* it. How does any mother allow such a thing? But who started it? He took a page out of his mother's book." She paused and looked at my mother with sorrowful eyes. "We pay for our mistakes, my girl. Make no mistake that we pay. Ignorance is a terrible thing."

My mother took her hand. "Oemie mustn't worry anymore. I'm happy to have Oemie with us. If Mummy could see us, she'd be happy that her mother's here."

Mention of my mother's mother made me drop two stones. All

I knew about this grandmother was that her name was Soemaya, and that she'd died before I was born. Other than that I knew nothing. I didn't know if she'd had a husband – there was no grandfather ever mentioned. The only grandfather I knew was my father's father, Braima. I waited to hear more about my mystery grandmother, but the afternoon of secrets was over. My mother said nothing more. Stealing a look at my great-grandmother's fine hair and delicate features, I wondered if this was where my sister had got her silk strands, and if it was the black great-grandfather's blood which accounted for my mother's and my blush complexions and curly hair.

My great-grandmother stirred in her seat. "It's been a long day. I'm tired."

My mother got up. "Oemie must have a rest before supper. I was thinking that one of the girls can sleep with me, and Oemie can share with the other one."

Suddenly I had the perfect name for her.

"Little granny can stay with me," I blurted out. I couldn't afford for Murida to get her hands on her first, and staying in the same room with little granny would make things stronger between us. But I had spoken without being spoken to. They looked at me as if seeing me at their feet for the first time.

"You want to share with – little granny?" my mother asked in surprise.

"Yes, Mummy. Little granny won't even know that I'm there. I'm very quiet." I surprised myself that I had come so easily to calling her little granny. I was even more surprised that my mother had used the name.

My great-grandmother fixed her gaze on me. "You'll be quiet?" she asked, her grey eyes much amused. "I haven't known any child to do that for more than a minute. How will you be quiet?"

I looked at my mother to make sure I had her approval to speak. "I can read, Granny."

Her eyes brightened. "Do you like reading?"

"Yes, Granny. I have six books in my room."

I'll never forget the smile that washed over the wrinkled features, starting in the eyes and spreading slowly to the mouth, revealing all of her natural teeth except for one missing in the front. "You have the Kloot spirit then. There's a history in the family. Readers and writers. Maybe one day you'll also be one."

The words spread over me like a warm blanket. I was flattered that a grown-up had even noticed me, let alone talk to me of such important things. I didn't know who the Kloots were, but imagined them to be important.

When my sister arrived home from her friends on Bryant Street, she immediately saw the importance of the visitor and tried to take over. I waited with a sinking feeling for my great-grandmother to fall for Murida's charms. My sister was cleverer than me, and had a way of pronouncing words – something she'd picked up from her sturvy friend, Lorraine – that impressed people. When little granny asked Murida how she was doing in school, she said that she never had to study hard for exams, and that when she was big, she would become a doctor. Little granny's eyes opened wide. She asked if girls were allowed to become doctors. Murida said yes, especially overseas. Little granny turned to me to hear what I wanted to be. I had never given my future a thought, and mumbled something about giving first aid to injured children lying in the street.

That night I dried the dishes and waited to see what my sister would do when she found out that little granny would stay with me in my room. Murida opened her mouth in haste upon learning of this new development. But my mother was firm. "Khadidja was here all afternoon while you were out playing. She asked first. Let's not upset granny."

It wasn't lost on me that my mother had said granny instead of oemie, and I was happy that she had made a distinction from my father's mother. But I wished my mother hadn't been so stern with Murida. Whenever Murida was scolded, she took it out on me. Once she had even stolen a frikkadel out of the pan, hidden it under my pillow and had told my mother I'd taken it. It had been a bad day for my mother. Galiema on the corner had spotted my father with a woman in OK Bazaars and had told her. My mother had got out the feather duster and had worked it over me like an eggbeater, despite my screams that I hadn't taken the frikkadel.

Bedtime arrived. I got under the covers and waited to see what little granny would do. I didn't know if I should offer to help take off her clothes, if I should turn my face to the wall while she undressed, or if I should fluff up her pillow. We were going to be sharing my bed. To my great distress she asked if there was a chamber pot. My mouth opened to say no – I feared that I would have the job of carrying out that pot in the morning – but one look at the tiny figure on the edge of the bed as she rummaged through a box at her feet, and I hopped to it. Little granny reminded me of a delicate butterfly, all pretty colours and cellophane wings, fluttery, fragile, easily carried away on the wind. I didn't want her stumbling about with a cane outside in the middle of the night. I went to my mother's room and fetched the pot, glad to discover that no one had dribbled into it yet. Back in my room, I found little granny still rummaging through the box.

"Is Granny looking for something?"

"I don't know where I put my sleep things," she replied, "in what box."

"Does Granny want me to look?" I had spotted a bag of dried fruit in between the rolls of clothing and was hoping she would offer me some.

"Yes. There's a pink one, and a white one. I like the white one."

I slipped my hand into the soft clothing, and found it almost at the bottom of the box. "Must I help Granny put it on?"

"Yes," she said. "My left arm's a bit stiff." She raised her arms slowly, and I took off her dress and petticoat, and slid the nightie over her head. She looked down at herself, smoothing the sleeves. The nightie was pressed, and still had the ironing folds in it, but still had to be fussed with a bit before being crumpled in bed. She was a particular woman. Even her petticoat had little flowers sewn on it.

"Where are the books?" she asked unexpectedly.

"The books, Granny?" I realised then that she was referring to the books I'd mentioned that afternoon. I couldn't believe she'd asked me. She was interested. No one was interested in my books. Not even my mother who bought them but paid no attention when I tried to tell her about them. I was accused of having an imagination. An imagination was a bad thing. The stories were putting too many ideas in my head.

15

I went to the cupboard where my school uniform and blazer hung next to my two good Sunday dresses and my labarang outfit, and opened one of the drawers. The top drawer contained my school socks and bloomers and petticoats and ribbons. The second one held my winter jerseys and folded corduroy pants and shirts my mother had made on the sewing machine. Underneath this orderly pile in the second drawer, was my secret treasure of books. My favourite was the one I received for my eighth birthday, a nice fat one called *Fairy Tales of the Brothers Grimm*. I took out all six books and spread them next to my great-grandmother on the bed. I waited to see which one she would pick. My heart bounded as her hand reached for the one with the picture of a knight in blue and silver armour and a beautiful princess on the cover.

She picked it up, and peered at it, holding the book slightly away from her face. Her eyes weren't good. She opened the book and looked inside. My heart sank when I realised that she was looking only at the pictures. My poor granny couldn't read.

"Does Granny know Grimm's Fairy Tales?"

She looked at me and smiled. "Your granny only knows real stories. But you can read one of these for me, if it's not too long."

It was too much. No one had ever asked me to read. And I could read. That much I knew I could do. I had an ability for words, the Standard One teacher had told my mother the previous year when it was suggested that I be moved up to Standard Two. My mother had listened to the teacher's reasons, and at the end of it told her to keep me in Standard One. She didn't want me thinking I was too clever, have me elevated to a higher standard, then dropped back to Standard One again if it didn't work out.

"Does Granny know the story of Clever Gretel?"

"No."

I came to sit next to her on the bed. "I'll read that for Granny then. *There was once a cook named Gretel*," I started.

My granny leaned back on the pillow against the wall, and listened. I read how Gretel had roasted two chickens for her master and the guest who was expected to come and eat with them, and how – unable to wait any longer for the guest to arrive – Gretel started to eat first the one chicken and then the other. On and on I read, carefully pronouncing the words. I neared the end of the story.

"Just as she was in the midst of her meal, her master came back and called, 'Hurry, Gretel, the guest will soon be here!'

'Yes, sir, I'll get everything ready,' answered Gretel.

Meanwhile the master checked to see if the table was properly set and took out the large knife with which he wanted to carve the chickens and began sharpening it on the steps in the hallway. As he was doing that the guest came and knocked nicely and politely at the door. Gretel ran and looked to see who was there, and when she saw the guest, she put her finger to her lips and whispered, 'Shhh, be quiet! Get out of here as quick as you can! If my master catches you, you'll be done for. It's true he invited you to dinner, but he really wants to cut off both your ears. Listen to him sharpening his knife!'

The guest heard the sharpening and hurried back down the steps as fast as he could. Gretel wasted no time and ran screaming to her master. 'What kind of guest did you invite!' she cried.

'Goodness gracious, Gretel! Why do you ask? What do you mean?'

'Well,' she said, 'he snatched both chickens just as I was about to bring them to the table, and he's run away with them!'

'That's not at all a nice way to behave!' said her master, and he was disappointed by the loss of the fine chickens. 'At least he could have left me one of them so I'd have something to eat.'

He then shouted after the guest to stop running, but the guest pretended not to hear. So the master ran after him, with the knife still in his hand, and screamed, 'Just one, just one!' merely meaning that the guest should at least leave him one of the chickens and not take both. But the guest thought that his host was after just one of his ears, and to make sure that he would reach home safely with both his ears, he ran as if someone had lit a fire under his feet."

I finished the story and waited, my eyes still on the page. I wanted my great-grandmother to be the first to speak, to tell me how much she'd liked it. But she didn't say anything. She was looking at me with a curious expression on her face.

"Did Granny understand the story?" I wanted to know.

"I understood it very well."

"Does Granny not like the story?"

"I thought a story out of a book would be a good story. It was called Clever Gretel, wasn't it?"

"Yes, Granny," I replied, feeling a sinking feeling in my heart.

"It seems Gretel had an evil heart," she said in a voice I was to come to know as the voice of disappointment. "And I'm wondering what's the point of the story. Evil is never good. Even when it looks clever."

I hid how her words crushed me. "Yes, Granny."

She started to button up her nightie. "Tomorrow I'll tell you a real story. Your granny has lived in the highest and driest of places, her eyes have seen much. Do you like stories?"

"Very much."

"But we'll keep these stories to ourselves," she said. "Can you keep such a promise?"

I'd never been asked to keep a secret by a grown-up. To be a keeper of confidences was a grand compliment. "I swear, Granny, I'll never tell."

"Good," she sighed, getting under the blanket, pulling it up to her chin. "Tomorrow I'll tell you about a place far, far away where the gods watch over the land with a jealous eye, and the land is so dry you can watch your spit disappear before it lands on the ground."

My white granny came today. She said there're slaves in the family. I like her.

~

Khadidja finished reading the divorce document Alison had placed on her lap and sat for a few moments looking out the windscreen of her car. Next to her, Alison was dragging nervously on a cigarette. They were in the parking lot outside the building on the Foreshore where Alison worked as a nurse for a gynaecologist.

"I'm so sorry, Alison. This is terrible."

Alison looked out her side of the window. "I feel like a lorry's run over me. I had no idea it was coming. We never even discussed it, and if anyone had grounds for divorce, it was me. And to have me served at the office. How embarrassing."

Khadidja reached over and hugged her. Alison started crying and sobbed into her hair. "How can he say that I'm an unfit mother? Leila comes first in my life, everyone knows that."

"He knows it too. He has no grounds. And she's a teenager already, she won't go with him."

Alison was inconsolable. "He says I won't raise her Muslim. What is she now, then? I converted, for God's sake. I should never have married him. I should just have gone through that pregnancy by myself, I would've been better off now. One child left and he wants to take her from me."

The eldest girl's dead face flashed before Khadidja. Southfield Road, the flashing lights of the ambulance, police, Alison screaming hysterically. She took a tissue out of her bag and handed it to Alison. Was Alison ever going to forget? Alison had never blamed her, but she was the one who'd driven the car. And when was *she* going to forget the night she'd had one joint too many and run a stop sign?

"You won't lose Leila. She's fifteen. A fifteen-year-old can decide. What would he do with a fifteen-year-old anyway? It's all just a control issue."

"The papers say that I –"

"I know what they say. You'll file your own papers. I'll talk to Saville."

"Saville Eisenberg? I don't know that I can afford him."

"Don't worry about the money. I just hope he can take you on."

Alison looked troubled. "You know how Leila and I always argue. She thinks she's my mother sometimes. Farouk'll bribe her. Maybe she'll go with him just to spite me."

Khadidja took her hand and squeezed it. "Never. Leila can't be bought. And she loves you." She started the car. "I'll talk to Saville.

He owes me for that profile I did in the magazine. Go and see him, have a consultation. If you don't feel comfortable, ask him to recommend someone."

Alison took out her cigarettes and lit a fresh one. "I told Farouk long ago that no matter what happened between us, I would never change back to my old religion. I turned Muslim before I even married him. It's that mother of his. Right from the start she was against me. What does she think I'll do? I'm the one who sent that child to madressah, who sees to her religious upbringing. He's too busy making money and getting up to nonsense."

Khadidja had met Alison's in-laws several times. Farouk's mother was like any other Muslim mother when it came to marriage and how the children of that marriage would be raised. But it was more than religion. Alison wasn't fair enough, her hair was nappy, her nose was too broad. Alison had come crying to her once when Farouk called her a hotnot. When Nazli was born, his mother had said the baby's nose wasn't from their side of the family. Nazli was the first child and should've had the lion's share of the grandparents' affection, but it was Leila, born two years later with her father's straight hair and sharp features, who got the attention.

"I have to pick up mango atjar for my mother," Khadidja said. "Let's take a run up to the spice shop."

"How's she?"

"Fine. She's looking forward to seeing you."

"Me too. And how is sies Moena?"

"Getting thinner and thinner, since boeta Amien died."

"God, it must be years since I've seen all of them. How many children were there again?"

Khadidja thought of her mother's next-door neighbours, the Gamieldiens. "Fourteen, I think, if you count all of them. Maybe one or two more with those who died during childbirth."

"I ran into Kulsum at Stuttafords the other day. She told me she had four children."

Khadidja laughed. "Yes. And she's happy. She and Gabieba and Fatima, they've all made good choices. Riaz is divorced now, seeing a white girl. Sies Moena's having a fit about that. Moosa's back from Canada."

"Still not married?"

"No."

"Are you thinking what I'm thinking?"

"Probably."

"Not girls?"

"Not girls."

"And the others? Do you see them?"

"Sometimes, when they visit sies Moena, they'll come next door to say hello to my mother. We were never really close. They were much older."

Alison became morose again. "Maybe it's not such a good idea for me to come for supper tonight."

"It's exactly what you need to take your mind off things. I'll take you back early if you want." They were at the top end of Wale Street. Khadidja stopped the car in front of the spice shop, and got out. "I'll just run in quickly."

She waited for a break in the traffic to cross the road. It was April, the air was starting to get nippy in the mornings, but the afternoons were still warm. Children were out playing in the street, waiting to be called in for supper. Below them, the offices had closed, the streets empty.

A barefooted boy came up to her. "*Argus*, lady," he held out the evening newspaper.

"No thanks." She didn't want any more news, and anyway had always preferred the *Cape Times*. Not only because she'd worked there once, but because she liked a morning paper, and liked the reporting. A reporter for *Drum* in the seventies, it was in 1980 that a friend had introduced her to the editor of the *Cape Times*. This was the time of the school and bus boycotts, and the killings on the Cape Flats where an unknown number of people died during a two-day stayaway to commemorate the Soweto uprising of 1976. Police refused to supply the *Cape Times* with a casualty list. A week after the shootings, the editor called her into his office. She was a reporter of colour, and had developed a high profile in the community. She tracked down twenty-six families. The security police arrested her, and she was detained for four days. Her husband, Rudy, balked at the dangers of her work. He had never liked the idea of her being a reporter anyway. A few years later they withdrew her passport. She became disgruntled with journalism, left the *Cape Times*, and entered the world of magazine publishing. Six years later she was the editor of an up-market women's magazine. The first coloured woman in such a position.

She reached the other side of the road and stepped up onto the pavement. She saw a couple come out of the spice shop and realised with a jolt who they were. She hadn't seen the man in years, and recognized the woman from the mole above her right brow. She turned and quickly retraced her steps across the road. At the car she turned to look. The man had seen her, and had seen her walk away. His mouth moved, as if to call out to her, but he just stood there, his hands hanging limply at his sides. Time had tossed him about, she thought; gravity had loosened his jowls.

"You look like you've seen a ghost," Alison said when she got back in the car.

"I've just seen my father."

"That's him?" Alison looked in the direction of the man still standing on the other side of the road. "Did you talk to him?"

Khadidja started the car and drove off. "No."

"What about the mango atjar?"

"I'll get it tomorrow. Light me a ciggie."

Alison lit two Stuyvesants and handed her one. "You're smoking?"

Khadidja inhaled the smoke deep into her lungs. "You know I quit. I just got a bit of a shock."

A few minutes later they turned into Sachs Street. She noted her husband's BMW in front of the door. She parked behind his car and led Alison into the house. Khadidja caught a glimpse of herself in the hall mirror. After years of straightening her hair and sleeping with a stocking on her head, an Adderley Street hairdresser had shaped, coloured, and turned it into a wanton burst of copper ringlets reaching into the small of her back. It was so naturally wild that people asked to touch it, not believing the corkscrew curls didn't come from a hot comb or out of a bottle. But it wasn't a look that pleased her husband, and it worried her mother who was always concerned with what people were going to say about a daughter who not only didn't wear a scarf, but displayed her hair for all to see.

Khadidja led Alison down the short passage into the kitchen where three people sat at the table: her mother, Ateeka, in a biscuit-coloured cotton dress with orange dots; the next-door neighbour, Moena Gamieldien, smoking a cigarette; and Rudy, a plate of chicken breyani in front of him.

"Salaam aleikoem," Khadidja greeted everyone in general.

"Hello everyone," Alison said, right behind her.

"Alison!" Ateeka exclaimed. "How're you?"

"I'm fine. How's Aunty?"

"I can't complain. I haven't seen you in such a long time."

"I know." She turned to Moena Gamieldien. "How's sies Moena? I ran into Kulsum a few weeks ago. She says she's still up on Bloem Street."

"She is. You must take a walk up there with Khadidja. She'll be happy to see you. Do you know boeta Amien died?"

"Khadidja told me. I was sorry to hear it. How's sies Moena coping?"

"I must maar cope. What can I do? Moosa stays with me, and Riaz. He came back home."

"Really?" Alison didn't let on that she knew Riaz was divorced. Divorce was an embarrassing thing for some people to admit to – the same way sies Moena couldn't admit what boeta Amien had died of. She might say sugar, a bad stomach, heart attack, but never cancer.

Rudy pulled out a chair. "Sit, Alison. I'm sorry to be eating already. I have an appointment at seven."

"Not at all. I didn't expect to come for supper."

"How's your daughter?"

"Fine."

"Farouk's still in the building trade?"

"Yes. We're separated."

The two older women looked at each other. Khadidja lifted the lid of the pot on the stove. "I'll dish up. I hope everyone's hungry."

"Separated?" Ateeka asked.

"He served me with a petition today."

"You mean he's divorcing you?"

Khadidja lowered a platter of chicken breyani onto the table. "Alison doesn't want to talk about it. It all just happened this afternoon."

"You didn't know something like this was going to happen?"

"You always know something is wrong," Alison sat down. "I thought we would work things out."

"There's another woman?"

Khadidja became aggravated at her mother's persistence. "I brought Alison to come and have supper, Ma, not to be cross-examined."

"It's all right, Titch," Alison said. "I don't mind."

Rudy pushed back his chair and got up. "Sorry to break up the party, but I'm late already."

Khadidja watched him. Appointment was a nice word for it, she thought. She wondered where it would be that night; if it was the same appointment, if it was Muslim, if it had a brain. Still, she was strangely relieved by these nightly migrations. It freed her to have her own thoughts, and spared her from his touches at night. She watched him put his plate in the sink and dust the crumbs off the front of his shirt; a tall, good-looking man with a moustache, and too much hair.

"See you later, Titch. Don't wait up."

She waited for him to leave, and returned her attention to the people at the table. "Alison and I went to the spice shop," she said. "I saw Daddy."

Ateeka stopped with her fork in mid-air. "You saw your father?"

"With Hajiera. I don't know what they were doing here, so far out of their neighbourhood."

"Did he see you?" Moena asked.

"I think so."

"You didn't talk to him?"

"No."

"It's an old thing between them," Ateeka said.

"It's not that I hate him, sies Moena. Anyway, I don't want to discuss it."

"He's still your father," Ateeka reminded.

24

"So Mummy keeps telling me. The whole notion of fatherhood's overrated. As I said, I don't hate him. I just don't have anything to say to him. He can bond with my sister."

They heard footsteps in the passage. A tall man dressed in jeans and a cashmere sweater entered the kitchen. It was Moosa. "I'm knocking and knocking," he said. "I thought I'd just come in. My goodness, Alison! What a surprise."

"How're you?" Alison got up and hugged him. "I hear you were in Canada."

"I was. You look great. And still keeping your figure." He sat down next to his mother, and kissed her.

"You didn't like Canada?" Alison asked. "Too cold?"

Ateeka handed him the breyani platter and a clean plate.

Moosa dished up some food. "I liked it. Toronto's great, and the cold didn't bother me. But it's not for me, not to live."

"A Muslim can't live there," Ateeka said. "How can you live in a place with no mosques and no Muslim people? How do you raise children in such a place?"

"There *are* mosques, and quite a lot of Muslims from other countries. But you miss your own culture. Even if you live in Wynberg or Simon's Town, it's different from Bo-Kaap. Now imagine a place like Canada. It's an immigrant country. People from all over the world come to live there. It's not easy for anyone. And there's just something about this country that pulls you back."

"It's Table Mountain," Moena said. "Moosa's a Capie. I keep asking him when he's going to settle down and give me grandchildren."

"Mummy has enough grandchildren," Moosa laughed. "There must be thirty of them by now."

Khadidja listened to the banter back and forth between mother and son. Did Moena Gamieldien know the real reason Moosa had gone to Canada, she wondered? It wasn't something the family, especially the older brothers, would easily accept. Khadidja knew because she'd seen him at a Kloof Street restaurant in an intimate embrace with another man. He'd seen her also, and they'd talked. He'd accepted the contract in Canada to get over a break-up with an actor.

The next morning at work she called Saville. It wasn't a number she'd dialled in a very long time. He was on his way to court, his secretary said, but would take the call.

"Khadidja Daniels, how *are* you?"

She smiled at the effusiveness of the greeting. She'd met him on the steps of the Supreme Court in her heyday as a reporter more than a decade ago when he'd won a half-million-rand settlement in a paternity suit for a black girl against a well-known Constantia developer who claimed he wasn't the father of her four-year-old boy. They'd met again at a fund-raising breakfast at the Mount Nelson Hotel, and became involved. But there was apartheid, their different faiths, his mother terminally ill in Israel. They could sit in the car up on the hill at Rhodes Memorial and exchange saliva, but it was awkward out in public. It was almost a relief when he said he had to go away. She had met Rudy, and got married.

"I'm fine. How's your wife? The kids?"

"Everyone's well. Chaya hasn't thrown me out yet. But I haven't seen you since that profile you did. It prompted lots of calls. How're you?"

"Working hard. Still trying to finish my book. I know you're busy, so I won't keep you. I want you to see a friend of mine, Alison. She was served with a divorce petition. The husband's asking for custody of a fifteen-year-old. It's all a ruse to hold on to some properties. The lawyer's Jeremy Fingerhut."

Saville groaned. "Do you know my case load? I'm not taking on any more … but tell her to give me a call."

"Thanks."

"When you're rich, you can take me away for a dirty weekend."

She laughed. "Don't tempt me."

A voice in the background interrupted him. He came back on the line. "I have a judge holding. I have to take the call. Tell your friend to call me."

"There's no retainer," she said quickly.

"Anything else?"

"You'll probably wait for your money. Don't charge too much."

She replaced the receiver and sat for a moment staring at it. Then the art director entered, the sub-editor hovered at the door, the receptionist popped her head in briefly to say that there was another call holding, and Khadidja was swallowed up again by the demands of her work.

APRIL 26
Spoke to Saville today about Alison. I really should invite him to the house again for supper, just for old time's sake ...

≈

I didn't fall asleep easily that first night next to little granny. It was strange lying behind someone's back, listening to her breathing, so close to her smells. I tried to imagine this place, Paarl, where she'd come from. Was it like Bo-Kaap? Did it have Moslems? Were the houses stacked on a hill? Were there children? Did you hear the bilal in the bedroom, in the kitchen, in the classroom – five times a day from all directions?

Our house was one of five on a clay road no longer than a soccer field. Tar and asphalt hadn't reached us yet, and we weren't grand like Pepper, Leeuwen or Bloem, which were cobblestoned long ago to stop the horses from sliding down the hill with their loads. The houses were all on the same side, the stoeps facing the field rising up into Signal Hill, the kitchens overlooking the city below. Bloem Street came down in a dirt road and ended abruptly on our left. Pepper Street flanked us on the right. Our street was pressed in between those two – a small, forgettable crack in the wall that the Council couldn't be bothered to stretch its brain about and simply named after a Jewish man, Mr Sachs, who'd lived there long ago. Sachs Street was where I was born, and where my mother lived her whole life. A few hundred feet up was the Schotsche Kloof flats with the funny names. The Bakgat flats for those with venetian blinds. The Hollywood, for the sturvies. The Krieste flats for the ones with Christian families. Behind all this, at the top end of Longmarket Street, was the cannon which boomed over our heads every day exactly at noon.

We played many games on this hill: aan-aan, kennetjie, rounders, hide 'n seek. Sometimes we took an old blanket, a bottle of water, jam sandwiches, and sat high up on the hill, searching for vrietangs in the grass, picking bessies off the trees. When the wind blew, we held on to each other. When it rained, the water rushed down the hill in torrents and turned Sachs Street into mud. When we heard the bilal at the mosques calling us to prayer, we ran like the devil to get home. Even our Christian friends would shout, "Daar's die bilal. Hardloop!" There's the muezzin. Run! Everyone knew that Moslem children had to be off the street at sunset.

On the short little cul-de-sac, every resident knew every other resident. We knew one another's secrets, one another's smells. There was the woman at the end of the road, Galiema, who'd married a Christian who everyone called *die jahanaam se blok* – the block on which you would burn in hell for your sins. Then there was the African man, Vilele, and his wife Ayanda and their three children, who roasted sheep heads on the field and caused the stink to drift into our homes. There were the Gamieldiens next to us with the twelve children, whose eldest son, Ismail, had joined a District Six gang and sometimes made an appearance in the middle of the night to bring his mother an envelope. Sies Moena cried and reminded him of God's commands, but took the envelope. Feeding a small army three times a day took a Christian miracle, she told my mother over their eleven o'clock serial, *Life can be beautiful with Chichi*, which she sometimes came to listen to at our house on the small wireless in the front room. There were the Benjamins on our right with the pretend-white daughter, Sandra, who kept to themselves, never borrowed anything, and had a mad uncle living with them who'd twice been taken to Valkenberg with a stick stuck between his teeth so he couldn't bite his tongue. Next to them on the corner, in Mr Sachs' old house, was boeta Tapie with his sister and her four children. People said he'd had a disappointment, and spent too much time in the duiwehok with his racing pigeons. I didn't know what a disappointment was, but boeta Tapie was the one who fixed our taps and drove my mother in his car to the shop for material and fasteners and ribbons and thread. Last, there were us, in the middle of this mix, the only family where just three people – now four – occupied a whole house, and with the only Moslem children who went to St Paul's Primary instead of Schotsche Kloof. *Die kinners sonner pa,* people whispered about our fatherless state. I knew that the Gamieldiens, burdened as they were by a house full of children, felt sorry for Murida and me.

The Gamieldiens struggled more than we did, but the father, Amien, was a tailor, and after the holy month of fasting, on Eid, his sons wore suits with buttons on the sleeves and tickey pockets on the vests, and the girls looked like fairy princesses. My mother also made very beautiful clothes, and we had dresses with smocking and braids and embroideries and cutwork patterns. On this day of high celebration, when all the front doors were open and tables were laid with pastries and tarts and peanuts and sweets, we zigzagged through lanes and alleyways in our patent leather slip-ons and cream crocheted socks, getting silver tickeys which we swiftly deposited in our sling bags, stopping at almost every corner to count our money, and coming home with pains in our legs and the pattern of the socks still stuck to our feet when we took off our shoes.

The Gamieldiens were our best friends. Eleven children with Ismail gone; eight boys in one room, three girls in the other. At night, three of the boys slept on the pull-out divan in the front room. With the mother and father, thirteen people waited their turn in the morning to use the toilet; thirteen sat down for supper. The boys who worked, ate with their parents at the kitchen table where the food was dished up in bowls and they could help themselves. The rest ate in the boys' bedroom where a kerem table was set up between the two beds, and they gathered around it, their food coming from the kitchen dished up on their plates. When they went out, thirteen people crammed into Lizzie, the fat, eight-seater Plymouth, and sat on each other's laps.

Thinking of the crowded conditions next door always made me feel better about my own life. We didn't have a father in the house, but I could at least point to the food on the table and show my mother which potato and piece of meat I wanted. There wasn't a scramble for food, and I didn't have to be fifth or tenth in line for a bath and use someone else's wet towels. The towel for my bath was fresh from the line. Sometimes you could even smell the soap in it, or the apricot crystals my mother kept in the drawer. Sharing a bed with little granny also wasn't so bad. Kulsum, who was my age, had to sleep at the foot end of a bed. All night she got kicked in the chest by Fatima and Gabieba who slept at the other end.

That first night next to little granny, feeling warm and safe, I listened to her snore and thought of all the things I'd heard that afternoon. It was always at night, when everything was quiet, that I brought out the happenings of the day. I wondered about little granny's son, Solly, and his wife, Olive. I wondered how little granny could've lived in a house where she had to keep herself in. Muslim people didn't keep themselves in, especially not about things like religion. They blurted out feelings no matter who was there. I wondered whether my little granny would ever become used to our Bo-Kaap world which must surely be different from where she had come from. The thoughts went round and round in my head almost the whole night.

The next morning I helped little granny get up, and started a routine that was to be mine for as long as she was with us.

"I would like a bath," she said to me when she sat on the edge of the bed, wondering where she'd put her clothes the previous night.

I shuddered at the request. A bath was a big performance. "Does Granny know how we take a bath in this house?"

"No," she said, looking at me with eyes still filled with sleep. "Don't you just put water into the bath?"

I knew then that wherever she'd lived, they didn't wash themselves like Moslems. Moslems didn't sit in dirty water. Water had to run. Clean water had to rinse off the soap.

"No, Granny. We don't have a bath. Granny can wash in the toilet, and I'll put the water on a chair and Granny must use a skeppertjie to pour clean water over Granny. Or Granny can wash in the hok in the yard. There's a bucket with a tap in it on a shelf, and Granny stands under it on kaparangs. Does Granny know what's kaparangs? Those wooden things you put on your feet when you wash. The warm water runs down on Granny's head. I wash in the hok, it's less to clean up." Seeing the look on her face, I quickly added, "But it's too cold for Granny, I think. It'll be better for

Granny in the toilet. And if Granny washes in the toilet, Granny can rub Granny's heels on the cement floor to rub off the dead skin." I could see that she didn't know what I was talking about. The best thing would be simply to put the kettle on the stove and get everything ready.

"Can you find my gown, my girl?" she asked. "I'll wash in the toilet. Will you help Granny?"

"Yes, Granny," I said, waiting for her to tell me where I should look for the gown. And for a granny to *ask* me if I would do something for her spoke of someone who didn't know how mothers and grandmothers treated children in our neighbourhood. You weren't asked. You were told. And only once.

I found little granny's gown, helped her on with it, and walked with her to the kitchen where my mother had taken out all sorts of things and set them on the table. I could tell from the variety that she didn't know what little granny expected for breakfast. Usually we had Jungle Oats or mealie-meal porridge with lots of sugar and cream or condensed milk stirred into it. On Saturday mornings we had tomatoes and eggs. On Sundays, koeksisters that we bought from the Gamieldiens. On this morning, there was peanut butter, melon jam, a dish of butter, white bread from Motjie Janie's shop, a block of sweetmilk cheese, even a packet of Marie Biscuits.

"Would Oemie like some porridge, or eggs?" my mother asked.

Little granny lowered herself into a chair. "I'll just have some porridge, please. I don't eat much in the mornings. Where's the other child?"

She'd forgotten Murida's name, I thought, and wondered if she remembered mine.

"Murida leaves early for school," my mother said. "It takes twenty-five minutes to walk to Trafalgar. She's in high school already." Turning to me, in her no-nonsense, get-ready-for-school tone, she said, "It's ten to eight. Why aren't you dressed?"

"I have to help Granny. Granny wants to have a bath."

"It's too late now, I'll do it. Get on your clothes and come and eat. And get the tangles out of that hair so I can plait it."

"I don't have to bath this morning," little granny said. "Khadidja can help me when she gets home."

I smiled. She'd remembered my name. Not only that, she didn't say Didja, but Khadidja. If people were going to call me by the name my parents had given me, it was better they said it in full. Didja was common. I knew three Didjas, and their full names weren't Khadidja, but Gadidja. I didn't want to be confused with these Didjas, and would've liked a name like Nazli or Tamara, but instead I had to get the name of the Prophet's wife, which was a huge responsibility as people always mentioned it as if they expected something holy of me.

I got ready quickly, ate my porridge, took my sandwich which was neatly wrapped in greaseproof paper, and ran down the thirty steps between our house and the Gamieldien's to Bloem Street below, down to St Paul's on the corner of Bryant. The bell had already rung, and the teacher made me stand outside for five minutes before I was allowed in. I was hardly in the classroom when I blurted the whole thing into Alison's ear. *There's white blood in the family. You can't tell anyone.*

Alison, who had worse hair than mine – mine could at least lie flat against my head with coconut oil on it – but who was probably the toughest girl in school, opened her eyes wide, her eyebrows shooting up under a stiff piece of hair she thought was a fringe.

"White blood!" she nearly shrieked.

Miss Van Niekerk turned from her writing at the blackboard. "Who was that talking?"

We looked straight ahead.

"Who was that talking?" she asked again.

No one answered.

She put down the chalk and walked to the front row. She looked around the class. "If no one tells me who just talked in class, all of you will stay half an hour after school."

"*She* did, Miss!" Penelope "Four-Eyes" squealed behind me. I didn't have to turn. I knew her fat finger would be pointed at the back of my head. She would be too scared to blame Alison. I looked up at Miss Van Niekerk.

"Did you talk in class?" she asked.

"Yes, Miss."

"Come up here."

I looked at Alison. Alison's expression said that Penelope was going to get it. I stepped up to the front of the class.

"You're not so good at sums that you can afford not to pay attention. Tell this class what's so important that you should interrupt it."

I looked at the children sitting in their benches staring at me. A few of them looked happy that I was up there being humiliated. A few looked sorry. Some of them had been there before. Mr Cairncross, the principal, once hung Muggie – we called Christopher "muggie" because he was tiny like a midge – by the neck of his blazer on a hook next to the blackboard to punish him for copying answers out of Jeremy's book. I glanced at Penelope. My eyes promised revenge. She would have no ribbons left when Alison was finished with her.

"I'm waiting," Miss Van Niekerk prompted.

"I told her that my great-grandmother had moved into our house, Miss."

Miss Van Niekerk was tall as a street pole and had the same hairstyle that I'd seen Queen Elizabeth wear in *Woman's Illustrated*. This hairstyle was the same every day. Whether the wind blew, or it rained, or she sat in Mr Dudley's car with the window open, it never moved, and never had a strand out of place. She leaned forward with her neck, very much like those birds with the long necks and legs which stood in rivers and snatched at passing fish.

"This is what you interrupt the class for? The story of your great-grandmother couldn't wait?"

I could've said sorry, and saved myself, but she'd embarrassed me. "My great-grandmother *is* important," I said.

She straightened up and looked down her nose at me. "Say you're sorry right now," she demanded.

I could feel the tension in the room. I'd done a terrible thing, backchatting a teacher. Teachers were just below God, higher than a parent even, in the school.

"Did you hear what I said?"

I looked up and said nothing.

Her nostrils flared – wide little black holes you could stick a fat peanut into. She wasn't going to waste any more time with me.

But the cane was too easy. She had something better. Moving her head back like a cobra getting ready to strike, she said, "You'll stay behind after school, and write out one hundred times, *I was rude to the teacher.* I'll give you a note for your mother which you'll bring back tomorrow with her signature."

My mother! My mother didn't like complaints about her children. *She* could criticise her children, but no one else had better. I returned to my seat and saw the note in Alison's handwriting on the spot where I sat – WE'RE GOING TO MOER YOU. I didn't even know you could spell that word moer. There was no English word that promised so sincerely to beat you up good. Alison slid the note up behind my back where she held it for Penelope to read. There was a gasp. We waited to see if Penelope would blurt out this threat to her life, but she was silent.

The bell rang for break. Penelope stayed in class with a friend. She knew what would happen if she came out. Alison and I sat just outside the door and exchanged sandwiches. I had smoorsnoek – fish braised with onions – on mine. Alison had sweetmilk cheese and thin slices of tomato. We weren't allowed to eat from Christians, but I didn't see the harm in it as long as it wasn't meat. Still, I wasn't hungry. My mind was on the note I would have to take home.

"We'll wait for her by the steps, and moer her," Alison said. "That bitch!"

"I have to stay after school," I reminded her. "I'm going to start writing. A hundred lines is a lot. My mother's going to ask why I'm late."

"Don't show her the note."

I'd thought of the same thing. "What about the signature?"

"*We* can sign it."

"We can't sign like that, and I don't know my mother's signature."

Alison grinned. "Neither does Miss Van Niekerk. We can ask my brother, Willie. He's in Standard Six, and writes just like a grown-up."

"Are you sure?" I wasn't comfortable with the idea. Our plans to outwit adults had backfired before.

When the final bell rang, I remained in my seat. Miss Van Niekerk was marking test papers at the table up front. The halls had emptied. Outside on Bryant and Bloem Streets I could hear the grinding of gears as cars struggled up the hill. To make sure I didn't cheat, Miss Van Niekerk handed me several sheets of paper on which to write out my crime one hundred times. She wasn't interested in the forty-three lines I'd already written in my exercise book. I felt angry as I sat there writing. Even if I managed a way around the signature, I'd still have to explain why I was late.

At last, I was done and took my sheets up to the front. Miss Van Niekerk didn't look up from her marking and made me stand there, shifting from one foot to the other. Finally, she looked up.

"I'm done, Miss."

She took the sheets from me and counted the pages. Mmmm, she grunted, pointing to several lines where my e's sloped to the left, especially on the last page where I'd got tired of writing the same thing over and over again. I waited for the verdict. I had a pee waiting to burst out of me, and one wrong word from her ... I didn't know what might happen.

Then she said it. "Your handwriting's sloppy. Write it fifty times more."

I hated her, and was ready to say something, but couldn't hold my pee in any longer, and ran from the classroom. I didn't make it round the corner. Right there on the quadrangle in full view of anyone who cared to look down from Bloem Street, I tore at my navy blue bloomers, squatted, and let go. Miss Van Niekerk came to the door and watched me. I kept my head down. I was peeing on the grounds. No words would save me, and I didn't try. And my pee was noisy, rushing out of me like an angry little stream. I shook off the last drops, pulled up my underwear, and left. I didn't want to think of the consequences, and felt the first of the cramps coming on. I hated these cramps. They came on suddenly, and when they'd first started when I was very little, usually after my mother had had words with my father, my mother thought I needed castor oil, which she forced into me with terrible results.

When I got home, I went straight to my mother. She was at the kitchen table sewing buttons on a customer's dress. Little granny was at the other end, shelling peas into a bowl. My mother looked up when she saw me. I greeted them and put down my school-case.

"It's after three," she said. "Didn't I tell you to come straight home from school? Murida comes all the way from Trafalgar and is here before you. I can spit on the school roof from the kitchen window, and you only come now."

"Miss Van Niekerk kept me in."

She rested the customer's dress on her lap. "Why?"

Before I could answer, Murida came into the kitchen and said that a teacher from St Paul's was at the door. The heat rose to my face. My minutes were numbered. I noticed the frown forming between my mother's brows. She rearranged the scarf on her head, and went inside.

"What happened at school, Titch?" Murida asked.

I glanced at my sister. I always knew how she felt about me by what she called me. Titch was my mother's special name for me, and one I liked. Murida had to be in a good mood, I thought. "I talked in class. I had to stay after school and write a hundred times that I was rude."

Little granny took off her glasses and put them next to the peas. She peered up at me from under her brows. "*Were* you rude?"

"No. I just said that I told Alison that my great-grandmother had moved into our house. The teacher asked if that was important enough to interrupt the class. It wasn't even me. She kept on. I told her that my great-grandmother *was* special. She didn't like that I said it, and told me to say sorry."

"Did you?"

"No."

"Why not?"

"She embarrassed me, and said in front of everyone that I'm not good at sums."

We heard the front door close. Everyone looked towards the entrance. My mother came into the kitchen. I wish I could describe the look on her face. Anger would've been easy. She would've reached for the wooden spoon or the feather duster, and a few taps on the hands would've ended it. Her stillness made me feel as if I'd stolen money out of her purse.

"I'm disappointed in you, Khadidja."

The dreaded "d" word. And my full name.

"A teacher coming to the house and telling me I have a rude child. Imagine that. A rude child. You twice-fived her, then ran outside and peed on the grass."

"Tell your side of the story," little granny said next to me.

I looked at my great-grandmother. My great-grandmother believed I had a point of view. I took a deep breath, hoping I'd get the whole story out, and started with how Miss Van Niekerk had made me stand outside when I arrived late. I told my story without begging anyone to believe what I said.

My mother listened. When I was done she got up and stirred the pot on the stove. She stirred it for an eternity. I didn't know if this was the end of the matter, if I could get up, or if there was more to come. She was an expert at keeping us trembling. Finally, she put the lid back on the pot, and sat down where she could look me straight in the eye.

"Go put on your pyjamas and stay in your room. I want you to write Miss Van Niekerk a note and tell her you're sorry for being rude. I never want Miss Van Niekerk or anyone else ever coming here again to tell me my child has no manners. Do you understand?"

"Yes, Mummy."

"Now go to your room and stay there."

I went to the bedroom I shared with little granny, and took off my clothes. It was half past three in the afternoon. Outside I could hear my Christian friends playing. The Moslem ones were at madressah learning how to be good Moslems. My room was next to the kitchen. From its window with the wide window-sill your eyes smacked straight into the vastness of Table Mountain and Devil's Peak. It appeared so near, you could see rocks and bushes and paths. Below, to the right, was the silver roof of St Paul's Primary. I watched the goings-on of life outside my quiet little room: cars travelling along Buitengracht Street; a man pulling a cart with vegetables in it and a boy shoving from behind, making slow progress up Bloem. I counted the boats in the harbour – something I often did in the afternoons – to see if any new ones had docked while I was at school. I was hungry, I hadn't had tea and bread. The yellow loquats on the tree ten feet below in the yard tempted me, and I thought of the Marie Biscuits I'd seen on the table that morning. But there was nothing I could do except wait for evening to arrive. The stone in my heart was my mother's disappointment. Only God knew how long it would take her to have faith in me now.

It was about five o'clock, an hour before supper, when there was a knock on my door. Kulsum Gamieldien from next door stood in the doorway, surprised to see me in my pyjamas lying on the bed. She went to Schotsche Kloof Primary and we didn't see each other until madressah on Pepper Street in the afternoons. When I hadn't shown up, she came to see where I was. My mother told her I wasn't allowed out, but that she could come to my room. Kulsum had a round face with brown eyes and straight black hair, and her eyes were so expressive of how she felt, I knew immediately that she had something to tell me.

"Why are you in your pyjamas?" she asked.

I told her what had happened at school, but left out the part about Alison. Kulsum didn't like Alison because she thought Alison was becoming my best friend, and was always telling me things about Alison or her brothers to break us up.

"Have you written the note yet?" she asked.

"I don't know what to say."

"Just say, 'Dear miss. My mother told me to write to you and say sorry. I'm sorry.' That way you're not really saying sorry."

"My mother will want to see the note."

Kulsum thought for a moment. "Write two notes. Show your mother one, and give the teacher the other one."

I hadn't thought of such a strategy myself. Then she asked the burning question, the one I'd expected her to ask first. "Is that woman in the kitchen your family?"

I wondered how much I should tell her. It wasn't that I didn't trust her, but that trust had to include her brothers and sisters in the event she needed to trade secrets with them. "Did *you* have something to tell me?" I asked her instead.

"Yes," she said, sitting down on the edge of the bed. "But you can't tell anyone. Booia doesn't want the whole world to know."

"What is it?" I asked.

She took a Star sweet out of her pocket, bit it in half through the paper, and gave me a piece. I struggled to get the paper off the sticky pink sweet and put it in my mouth. Stars were our favourite, especially when we'd sucked them to the end and had shocking pink lips.

"Booia asked Gabieba if she would stay home and help mama."

"What do you mean?" I asked. Gabieba was fourteen years old and the cleverest of the Gamieldien girls. Her report card placed her in the top ten of all the Standard Eights in the whole of Trafalgar. Everyone knew Gabieba wanted to be a teacher.

"He said to Gabieba that it's too much for my mother to do all the work, that she needs help with the washing and cooking, also so that my mother could work on her sewing. If Gabieba would stay home, he would make her a new outfit every month."

I'd seen the washing loads on Mondays and Thursdays at the Gamieldiens. Ironing took a whole day. And cooking food for thirteen people was a lot of onions and potatoes and garlic and ginger that had to be cleaned. It was cruel to ask someone to give up school to do this. I couldn't believe that anyone would agree. "When did your father ask her?"

"Last night, at the supper table. Gabieba eats with us in the room, but he called her to come and eat with them in the kitchen. If you eat in the kitchen, you can dish up your own food."

"Your father asked? He didn't say she had to do it, he didn't force her?"

"No. He said twice that if she wanted to continue to matric, she could. But if she helped our mother, he would make her a new outfit every month."

"Every month?"

"That's what he said."

"Is she going to do it? I wouldn't."

"Me neither. She asked if she could think about it, then for the rest of the night she said nothing. She wouldn't talk to me or Fatima about it. We were in the same bed, asking her what she was going to do, but she didn't tell us anything. The whole night she fidgeted, keeping us awake. This morning when she got dressed, she didn't put on her uniform, and didn't say anything. You know

Gabieba. I told you about that time when Riaz was born and she had to bring the hot water to the door. She wouldn't tell us what she saw. She's very secretive. Anyway, my father was in the work-room when Gabieba came into the kitchen. My mother went to tell him that Gabieba wasn't dressed for school. He came out and talked to her, then called Fatima and me and Moosa and Riaz, and told us that Gabieba was going to stay home and help with the work in the house, and that we must appreciate our older brothers and sister – that they were working to help the family so the four of us could continue our schooling. One day when we were teachers and principals, we were not to forget those who'd sacrificed their school years for us."

The story upset me, and I felt sorry for Gabieba. I blamed her mother and father for all those children. I wasn't supposed to blame parents because parents could commit any crime against a child and it would be okay by God. You heard all the time that a parent could hit you and chase you out the front door, and you had to eat humble pie and come in through the back. No matter what they did, even if they were wrong, you had to keep quiet. A parent had rights, and a mother's rights were the highest of all. But what about the rights of Gabieba?

"Does your father keep his promises?"

Kulsum took off her scarf and combed out her plaits with my comb. "He keeps a promise better than my mother. My mother will just tell you she didn't have time, that we must be grateful for what we have."

"What does Gabieba say?"

"She doesn't say anything. She's making tomato bredie for supper."

"Can she make tomato bredie?"

"It's the only thing she can make. You just braise the onions with the meat and the garlic, then throw in lots of tomatoes. The potatoes go in at the end."

Murida appeared at the door and told me it was time to eat. I could tell from her face looking at the two of us skindering on the bed, that she knew we'd been discussing a secret. We waited for her to leave, then Kulsum got up and walked to the door. "You never told me about the woman in the kitchen," she said. "Who's she?"

"It's my mother's grandmother. From Paarl."

Kulsum's eyes opened wide with this news. "She looks like a white person."

I couldn't tell the truth – it was too ordinary – but couldn't not. "Does she look white?"

"Yes."

"I think she is. She's come to stay with us. She sleeps with me in this room. Last night I read her a story. She said she also had some to tell me."

Poor Gabieba. I'm glad I'm not her. The teacher came to the house and squealed on me. Little granny took my side.

Khadidja was in her office with a layout artist selecting shots for an upcoming issue when her secretary knocked on the door. "It's Alison."

Khadidja glanced at her watch. It had been a busy morning with artists and photographers, the hours had flown by. "Tell her to come in. I'm just wrapping up with Carl."

It was the holy month of Ramadan, she and Alison were fasting, but had agreed to meet at Khadidja's office to go to the bookshop during the lunch hour.

Alison appeared at the door. "Hi."

Khadidja turned, surprised by Alison's new hairdo. People never said about Alison that she was pretty. Words like exotic and sensual came to mind. Alison had an athlete's narrow hips and legs, and looked like the girl blue jeans had been invented for. But Farouk hadn't liked jeans, and Alison had given them away. That, and the hoop earrings, the nail polish, and the mini skirts. It was two months since Farouk's departure. The jeans were back, and the hoop earrings – big silver ones that dangled like disks from her ears – and a new look. "You cut your hair. I like it."

Alison waited for Carl to leave. "I needed to do something. I don't feel very attractive these days."

Khadidja picked up her bag, and walked with her to the door. "Don't be silly. You look great. If you keep it short like this, you don't have to do anything to it."

Alison felt about her head. "You can see my scalp, you mean."

"Almost. Come, we have an hour. I ordered this book three weeks ago. They called yesterday to say it was in."

Out on Burg Street, they walked quickly up to Long. "Did I tell you I've got a title for my book?" Khadidja asked. "*First Wife.*"

"I like it. Polygamy? Divorce?"

"Sort of." She had never discussed the plot with anyone before. "It's about a woman who sees her life fading away, and seems unable to stop it. Her husband takes a second wife. She's hurt, but has no choice. Then she meets a younger man. Younger than her husband."

"I like that. Does she leave the husband?"

Khadidja stopped to dislodge something that had found its way into her shoe. "You'll have to read it," she said with a mischievous smile.

"You mean you don't know."

"I do. I'm on the last chapter. I'll let you take a look soon. I want your honest opinion before I submit it. It's just a bit hard right now to write while we're fasting. There's no sugar to the brain, I can't create. I need coffee, chocolate. A cigarette would be even better, but I've given that up. How did the meeting with Saville go?"

Alison sighed heavily. "I've signed the affidavit, and he's spoken to Fingerhut. There's no problem with Leila – Farouk's accepted that she has to stay with me – but there's going to be war over the business and properties. He's made an offer. Fifty thousand."

"Already?" They stopped at a curio shop and looked in the window. "He seems anxious to settle. Are you going to accept it?"

"No. I helped set up that business. I know what it pulls in, what it's worth. Saville's asked for profit and loss statements." She became distracted by a silver bracelet with turquoise stones. "What a beautiful piece," she pointed to it in the window.

Khadidja looked at the price tag. Alison turned into a shopping fiend when she was depressed. "You have that kind of money on you? It's five hundred."

"I'll put it on my card. Why not? I've already spent fifty on my hair."

Khadidja didn't say anything. Ramadan wasn't a month for hairdressers and tight clothes, but these things provided the same fix as a cigarette – something to tide you over a rough patch. She led Alison into the shop. The shop owner was an elderly man with black-rimmed spectacles. He handed the bracelet to Alison who fitted it on. "How does it look?" she held out her wrist.

"It suits you."

"I like silver much better than gold." She took out her card and gave it to the shop owner.

Khadidja watched her delight over the new bracelet. The bracelet would be a novelty for a week or two, then Alison would drop it into a drawer and forget about it. She hoped this was the end of the shopping spree. She noticed a sign behind the counter. "Do you buy gold?" she enquired of the man behind the counter.

"Yes."

Khadidja slipped the ring off the finger of her left hand. "Just as a matter of curiosity. I never know what these things are worth."

He placed a credit card form in front of Alison for her to sign, and took the ring from Khadidja. He poured a drop of liquid onto it, examined it. She imagined he was doing some kind of test. "I'll give you fifty," he said after a while.

"This is what my ring's worth?"

"That's what I'll pay for it."

"Why do you want to sell your ring?" Alison asked.

"I don't want to sell it. I just want to know what it's worth." She took the ring back, and slipped it onto her finger. "It's twenty past. We have to hurry."

Back out on the street, they walked quickly up to the bookshop, picked up Khadidja's book, and left.

"Ramadan's nearly over," Alison said. "I haven't had you and Rudy over for supper yet. How's he?"

They were almost at the corner where they had to part to return to their respective offices. "Fine."

Alison glanced at her quickly. "That didn't come out right."

"Didn't it?"

"No."

Khadidja walked for a few moments in silence. At the corner she stopped to wait for the traffic. "I think he's seeing someone."

"What?"

"Don't ask me now." She squeezed Alison's hand and darted across the street to avoid an oncoming car.

Walking home after work that evening, Khadidja thought about what she'd told Alison. Telling had made it real. It was out now. Irretractable. The doubts, suspicions, were complete in that moment. She couldn't deny it anymore. At home she found her mother busy at the stove.

"It smells good in here. What's Mummy making?"

"Curry. Your sister brought crayfish tails."

"My goodness. We're getting extravagant."

"It wasn't extravagant. Maan got them through a connection. They invited us also to come and eat with them on Sunday night."

Khadidja put down her bags and went to her room to change out of her suit. Murida was a different girl from the old days, she thought, and it amazed her when she heard the things Murida did for her husband. Setting out his clothes in the mornings; picking his tie, socks, shirt; frying his eggs with a tablespoon of butter; toasting his bread a golden brown. Every morning before he left for the office, she asked what he wanted for that night's supper. Murida selected the movies and plays they went to. If her sister could play cricket, Khadidja felt sure that she would've joined Maan's team and batted with them on Saturday afternoons.

Khadidja went back out to the kitchen to help her mother fill four small plates with coconut pancakes. Every night she told her mother that they didn't need all these cakes and samoosas and koeksisters from the neighbours, and every night her mother reminded her of the tradition of exchange. She ate enough pumpkin and banana fritters during the holy month to last her a year.

Rudy arrived home shortly after six. Usually, he performed as'r prayers, then relaxed in the front room with the *Argus* until supper. This evening he came straight to the kitchen and sat at the table, fanning the pages over the plates.

From where she stood at the stove fluffing up the rice in the pot with a fork, Khadidja watched him. He was skimming the articles, hardly reading. The sunset hour was one of solitude in a Muslim home. No radio, no television. Often, while waiting out those last minutes for the muezzin to signal that it was maghrib, Ateeka would read from the Qur'an, and Khadidja would be on her prayer mat in the bedroom.

Presently they heard the call to prayer from the Chiappini Street mosque. Ateeka passed around the dates. Khadidja took one, and broke her fast with a glass of water. She watched Rudy take a samoosa from one of the plates. No one spoke. A few minutes later they went into the front room to perform maghrib prayers. Rudy stood in front, Khadidja and Ateeka on their prayer mats behind him. Khadidja listened to his voice as he recited the Fatiha in Arabic. *Thee do we worship, and thine aid we seek. Show us the straight way.* He had a beautiful reciting voice, she thought, and had always marvelled at his ability to memorise the Qur'an, a feat accomplished in childhood.

She caught herself thinking worldly thoughts, and tried to concentrate on her devotions. But concentration on the prayer mat was an art, especially if you prayed in a language that wasn't your own. The mind wandered while the mouth mumbled, and in the beginning performing salaah had been ritualistic and mindless. But she'd rediscovered her faith. God didn't want meaningless words. The heart had to follow the words and prostrations, and the heart wasn't always a willing partner. A born-again Christian at the office some years ago had prayed for her back to heal when she'd injured it at the gym, and touched her so by his words, his reverence, the love that filled his eyes and voice when he spoke to God, that she vowed to change her own way of communicating with the Almighty. She still performed salaah as prescribed by the Prophet, but when it was over, sat a few extra minutes on her mat with her eyes closed, just saying thank you over and over again in her heart. She didn't talk, she didn't think, she just allowed all God's goodness to flow into her.

Prayers ended and she returned to the kitchen. She dished up the food, and took a seat on Rudy's left.

Rudy handed her mother the bowl of rice. "Go ahead, Ma."

Khadidja watched him. He'd said six words to them all evening. Dishes were passed around in silence. No one seemed to have anything to say.

"A few more days, then it's all over," Khadidja said. "Are you going to tarawih?" He'd gone to mosque every night for tarawih prayers. She'd spoken for the sake of breaking the silence.

The question revived him. "I'm not going tonight. There's something I want to say, and the best way, I think, is just to come out and say it." His head moved in her direction without really focusing. "I didn't plan it, Khadidja, or look for it. It just happened. It's not my intention to hurt you. But Islam allows a man to take a second wife ..."

The words struck her in the heart.

"... there'll be no difference, no favourites. I'll divide my time equally between the two homes. I'll come home Fridays and spend the weekend with you."

She listened in a daze, her eyes focused on the pinhead of decay between his front teeth. She hadn't noticed it before. "This was where you went on all those appointments?"

He met her eyes with weak defiance. "If God allows a man to have a second wife, there has to be a time for him to see her and develop the friendship."

The arrogance stunned her. She glanced at her mother, who'd gone pale. "You don't have to divide your time, and you don't have to come here on Friday nights."

"What do you mean?"

"I mean you don't have to divide yourself up like a cheap loaf of bread – a piece for you and a piece for you. I'm not good with charity. When you're ready, you can go. No one's going to stop you." The calmness in her voice, her rational responses, belied what she felt.

"Look, I know you're upset."

"Upset?" She gave a sarcastic laugh. "Upset's when you break a fingernail, when you put too much bleach in the wash and spoil

46

a sweater. Anyway, do what you must. I won't stand in your way. And I'll sleep by myself tonight. You can move your things into the dining room until you decide."

His face turned purple. "It doesn't have to be this way. It doesn't have to separate us."

The breath felt heavy in her chest. "We separated long ago, Rudy. Jesus said that when a man looks at a woman with lustful eyes, he's already committed adultery in his heart. Women aren't hurt by the act. They're hurt when the thought first enters your brain."

His cheeks puffed up at these words. "I don't need someone who's afraid to wear a scarf to quote the Book to me. Read the Qur'an and see what it says in there."

"I think *you* should read it. But I'm not going to get into religious debate. What's happened is for the best. I always felt guilty that I couldn't give you children. The weight's off me now." She looked at a spot on the tablecloth. He had shocked her, utterly, but it had made it easier for her to speak.

He took hope from her words. "That's why I don't see why we have to end it. I want children. I can support both of you. You won't lack anything." He turned to Ateeka. "Tell her I'm within my rights, Ma. A woman must allow a man a second wife if she can't have children."

"My daughter must make her own decisions. I can't tell her what to do."

"But it's not wrong for me to have more than one wife."

Ateeka gave a thin smile. "That's what men keep telling women, and women cry long tears at night. Men bend the words of God, then quote God to justify their behaviour. God says a man can take a second wife, yes, but says also that it's hard for him to be fair. If he can't be fair, he must only have one. It's permitted. Not recommended. And a first wife doesn't have to accept it."

He paled under the reprimand. "I'm willing to compromise."

"Compromise?" Khadidja laughed. "Don't make me swear during this holy month. When you asked to marry me, did you say I want you now, but in ten years' time I might want someone else? You should've said that. Besides," she moved a potato around on her plate, looking up at him slowly, "I don't love you."

He looked at her in stunned silence.

"That's right. And don't look at me like that."

"You *never* loved me? All the time we were together?"

"I thought it would happen. It didn't. I married you because I thought it would stabilise me. It did. I calmed down. But I didn't grow feelings."

His face was flushed. He pushed back his chair and it made a scraping sound. "Was this necessary?"

Her voice crackled with sarcasm. "Well, it seems it's a night for truth."

"Maybe you have someone yourself. Maybe you're even glad I'm going, making it easy for you."

She gave a little laugh. "Don't make yourself out to be the injured party, Rudy. It doesn't suit you. You weren't happy, you looked elsewhere. Be glad I'm not making a fuss. Do what you have to do. And don't wait three months to send the imam. We all know there's no chance I'll be pregnant, so send the imam any time."

Rudy looked at his mother-in-law. Ateeka didn't meet his eyes.

"That's it, then," he said, stepping away from the table. "I'll sleep on the sofa and move out after Ramadan. It didn't have to be like this, Khadidja. I don't want to hear tomorrow that I left my wife for another woman. I wanted to keep you, remember that."

"Oh, fuck off, will you. Don't be pathetic."

She called Alison as soon as the dishes were washed, and told her.

"A second wife? Rudy? I don't believe it. I never would've thought that of him."

"Remember that night you were here for supper and he said he had an appointment? According to him, he's allowed to have these appointments if he's to develop the friendship. How do you like that? *Develop the friendship.* I've never heard cheating on your wife called that before. He actually believes he has God's permission."

"Unbelievable."

"I wasn't happy in the marriage, but I stuck it out. *He* wasn't happy, and got a replacement. We do this to ourselves, Alison. The thing looks jaundiced, but we hang on. In the end they stick it to us. Exactly like in my story. Only, I wrote the story first, and *then* it happened. How can that be?"

"Maybe you wished it."

"In the story, the wife meets a younger man."

"You told me. Is there a relationship between those characters?"

"He comes to the house. They sit in the living room and have tea. She doesn't allow him to come after sunset. The curtains are always open. He asks if she'd like to go for a walk with him the following Sunday. I guess that's a friendship. But I don't want to talk about my story. The story's fantasy. Do you think it's us, Alison? That there's something planted in our brains that makes us wait for the last bullet?"

"It's our mothers. They're to blame. They train us to be these patient handmaidens. Don't make trouble, they say. If he says yellow is green, let him believe it even though you know it's not so. *Let him win. It's important for the man to win.* So we give them the biggest piece of meat, the last word, the benefit of most of our doubts. We wash and fetch and overlook, and they sell us down the river faster than you can wash between your legs. There's nothing dignified about being replaced. It's the golden handshake for years of loyal service. The last thing you want to be is charitable. You were still nice. I would've thrown the pot at him. But at least you had it face-to-face, you got it straight from him. I found out about Farouk from other people, and then when I confronted him with it, he still lied. You really want to make money with your writing, Titch? Write a handbook for people contemplating marriage – *how to recognise a prick before you get pricked* – and dedicate it to him."

Khadidja laughed. "It's late. In a few hours we have to be up for fajr. In a way I'm glad the fast is ending."

"Me too. This was my first Ramadan alone. It was tough."

"You miss him?"

"You can't help it. And you don't want someone else to have him even though you don't want him yourself. It's all a fuck-up. I was thinking. There's this women's class on Wednesday nights at Imam Adams' house in Duke Street. I was thinking of going. Every year I promise myself to attend one of his classes, and every year I don't do it."

Khadidja knew what was meant by every year. The anniversary of Nazli's death. It was a hard time for Alison, and a painful time for Khadidja. Alison never spoke about it directly to her, but one day Khadidja would bring it up. One day she would force Alison to speak of that fateful night.

JUNE 14
Rudy wants a second wife. The irony of it. The cheek. I never thought that he would be the one breaking us up.

~

On a Saturday afternoon, a few weeks after Kulsum told me about Gabieba, we saw the first evidence of boeta Amien's promises. The sky had been purple and broody all morning, promising rain. After lunch, the heavens swelled up like a mushroom and exploded over our heads.

I was in the front room looking out the window at the water rushing down the slope, and saw Fatima and Kulsum outside. I went to my room, put on my navy-blue raincoat, and went out to join them.

"Guess what," Kulsum said. "Gabieba got her first outfit. A dress and a coat."

"Really?" I knew that boeta Amien had a big winter order for blazers and that everyone in the house had been helping.

"You must see it," Fatima said. "The coat has twenty-four buttons. Gabieba's going to the matinée."

"The matinée!" I said enviously. "Where?" I'd only been to the bioscope once with my mother, and had never forgotten the experience of sitting in the dark with a packet of crisps and a cool drink, watching John Wayne chase after a swarm of Apaches.

"To the Alhambra. She's going with her friend, Reedie, from Trafalgar. Reedie's father's coming to pick her up with the car and dropping them off."

"They're going alone?"

"Yes. She's already dressed, waiting for the car to come and fetch her."

"Take off your shoes," Fatima said. "They're getting dirty."

I looked down at my boots with the white fur inside. They were my special shoes, not to be worn on school days or in the rain. I removed them, and flung them over the low wall onto the stoep. The three of us dragged our feet through the warm mud to the other side of the road where Riaz and Moosa and Vuyo, each with a jar in their hands, were getting ready to go up the hill.

"Where are you going?" I asked.

"To look for tadpoles," Riaz said. "No girls allowed." Riaz was the youngest of the Gamieldiens, but the most adventurous, and the one who got most into trouble. No one had been sent home from school more times than him. Playing in the rain was a great time for us, and if there was a puddle anywhere with even one tadpole in it, Riaz would find it.

The three of us watched them clamber up the hill. "A car's coming," Kulsum said as a black car turned into our street.

She'd hardly said the words when the Packard clugged to a stop in front of boeta Tapie's house. We sloshed over to go and see. A big man with a red fez was behind the wheel, with a girl next to him in the front seat. The man tried to get the car moving by stopping and starting, but it was no use. The wheels spun in the clay, splashing us with orange mud. The boys saw what was happening, and came running down the hill.

The man rolled down the window. "Can you children give us a push?"

We looked at one another. We knew it was Reedie's father, and Reedie sitting next to him.

"It won't work," Moosa said.

"What do you mean?"

"This is Sachs Street. People park on Pepper Street when it rains."

The man sighed. "Maybe if you push backwards."

We moved to the front of the Packard. "I'll tell you when," the man called from the window. "Now!"

All together we heaved our bodies against the car and pushed.

The wheels turned without moving the car forward, whirring mud at us until we were soaked to our necks.

"Khadidja!" I heard my mother's voice.

I left my friends, and walked to the house, my clothes plastered against my body.

"Look at you," my mother said in a harsh tone.

"We're trying to push the car out," I said. "It's people for next door. Gabieba's going to the matinée."

Moosa came up. "Aunty Teeka, the boeta wants to know if we can make a phone call to the Council. I told him the Council can get the car out."

We were the only ones on Sachs Street with a telephone, and made these calls at least once every winter. "I'll phone," my mother said. She turned to me. I expected to be ordered into the house. "Look where you threw your shoes," she said. "Make sure you clean them properly when you come in."

I ran out to the other children, happy to be free to play in the rain. Reedie had gone inside the Gamieldien house with sies Moena. Her father stood with boeta Amien on the stoep, looking frequently at his watch.

"Daar kommie vlooi!" Riaz shouted as the small City Council car with the pointed nose turned into our street.

We watched the men get to work: one in the vlooi – we nick-named the Council car the flea for its smallness and agility – the other standing with his boots in the mud, directing him; a third behind the steering wheel of the Packard, the front of which was sunk lower into the mud than the rest of its body. The vlooi positioned its nose up against the front fender. There was a command, a whirr of engines, and the Packard lifted gracefully out of the mud like an old camel getting up on its haunches.

When the Council people left, Reedie and Gabieba came out on the stoep. I couldn't take my eyes off Gabieba. She was wearing stockings and shoes with a small heel much too grand for the muddy steps to the car, and a black tailored coat with narrow sleeves and buttons that ran all the way from her neck in a tight row down to her waist.

"We're late for the matinée now, Booia," she said to her father. I could see she was nervous saying this to him in case he changed his mind.

Boeta Amien looked at the man next to him. "They *are* late," he said. "What about the five o'clock show? I'll drive them and bring Reedie home."

A five o'clock show, I thought. You had to be at least sixteen to be allowed to go out that late and come home after dark, and everyone knew that to sit in a place of entertainment during maghrib prayer time was to have no respect for your God. I'd hardly thought it when Reedie's father said, "But they'll be sitting in bioscope right through the waqt."

"That's true," boeta Amien nodded gravely. "But it's not their fault. Of course, it's only this one time. It won't happen again."

Reedie's father had already decided, I could see, but was pretending to think about it so his daughter could appreciate how difficult the decision was for him. "Of course. All right, just this once. In future, if they want to go to bioscope, it'll have to be the matinée show."

I felt happy for Gabieba, and liked boeta Amien for breaking his own rules so she could go. Gabieba wasn't like me or my sister or even Kulsum and Fatima, who argued with older people. She just took whatever they gave her. I don't know if this was intentional, but sometimes it worked for her when she said hardly anything.

"Do you want to come with us when we take them?" Kulsum asked.

I jumped at the chance of riding in Lizzie, and went home immediately to wash. There wasn't enough hot water on the stove, and I stood shivering under a dribble of lukewarm drops from the overhead bucket in the shed, scrubbing myself with Lifebuoy soap. My mother put out my green corduroy pants and beige jersey, and warm once again, I went with Kulsum and Fatima and Moosa and Riaz and boeta Amien in the Plymouth, and delivered Gabieba and her friend to bioscope.

"When can *we* go, Booia?" Riaz asked as we watched the two girls disappear into the foyer. They had money for ice-cream and chips, and we could see the back of Gabieba's coat as they stood behind a line of people waiting to buy something.

Boeta Amien turned to look at him sitting in the back seat. "You and Moosa help with the bastings in the afternoons instead of playing in the street, and you can also go."

I knew about those bastings, especially at Christmas time when boeta Amien had orders for the cricket team and the Malay Choirs, and a mountain of blazers lay waiting. Every blazer had long white threads up the sleeves, over the lapels, across the pockets, alongside the back slit. A blazer couldn't go to a customer with even one thread or knot showing. At the end of the year all the Gamieldien children sat with a blazer across their laps snipping and pulling. It was a tiring job. There were no deals. They just had to do it.

Not long after Gabieba's outing to the matinée, oemie Jaweier called at our house on a Saturday morning to come and visit. She was my father's mother, and as my father seemed to have forgotten he had children, she felt it her duty to come and see how we were. I don't know why I never took to her. She was a good grandmother and only wanted to see us grow up with God in our hearts and a scarf on our heads, but I couldn't take her strictness and the way her eyes narrowed and her lips thinned when she told Murida and me what would happen to us if we didn't do God's bidding. She had no shame pulling my sister's plaits in front of people when she saw Murida without a scarf.

The day she arrived, little granny and I were sitting on the stoep – me on a Pepsi Cola crate, little granny on a wooden chair with two cushions – both of us with newspaper on our laps, cleaning garlic for my mother for the week. Sitting on the stoep in the morning sun and telling me stories was little granny's favourite thing. Her grandmother was the daughter of a slave woman and an Afrikaner, she said – I knew this already from what she'd told my mother that first day – and had lived briefly in a foreign land, married first to a German, then to a Mohammedan. It was this second husband, her dark great-grandfather she was telling me about, when suddenly, up stepped oemie Jaweier onto the stoep in a puff of robes and veils and camphor fumes from the bandage around her bad leg.

"Oemie," I said, greeting her quickly. She was dead strict about the way children had to greet older people. You had to say salaam aleikoem, then kiss her on the cheek, after which you had to ask, "How's Oemie?" I did so. She kissed me back, her eyes fastening on little granny sitting there in a maroon dress and stockings and black shoes.

"This is little granny," I told her. "From Paarl."

Her eyebrows lifted. "Little granny?"

My mother came out. "Mama ... what a surprise ..." They kissed and greeted. "This is my oemie, from Paarl," she explained. "My mother's mother, Janey."

Oemie Jaweier was veiled, with only her eyes and nose showing. But she was in the company of women now, and so she unpinned something at the side of her neck to release the veil from her mouth. "I didn't know you had a grandmother, Ateeka. From Paarl? I didn't know that. Did Hassiem know?"

You could see from the way her eyes darted back and forth between my mother and little granny that she was trying to work things out in her head. Little granny looked like a proper white woman. Not like Sandra, next door, who put powder on her face and sat in the white tearoom cinema. From far away, Sandra could pass for a white. Up close you could see the hair at the ears and in the neck where the hot iron couldn't straighten it properly. Little granny could've been the queen's mother, so fine and delicate she was. You could inspect her from any angle. What probably added to oemie Jaweier's confusion was that a woman of little granny's age was sitting there bareheaded. She would never have thought little granny was Moslem.

"I can't remember if I told Hassiem about my grandmother," my mother said. "But Oemie's out early today. Shopping? Who brought Oemie?"

"Mietjie had to see a customer in Leeuwen Street. He dropped me. I have some things for the children. Their father sent them comic books and chocolates."

"Comic books and chocolates?" my mother choked back a laugh. "They need shoes on their feet and food in their stomachs. Does he think sending chocolates and comics cancels his duty as a father? He hasn't seen them in months. What kind of father is that?"

"Ateeka ..." little granny said in an embarrassed tone.

"He's a thoughtless, selfish –"

"It's your mother-in-law … she's not responsible …"

"It's all right," oemie Jaweier said. "Ateeka's right. Children need to see their father, even if the father and mother don't see eye to eye. You can't take it out on the children. The two of them have to work things out."

"There's nothing to work out," my mother said. "He made his bed. He must just do his duty by his children. I want nothing for myself, but he has to pay for his children."

Oemie Jaweier slipped her hand into her robe and brought out an envelope. "Boeta Braima gave this. He wants them to have new outfits and shoes."

"No," my mother pushed back her hand. "I won't let a grandfather give his pension money to my children. Thank you, but I can't."

Oemie Jaweier looked hurt. "He niyatted this for them. He'll be upset if you don't take it." A niyat was an intention, from the heart, that you couldn't deny someone the pleasure to give.

"I know, but it's not right. I can't take it. Please, come in, I'll make tea. It's getting hot on the stoep." She looked at little granny. "Is Granny coming?"

"Yes," little granny said, and one, two, three, the envelope changed hands behind my mother's back. I was shocked. These women were strangers, but without words, one passed it to the other, and the other took it without question. Oemie Jaweier had given it to little granny because the money had been niyatted for us. It was almost a burden for oemie Jaweier to continue to have it. I helped little granny out of the chair, then plunked myself back on the crate, wondering how she would give this money to my mother who had far too much pride to take my grandfather's money when my sister and I needed going-out shoes and school blazers.

I was still thinking about it when Murida, who'd been sent to motjie Janie's shop for a tin of tomato paste, appeared on the stoep.

"Guess who's here. Your favourite."

"Who?"

"Oemie."

Murida made a face. "She's not my favourite. Did she say anything?"

"About what?"

"About my father."

She said it as if he were her father alone, but I didn't mind. She could have him.

"He sent chocolates and comics."

"That's all?"

I didn't bother to answer. I didn't know what else she expected. The question was stupid considering that my father never called or sent anything.

"I'd better put on my doek," she said.

"Why? I didn't."

"You're only eight. She won't do anything to you. I'm twelve."

I looked at her. A few months ago Murida had found a stain in her panties and the fuss made over it was as if gold had been discovered under Table Mountain. First my mother took her into the bedroom for a talk, then little granny added her own sixpence. I wasn't allowed to listen, but knew these things already from Alison who'd told me about this horrible thing that happened to girls every month. Murida was treated almost like a grown-up, and when her lentils sprouted and swelled into breasts, she was told she had to wear a scarf, she had to pray, she had to fast full days during the holy month except when she was sick, she wasn't to be alone with a boy, and she had to be careful how she sat with her legs. No one was to touch her anywhere.

I finished cleaning the garlic, rolled up the paper with the skins, and took the bowl into the kitchen where the grown-ups were seated at the table having tea.

"I'm finished, Mummy. Can I go play at Alison's?" I was taking a chance asking to be let out this time of the morning, but thought that since my mother was occupied with people, she wouldn't say no. But it was my grandmother's nosiness I'd forgotten about.

"Alison?" she asked with big eyes. "A Christian friend? You allow the children to play with Christians?"

"Alison's a nice girl," my mother said.

"Doesn't matter. You want them to mix with their own kind."

"They mix with their own kind, but they mix with other kinds also."

Oemie Jaweier sat back in her chair, looking a little hurt. "Well, it's not my business. They're your children. I'm only their grandmother. You know what's best for them."

I hated it when she did this – making my mother feel guilty. The last time oemie Jaweier pulled this stunt was when she saw Murida in corduroy pants and told my mother that Murida was big now, she shouldn't show the outline of her body. My mother had said Murida was just a twelve-year-old girl, but afterwards removed all the pants from the cupboard.

"Can I go, Mummy?" I asked again, feeling my chance slip away. "I always play at Alison's house. It's Saturday."

"Must you interrupt?" she turned on me suddenly. "Stay here now, and do your homework."

"I don't have homework."

"Well, do something else. Read a book."

I looked at my grandmother in her ugly black robe. "You have no say here," I said. "This is our house."

She covered her mouth in shock.

"Apologise to Oemie immediately!" my mother ordered.

"I *won't* apologise, and I won't stay! I'm going to Alison's!" And before she could do anything, I ran from the kitchen. I don't know what made me do it, but there I was out on the street, not knowing which way to go. My mind wasn't working properly, I felt the blood pumping through my veins. I'd never done such a thing before. And where would I run to? Alison's house was out of the question. I headed for the steps leading down between the houses to the street below. I heard my mother's voice, "Khadidja, come back here!" It was Khadidja now, not Titch. I darted down the steps as fast as my feet could take me, down Bloem Street, to Lion, to Bryant, until I found myself on Buitengracht Street. I paused briefly to look behind me to see if anyone was following. There was no one. I went down Wale Street to the Gardens, but I'd been there a few times with my father when he first came to see us on weekends, and decided to go to Darling Street rather, to the Grand Parade, and just walked and walked, all the way into District Six.

My first hour was filled with dread. I couldn't undo my crime. Nothing short of a Christian miracle, to use sies Moena's words, would save me. My destruction was being planned as I wandered around, and for a moment I almost considered running to my father's house in Duke Street in Walmer Estate.

I heard the boom of the cannon in the distance. Suddenly Bo-Kaap seemed far away. This was a new world, one I wasn't used to on my own. Hanover Street was long and winding, puffed up like a caterpillar with people and buses and cars, moving slowly, oozing smells.

I wandered past an old man sitting on a crate in the entrance to a building that looked like it was ready to collapse, fixing a guitar string. In the doorway next to it, two girls in high heels leaned against the frame, as if in a picture, posing for no one in particular. All around me were fish 'n chips shops and cafés and butchers and stalls and places with curry smells drifting out of them. I had no money to buy anything.

A place with a glass window and the words *Bennie's Hairdressing Salon* on the other side of the road attracted my attention, and I made my way over. I looked through the window. A man with a woman's hairstyle and very thin eyebrows was the first person I saw. I guessed that this was Bennie. The salon was full, with women sitting in front of mirrors reading magazines, smoking cigarettes, some with a cup in the hand, waiting their turn.

I looked longingly at a woman whose hair was being puffed up on her head. I'd seen people after they'd been to a hairdresser. Even Alison's hair looked real after her Christmas cut. But Alison's hair lasted only until it got wet, then it turned into a pot scraper, thick and clumpy, and she fought with it again. People judged you just for your hair, even if they knew nothing about you. Once, my own sister asked me why I was friends with a kroeskop like Alison. And grown-ups said things about it too, people who told you all day long not to fitnah about others. They were the worst.

An exchange of words between Bennie and one of the other hairdressers made me press my face into the window. The glass was too thick for me to hear, but I could make out from the way the other hairdresser's eyebrows lifted and the way he suddenly dusted off the customer's neck in a huff that he'd been told to do something. Bennie took money out of the till and handed it to him. He

59

took the money, said goodbye to the customer, and came out, grumbling under his breath.

"*I* can go," I stepped in front of him.

He took a step back at my sudden appearance. "Who're you?"

"I ran away," I blurted out, as if that explained anything.

He stared at me, not sure whether to trust me, then stuck some coins into my hand, "Go over there to the fish 'n chips shop for two packets of chips with salt and vinegar, and two Pepsis. Tell them it's for Niefie, they mustn't be stingy with the chips. And don't run off with the money."

I looked at the silver coins on my palm, but didn't let the money get hot in my hand. I dodged through the crowd, got the chips and drinks, and returned to the salon. I was nervous. I had to go inside. All those people would look at me.

I opened the door and didn't glance at anyone as I made for Niefie at the third chair. He took the chips and drinks. I held out my hand with the change. "Keep it," he said.

Bennie was at the next chair, snipping a customer's hair. "Sweep the floor," he said, "and there's more."

I realised I was being offered a job. I looked at the floor. There was hair everywhere around the chairs. That didn't bother me. I swept the stoep every morning before going to school. "I don't want money," I heard myself saying. "I'll do it if you fix my hair."

Bennie stopped snipping, and stood with the scissors poised in the air. "What's wrong with your hair?"

"I hate it."

His right eyebrow shot up. "You hate it?" He looked at me properly for the first time. "Who're you? I haven't seen you before."

"I ran away from home."

"You ran away? A little girl like you? Where did you run away from?"

"Sachs Street. In Bo-Kaap. And I'm not little. I can sweep up, *and* I can make tea."

"You ran all the way from Bo-Kaap? Do you know people here?"

The women in the chairs were staring at me now. I didn't answer.

"Your parents must be looking for you," he said. "Don't you

know it's dangerous? They steal girls, even little ones like you. Anyway, sweep up, make tea for the ladies, and I'll see what I can do. But we don't want pee tea. And don't put rooibos in it. I'm taking you home afterwards. What's your name?"

"Titch."

"Moegsien!" he called to someone at the far end. "Wys vir asterpoester daar waar's die goeters." Show Cinderella where everything is. When someone called you asterpoester, they didn't mean the princess who got to go to the ball, but the scrappy one with the dirty face who had to sweep out the chimney. I didn't mind. The way he said it wasn't mean, and I didn't want a glass slipper or a prince. All I wanted was hair that didn't shrink when someone breathed on it.

Moegsien took me behind a curtain and showed me the kettle and the tea things and the red plastic basin in which I had to take all the dirty dishes to the outside tap to wash. I rolled up the cuffs on my dress and got started. I had enough practice making my mother's tea, and in no time had seven cups filled with the strong brew. There were no complaints, and for the rest of the afternoon I swept up clumps and curls and strands, made tea, and listened to stories of children and husbands and things my mother would box my ears for. I liked it in the salon, and liked the hairdressers who were nice to me. Still, as the afternoon wore on, I became more and more worried about going home. I didn't know which crime would be considered worse – being rude to my grandmother, running away, or tampering with my hair. But frightened as I was of the hiding I would get, my decision to cut my hair wasn't going to change. I could get only one hiding.

The sun was almost setting when Bennie finally locked the door of the salon, and we started the walk back to my house. I had money in my pocket, two toffee rolls, and a hairstyle that brought tears to my eyes. But I said nothing. Bennie had cut my hair to my ear, then when I'd panicked about him putting on straightener, he'd simply worked his hand through it and stuck me under a burning hot hood. I came out with a frizzy helmet several inches thick on all sides of my head, ten times worse than before. I had to bite my lip not to cry when I had seen how it looked. It was in this frightening condition that I walked alongside him, hoping that somehow his presence would keep matters under control when my mother saw me. Bennie must've sensed my fear for he asked about my school and my parents, and what I wanted to be when I grew up. I don't remember anything I said. Finally we turned into my street. My heart jumped in my chest when I saw the commotion and all the people. It was a small street, but there was a police van, cars, Mrs Benjamin and Sandra, Galiema and her Christian husband, boeta Tapie, talking to the man on the fish cart, and all the children of the street. The whole community knew what I'd done, and were waiting for me. As I came nearer, I saw the tall figure of my father.

"Hey, toetkuif!" someone shouted at Bennie. Toetkuif was a very bad word having something to do with hair on people's private parts. Bennie ignored the remark and steered me through the crowd without looking at anyone. My father saw me and rushed forward. I walked past him to my mother. I was ready for my punishment, and just prayed it wouldn't be out there in front of everyone.

The policeman was a big white man in a blue uniform. He cleared his throat and started to speak Afrikaans in a gravelly tone. I couldn't understand all the words. Voices buzzed all around my head, bombarding me with questions. Why had I run away? Where had I been? What had happened to my hair? Who was this moffie in the Bette Davis hairdo? Didn't I know the worry I'd caused my poor mother?

Bennie explained that I'd been at his salon in District Six. Nothing bad had happened to me, they had even given me lunch, and done my hair. My mother trembled and burst out crying. Oemie Jaweier clucked like a turkey, saying it was all her fault. Sies Moena grabbed me to her like one of her own children, and said they'd all thought I'd been kidnapped. Kulsum stood between her brothers and sisters, actually crying. And little granny leaned on her cane on the stoep, watching as if from a great distance. I waited for my ear to be pulled, for my backside to be spanked, but nothing happened. My mother took my hand and walked me into the house. Out of the corner of my eye, I saw my sister with Gabieba, a dumb look on her face.

When I finally dropped dead tired into bed, having been given a glass of Ovaltine with lots of milk in it by my mother, I remembered the question I'd wanted to ask little granny that morning when we'd been interrupted by oemie Jaweier's arrival on the stoep.

"Granny, can I ask something?"

"What is it?"

"Did my mother have a father?"

"A father? Of course she had a father. Everyone has one."

"Then why don't I have two grandfathers? Like oupa Braima?"

She looked at me, her grey eyes thoughtful. "Not all fathers want to be fathers. But the thing to remember about fathers is that even a bad father is a father even if he doesn't act like one."

~

The winter rains came, spring fused into summer. Khadidja received her second talaq, and was divorced by Muslim rights. Not long after, she heard from her half-brother, Ishmail, that Rudy had married a legal secretary. She had expected that there would be a marriage, but still the news came as a surprise. There was information now about the woman who'd replaced her. The woman worked for lawyers. Possibly she was young and smart and would produce a string of children. Hearing of the marriage affected Khadidja in a way she didn't expect. She felt a loss. A loss of another time. A loss of community and closeness. But she got used to that too. Time scrambled the memories. She hadn't wanted to be a first wife. She'd never loved him. Her thoughts of him dwindled and after a while she regarded the decade they'd had together as kindergarten for the bigger picture to come. She surely wouldn't make the same mistake again.

On New Year's Eve she was lying on her bed with a typed manuscript, trying to edit the book that had taken her almost two years to write. The frenzy of the past weeks was over. Her mother had finished the enormous task of measuring, cutting and sewing thirty-two yellow satin jackets and pants for The Velvet Boys. The year before it had been The Emeralds; the year before that, The Pink Phantasias. Every year her mother vowed that it would be the last, and every year she couldn't resist making the outfits for the Coon Carnival. Every year when the sewing machine was finally put away, and New Year's Day arrived, her mother and sies Moena packed a basket with chicken sandwiches and biscuits and a flask of tea and went to Green Point Stadium. They would sit all day in the stands with their sandwiches and tea, and watch troupe after troupe of satin-dressed, black-faced, cane-tapping minstrels with their banjos and tambourines sing and dance in front of the judges.

Khadidja heard the tap at the door. It was her mother and sies Moena, in loose white pants and long tops, ready for their night on the town. Sies Moena's scarf was tied in front. Her mother had on a turban, emphasising her oval face. The women inspected themselves in the full-length mirror. Their New Year festivities started with the Malay Choirs on New Year's Eve.

"We're going now," Ateeka said. "I left some things on the table for when that man comes. He'll be here anytime now. When are you getting ready?"

"I'm not. I look fine." She turned to Moena Gamieldien. "I don't know why I allowed myself to be talked into this, sies Moena. My mother meets this man at a wedding, and one, two, three, she invites him over to come for tea."

"Be glad I did," Ateeka said. "You never would've asked him. Everyone could see how he was watching and listening to you."

"He's a lawyer. He knows how to listen."

"There you go. A lawyer, as if that's a bad thing. Anything wrong with having a man who can take care of you?"

"I just got divorced, Ma. I can take care of myself. And I don't need my mother to set up dates for me. I'm not interested in any man now."

"I saw how you laughed at his jokes. You liked him."

"Of course I liked him. I like a lot of people. It doesn't mean I want to play housie-housie."

"This child, Moena, I tell you," Ateeka laughed. "Smart with the mouth. No one's good enough."

"Who's this man?" Moena asked.

"Yusuf Arendse, a lawyer," Ateeka explained. "He just lost his

64

wife. En jy weet, Moena, 'n man verloor sy vrou, en veertig treë van haar qub'r wag die vrouens. En moenie praat as dit 'n dokter of a lawyer is nie. Hulle't niks skaamte nie." A man loses his wife, and forty steps from the grave, the women are waiting for him. And if it's a doctor or a lawyer ... they have no shame.

"Kyk wie praat," Khadidja said. Look who's talking. "Don't forget to tell sies Moena where he lives, and what he drives. My mother went and asked Maan about him, sies Moena. Can you believe that?"

"So what if I asked? You would too if you were interested." Ateeka looked at herself one last time in the mirror. "And don't be nasty to him when he comes. You know you can make someone feel very uncomfortable if you don't like them. Don't let him sit here on a New Year's Eve with a dry mouth. Make tea. The lemon cake's on the kitchen table. Come, Moena. Farieda's waiting." Farieda was the third musketeer, the only one who still had a husband, and the only one of the three who could drive.

Khadidja listened to their fading chatter as they left. It was hard to concentrate on the manuscript. Outside her window, fireworks pockmarked the sky. The night resonated with distant laughter and music, and loud caterwauling drifted up from Adderley Street where pink, red and green lights in Father Christmas and fir-tree shapes twinkled like a little Las Vegas for the partygoers and coons and choirs who would be there to sing in the New Year and celebrate. It wasn't a night for editing stories, but for dancing and laughing and holding a man tight. But there was no man, and she didn't know the kind she wanted anyway. Still, it thrilled her to know that she was free, free to fantasise, free to do it again. A pop outside the window made her get up. She looked out. There was no one there.

Khadidja caught a glimpse of herself in the full-length mirror. She wasn't ever satisfied with what she saw, but thought it ironic that the thing she'd most hated as a child – her hair – was her best feature now. Her breasts were too small. Her lips too fat. Admittedly, her eyes were good, her hips were narrow, her bum still tight, but her legs didn't have as much definition as Alison's. Was Alison going out? she wondered.

She picked up the receiver on the table next to her bed and di-alled the number. The telephone was answered almost immedi-ately.

"Titch! Happy New Year!"

She was taken aback for a moment. Just two days ago Alison had been terribly depressed. "It's not midnight yet, but happy New Year to you too. You sound like all your horses came in."

"Farouk was just here to pick Leila up." She gave a nervous lit-tle laugh. "I don't know if I imagined it, but I think he – well, per-haps I just imagined it."

"What happened?"

"I had on this black gym top. He … kind of … his hand sort of brushed against me."

"He grabbed your boob, you mean."

"Well …"

"You didn't go there, Alison. Tell me you didn't."

"I didn't, but he asked me what I was doing tomorrow night. He wants to talk."

"Talk? What does he want to talk about? You must talk through the lawyers."

"He wants to talk about Leila, the business. He says we're doing all this fighting, and the lawyers are the ones benefiting, making money out of our misery."

"He's right, but they're a necessary evil right now. Don't mess it up. You're close to a settlement. He's smart. He knows where to push. You know what happens when you listen to him. He's per-suasive. A touch here, a move there, and you end up under him. If that's what you want though … Do you think there's a chance for reconciliation?"

"There's no chance," Alison said, suddenly despondent. "And I don't want it. I guess I was building up things in my head."

Khadidja took care with her words. "It's easy to do that when you're down. I know how it is. It's New Year's Eve. The year's end-ed, there's no one there. You're lonely. Farouk comes along and shows a little interest. He's familiar. He says the right words and starts to look good. You're willing to renegotiate." She looked out the window at a pink rocket flashing across the sky. "He *is* interested, Alison, he's always going to be interested. Men don't separate their aerials from their brains. But that's all it is. It's not intimacy, it's not love. Tomorrow he's back banging the bitch."

Alison sighed. "How two people could've cared for one another, and how it could break up just like this … I don't understand. And on a night like this, it sure as hell would be nice to have someone who cared."

"Your mother cares, Alison. Leila cares. I care. Farouk doesn't care. You've lived with him a long time, you know him. Cancel tomorrow night, and tell him to go through his lawyer. It's hard to walk away, but you have to. You can't skip this pain. It's necessary to move you through it." Khadidja peered under the bed for her shoes. "I also didn't want to deal with stuff when Rudy left, and when I heard he'd got married, it was worse. Someone else wanted him. Suddenly I didn't know if I'd done the right thing. I went from one emotion to the next, from feeling glad that I'd left him and was free, to feeling unloved and rejected, not good enough. I allowed myself to feel it. I dared it to hurt me even more. I told myself that maybe there had even been girls from the start. So what. What had I lost? Not anything I wanted or couldn't get for myself. Today, nothing Rudy says, nothing he does, or nothing he's done, disturbs me. In fact, I hope he finds happiness with his new wife. I hope he has a string of babies. I have no feelings of animosity."

Alison was silent for a while. Then she said, "You've always been strong. Even that time when you broke up with Saville."

"Oh yes? I broke up with Saville, and I married someone else to get over him. And look what happened."

"You're not saying it would've worked out with Saville?"

"I'm not saying that at all, but he was interesting, sexy, earthy, and totally scrambled my brain. I had the head thing going on with him. Every part of me was engaged. I didn't have that with Rudy. There was no laughing, no playing, no after-dinner conversation except for the smorgasbord of crime the *Argus* offered every night. I had a husband I could show up with at weddings and teas, but couldn't stand his touch in the bedroom. It's an art, Alison. Your heart has to be in it. Foreplay doesn't start under the sheets. I don't think I can ever be with someone who doesn't do it for me in the head."

Alison laughed suddenly. "I listen to you and I have to feel good."

"I know how you're feeling, Alison, trust me. I know the loneliness. But it passes. The reason you're taking a bit of time working through it is that there's ongoing contact: the law suit, he comes to the house to see Leila. You can't help that, but there're ways you can make it easier for yourself. Do your business through the lawyers. And Leila's a teenager. He can pick her up in town, or some other place. Don't make your house available to him."

"The imam said he was entitled as a father to see his child in the home. If someone was there with me, of course it would be better."

"Is the imam there when he's feeling you up? Is aunty Mavis? Protect yourself. We've had a rough year, but in three hours' time it's a new one and we can start again. Look at this real estate thing we just did. That was a good thing. Did we do well, or what?"

"We did. Have you told your mother yet?"

"No. Transfer's only in March. I have time." She looked at her watch. "I've got to go. I have this man coming at nine. Hell, there's the doorbell."

"Who's coming?"

"I'll tell you tomorrow. I have to go." She hung up, pulled her hair back off her shoulders, and walked to the front door.

Yusuf was dressed in a suit. In his left hand was a bouquet of pink roses. "For you," he said. "I won't wait for midnight. Happy New Year."

"Thank you," she smiled, taking the roses. "And a great New Year to you too. Come on in." She led him into the kitchen where she took out a vase. "I thought you might've forgotten to come over, New Year's Eve being such a night of excitement."

"Not for me," he said. "This is one night I don't like to be on the road. Too many accidents."

She arranged the roses. "I'll make us something to drink. What would you like? Coffee, tea? Lemonade made with real lemons?"

"It's too hot for tea. The lemonade sounds good."

She took out two tall glasses and filled them from a glass pitcher. "Some cake?"

"That would be nice."

She cut some of her mother's lemon cake, emptied a packet of salted peanuts into a bowl, topped up another with ginger chocolates, and put everything on a tray. "Let's go sit on the stoep. It's much cooler there."

Yusuf followed her out. "Just you and your mother live here?" he asked.

"Yes." She sat down and offered him one of the glasses. "I've lived here all my life. It's my mother's house. When I was married, my husband lived here with me. In the same room I had as a child."

"I have a brother on Rose Street. He also likes Bo-Kaap. My mother lives with him."

"I believe you have twin daughters?"

"Yes. Sawdah and Shamiela, nine years old. They're with their cousins tonight. In Wynberg."

"I just bought a house there, on Rosmead Avenue."

"Really? You're moving out then?"

"In March, hopefully."

"You'll stay by yourself?"

"Yes." She offered him the peanut bowl. He took a handful.

"So tell me, Khadidja –"

"Titch," she corrected.

"Tell me, Titch, how is a girl like you dateless on New Year's Eve?"

She smiled. "By choice. And I can ask the same thing of you."

"I just lost my wife. My daughters are my first priority."

"It must've been hard for them losing their mother. They're so young."

He looked down at the glass in his hand. "It all happened very suddenly. She was having a shower and collapsed. Fell with her head on the hard edge of the tiles. Her doctor told me afterwards that she had angina and that he'd prescribed medication to lower her cholesterol."

"You didn't know?"

"I knew nothing about it. There was some dieting going on, but I never saw any pills. It was a shock when I heard about it. The twins took it very hard. They don't talk about it."

"How long has it been?"

69

"Five months. Their mother's sister came to the house recently to sort out her personal things. The twins asked if they could keep the little red leather bag with the gold studs, and the fox fur stole she had when she was young. It was the first time they acknowledged her absence. I don't know if you know about identical twins. They're very close, and confide in each other, not in anyone else."

"Not even their father?"

"When I ask them, otherwise I don't know."

"Would it help to take them away on a holiday?"

"A holiday?" He gave a little laugh. "I haven't had a holiday in years. I have a business with secretaries and clerks. I can't just take time off when I want. I have other things to think about. I'm looking for someone right now just to do some cooking and cleaning. Finding help would be a good start."

The words popped out before she could stop them. "So you're looking for a woman."

"Yes."

"One to clean up for you, or one to marry?"

He reached forward and took a chocolate out of the bowl. "Whatever I find first."

"So it's a question of necessity. A maid or a wife – either one will do. Not love."

He settled back, and his jacket fell open to reveal the crispness of his shirt.

"I'd like to have love. Who wouldn't? But I don't have time to wait for it to roll up to my door. My children are changing right before my eyes."

"That's certainly to the point."

"I know what I want."

Khadidja smiled. "Is that why you're here?"

He looked her straight in the eye. "It's why I'm here. I'd like to see you."

She took a handful of peanuts. "This is very, very direct."

"*You* are very, very direct. I'd like a woman in my life. One who's modern, but knows her Islam. A woman who can be a mother to my children."

She sat with her mouth full of peanuts, staring at him.

He continued. "I like what I see, what I hear. I'd like to see you, with a view to marriage."

"Marriage!" The peanuts spluttered out of her mouth. "You know nothing about me. You don't even know how I think."

He smiled. "How do you think, Khadidja? Do you think differently from any other woman? Falling in love is for sixteen-year-olds. Did the Prophet fall in love?"

She was astounded by the reference. "You're comparing yourself with the Holy Prophet?"

"No, but why do people get married?"

"I don't know. Tell me."

"For comfort, companionship, to help each other through life. Falling in love was invented by human beings. It wasn't how things happened in the old days. In the old days marriage discussions took place at the well and the boy's father came over and the whole thing was arranged." He smiled at the look on her face. "Of course I don't want an arranged marriage, and I do want love. But love is one thing. Being *in* love is another."

"Well, it's one way to look at it. Would you want to be with a woman you had no feelings for?"

"I wouldn't be here if that were the case."

"You're contradicting yourself."

"Not really. You have to like the person at least, and go from there."

"But how do you know you even like me? People are on their best behaviour when they first meet. Like you are now, like I am. I'm quite mean. You don't know me."

His eyes twinkled. "I don't know if you're mean or just saying so, Khadidja. I get the feeling you like to shock people. But you're right, I don't know you. Still, one can have a hunch. Lawyers have hunches all the time. I wanted to see if I was right."

"And were you?" she asked, feeling quite good sitting there with him. He was delicious to flirt with.

"Yes. Your jeans are too tight, but I like you."

"Too tight?" she laughed. "You think I should change them?"

"I don't know. Stand up. Let me see how they look from behind."

She got up, and turned slowly, fully aware of her assets.

"Nice," he said. "I wouldn't want to be sharing this."

The words had a strange effect. "I have difficulty loving people."

"What do you mean?"

"I mean, I don't think I loved my husband. I don't know if I have it in me. To love."

He laughed. "This is what you're worrying about? Whether you can love me? I don't love you, Khadidja. Not yet anyway." He reached for his glass. "Would you like to see me?"

"Can't we just play it by ear? I thought this was a preliminary round, to see if we liked each other."

"I do. Do you?" His right brow was raised, a smile curling his lip upwards.

"Of course I do. I like a lot of people."

"Don't play with words, Khadidja."

She was on the witness stand. The answer was yes or no. "We just met. You're practically asking for my fingerprints."

He chuckled, and looked at his watch. "Would you mind if I used your telephone? I want to check on the children."

"It's in the kitchen, go ahead." She waited while he went inside and made the call. After a few minutes he returned. "My brother's having a small party at his house. Do you want to come?"

She would've liked to get all dressed up and go with him, but he'd not mentioned the party before. "I don't think so. You go ahead and have fun."

He didn't try to persuade her. "I'll finish my drink. Your magazine's good, I meant to tell you. A friend pointed it out, I read a few of the articles. I knew a little about you when we met."

"You mean it wasn't a chance meeting at the wedding?"

"No."

She walked with him to the gate where he gave her a brotherly hug. "Goodbye, Khadidja. We'll talk again."

She watched the car pull away from the kerb, and returned to the little table on the stoep. The cake was untouched. The bowls seemed dressed-up with peanuts and chocolates, with nowhere to go. The night was suddenly cold.

She sat outside for a while, then returned to her room, and wrote in her diary.

Alison very depressed. Farouk came around and fiddled with her feelings. The three musketeers out on their night on the town. Yusuf Arendse came for tea. First date since divorce.

∼

"**A**nd that's that, Ma," Khadidja concluded the next morning over breakfast with her mother. "It was a nice visit, but don't invite anyone over for me again."

"What did he do wrong? He went to a family twenty-first."

"You don't visit someone on New Year's Eve, then after forty-five minutes, say you have to go somewhere else. He obviously had lost interest. It was right after I couldn't give him a straight answer about whether or not I wanted to see him again that he said he had to go. He's in a hurry for a wife. And I'm too mouthy for him."

"He asked you. You didn't want to go with him."

"He was being polite."

"He'll call again. I'm sure of it."

"I don't want him to call. Anyway, sit down, Ma, there's something I want to tell you."

Ateeka wanted to know more details, but sat down. "Can I butter my toast at least?"

"Mummy's not supposed to have butter. Yusuf's wife was young. She had angina like you. Look what happened."

"It was her time, that's all. Nothing's going to happen to me."

"Okay, Ma, have it your own way. Anyway, I have something to tell you. Remember this thing I mentioned some time ago that Alison and I wanted to do to make a little extra money? We did it. On Saville's advice, we borrowed some money from the bank and bought an old house in Claremont, got a contractor, and renovated it. We fixed the bathroom, put in a new kitchen, laid tiles on the floor, and sold it for sixty thousand more than the purchase price."

Ateeka's brows shot up in surprise. "What? How come I don't know anything about it?"

"I didn't want to say anything just in case it didn't work out.

We took a chance, and got lucky. Alison's planning to open a little shop with her share of the money. I'm buying a house. I've made the down payment already."

"A house for yourself, you mean? To live in?"

"Yes, Ma. It's on Rosmead Avenue in Wynberg, opposite the fire station."

Ateeka stopped buttering her toast. "You're moving out?"

"It's not the end of the world. Mummy can sell up, and come and live with me. The house has three bedrooms, a large kitchen, and a pretty garden. Mummy won't have to worry about anything."

"I'm not worried about anything. I didn't know you weren't happy here."

"I'm happy, Ma. I've always been happy. But I can't live forever with my mother. I'll be forty in March. The deal will go through roughly at the same time."

Ateeka looked pained. "You can't live forever with your mother?"

"I don't mean it in a bad way. It's just that I've never been on my own. I would like to have my own place, where I pay the accounts and where I make the rules."

"There're rules here?"

"Of course there're rules, but that's not why I'm moving out." She pulled her chair closer to her mother and put her arm around her. "I need to do my own thing, Ma. It's time."

"Your own thing? What's your own thing? I don't allow you to do what you want?"

"That's just it, Ma. I'm too big to be allowed. I'm not a little girl anymore. You looked after me, then Rudy thought he looked after me. I'd like to look after myself now. And let me look after Mummy. Come to Wynberg. There're no hills to climb there."

"I don't care about hills. I was born here. My friends are here. My masjied is here. They carried my mother out of here, and your great-granny. That's the only way I'm leaving this house. And sies Moena and I have a pact. We're not going to live with children."

The day before the move, Alison came to help with the packing. Sies Moena and Ateeka had already wrapped the cups and plates and glasses with newspaper, stuffing little packets of spices and condiments in the hollows and crevices for Khadidja to discover in her new home. The clothes were in suitcases, the linens and bed covers pressed and in the kist. All that remained were the magazines and books, and small items. It was early afternoon. Khadidja was on her knees in the front room surrounded by boxes, wiping the cover of each book, photo frame and record album. Alison and Ateeka were looking through a shoe box containing old photos.

"Look at this one here." Ateeka held up a faded photograph to Alison. "Here they are in their tartan outfits."

Khadidja didn't have to look. She remembered the black and red check pleated skirts and white blouses she and her sister had worn with their black patent leather shoes, and cream crocheted socks that left patterns under their feet. She and Murida were the same age as the queen's daughter, and whatever fashion was sported by Princess Anne in *Woman's Illustrated* at the time, out came the chalk and the pins and the sewing machine, and her mother made them each an outfit.

"We didn't have money, Alison, but my children never wanted for anything. You should've seen the dresses when they were little."

"I know, Ma. Titch and I were friends from long ago, remember? I remember their outfits on labarangs."

"The prettiest dresses they had, with smocking and cutwork patterns, and ribbons, and laces, and stiffning petticoats. Murida was bridesmaid and flowergirl five or six times. I made all the dresses."

She would miss her mother, Khadidja thought. Ateeka was keeping up a good front, but several times Khadidja had found her staring out the window, deep in thought. She didn't have to be told what her mother was thinking, and didn't ask. Listening to their chatter now, Khadidja wondered whether she was making a mistake. Bo-Kaap was much more than just a place where she'd grown up and lived for forty years of her life. It would be hard to leave a place where you woke up with sea smells and big city sounds and the call to prayer five times a day.

"I left some books in the other room," she said to no one in particular. She hadn't left any books anywhere, but wanted to see the room suddenly. She'd been with her sister in that room, her great-grandmother, with Rudy. The room had a history of childhood secrets and games, and over the years had been converted from a sewing room to a child's room to a bridal chamber. The only thing unchanged was the position of the bed facing the window, and the bookcase her great-grandmother had bought for her on her tenth birthday. The bookcase was empty now, stripped of its sagas and biographies and gossips and lies, awaiting removal to its new home. For a terrifying moment, she wanted to run inside to her mother and tell her she wasn't leaving.

The doorbell sounded. Another neighbour, she thought. Neighbours had come to say their goodbyes, and came with words of advice and a little something for the new house. Sies Farieda brought two embroidered pillowcases, and pickled fish. Sies Moena gave her a toaster and steak-and-kidney pies. Moosa presented her with a watercolour painting of Sachs Street that an artist friend had painted for him. Boeta Tapie offered to come to her house the following week and take a look at the tiles she wanted changed in the bathroom.

"Khadidja!" She heard her name called, and returned to the front room. Her heart lurched when she saw who it was.

"Daddy ..."

Hassiem stood awkwardly in the doorway. He didn't know whether to embrace her or shake her hand. "Hello, Khadidja." He had never learned to call her Titch. "How're you?"

She made no movement to embrace him. "I'm fine. How's Daddy?"

"I'm fine. I have a bit of an ulcer, otherwise I'm all right."

Ateeka lifted books from one of the chairs and invited him to sit down. "Do you remember Alison? She's Alia now."

Hassiem turned to Alison. "No, I don't. Hello, Alia."

Alison shook his hand. "We did meet once, long ago."

He took the seat offered to him. "I saw Murida last week." He turned to Khadidja. "I told her that I have to buy *Lifestyle* to find out what my other daughter's doing." It was meant as a joke, but came out stiff and unnatural.

"Well, Daddy knows where to find me."

"She also said you were moving to Wynberg. I was on Rose Street. I thought I'd come and see you."

"Does Daddy want tea?"

"I'll make it," Ateeka said. "Tell your father about the house. Did you know she's writing a book? She sent it off to a publisher."

"Is that so? A book? What about?"

"It's about divorce. About men who mistreat women, and the women who stay with them."

"You are interested in this subject?"

"I'm divorced, Daddy. My mother's divorced. My father's been divorced twice. It's also about the misery of first wives."

Ateeka shot her a warning look. "Tea, Hassiem? Coffee?"

"Tea, please," he said. "You look well, Ateeka. Your health is good?"

"Algamdu lilah, very good. You were on Rose Street, at the janaaza?"

"Yes. Mogamat Zane, the carpenter."

"We heard about it. I believe he had a heart attack last night in the mosque. He was taking off his shoes and collapsed. Did he have heart problems?"

"I don't know. It just happened, they said."

"Heart attacks don't come out of the blue," Khadidja put in. "Our people like their heavy meats and creams and fried foods. And they don't like doctors."

Ateeka got up from her chair. "Let me go and make the tea," she said. "Come, Alia. Give me a hand."

Khadidja watched them depart, leaving her and her father sitting there like brooding eagles. Her father looked at the boxes in the room, the books on the floor still waiting to be packed. "When are you moving?"

"Tomorrow morning."

"Rosmead Avenue's a nice area. A lot of traffic, but some beautiful trees. Near the sports grounds?"

"Opposite the fire station."

He looked at a rakam with the words, *God is great,* in big Arabic letters, on the wall. To look anywhere else was to be caught in the crossfire of her stare.

"Why didn't you support us, Daddy?" The question came out of the blue and made an ugly sound in the room. He looked at her, the colour draining from his face.

"Mummy had to sew for other people to earn money to feed us," she continued.

"That was long ago, Khadidja. You wouldn't have understood."

"I'll understand now, Daddy. Why? The poorest child in school had a father. We didn't."

"People make mistakes. We were young, your mother and me. We did things in a hurry."

"Did you also do things in a hurry with your second wife? That's why you took a third?"

He fixed his woeful eyes on her. "You're angry. Why can't you let the past be the past?"

"I'm not angry. I don't care."

"You don't care about your father?"

She looked him full in the face. "We were your children. We still needed to eat, we still needed clothes, and we still needed to be taken care of."

His eyes left hers slowly. He hunched forward in his chair, then got up. "I won't stay for tea. Tell your mother."

She walked ahead and opened the front door. She stood on the stoep and watched the car drive off and turn right at the corner. As a child, she had run to her bedroom window and had watched the taillights flicker down the hill, counting the stops before it turned left into Buitengracht.

Ateeka came out onto the stoep and looked about. "Where's your father?"

"Gone."

"What'd you say to him?"

"I asked him why he didn't support us."

Ateeka's scarf was in her hand. She wrapped it around her head, ending with a knot on the side. "What did he say?"

"He said it was a long time ago."

"It *was* a long time ago. You must forget it."

APRIL 10

Moved in on the 1st. My own place at last. First few nights a bit scared to sleep alone in the house. Will get a dog. Father came unexpectedly to Sachs Street.

~

Shortly after my ninth birthday, my mother thought she'd found a way to make some money to support us. Boeta Rakiep from Dorp Street – Kiepie, the people called him – had lost his wife to a gangrenous foot the previous year. Boeta Rakiep did the rounds on Fridays on Sachs Street, selling fruit and vegetables from the back of his cart. A few months after his wife's death, he started putting in extra tomatoes, onions and potatoes in our packet, and always put in a mango or a cling peach. My mother didn't notice any of this. It was little granny who remarked on how many vegetables my mother was getting for her money. When my mother did notice, she got the idea to start a little business of her own.

"I'm going to ask Kiepie to bring me two dozen chickens from the market to sell. What does Granny think?"

Little granny was mending the sole on her shoe with a thick squirt of glue. "To sell? You mean you'll keep chickens here in the yard?"

"No. I'll slaughter them and clean them and sell them. There's not enough money coming in from the sewing. Murida's in Standard Seven. Khadidja's going to Standard Three. I want them to finish school. One day when they put their feet under their own table, they won't have to take a man's nonsense. If I have to sell chickens to pay for their education, I will."

I was horrified. My mother selling chickens! I could see my sister and me being dragged into this.

"You know that man's interested in you," little granny said. "I'm sure he'll bring the chickens, and probably sell them for you also, then come and knock on the door with the imam."

"I'm not interested in him that way."

"You're not, but he is. Men do favours, but some favours come with a price."

"Don't Granny worry about that. He'll know soon enough there's nothing in it for him."

This wasn't unusual talk for my mother and little granny. I'd heard little granny before asking my mother whether she thought she would marry again. My mother always had the same answer:

she was almost forty, there were only married men looking for second wives, and a widowed man with children would put his own children first.

Boeta Rakiep came that Saturday afternoon, took tea in the kitchen, listened to my mother's idea, and agreed to pick up the chickens on the following Friday morning. It was a school holiday, he would come straight from the market to drop them off. My mother dipped her hand into her overall pocket where she had the money ready and put what she thought would cover the purchase of the chickens on the table in front of him.

"Nie nou nie." He pushed it back. "Give it to me when I come with the chickens."

Young as I was, I knew what that meant. And everything about boeta Rakiep's appearance that day – a jacket, the shiny black shoes – said that the visit to my mother was special. We noticed also that he had trimmed his hair, which seemed to have spread like wild grass over his ears since his wife's death.

"I don't want them for nothing," my mother said.

"Don't worry, siesie. Siesie sal betaal." Don't worry, lady, you'll pay.

"Ek weet ek sal, maar met geld," my mother laughed. I know I will, but with money.

Boeta Rakiep also laughed, but not with the same confidence as before.

On Friday morning, shortly after seven, there was a rap on the door. My mother was already up and making our porridge, and went to answer it. I couldn't hear what was being said from where I lay in a half-sleep next to little granny in the back room, but heard the racket of squawking chickens.

"Khadidja, Murida, get up!"

My mother's voice got shrill when she was under pressure, and I wondered what it was that made her shout so early in the morning. I got hastily out of bed and walked in my nightie to the front door. There, on the cement stoep, were two wooden crates with a clutch of noisy chickens pressed in on one another, waking up the whole neighbourhood. Boeta Rakiep looked flustered, but carried the crates through the house and deposited them next to the shed in the yard.

"Who's going to slaughter them?" he asked.

"I'll ask one of the neighbours," my mother said.

Boeta Rakiep glanced at his watch. "It's late, I'm usually on my rounds already by this time. Give me a sharp knife. Quickly."

My mother went into the kitchen, produced a glinting, silver cutter, and handed it to him. Boeta Rakiep stuck his hand into one of the crates and brought out a chicken. Squatting at the drain under the kitchen window, he held the fowl down, flattening its neck on the cement ledge. *Bismillah*, he muttered, invoking the grace of God. The knife flashed briefly. The bird jerked under his hand, then lay fluttering on the edge, a scarlet ribbon trailing into the drain.

I stood mesmerised, unable to tear my eyes away from the headless bird. Boeta Rakiep stuck his hand back in the crate, brought out the next one, and the next, until all the chickens lay in a quivering pile of stained feathers on the damp cement.

"That's it," he said, washing his hands under the tap. My mother looked at the dead chickens. It must've dawned on her about then what she'd gotten herself into. The chickens were slaughtered, they couldn't lie around in the heat. She saw boeta Rakiep off, then came back and rattled off a list of instructions.

"You two, come and have your porridge, then get on your aprons. All those chickens have to be cleaned."

I looked at her. Did she think I was going to touch a dead chicken? "I've never cleaned a chicken," I said. "I don't know how."

"I'll show you. Eat your porridge while the water boils."

Murida tried the excuse that always got her out of doing household jobs. "I have to study. We're writing exams in two weeks' time."

"You have the whole weekend to study," my mother said. "There's nothing to cleaning a chicken. You dip it in boiling water, pluck the feathers, then pull out the guts."

Pull out the guts? I had to fight back the nausea rising up in my throat.

Little granny heard the commotion, and came limping out on her cane, her red hair aflame in the morning light. I could tell from her face that her leg hurt.

"So much noise this morning," she said. "What's going on?"

My mother stirred milk and sugar into our porridge and put a bowl in front of each of us. "Kiepie brought the chickens. The children are giving me a lot of lip."

"I can't touch a dead chicken, Granny," I said.

"And I have homework," Murida added.

My mother ignored us. She took a clean bowl from the cupboard. "Porridge for Granny?" she asked. Little granny said yes, and took a seat next to us. She said nothing. She wasn't afraid to give my mother her opinions, but my mother's face must've told her it was a bad time. We ate in silence. Ten minutes later, we were shepherded out to the work table in the yard.

"Watch," my mother said. She dipped a chicken into a paraffin tin filled with boiled water, letting it sink to the bottom, then dunked two more into the steaming vessel. The smell was horrible. After a few minutes of soaking, she lifted out the sopping bird from the bottom of the tin and placed it on the wooden table covered with newspaper.

"This is how you do it," she said, plucking the feathers in short, quick movements, the damp feathers sticking to her hand. "Make sure you get all of it."

We stood at the table, tight-faced and hateful.

"Get to it," she said.

I forced myself to the task, touching the spongy feathers, my first few attempts not very successful. Murida found it equally terrible, I could tell.

"Stop grumbling," my mother said. She was busy with a chicken herself, and kept looking over at us to see that we were doing it right. For what seemed like hours we dipped and plucked, getting the front of our clothes soaking wet, reeking of damp chicken. Little granny was seated on a bench with old rags and newspaper on her lap. We handed her the fowls one by one to inspect and to remove the needles and feathers we'd missed. Finally, the feathers were rolled in the soiled paper and put in the bin. I was inches away from throwing up. The smell from the hot cavities made me naar, and my mouth had a horrible taste at the back of my throat.

My mother placed the first chicken on a clean stack of newspaper, made a cut in the backside, and without blinking, stuck in her hand and pulled. Out came a slimy, dangling twist of intestines twined around her fingers, dripping with blood. The stink was so overwhelming that I vomited right where I stood – over my shoes and the front of my dress, a grey mass of porridge sliding off the side of a pimply-skinned carcass.

"Sis!" Murida jumped back with a scream.

"Stop that!" my mother ordered.

Little granny got up, limped with me to the tap where she took water in her hand and washed my face. "Did I tell you about the time my grandfather found a snake in the house and couldn't kill it? My grandfather hated snakes. A brother had died of a snake bite when he was little, and –"

"There's no time for stories now, Granny," my mother interrupted. "That girl's head's full of stories. She has too much of an imagination already. Come here, Khadidja." She was calling me Khadidja. I wasn't her Titch now.

"I can't do it," I said.

"Stop acting like a baby. Come here!"

"For God's sake, Ateeka." Little granny finally spoke to her. "Not everyone's got the stomach for it."

"Granny, please, I'll do it my way." It was the first time I heard her tell little granny to mind her own business.

Little granny stroked my hair back, then turned and went into the house. My mother realised that she'd been nasty, which made her even more irritable.

"Make a cut here," she instructed, "and put your hand in."

I was shaking so badly, I thought she would smack me. I couldn't get my hand to leave my side.

"Do it!" she ordered.

Murida quickly put in her hand. I waited to see how she would do it, but nothing happened. Funny sounds came from her nose and mouth. Murida dropped the chicken and both of us ran from the yard.

My mother came after us, huffing and puffing, whipping after us into the kitchen, around the table, into the front room, where she finally cornered us with the feather duster. But the hiding was a relief compared to having to stick my hand into a chicken's ripe behind. Eventually she stopped, dropping exhausted into a chair. Little granny sat near the stove. She didn't say a word. I'd heard her tell my mother once that she had never hit her children. A child could learn just as well from a good dose of the silent treatment and being sent to bed.

When my mother was sufficiently recovered from the morning's performances, she gutted the rest of the chickens herself, and dispatched us all over the neighbourhood. One chicken for boeta Tapie, two for sies Moena, one for sies Farieda, one for Galiema on the corner, one for the imam's wife, one for the man who lived in Dorp Street with six children and no wife, the rest to Ali, the butcher, for customers. Not one chicken was roasted in our oven. And just as well. I never wanted to see another chicken, dead or alive, and my mother never again asked boeta Rakiep to do her any more turns. The incident was enough to quash all further chicken ideas. Not long after this, we heard from sies Moena that boeta Rakiep had found and married a woman from Woodstock. She was a bit long in the tooth, sies Moena said, but could still run the mile.

The chicken incident also reminded little granny of her grandfather's farm in Philippi when she was a child, and later that night when we were alone, she told me about him. I don't know if it was the chickens that made her tell me, or boeta Rakiep using the chickens to make a footpath to our door – her stories usually made a point – but the story was about love.

We were in our bedroom, going through our nightly rituals before getting under the covers. I had helped her take off her dress and petticoat, and she sat with her nightie bunched around her hips on the edge of the bed.

"My grandfather wasn't an easy man," she began. "If you didn't know him, you would think him hard and unfeeling, but I didn't know what love was until I saw him bent over my grandmother. I saw my mother with my father all the time, and knew there were strong feelings between them, but I hadn't seen two people like this. He was a big man, my grandfather. Dark, with sharp features, and quite a temper. My grandmother was the opposite. She was a bright little jewel with hair the colour of weak tea, her eyes so green that they reminded you of a stormy ocean. She was of the faith, but had been born of an Afrikaner father, and had had a German husband. My grandfather was the second husband, and loved her more than anything. He was a hard man, a smile didn't come easily to his face, but with her, he was weak. The first time I remember seeing him I was very little, and had gone with my mother to the farm. He met us at the gate on his horse. I remember the moment, this big man sitting erect on a black horse, the way he glanced at me propped between my mother and the driver of the wagon, not sure whether to snatch me up or ignore me. He was strong, unafraid, and when I saw him bent over my grandmother in the chair with the big cushions where she liked to sit on the stoep in the afternoon sun, I saw something I'd never seen before. I don't know if it was his voice, his eyes, if it was his arms when he put them around her and leaned his cheek next to hers, if it was the way his big body just folded in on itself in her presence, but I knew then, looking at them, that when I grew up I would want love like that."

I listened with interest, and wanted to know if she'd found love like that, but to interrupt would send her off in another direction.

"On the third day I was there, he took me with him into the veld to check on the cattle. I had never been on a horse and was afraid to say so, but sat where he placed me in front of him on the stallion, and smelled the tobacco in his clothes, and the sweat of his body. The next day it all came to an end. I woke up and there was the smell of incense. I knew immediately that something was wrong. I saw the house filled with people. People with sad faces, talking in whispers. I'd gone to bed and everything had been all right, then I woke up, and my mother was crying. I knew. The door to the bedroom was closed. They were washing her in there."

"Was it your grandmother, Granny?" I asked.

"Yes," she sighed. "It's a day I'll never forget. Scorching hot, we hadn't had rain for weeks. Girls don't go to the cemetery, but someone had put me on one of the wagons and I ended up there. I stood on one side and watched them put my grandmother's body into the ground. All wrapped up in white, two men getting right into the hole to put it in a sitting position, facing east. When the planks were fitted over the grave and they started to fill it with sand, my grandfather stepped forward. He hadn't spoken, he hadn't cried. Could they wait for him at the gate, he asked. The other men looked at him. It was an unusual thing to ask, but the imam made a sign and they walked off. My grandfather took a shovel and started to fill the grave. When he was done, he stood over it, and looked up at the sky. It was early afternoon, I didn't know what he was doing, but as he stood there, he frightened me. I watched from about ten graves away. Then something happened that was almost biblical. The day had been hot and airless, but out of nowhere a darkness formed overhead. I heard a cry, like someone in pain. Minutes later the sky roared over our heads and the rain came."

My mind opened and closed like a concertina with questions. I didn't know if the cry was from the grandfather, or from God. "Did he cry for her, Granny?"

"I don't know. I didn't see."

"What was Granny's grandmother's name?"

"Oh, she had a beautiful name. I don't think they know it here in the Cape. It was a name her slave mother gave her. Sihaam."

I liked the name also, and wondered why I couldn't have had a name like that.

"Did he marry again, Granny?"

"Oh no. My grandmother was the only one for him. He was in good condition still for his age. Had all his teeth and his hair, and the fewest of words, but never took another woman into his house. People said he'd loved her too much, that he would pine himself into the grave, but he didn't. He ran that farm for a good ten years after she died."

I thought about this grandfather, and wished I had a grandfather like that.

"If you're white, Granny, is it better to be Christian or Moslem?"

"Christian, I think. There're not so many rules."

I agreed with her about the rules. Alison had hardly any rules in her religion.

"But it doesn't matter whether you're Christian or Moslem. The important thing is to love God, and not be a hypocrite. Hypocrites don't believe in God and the last day. Your granny has sins, but she's not a hypocrite."

This admission of sins astounded me. I didn't think adults could have sins, and then to tell someone about them. "Does Granny ask God to forgive them?"

"Granny's always talking to God."

"How, Granny?"

"Like I'm talking to you. You don't have to be on a mus'lah to talk to God. And you don't have to talk in a language you don't understand. Any language you understand, God understands. And anytime you want to talk, He's right there. But as long as God's asleep in your heart, no one's listening."

"Does Granny *love* God?"

"I love God, but I don't take chances. I don't do bad things, then say God will forgive me. There're small sins and there're big sins. I stay away from the big sins."

"What's a big sin, Granny?"

"A big sin's when you say something bad about someone behind his or her back."

I thought of all the things I'd said about my sister to Alison, and vowed to recite the *Fatiha* seven times before I fell asleep. Seven was my lucky number. I did everything in sevens. "And if you don't wear a scarf?"

"I think that's a small sin."

"Oemie Jaweier says God's very, very strict, and if I don't wear a scarf, when I die I'll swing by my hair and the snakes will pick out my eyes."

She smiled. "I don't want to argue with your oemie – she's cleverer than me about these things. But you mustn't fill your head with frightening thoughts. You mustn't be frightened of God, you must love God. When you love God, you'll try to please Him. If you please Him, you can't go wrong. He doesn't want you to be good because you're afraid. He wants you to be good because you want to be. It's no use if you wear a doekie, then do other things, like tell lies or take money from your mother's bag."

"I *never* take my mother's money, Granny!"

"I know, but I'm just saying it to make a point. I knew this man who carried a big Bible under his arm and went knocking on doors talking to people about God, but committed some of the worst sins. One can have the appearance of being good, or one can be good. It's important to know the difference."

∼

On the day before little granny's eighty-fifth birthday, a telegram arrived at the house. As my mother had her hands covered in flour, rolling out pastry for coconut tart, I was asked to open it. I fiddled with the envelope, careful not to tear the edges of the paper inside. I took out the slip, and said it was from little granny's son.

BESTE WENSE MET MA SE VERJAARSDAG. ONS KOM KUIER MORE. SOLLY.

My mother and little granny looked like they'd seen the Angel Gabriel. In the year that little granny had been with us, no one in Paarl had made any contact. Little granny had waited to hear from her son, but the months had drifted by in silence, and she spoke no more about him.

My mother wiped her hands on her apron and took the telegram. "Uncle Solly's coming tomorrow, Granny."

Little granny lowered her head and looked at her hands. Old hands, arthritic, wrinkled, blue veins pulsing under cellophane skin. Hands that had helped birth calves and other people's babies, and that had lifted her grandfather's head for the last time on his death bed.

"I thought he'd forgotten me," she said.

My mother's voice became tender. "A child doesn't forget his mother no matter how things might seem. We don't know what happened."

Little granny wasn't much comforted. Before she'd stopped talking about her son altogether, she'd often talked about her son's wife, Olive, to my mother. I'd got the feeling that it was Olive who stopped him from coming to visit. "Well, at least he remembered my birthday. Perhaps he will bring the family."

The next morning saw the effects of the telegram. It wasn't our day for baths, but the black kettle hummed and was emptied and refilled several times. By breakfast my mother was baking a chocolate cake in addition to the tarts she'd made the previous day. We wished little granny a happy birthday, and piled our presents of chocolates, slippers, gloves and a scarf next to her plate. I don't know what my mother was hoping to achieve with this scarf. Little granny put one on when she prayed, and took it off again when she was done. Maybe my mother thought that if she gave little granny a chiffon one, it would stay on her head.

The morning turned slowly. We didn't know when the visitors would arrive. We ate cheese sandwiches with tomato for lunch and were careful not to soil our clothes. Finally, when my crocheted socks sank around my ankles, and little granny was nodding off in the chair, a black car drove up and stopped in front of the house.

"Granny, wake up! They're here!"

We gathered behind the lace curtain in my mother's bedroom, and watched little granny's son, oupa Solly (Murida and I had been instructed to call him this) – a tall, very fair man with a balding head and a fringe of light hair – step out and open the door for the passengers. Two women and a young boy stepped out. The women were dressed in pleated skirts – one wore a hat – and looked nervously about them. Even from where I was behind the lace curtain, I saw their disappointment. They didn't like this place, I thought. One said something to the other. The man said something to both of them. The boy was already on the pavement. Something about him made me look at him closely. He was barefooted, dressed in khaki shorts, his cropped hair poking out of his head in short needles. He looked like the tree-climbing kind who got into trouble with teachers, and reminded me of sies Moena's Riaz.

My mother and Murida walked with little granny to the front door. I stayed where I was, watching everything from behind the bedroom curtain. I saw Mr Benjamin and his wife at their gate, and Vuyo and Moosa and Riaz kicking a football in the street. They'd seen the car and the people getting out.

From where I stood, the front door just feet away, I could hear and see everything. Little granny, delicate and pretty in her blue gabardine dress with the lace collar, stood on the top step of the stoep. Her son hugged and kissed her, and turned to my mother. Then just like that, his arms were about her. Very different from the first time.

I watched my sister. Speechless for once, she stood as serious as Queen Elizabeth waiting for someone to put the crown on her head. Oupa Solly said something about the colour of her hair. She smiled. She was used to people making a fuss over her looks.

Finally, he introduced the women and the boy. "These are my daughters, Helga and Liesl, and my grandson, Joachim. Helga's child."

I had never heard such names. I'd thought the children would be Moslem. And I didn't much like Helga's looks. She had slitty, pig eyes, with short, yellow hair. The hair didn't look real. Liesl, the one with the hat, was darker, a little fat, and seemed friendlier. I watched Murida. They had shaken my mother's hand, but not hers. She was having a taste of what it was like to be smiled at and dismissed.

A movement at the bedroom door caught my eye. It was the boy. Somehow, he'd slipped past everyone on the stoep, and come into the house. I felt nervous. He looked like a white boy. He was so close that I could count the freckles on his face.

"Do you live here?" he asked.

I didn't know what he was to me – an uncle, a cousin, I couldn't work it out in my head – and realised that he didn't think I was one of the family. The stupidest thing came out of my mouth. "I'm the dark one of the family."

He frowned. "You're not dark. We have Africans on the farm. *They're* dark." He touched his hand to the dried rose petals in a glass bowl on my mother's dressing table, feeling the papery texture between his fingers. "Where do you play?"

"In the street and on the hill. In the yard also, but it's not big."

"Do you have lots of friends?"

"Yes."

"And brothers and sisters?"

He had too many questions, I thought. "Yes. A sister. You met her on the stoep. Do you?"

He fiddled with a small round container on the dresser. "My mother can't have more children. What's this?"

"It's my mother's kohl. She puts it under her eyes."

Just then little granny appeared, leaning on her cane, leading the visitors inside. "Dis Titch, my asterpoester," she said fondly.

My face reddened. I didn't mind being called asterpoester – I knew I was her skattebol – but wasn't sure that these people would know how she meant it. Helga's next words proved me right.

"'n Wittetjie en 'n blassetjie," she said, referring to me as the brown sister and Murida as the white one. I saw my mother's eyes. She said nothing.

Helga's father knew she'd said a bad thing, and tried to fix it. "Jy's die jongste?" Was I the youngest?

I pretended not to understand him and kept silent. He dipped his hand into his trouser pants and took out a handful of change. I knew what he was going to do. He was going to pick out a tickey or sixpence and give it to me. As if money could change what she'd said. "I have cramps," I said to my mother, and walked past them, out to the shed in the yard. I knew my behaviour wasn't good, but I didn't care. In the shed, I took the bath bucket from its shelf, turned it upside down, and sat on it. Moments later a shadow filled the doorway. It was Joachim. In his hand was a small black snake weaving between his fingers.

"This is Piet," he said.

"It's a snake! Where'd you get it?"

"He came with me, in my pocket. He's not poisonous."

I stepped back. There were terrible stories about snakes. Snakes travelled in pairs. If you killed one, the other one came after you. In Standard One, the teacher had taken the class to Groot Constantia, and a snake was spotted in one of the vineyards. A screeching bird had alerted the workers to its presence, and one of them had trapped it with a rake, and hit it mercilessly with a spade, burning it afterwards on a small fire. The class watched as it burned, the body twisting on the coals long after it was dead. It haunted me, this memory of the wriggling dead snake, and I always checked under my pillow at night to see that nothing was there. Then there were the snakes who would poke out my eyes for not wearing a scarf, and the biggest creeper of them all, the one who'd caused all that trouble in God's beautiful garden. I didn't care that Piet wasn't poisonous. I hated snakes.

"Do you want to hold him?" Joachim asked.

The thought of that slippery snake in my hand made me shudder. A year's supply of comics wouldn't get me to touch it. But I also didn't want to be considered a weakling. It was his mother who'd insulted me. It hadn't stopped him from coming to look for me.

"Won't it bite?" I asked, wanting desperately to be brave.

"No. Feel him, he's quite friendly."

"Friendly?"

"Yes. I don't let any old one hold him."

That decided everything. I had to do it. "I'm scared."

"Hold out your hand," he said. "I'll put him on."

In my head I prayed silently. I held out my hand, my eyes tightly shut. When it touched my skin, cold and slippery, I wanted to scream. It was the strangest sensation. The weight of the snake in the palm of my hand. Balling up. Uncurling. Slithering. But I didn't scream. And I didn't let go. I opened my eyes. The snake had its head raised a few inches, licking at the air. I almost dropped it. The touch of its clammy skin on my palm and fingers was the queasiest sensation, but as I stood there, I knew I'd done a very big thing. I counted backwards from twenty in my head. When I reached one, I held out my hand to Joachim.

He took it from me. "See? I told you he's friendly." He stroked the snake's head and put it in his pocket. I saw him look around the shed. "That's a strange bucket." He pointed to the big silver bucket with the small tap on its side.

"We use it to take a shower. We don't sit in standing water. We have to have running water. We fill up the bucket, and put it on the shelf, then stand under it, on this plank, and open the tap. The water runs over us into the drain."

"Really? You wash in here? We wash in a bath, or in a tin tub in the yard, when it's hot." He looked about. "Does my oumagrootjie like it here at your house?"

I realized that little granny was also his great-grandmother. "Little granny likes it here very much," I said with quite a bit of emphasis in case he had any ideas that she might want to return to Paarl.

"Little granny?" he asked, his blue eyes curious.

"Yes. I gave her that name. She's little and she's a granny. Everyone calls her that now. She likes it. And she likes living here."

"Better than on the farm? Have you been to a farm?"

"No, but little granny told me about it. She says you have horses and chickens and rams and ewes. There's one with round curly horns that chases people away. Is it true?"

His eyes brightened. "We still have him."

"Don't you keep them forever?"

"No. We slaughter sheep regularly for our pot, but that ram's used to cover the ewes. Oupa won't slaughter him, but he won't give him a name, just in case we get too fond of him. There was a turkey once which belonged to the workers. The children adopted it as a pet, and called him Koeloe. One was in charge of his feeding, the other taught him tricks, another tied a string around his neck and took him for walks. The turkey's whole day was divided up. The day before Christmas, Kleinjan's father told him to slaughter the turkey. Kleinjan didn't want to do it, and the other children asked how they could kill Koeloe, who was their friend. His father ordered Kleinjan to do it. Kleinjan had the axe in his hand, the turkey's neck flat on the ground. 'Koeloe's going to feel it,' one of the children cried, 'you can't just chop off his head like that.' Kleinjan said he had an idea, and went to fetch the chloroform my grandfather kept in the barn. He put some on a rag and held it over the turkey's face. Koeloe struggled and flapped his wings, but after a while he lay still, and Kleinjan chopped off his head. The children cried, and the next day at lunch, wouldn't eat him. They couldn't eat their friend, they said. The grown-ups went ahead and cut the turkey. They took a bite, then ran outside to spit it out. They couldn't understand why the turkey tasted like medicine. In the end they gave it to the dogs, and had pumpkin and roast potatoes and yellow rice."

"Did Kleinjan's father find out about the chloroform?"

"I don't know, but Oupa said it was a bad thing to get yourself attached to animals like that. Our horses have names, but that's all."

"You have a snake with a name."

He slipped his hand into his pocket and brought Piet out. "Piet doesn't count. I can let him out anytime. I have other pets also, even an old tortoise, but I haven't seen him lately. Sometimes they bury themselves somewhere, and come out again in a few months. We also have dogs."

"Do they have names?"

"They have to have names so we can call them."

"And no one has feelings for them?"

He laughed. "Of course, but it's not like a turkey or a chicken or a rabbit that you're going to eat." He looked about the yard. "Don't you have dogs?"

"Moslems don't like to keep dogs, unless they're watchdogs. If a dog licks your clothes, you can't pray in them."

"Moslem?" His eyes burned with curiosity.

I looked at him. "A Moslem is – Moslems don't go to church. We don't get buried in a coffin." I knew this wasn't a good explanation or nearly enough because I could go on and on about the things a Moslem had to do, but I didn't know how to describe exactly what a Moslem was and, anyway, found it strange that he didn't know. "I think Christians believe in Jesus. There are Christians in my school. They talk a lot about the Lord Jesus. And every day at school we have to say the Lord's Prayer. Are there no Moslems where you are?"

"No," he said, shaking his head. "I've never met any. Do you not believe in God, then?"

"Oh yes. We call him Allah."

"Really? And about the dogs. Do *you* like dogs?"

"I don't know. I've never had a dog. The Christian people next door have one. He makes enough noise for the whole street. No one goes there to play."

He put Piet back in his pocket. "You must come to the farm. I think you'll like it."

I was surprised that he would ask me to come to his house. Me, a girl and a Moslem.

Murida came into the yard. "You have to come in. We have to sing happy birthday to little granny."

I could tell from her face that she was surprised to see Joachim and me talking there, and wondered what she would say if she knew there was a snake in his pocket. Murida would never have been interested in talking to him if he was from around the corner, but she hung around, asking him where he went to school and what standard he was in. I watched to see how interested he was in her. He didn't seem very interested because he didn't even take out his snake, and he just answered the questions. He didn't ask her anything.

The afternoon turned out like one of those *School Friend* or *Girl's Crystal* episodes where the ugly girl has something good happening to her in the end, like winning a prize or saving a child from drowning, and everyone wants to be her friend. The table was laid in the front room with puddings and cakes and sweets, and we were asked in. We were seldom allowed to sit in grown-up company, but it was little granny's birthday and children were part of family celebrations.

Throughout tea, I studied the two women: their clothes, their hair, the way they moved their hands, rolled their eyes. I was a studier of people, and liked to watch them, and these two I found more interesting than little granny's son. Pa, the two women called him. My mother called him uncle. Murida and I had to say oupa Solly. But I was interested in the sisters. One was fair, the other was nice. Liesl even offered Joachim and me the bowl with the cashew nuts in it. Was Liesl nice because it was the only thing she could be? Was I nice? Helga had slitty eyes, but was still the prettier of the two. People paid more attention to you if you were pretty, and no matter what stupid thing you said, it would be seen as funny or cute, or some excuse would be made for it.

I was having a good afternoon. I was sitting between little granny and Joachim, trying not to look in people's mouths as they talked, but listening to everything that came out. Adults became used to your presence, and some of them got silly after the icing sugar hit their brains, and said things that made your toes curl in your shoes. But conversation was about ordinary things; no secrets came out.

Little granny asked about Olive and the people on the farm, and her son talked about crops and workers. He said that the farm kept him busy and that he'd been very neglectful, but that he would make an effort to come to Sachs Street to see little granny more often. Perhaps she could even visit them for a week or two. I didn't like to hear this because I knew what it was like if someone said they would fetch you, and then didn't show up. There was also the danger that little granny might not come back. Still, I liked oupa Solly. He could talk, and little granny laughed at all his jokes. I liked Liesl also. Liesl fussed over her father. She put sugar in his tea and stirred it without asking, and cut him a slice of cake, and said things like, "Pa must keep a little space for supper tonight."

When the visitors had gone, my mother brought out the presents. Little granny had got six presents from the Paarl family. She looked at the labels and said they were just what she needed, then left them in their wrappings so she could look at them from time to time. I don't think she ever planned to wear those nighties and petticoats. And the little basket with the glazed fruit and nuts that she got from Liesl grew hair before she removed the cellophane and said we could eat them.

It was little granny's birthday today. Her son from Paarl came. And his family. I had a snake in my hand. I met Yagiem. He asked what a Moslem was. I can't believe how stupid my answer was. I don't like his mother.

〜

Khadidja was in a deep sleep when she heard the doorbell. She switched on the light and looked at the bedside clock. It was ten past four in the morning. A telephone call or a knock on the door in the middle of the night always meant bad news, and her first thought was that something had happened to her mother. Why hadn't she heard Sief barking, she wondered? Sief was a puppy still, but an alert and vigilant German shepherd. She pulled on her gown and walked barefooted in the dark to the front door.

"Who is it?" she asked without opening.

"Fireman Morris from the Wynberg Fire Station, ma'am. We found an Alsatian wandering around Rosmead Avenue. One of the other men said he thought the dog belonged to this house."

She opened the door and saw the outline of a tall man at the gate holding on to her dog. "He was on the road?" she asked incredulously. "I don't understand it. My property's fully enclosed."

"He must've got out somehow. Maybe he dug a hole under the fence. I brought him here as soon as we found him." He waited for her to come and unlock the gate, and removed the rope he'd tied to Sief's collar. "It's dark now, otherwise I'd take a quick look to see where he escaped. I would keep him in the house if I were you, ma'am, until you can see where he's getting out. I wouldn't like to see him run over."

Khadidja thanked him and said goodbye. "Naughty Sief," she said, patting the puppy's head, grateful to the man at the fire station who'd found him and brought him back. But what was she to do now? She loved Sief, but upheld the law of cleanliness regarding dogs in the house. At the same time, she couldn't leave him outside with his escape route wide open. She took him inside and wandered from room to room, trying to decide where to put him. The bathroom was too small, her study had books in it, the kitchen had foodstuff. In the end she brought her blanket to the couch in the sitting room to continue her sleep, and settled him down on the carpet.

As soon as it was light enough, she went to inspect the fence to see if she could determine how he'd escaped. There was an opening between two slats of wood where he'd dug a hole, and squeezed out. She fetched the shovel and proceeded to fill up the hole. Her neighbour, Pietie Adams, came out and talked to her at the gate. She told him about Sief's escape and the fireman who'd found him and brought him back.

"They're good at this fire station," the old pensioner said. "They're all white, you know?"

Khadidja smiled at this reference to white people.

"But what you have to do to prevent this from happening again, is to bury your dog's shit on the spot where he got out, and then bury it all along the fence. Once a dog gets a taste for the road, he's in trouble. This is a busy road. He could've got knocked over."

She worked at home that day, and was busy with her notes at her desk in the study when she looked out the window and saw Sief at the fence. His front paws were working vigorously in the earth, sand and grass flying out behind him.

"Sief!" she shouted, and ran out. He turned to look at her. His nose was covered with dirt. "You naughty dog!" she scolded. He bounded off and watched from a distance. He hadn't gone back to the hole she'd topped up with his excrement, but had made one in a different spot. This time she stopped it up with two bricks, then a fresh pile of shit. She was leaning with her arms on the shovel admiring her handiwork when she heard the voice at the gate.

"Ma'am?"

She turned. She didn't recognise the man at the gate. White, young, reddish-brown tan, long hair glinting like copper. The laces on his boots were undone, as if he'd just slipped them on, and he stood with both arms raised above his head, leaning forward on the grille of the tall driveway gate.

"Ma'am, I'm from the fire station across the way. This morning we were out on a call, and found your dog on the road. I understand one of our boys brought him back. I just wanted to say that he's a very beautiful dog, ma'am, and that if you couldn't take care of him, or didn't want him, we'd like to have him as a mascot at the fire station."

She laughed. "Thanks, but he's not going anywhere. I found the spot where he got out, and I've filled it. The thing is, he made another hole elsewhere. I've just finished stopping it up too."

"And he'll make another, ma'am. I know about dogs, having three of my own. What you need is a trench along the fence and some chicken wire in the ground."

She nodded. "Makes sense. Thanks."

"How old is he?"

"Almost seven months."

The fireman grinned. "Well ..."

"Well what?"

"Well, he's getting to be an adult, ma'am, six months is when they want to go sniffing about. What you don't want is for him to go chasing after a bitch. I've seen a Rottweiler hit the bricks like that once. Dogs have no road sense, ma'am, not when it comes to chasing bitches."

She looked at him. There was something about the way he'd said that, his eyes, the half-smile on his lips. "I guess I'll have to do something."

"I'm off duty now, but I have a rubble business when I'm not at the fire station. I could fix your fence for you."

She looked at the truck parked on the other side of the road, and the three men sitting in the back. "How much would you charge?"

"Nothing."

"Nothing? Why would you do it for nothing?"

He smiled. She noticed the straight white teeth – *the better to eat you up, the wolf said to the little girl* – the full mouth, the Daffy Duck lips. He reminded her of someone but she couldn't say whom.

"You don't have to get paid for everything, ma'am. Some things you do for free."

Something in her stirred. "No one does anything for free. There's always a price tag attached at the end of it."

"No price tag here, ma'am. Just love ..." He saw the alarm on her face. "... and a cuppa coffee," he added quickly.

"I beg your pardon?" *Just love, and a cuppa coffee.* It sounded like a good title for a short story, she thought.

"Oh no, not the grabbing kind, ma'am," he motioned with his hands through the grille of the gate. "I mean love as in friendship, an exchange of ideas. Do you believe in God?"

"There're still people who don't?"

"What are you, ma'am? Catholic? Protestant?"

"Muslim."

He was thrown for a moment. Then he said, "Doesn't matter if one's Muslim, ma'am, if one believes in God. That's the important thing. Maybe we could talk about God. That would be payment enough. And the coffee."

Suddenly she knew who he reminded her of. Mick Jagger. The same lips, eyes, ultralean panther-like sensuality.

"What about God?"

"Not now, ma'am. I have my boys waiting in the van, we still have three pick-ups. I'll call to arrange a time."

"All right."

"The number, ma'am?"

She gave it to him. He wrote it on the palm of his hand with a ballpoint pen he took out of an inside pocket of his jacket.

"And your name, ma'am?"

"Khadidja. Or Titch." She spelled it for him. "And yours?"

"Storm Callaghan."

"Like the weather?"

He smiled. "My mother chose it. Don't know why. She did the same with my brother, Arch – named him Archibald after a movie she'd seen. Women do strange things." His dimple deepened in his left cheek. "And your husband's name, ma'am?"

"Who wants to know?"

He put the pen back in his pocket, and smiled. "All right, Khadidja. I'll call. I'm off duty on Saturday. Maybe I'll come and do it then."

By Saturday afternoon Khadidja still hadn't heard from him. She was angry. Sief had made four new holes. As soon as she filled one up, he made another elsewhere. She could've called boeta Tapie to make her garden escape-proof, or asked her neighbour to recommend a handyman, but she didn't. Storm had said he would come, and he hadn't. He hadn't even called.

She worked on her novel at the weekends, and was in her study trying to edit. She had finished *First Wife* and sent it off to the publisher, but the more she looked at the copy, the more she found to correct. Still, she couldn't concentrate on the pages in front of her. She got up and fetched the telephone book and looked up the number for the fire station, then remembered he'd said it was his day off. She looked under Callaghan, and found three listed: one in Muizenberg, two in Kenilworth. She had a feeling that he was one of the Kenilworth listings. She wrote down the numbers and reached for the receiver.

Now don't be a silly goose. Put the phone down.

She threw the numbers in the bin, put on her coat, and got in her car. She arrived at Alison's house high up on the hill in University Estate.

"Titch!" Alison opened the door, hugging her. "Come in. You must've picked up my SOS. Leila's at my mother's house, I'm at a loose end. I was thinking of going to a movie. Do you want to go?"

"Not really."

"What's wrong? You look upset."

"I am." She followed Alison into the kitchen and sat on one of the stools, watching Alison switch on the kettle and set out mugs. "Sief escaped during the week. He dug a hole under the fence and got out. A fireman found him on Rosmead Avenue and brought him back. Later that day another one appeared at my door." She related every detail of their conversation at the gate, including his offer to fix the fence. "Today's Saturday," she concluded. "He never showed up."

Alison lit a cigarette. "And that's upsetting you?"

"Well – I can't get much work done. I sent off my book as I told you, but I'm still fiddling with it. I'm totally distracted."

"Is it the fence or the fireman?"

Khadidja gave a sheepish smile. "I think it's the fireman. I've thought of nothing else."

"A white boy. My, my. I must say that line's a good one, and very original – *just love, and a cuppa coffee*. What does he look like?"

"Mick Jagger with coppery red hair. Quiet, cool, very contained. The same bad eyes, the same build, the same sensuality. I swear to you, as he stood there leaning into the gate, I had this incredible urge to bite his lips."

Alison laughed. "I was beginning to think you didn't like men any more." She switched off the kettle. "This is too good for Milo. I have something much better. Come. Let's celebrate."

"What are we celebrating?"

"The affair you're going to have."

"I'm not going to have an affair. He didn't even call."

Alison slipped her hand behind a jam jar on the top shelf of the dresser and brought out a white envelope. "We'll see. Let's go sit inside. It's more comfortable."

Khadidja followed her into the living room. She liked Alison's house. A neat kind of untidiness – records, books, dried flowers, wide couches with fat cushions. "Any peanuts?"

"On the top shelf, above the sink."

Khadidja fetched the peanuts and a half bottle of ginger beer she found in the fridge. She picked a stuffed chair near to Alison, and kicked off her sandals. She watched Alison take a cigarette paper and rub the dry grass between her thumb and index finger. Alison was an expert at rolling joints.

"So … what to do about the fireman," Alison smiled naughtily. "Because you have to do something. I don't know when was the last time I heard you talk about a man. Must've been Saville. What're you going to do?"

"Nothing. I'll ask my neighbour to recommend a handyman."

"No. Call him. You have reason to ask why he didn't come. Your dog's an escape artist, he left you in the lurch. You could've got someone else if you'd known." She licked the edges of the cigarette paper, pressed it into place, and lit it.

"I don't have your courage."

Alison's eyes narrowed as she inhaled. "You? You're the queen of bold. Here," she handed the joint to Khadidja.

"You know I quit." She wondered how Alison could've forgotten the circumstances under which she quit. But perhaps Alison hadn't. Perhaps it was her way of saying the past was over and done with.

"Oh, come on. Just a little one. I don't want to smoke alone."

Khadidja couldn't resist. She took three rapid drags and blinked her eyes. "Whoa. Where'd you get this?"

"Farouk."

"What?" She could feel the heat spreading through her shoulders and relaxing her. "He came over and you had your talk and it was all a nice little party over a coupla joints? Did you get into bed with him? What happened to that women's class at the imam's house you were going to go to?"

For Alison, dagga had a different effect. Her eyes got slitty, she became morose. "I'm not ready."

Khadidja handed the joint back to her. "Farouk's not going to change, Alison. This isn't a new thing, or the first time he's done it."

"You get really nasty when you smoke."

"I tell the truth without the sugar coating. You want sugar coating? I can play around with words, I'm good with words. I thought you were going to end it."

"I have to do it in my own time."

Khadidja rested her head against the cushion and closed her eyes. Alison was right, she thought. It was easy to stand on the outside and judge. How hadn't she seen and judged her own situation with Rudy, and done something about it? "Of course you're right. What about the shop you were going to open?"

"If I start my business now, I'll get screwed on the property settlement. Farouk can't know I have this money. I'll just have to twiddle my thumbs for another six months. I don't mind. The money's in a fixed deposit. What about you? Are you buying another house? It was so easy, I'm tempted to do it again."

"There's no spare money now. And I'm not interested in making more money just for the sake of having more. I needed a house. I have one. And two or three more deals, and Revenue would've latched onto us."

Alison lit another joint. "Leila told me last night that when she's finished matric, she wants to study in America. She's not going to stay in this place."

"What? You're going to let her?"

Alison looked at her with woeful eyes. "You know Leila. You can't stop her once she gets something into her head. You can't stop kids today when they want to do something. It's not like in our day; when your mother said no, it meant no. They don't have money, but they tell you they're going overseas. She's applying at several universities in the States."

"She still wants to be an astronaut?"

"Can you believe it? Whoever heard of women astronauts? She likes maths, she loves space. And she's got the marks. Go into her room and see what she reads. You won't find one romance novel like we used to read at that age."

"What does Farouk say? He knows?"

"He says it's a phase. She'll get over it."

"He doesn't know his own kid. And your mother?"

Alison laughed. "Old aunty Mavis. My mother brags to all and sundry about her Muslim granddaughter. She doesn't mention that Leila bunks school, or that she cuts off the teachers, or that she's intolerant. Leila can do anything with her. I told you about that computer game last year. Leila needs something, she goes over there and gets it. Not even Willie and Mark's kids are spoiled the way she is."

Khadidja closed her eyes for a moment to relish the luxurious feeling in her body. Dagga always made her relax. But two hits were enough. More made her reckless. She thought of Alison's precocious teenage daughter. She liked Leila, but always knew that Alison wouldn't have Leila with her for long. Leila didn't run with the pack, she didn't get close to you. The only person she was really close to was her grandmother. Aunty Mavis covered up all her faults.

And there were plenty. When a doctor first diagnosed a behavioural disorder and recommended medication, Farouk agreed, Alison didn't. Another doctor made a different diagnosis. When a child blurts out an answer before the question is posed, he said, or spars with the teacher, or daydreams in class, it's an indication of giftedness. Leila needed enrichment, and needed to be with children like herself. The problem was that the few schools with enrichment programmes were all white.

"She still has a private tutor?" Khadidja asked.

"Yes. And she belongs to a chess club, and is a member of a general knowledge team. She has a certificate for a competition she won last year."

Khadidja smiled proudly. She felt about Alison's daughter as if she were her own. She'd been to all the birthdays, school plays, hockey games. "She will go, you know."

"I know. And I want her to. But I don't want her to know. Not yet. I have to get used to it first. My only kid, Titch. What will I do?"

My only kid, Titch. Khadidja got up. "I want to take a run up to my mother. She's complaining that I don't see her enough, although

I go there twice a week after work. Are we going to movies on Tuesday night?"

On Monday afternoon at the office, Khadidja closed her door and dialled the number of the Wynberg Fire Brigade.

"Can I speak to Storm Callaghan, please?"

"Fireman Callaghan's not on duty today, ma'am. Is there a message?"

Khadidja thought quickly. Her courage would hold only as long as she held the receiver in her hand. "Tell him the lady with the dog called. He never came to fix the fence."

"Right, ma'am, I'll leave this message for him."

She was in the bathroom the next morning brushing her teeth when the telephone rang. She walked toothbrush in mouth to her bedroom and lifted the receiver.

"Is that the lady with the dog?"

She swallowed the foam in her mouth. "You never came. I waited."

"I'm sorry. Didn't I say I would call?"

"Why didn't you? I could've had someone else fix the fence."

His voice was measured and calm. "I didn't know you were serious. I have to know for sure about these things."

"What things?"

"I have to know how people feel about me, if they really want me around."

"You have to be liked to fix a fence? I offered to pay."

"With some people it's different. Is there something in your mouth? You're mumbling."

She removed the toothbrush. "Why's it different with me?"

"I don't know. You might be able to teach me something. I like people who walk their own paths. I sense that about you. Am I wrong?"

She wondered if he could hear her pounding heart through the telephone. "What do you think I can teach you?"

"Have you heard the words, *in the beginning there was the Word and the Word was with God?*"

Khadidja was stunned for a moment. "Actually, yes. I was talking to a friend about those words just the other day. It's strange that you should ask me about them."

"You know these words?"

"I know that passage, yes."

"What do you think it means?"

"I'm sure you're going to tell me."

"I think it means Jesus was the Word, that he was there from the beginning, that he's God."

She hadn't expected that he would launch immediately into religious debate. "Who do you think wrote those words?"

"What do you mean?"

"Those words you just quoted. Who do you think wrote them?"

"Does it matter who wrote them?"

"Of course it does."

He was quiet for a moment. "How come you know this stuff? You're Muslim."

"Muslims read the Bible also. And I like stories. Have you read the Dead Sea Scrolls?"

"No. Why confuse myself? The Lord says, too much knowledge causes grief."

"I thought he said, seek and you shall find, and when you find, you will become troubled, and when you become troubled, you will know the All?"

"Where does it say that?"

"In the Gospel of Thomas. It's not in the Bible, but you can find it if you look. Do some research. A friend gave me a copy of the Gospel of Thomas and the Gospel of Barnabas. Both these gospels have been rejected by the Church. Anyway, I don't think God would want you to bury your head in the sand. You believe Jesus is God. That's fine."

"I don't believe he's God. He's God's messenger boy. I don't believe like other Christians that he's going to come down in a cloud. I'm Apostolic."

"An Apostolic's not Christian?"

There was the loud sound of an alarm. "There's a fire! I have to go!"

"What about the fence? Sief's making holes all over the place."

"I'll call you."

Two days later she was on her knees pulling up weeds in the garden, when he rode up on a bicycle to her gate. "I have to pick up something from my place for one of the boys," he said. "I thought I'd come and see if you wanted to take a walk. My house is just up the road in Kenilworth."

She had two book reviews to edit, and her own manuscript to work on, but she didn't hesitate. "Let me lock the door."

He waited for her to come back, then got off his bike and walked alongside her. "It's not far. Just off Rosmead."

She wondered what he would say if he knew she'd looked him up in the phone directory and knew where he stayed.

"I've been thinking about what you asked me the other day, about who wrote those words in John."

"I also asked whether an Apostolic wasn't a Christian. The alarm interrupted us."

"We don't follow other Christians. We have our own interpretation of things. Anyway, I asked my leader about that opening in John. He says it doesn't matter who wrote it."

"Doesn't it matter to you?"

"I can't see how it will make a difference to what I believe."

"Really? Me, I'm a skeptic. I'm a glutton for this stuff, I have to know the source. It can drive you crazy because you can go on and on doing research, and never get anywhere."

"That's what I mean," he agreed. "It can get too much, and you can end up being an atheist. You're quite religious then."

"I'd like to think I'm spiritual. But reading the Bible or the Qur'an doesn't make you spiritual."

"What about people who go to church?"

"Same thing. We get caught up in rituals and forget about the larger picture. I'm not saying though that you're not spiritual if you go to church or mosque or synagogue. Spirituality isn't a *doing* thing, it's a *heart* thing."

He walked in silence for a moment. "We go to church six times a week."

"My goodness." She saw a woman with three poodles on one leash walk towards her, and made a mental note to take her dog for a walk. Perhaps Sief wasn't getting enough exercise.

"Saturday nights we get off."

"Sounds like a prison with weekend privileges for good behaviour." She realized that she was being insensitive. "I'm sorry, that was inconsiderate."

"It's all right. People make fun of us all the time. When I was nineteen I was looking for a church to belong to, and found one called Church of Christ. I'd seen that name in the Bible. Anyway, I went to this church for about a year, but didn't like its philosophy. I told my father that I wanted a change, and he and I went to ten different churches, and ended up in this one on Allenby Street. It was an evening service, I'll never forget. When it was over and we were getting ready to leave, this man crooks his finger at me. I looked over my shoulder to see if there was someone behind me. He said, 'No *you*, come over here.' I remember I had on these big boots with spurs. I was riding a motorbike then. He took me into a room and asked me what I was doing with my life. He told me that he wanted to see me there every night from that night on. He made me sign a form."

"What did the form say?"

"There were five things I had to agree to. I wasn't to stand guarantor for anyone. I wasn't to lend money. I had to give ten per cent of my earnings to the church. I had to come to church six times a week. I can't remember the other one."

"You signed it?"

"I had to. If it was left up to me, I would never have gone there again. If I wasn't forced, I might still be where I was, godless, with no direction, no place to go. That's why we go out and knock on doors. We're sinners, we have to be shown the way. At my church we're one big family, and the philosophy makes sense. Take adultery, for instance. I don't think it's wrong if both people want it. If I pay a woman one hundred rand for sex, and she likes it, and I like it, I don't see the sin in it. Adultery to me is if the Pope wants to plant a seed in my head and change my thinking and turn me into a Catholic. *That's* adultery."

"This is the view of your church?" She was taken aback by his interpretation.

He glanced at her guiltily. "I didn't say so."

"Have you paid a woman for sex?"

"I'm a healthy man, I have needs."

"But have you?"

"Once, yes."

"A married woman?"

"I don't know. I don't think so. It was in a massage parlour. She charged and I paid. It was a straight transaction. No one was hurt."

"What about how you felt? Afterwards?"

"I didn't feel anything. I'd shot a load. I felt relieved. Don't you have needs?"

She could've answered several different ways, but didn't think that he would appreciate any of the answers. "Women want love. Not a drill operator."

He smiled. "Love's overrated, if you ask me. What's love anyway? Who can explain it? It's a flesh thing. It won't get you anywhere. You must come to my church. You'll learn some valuable truths. We're different. Not like other Christians."

"Are you trying to convert me?"

He frowned. "I never would do such a thing. If you didn't have God, yes, I would try, but I can see you have a God. Actually, I would like to read the Muslims' holy book. Where can I find it? And is it Muslim or Moslem? I don't know which is the right word."

"You can say either. When we were children, we said Moslem. Now we say Muslim. About the Holy Qur'an ..." She thought about the copies she had on the mantelpiece above the fireplace. "I have three copies. I can lend you one."

They were a block away from his house. The walkie-talkie crackled on his belt and he spoke into it. She walked on, listening. He latched it back on his belt. "What do you do for a living?"

"I'm the editor of a women's magazine. *Lifestyle.* Maybe you've seen it on the shelves. I used to be a journalist."

"Really? So you're a clever girl, then."

"I can string a sentence together if that's what you mean."

"You check the grammar and so on."

She smiled. "A little more than that. I commission articles, I decide what gets published, what pictures, what what."

"And men? You are married now, or were before?"

"I was."

"I was married also, for about a year. It didn't last long. One morning she just stuffed her clothes into two carrier bags and walked out. I have a daughter, Sammy, about twelve. She's with her mother in Jo'burg. I'm not allowed to see her. Do you have children?"

"No."

He kicked a can out of the way with the tip of his boot. "Do you think you'll marry again?"

"If I find the right person. I'm an optimist. And you?"

He took a moment to respond. "If I'm with someone, I have to consider feelings. I don't want to be responsible for another human being."

She looked away so he wouldn't see her face.

"Women expect too much. You can't be with your friends. You have to say what time you're coming home. They want to know all the time where you are."

She would finish the walk, she thought, say goodbye, and never see him again. Presently they reached his house. Three dogs rushed to the gate.

"Come in," he said, "they won't bite."

She followed him through the gate into the yard where she saw a furry blanket of cats curled up together in a wheelbarrow. "Quite a zoo here."

"Three dogs and seven cats," he smiled, proud of his children.

She saw two trucks, and a cream Ford with rust marks on the bonnet up on blocks. The yard was big, with wheelbarrows, bricks, sand, bags of cement. "I'm building a garage for my trucks," he said. He opened the back door. "Come in for a minute."

She stepped into the house and looked around the dark living room at the disarray. Clumpy brown sofas with crumpled blankets, green carpeting with food stains, a coffee table with a clutter of wooden elephants and giraffes and seashells, a dusty old sideboard with mouldy books and ragged spines, studded high-back chairs with faded rose velvet seats, an outdated television and hi-fi set, and cream tattered woollen curtains shutting out the light.

As her eyes got used to the gloom, she saw the cat hair, dust, the dirty walls. Everything looked like it had been hauled from someone else's junk pile. She didn't touch anything.

He reappeared. "My boarder's here, come and meet her. She's had a baby."

Khadidja followed him to the door of the first bedroom. She looked in. The room was in semi-darkness. A girl with short black hair in her twenties sat on an unmade bed with crumpled grey sheets, a baby in her arms. The scene was Gothic and grim. There was the girl's strange smile, the way she held the infant – not close, but disconnected from it, as though it wasn't hers. The room had no warmth, no sign of new life in it.

"This is Carol," he introduced them. "Carol, this is Titch."

"Hello, Carol."

Carol grimaced.

Out on the road, they walked in silence. "What do you think of my house?" he asked.

She wanted the walk to be over, and picked up her pace. "It's all right."

"My mother used to come once a week to dust a bit and clean up, but she doesn't anymore."

"Doesn't the boarder do anything?"

"She's lazy. Sits all day with the baby, borrowing cigarettes and money. I'm going to get rid of her." They stopped at a tree. "Look at that," he said in wonder, "a witogie."

She saw the twittering bird in the branches, and stood with him for a moment admiring it. He was like a child, she thought. Innocent, filled with wonder, yet there was also something predatory and wolfish about him.

"Do you know anything about birds?" he asked.

"No."

They walked on. The minutes passed. She wondered what her family or her neighbours would think if they saw her walking along the street with a white man. Her mother wouldn't be surprised. There had always been a smorgasbord of friends, and there'd been Saville. She and her mother had had the conversation already in the heyday of the 1960s when Section 16 of the Immorality

111

Act saw late-night raids on unsuspecting couples by the police. The dreaded Act had now been scrapped, but there was still apartheid, and heads still turned to see a white man and a coloured woman together.

"Is something wrong?" he asked after a while.

"No."

"You're a fast walker," he said.

"My friends sometimes complain about that too. I'll slow down."

They walked for a bit in silence. Finally, they reached her gate. "Wait here. I'll get the Qur'an."

He waited. She reappeared with the book and handed it to him. "You don't have to return it."

There was finality in the way she said it. His eyes searched hers for an answer. "That's it?"

"That's it. Thanks for the walk."

Inside the house, she made tea, had a sandwich, and called Alison. Alison listened to the whole story. "Well, I like how it all began," she said, "but I agree with you, he's not interested in a relationship. And what kind of relationship can you have? There's not only the question of your different faiths; he's white. But why'd you give him the Qur'an?"

"What do you mean?"

"I mean, why did you give it to him if you'd made up your mind not to see him again?"

"I'd promised him."

"C'mon, Titch. You can break a promise for that. What did you care if he read it or not? It's a link. As long as he has it, he has a reason to come back."

Alison's words gnawed at her. As the days passed, Khadidja regretted that she'd written him off. Sief was digging up her garden, and the fence still wasn't fixed. On Saturday morning she was watering the geraniums in the front when the cream Ford pulled up at her gate. The door cranked open, and Storm stepped out, dressed in jeans, a faded red sweatshirt that didn't quite make it to his navel, and work boots. He reached into the back seat and took out a shovel and several plywood boards.

"Hey ..." he greeted.

She unlocked the gate and let him in. She didn't express any surprise to see him there with his gardening equipment.

"You're really barricading yourself in here," he said, patting Sief on the head.

"And you really came to fix the fence."

"There's coffee?"

"There is. How do you take it?"

"Tutu."

"Tutu?"

"Black. Two sugars."

She laughed. He took off his sweatshirt and flung it on the branch of a tree. She tried not to stare. His shoulders and back spoke of long hours in the sun, but his body was young like a boy's, hard and corded, his nipples shiny brown lentils in honey-coloured skin. She forced her eyes to his face.

"Do you want a sandwich with it?"

He had his foot on the shovel and pressed it into the ground. "I was hoping more for supper later on. Conversation."

"You can have both."

"Okay. Coffee now, sandwich later." He scooped out a huge mound of sand. "I read some of your holy book. I saw a mention of Adam in it. In the Bible, he was the first man created by God. Is it the same with the Muslims?"

"There're those who believe he was the first, and those who believe he was the first to be given a conscience. If you believe the latter, there's the implication that God created imperfect models before Adam."

"What do *you* believe?"

"That he was the first man created, and that Eve was created from his essence, but that there were other people created in the same way after that. That would account for yellow and white and black and red people. They all couldn't have come just from Adam and Eve."

He stopped shovelling. "I always wondered how all those people could've come just from those two. It would've been the first case of incest. I'll ask my leader what he thinks."

Khadidja went inside to make coffee, and brought him a mug a few minutes later. "Let me know when you're ready for your sandwich. I'm inside."

She went to her study and opened the file she'd brought home – an article on menopause, a book review and a short story. But she couldn't focus on the pages before her. It was the kick of the shovel outside her window. He was there, in her garden, his sweat dripping onto her land. She looked out. He'd dug a trench along part of the fence, and was tamping a board into it with the shovel. Sief was at his heel with his tail wagging, running around in small circles, then coming back to look at what was going on. Storn looked up and saw her in the window watching him. He wiped the sweat out of his eyes with the back of his hand and beckoned for her to come and see. *God, he's beautiful*. She put down her pen and went out.

"He can't get out now," he said, waving his hand over his handiwork. "The boards are long, he'd have to pull hard and evenly. He's not clever enough to figure it out. I have three more boards for the rest of the fence."

She nodded her head appreciatively. "This was a good idea. At least let me pay you for the boards."

"I had the boards lying around in my yard. You don't have to pay me. What time is it?"

"Almost noon."

He took his red sweatshirt off the branch and pulled it on. "I want to go to the shop before it closes, get something to celebrate our new friendship. Do you like champagne?"

She stiffened. "You can't bring liquor into my house."

He knocked his boot against the trunk of a tree to rid it of dirt, and fished a crumpled pack of cigarettes out of his jeans pocket. "Can you let me out?"

She unlocked the gate. "I mean it."

"Ssshhh," he put his finger to his lips.

She stood at the gate and watched the Ford sputter up Rosmead Avenue. She returned to her work and forced herself to concentrate. She was still huddled over her papers, editing, when she heard the car return.

He followed her into the house, admiring the wooden floors, the paintings on the walls. "My goodness." He came to a stop in front of a wall lined with books. "You've read all these books?"

"I can live without a lot of things, but not without books."

He turned to a watercolour painting on the wall. "Where's this?"

It was the painting Moosa had given her. "Sachs Street, in Bo-Kaap. I was born there."

He stood for a moment in front of it. "The old Malay Quarter?" He pressed a brown paper bag with a bottle in it into her hand. "Put this in the fridge."

"Listen, I thought you knew that Muslims don't drink."

He steered her along laughingly to the kitchen. "It's only champagne, it's not such a big thing."

"It'll bring bad luck into my house."

"Come on," he pleaded. "Just this once."

She felt strange with the bag in her hand, and the thought of putting it into her fridge irked her. "Keep it in the car."

"I have to get back to work, Riempie. Can I have that sandwich soon?"

Riempie? Where did that come from? A riempie was a little leather strip. But it had a nice sound to it. She opened the fridge reluctantly, and put the bag with the bottle in it on the bottom shelf, behind the lettuce and tomatoes. He could take it with him when he left, she thought. She made a fresh pot of coffee, cut a few slices of bread, placed the peanut butter on the table, a wedge of sweetmilk cheese, a sliced tomato, two figs, and went out to tell him it was ready.

He came in and washed his hands at the sink. "It's all done. He won't be able to get out now. I like your house, Riempie. You have a little palace here."

"Thank you."

He sat down at the table, and put a slice of bread and some sliced tomato on his plate. "So, why do Muslims pray five times a day?"

"We're going to talk about religion now?"

"It's good to honour God's name. I don't understand this about the Muslims, all this praying and washing and fasting. It's too much."

She took a fig and peeled back the skin. "A few minutes a few times a day to keep your connection to God?"

"It's too much. People have things to do." He took a bite of his sandwich. "And I don't need to pray five times a day to keep myself in line."

"A man without temptation then, free from sin."

"I didn't say that. Do *you* pray five times a day?"

"Not always."

"It's too much. And this Friday business. It's ridiculous to expect people just to cut off work in the middle of the day, and go to mosque. Why not on a Saturday or Sunday? Like normal people? Why must the Muslims be different?"

"Do you think they try to be?"

"Of course. They're self-righteous. And this business with all the wives – how can they think God would prescribe such a thing?"

She bit into her bread. He was becoming belligerent. She didn't want to continue. "Muslims didn't invent polygamy. One day, when you're ready to listen, I'll explain."

"The Muslims tell you that there was a holy war," he persisted. "Even if that was the reason, that was then, this is today."

She was becoming impatient with the conversation. "Women still outnumber men. Some of them are standing with crowbars at other women's marriages. Would it be better for a man to cheat on his wife and divorce her, or take the other woman into his household as well if he can afford both and be fair? Providing, of course, that the first wife agrees."

"You're in agreement with this kind of thing?"

She realised that she'd made a case for polygamy. "I'm in agreement with it for those who can live with it. Not for me. My own husband wanted a second wife."

"Oh."

"Men have rights, but women also have rights. They don't have to agree. Not agreeing has its consequences, though. Not all women have the same chances. Some have no skills, no money; they have children to support. They stay on out of necessity. These are the situations that bother me, when a woman is held in place with religious strapping – God's words taken out of context or conveniently omitted. I've just written a book about it. Well, it's fiction, but it deals with divorce and polygamy."

"You've written a book?"

"Yes. *First Wife*. It's at the publisher's now. I'm waiting to hear."

His face broke into a smile. "You're too much for me, Riempie. I can't keep up with you." He was an innocent boy again, the angst of religious discussion behind him. "I'm going home now, to have a nap. I have naps, you know. Those twenty-four-hour shifts at the station are murder. Sometimes you don't get any sleep, and even when you do, it's always with your feet in your boots. I'll see you at seven."

When he was gone Khadidja looked in the fridge to see what she would cook for their supper. The shrill sound of a hooter outside her gate made her go out. It was her mother and her heavily pregnant sister Murida, getting out of Maan's new black Mercedes. Her sister's third pregnancy had come as a complete surprise to her at forty-four.

"Must you hoot like that?" Khadidja asked Murida, who was struggling to get out of the car with a cake container. "I hate it when people hoot outside my door."

"Ag you," Ateeka said, pinching her. "Always grumbling. We thought you'd be happy to see us. I made shrimp breyani, and a fridge cake, and this is the welcome we get."

"Thanks, Ma. My favourite." She took the cake from her sister. "Should you be driving in your condition? You look ready to pop."

Murida stood for a moment holding her sides. "I wish I would. Two more weeks, then it's all over."

"How're the children?"

"Excited. I dropped them off with Maan at his mother's house, then went to pick up Mummy. We thought we'd surprise you."

Ateeka started to walk inside with the pot of breyani. Khadidja remembered the bottle of champagne in the fridge and walked ahead of her, removed it and stuffed it in the ironing cupboard.

"You've got the pots out," Ateeka said.

"I'm having a friend over for supper."

"Alison?" Murida asked, sitting down and kicking off her clogs to relieve her swollen feet.

"No."

"How's she? Is the divorce through yet?"

"The property settlement's holding it up. But as far as the imam, yes, that part's all over."

"She got all her talaqs."

"Yes."

"Do you think she'll go back to her old religion?"

"Never," Ateeka jumped in. "That girl wanted to be Muslim from the time she was little. She didn't even know what it was, but she went everywhere with Titch, even fasted with her."

"Did Mummy tell Khadidja about Moosa?" Murida asked.

Khadidja tensed. She had a feeling she knew what it was. "What about Moosa?"

Ateeka took out plates from the cupboard and set them out on the table. "Sies Moena had an anonymous phone call. People are wicked, you know. I wouldn't even have known about it if I wasn't there when it happened, she was so ashamed. She said it was the second time this person had called, saying this nasty thing, then hanging up."

"What did the caller say?"

"The woman said, 'Did you know your son liked boys?' Can you believe it? People are callous. How can they make an accusation like that? Just because he's not married."

"Is he gay, Titch?" Murida asked.

Khadidja busied herself at the sink. "What makes you think I would know?"

"You're good friends. Maybe you know and you don't want to tell us."

"That boy's not gay," Ateeka said. "How can he be gay? And Titch would know if he was."

Khadidja was glad her back was turned to them. "Moosa's always walked his own path. He's different. That's all."

"There." Ateeka relaxed. "I said he wasn't. Do you have any at-jar?"

Khadidja opened the fridge and took out a jar of mango pickle.

"So who's coming for supper?" Murida asked. "That Yusuf guy who came for tea? A lawyer, wasn't he?"

Khadidja smiled at the memory of the man who'd sat with her on the stoep on New Year's Eve and charmed her. "I didn't fit the prescription."

"You don't *want* to fit," Ateeka countered. "No one's good enough."

"That's right, Ma."

"So who's coming?" Murida persisted.

"No one you know. Sief dug a hole under the fence and escaped. A fireman found him on Rosmead Avenue and brought him back. Another one came and fixed my fence. He just left. He didn't want to be paid."

Ateeka and Murida exchanged looks. "Supper instead of money?" Ateeka asked. "What does he want?"

"Hopefully me, Ma."

Ateeka's brows shot up in surprise. "Hopefully you?"

"Yes," Khadidja laughed.

"My, my," Murida sat back, enjoying herself. "I'm hearing things this afternoon. My sister and a fireman." A sudden pain made her wince, and she massaged the side of her belly.

"Is it the baby?" Khadidja asked.

"It's too early. It's just a cramp."

"The doctors aren't always right," Ateeka offered. "You're carrying very low. Lower than last week."

"I hope Mummy's right." She turned back to Khadidja. "So tell us about this fireman. What's his name?"

"There's nothing to tell. He's just someone who came to fix my fence. Storm Callaghan."

"Storm? What kind of name's that?" Ateeka asked. "He's Muslim?"

"Has Mummy ever heard of a Muslim called Storm? And the man's only coming for supper. I'm not going to carry his baby."

"Very clever with the mouth," Ateeka said. "All the right answers. Just don't get yourself mixed up with Christians."

"I'm mixed up with Christians all day, Ma. Alison was a Christian."

"I'm not talking about Alison. And why do you keep calling her Alison? She's Alia."

"Alia, Alison, it doesn't matter. God knows who she is."

Her mother and sister stayed until four for tea, then left her to her preparations for the evening. Khadidja decided to serve her mother's shrimp breyani for supper and spent the time she would've used to cook to balance her personal accounts and fine-tune the editing she'd done earlier. Her mind at ease, she was able to do quite a bit.

At six-thirty she had a shower, tossed her towel-dried hair about until she was satisfied with the look, then set the table and warmed the food. The only thing she'd made to go with it was a sharp onion and tomato salad with chopped coriander and green chillies. There were some minutes to spare, and she jotted a few words in her journal. *Supper date with the fireman.*

Storm arrived shortly after seven, dressed in jeans and a cream top, and handed her a chocolate bar. "I don't know about these things, Riempie. Is this all right?"

"It's fine. I didn't expect anything. And I like chocolate. Thanks."

He saw the dishes on the table. "Can we sit in the room with the books? I like it in there."

She was aware of his smell, his wet hair. She walked into the living room where the hi-fi was. "Do you want music?"

He followed her in. "All right, but not loud. I want to look through your books. Supper smells good. What did you make?"

She slipped a Billie Holiday tape into the cassette. "I didn't make anything. My mother and sister were here this afternoon and brought seafood breyani."

"I like Muslim food." He sat down on the couch and picked up a green volume with gold lettering from the coffee table. He leafed through it, then picked up another, and another. "All these books on Jesus. My word."

"Jesus is revered in the Qur'an."

"Revered is a word, Riempie. You have to love him as a God if you want to be saved."

"I thought you said you didn't believe he was God. Have you changed your mind since last week?"

He didn't answer, and scanned through another of her books. Then he put that down, and looked around, at the hi-fi set, the couch he was sitting on, the paintings on the wall. "You live too much in this world, Riempie. This is the natural world. We live here for a short while, but we'll be in the hereafter forever."

"It doesn't mean we don't have to be happy or that we shouldn't live a good life. We're still here. Are you hungry?"

"Yes." He got up and followed her into the kitchen. "Where are the glasses and the champagne?"

"The glasses are in the cupboard above the sink, and I had to hide your package in the ironing cupboard." She pointed towards it. "Don't bring this stuff into my house again."

He took out the bottle and two glasses. "A little taste?"

"No thanks. I'll have ginger beer." She dished the breyani onto a platter and carried it into the living room. He poured their drinks and raised his glass. "To a new friendship." He took a sip, smiled at her, and reached for the spoon on the breyani platter. "Can I start? This food looks so good. I'm starved."

He was like a boy who couldn't wait to try out his new toy. "Go ahead." She watched him spoon breyani and salad onto his plate. "My mother's a good cook. This is my favourite."

"Very good." He smacked his lips together in approval. He waited for her to dish food onto her own plate. For a few moments they ate in silence.

"Do you want to fall in love, Riempie?"

The question surprised her. "Doesn't everyone? It's natural to want to be close to another human being, to want to be cared for and protected."

"Can't you protect yourself?"

She looked up from her plate. "Of course I can. I'm doing it now."

"Love is necessary for women, isn't it?"

"Yes. And we know right away when we meet someone we like. The man's still trying to memorise the phone number, we're pairing up names. For instance, I meet a guy I like, and his name's Adam Jacobs, for argument's sake. And I'm thinking, how does Khadidja Jacobs sound? The poor sod's just standing there. We're thinking what kind of hair and features the child will have."

"Really?" He looked at her over his fork. "You mustn't fall in love with me, Riempie."

She looked down at her plate to hide the shock of hearing him say it. "Don't overestimate yourself, Storm. Not every woman's in love with you."

"What I mean is –"

"I know what you mean, and this is the second time you've suggested it. I don't know why you feel you have to keep reminding me that you're unavailable. I don't lie awake at night thinking of you."

His face turned red, and for a few minutes they listened to the music while they ate. Billie Holiday's *Don't Explain* suddenly depressed Khadidja. She got up and changed the mood with Pink Floyd.

"You know," he said, "I've always wanted to be a ranger in a wildlife sanctuary, or work in the bush. I love animals."

"Why didn't you?"

"The opportunity for a position as a fireman came along and I took it. My mother said it was a good job."

"The two of you have a good relationship?"

His expression changed. "She doesn't want to become an Apostolic."

Khadidja didn't know what this had to do with having a good or bad relationship. "Does she have to be?"

"I want her to be saved. She goes to a Baptist church. They don't know anything there. In my church they tell you the truth. I gave up a Methodist girl once because she wouldn't switch. Girls are temporary. They can't give me what I get from my church."

She put her plate on the coffee table, glad that he'd killed any possibility of a relationship. "I don't understand you," she said, genuinely confused. "Didn't you love her?"

"No. But there was this other girl, Paula. I don't know if it was love."

"What happened?"

He hesitated. "She had a sister, Melissa. I touched Melissa."

"You had sex with her?"

"Melissa's in the same church as me. It just happened. Paula wouldn't take me back. She ignores me still."

"But how could you expect Paula to understand this? You betrayed her. And with her own sister. What happened to Melissa?"

"She's still in the church. We lived together for a few years. We're just friends now. She's like a little sister to me. A church sister."

Horny stormy pudding 'n pie, fuck the sisters and make them cry. She said nothing.

"Melissa knew I didn't love her," he continued. "I told her not to wait for me. I told you, it's not the same for men as it is for women. There are things that I like about her, but she's not what I want."

"How did it end?"

He looked away. "She found me with another girl."

"Yet another one? Where?"

"In the house. That's when Melissa stuffed her things into a carrier bag and threw a tin of tuna through the back window, and told me to make my own supper."

Khadidja tried to picture the scene. Two sisters. A betrayal. And then another betrayal. "And your wife?"

"She was long ago. We were just kids when we had Sammy."

"Do you see your daughter at all?"

"When she comes down with her mother, and she wants to see me. They'll come to my mother's house."

Khadidja leaned back into the couch and listened to the music for a few more minutes while he finished his food. "Did you have enough to eat?" The champagne was finished. She was ready to offer him fridge cake and see him off. It was clear to her that they could never have a relationship. Not even a friendship. He had too many issues, and she was too attracted to be just a friend.

"I had plenty. That was good food. Thanks." He picked up some of the dishes and carried them to the kitchen. She tidied up the coffee table, and followed him. In the kitchen, she found him washing the dishes in the sink.

"You don't have to do this," she said. "I have cake. Would you like some?"

"No thanks. I can't eat another thing." He stacked the last of the dishes in the rack, and dried his hands. "Turn the lights off."

"The lights? What do you mean?"

He took her by the elbow and led her to the bedroom, turning off the lights as he went.

"What're you doing?"

"Come, Riempie."

In astonishment she watched him pull his cream top over his head, step out of his jeans, and get in under the covers. "Storm ..."

He turned off the light on the nightstand. "Bring the candles ..."

She stood like an idiot at the foot of the four-poster. He was in her bed, waiting for her to hurry up. "You can't do this," she said.

"Take off your clothes, Riempie."

"Get out of my bed."

He got out, and started to tug at her shirt. His hands on her skin excited her. "Riempie, I know you want to."

"No."

"Come, Riempie." He pulled down the zipper of her jeans. "God wants us to be happy."

"No! I don't want it like this."

His hands tugged and pulled. The jeans came off, then the panties, and they fell into bed in a tangle of limbs. She felt the brush of his lips on her cheek, his anxious fingers. Her pulse raced, she was anxious for his touch despite herself. But there was no kiss, no intimate touching. He shoved himself into her, hard and greedy, and she gasped with pain. Then lay helpless under a pounding marathon punctuated by short bursts of excessive speed during which she thought he would rattle her teeth out of her head – pumping, disconnected, alone, his eyes shut tight against her tears.

Finally it was over and he slumped down next to her.

"Riempie ..."

She turned her face into the pillow.

"No, Riempie, don't cry." He put his arms around her. "Don't cry. I'm sorry. I didn't know you would take it like this."

She got out of bed, dragging the sheet with her. In the bathroom she turned on the shower.

"Riempie ..." he pleaded outside the door.

She stood under the stinging spray, peeing and crying at the same time.

"Come out, Riempie ..."

"Go home!"

124

Eventually, she turned off the shower. She brushed her teeth, but couldn't look at herself in the mirror. With the towel wrapped around her, she returned to her room. The light was on. He was still there, sitting up in bed with two mugs of coffee on the side table.

"I'm sorry, Riempie. Can you forgive me?"

"I thought I told you to leave."

"I don't want to leave like this."

She got into bed, drawing the covers about her. "I told you not to bring that shit into my house. I told you it would bring bad luck. Do you know what you've done?"

"I didn't know it would be like this. I didn't see anything wrong."

"That's because you thought of yourself. It wasn't what *I* wanted."

"I thought it would make you happy. God wants people to be happy."

"Stop talking about God. You know nothing about what God wants. And it didn't make me happy. I had no plans to bring you into my bed. Especially not someone who doesn't want anyone in his life."

"You *will* be in my life, you're in it already. I'm fighting against it."

"Why didn't you stay away, then? I would've paid you for the fence." She slid down under the covers, and curled away from him.

"Do you want me to hold you?"

"Get out of my bed."

He put out the light instead. "I won't do it again, Riempie. I promise. I don't want to hurt you."

She said nothing. Eventually everything was quiet. She lay listening to the traffic on Rosmead Avenue, heard the grunt of the fire truck as it pulled into the station. She turned to look at him. It was the face of a boy, innocent in slumber. His arm was around her, his ankle hooked around hers. She dozed off. Shortly after dawn she woke up. He was standing in front of the window with a mug of coffee, the curtains pulled open.

"I have to go home and feed the animals. I'm on duty at nine." He put down a steaming mug on the side table. "I'll call you."

She wanted to go back to sleep, but the harshness of dawn made her remember. She'd had sex and spent the night with a man. She was too ashamed to get up, shower, take ablution in preparation for prayer. What would she say on her prayer mat? Sorry, it won't happen again?

The telephone rang at her bedside. She picked up the receiver. "Titch?" Her mother's voice rang clear and excited in her ear.

"Hello, Ma."

"Murida had the baby this morning at four o'clock. A lovely boy. The image of his mother!"

"So those *were* labour pains."

"That was the beginning. She called the doctor when we got home, and he booked her in. She's at Medipark."

"She's all right?"

"Yes, and the baby also. Everything went well. Are you all right? You sound a bit off."

"I'm fine."

"Come down. I'm putting a chicken in the oven. Kulsum's here. She'll stay for lunch if you come. We can go to the hospital together."

Khadidja perked up a bit with the news. She needed to be around family and old friends, and hadn't seen Kulsum since she'd moved. They had things to talk about. Things that had nothing to do with her intimate life and which bore no resemblance to the kind of things she discussed with Alison. Kulsum was married to a mechanic and had four children. Her life revolved around fund-raising activities for the mosque and madressah, and working with a priest and social worker feeding and tending to the street children in the business district. After ten minutes in Kulsum's company, Khadidja always felt she should do more to improve her spiritual life.

~

A few months after the visit by the Paarl family, oupa Solly telephoned to invite little granny, Murida and I to the farm for the Easter weekend. Murida and I had never slept out, and my mother took a few days to decide if she would allow it. When she did finally make up her mind, she said that both of us couldn't be away at the same time, and that little granny had to decide which one of us she wanted to take along. Little granny didn't like to choose between us, but had to take a decision. I waited anxiously to see who she would pick. If it was to help her get dressed, and fetch things, I knew it'd be me. If it was a question of who would fit in better with the Paarl family, it would be Murida.

"I don't have any favourites," little granny said, dipping a Marie biscuit into her tea. "But Khadidja knows what pills I have to take."

My mother didn't say anything immediately. She looked at me sitting at the table with my books. "Does Granny not think it would be better perhaps if …" She couldn't seem to finish her sentence.

Little granny glanced at me. I pretended that I'd left a book in my room and had to go and get it. But I didn't go all the way round the corner, and leaned with my ear against the wall and listened.

" … Helga said that thing about colour. I mean, how will they receive her?"

Receive her? What did she mean? And little granny must've known I was listening, for I couldn't hear her reply. But my mother seemed satisfied with her response, and I heard her say, "all right". Still, it shocked me to hear this said about me, and I didn't know if I wanted to go anymore. What if I got there and no one spoke to me? Also, little granny choosing me instead of Murida threw my mother into a panic. There were other concerns. My manners were not the best. I couldn't be relied upon to behave. She said none of these things, but I felt it in the way she started to correct me about things. But I wanted to go. And I remembered very clearly Joachim's invitation that I should come to the farm.

My mother had a week to get me ready. She took a newspaper and cut patterns for two dresses, and took me to Spracklens for socks, a petticoat and white panties. I'd never had white nylon panties before, and couldn't wait to feel the softness against my skin. The biggest surprise was on our way home, when she stopped in at a hairdressing salon.

"You want it straight?" the hairdresser asked. She was a woman in a pink overall, and looked like she knew what I needed.

"Yes," my mother said.

"I'll have to cut it close to the scalp."

"She'll have no hair if you do that."

"A short cut will look very nice. She has an oval-shaped face, it will suit her. If you want to keep it long, and you want it straight, I'll have to put on straightener."

The salon was full. She had a customer waiting. My mother had to decide what she wanted. "Cut it rather," she said.

I couldn't believe it. After years of begging for short hair (not forgetting that one episode when I ran away and ended up at Bennie's Hairdressing Salon) I was finally going to have my ugly curls chopped off. The hairdresser got to work quickly. She washed, and cut, and snipped, the wet locks making dark ringlets on the white linoleum floor. I couldn't bear to look in the mirror, and kept my eyes on the book on my lap. Finally, she dusted my neck and asked me how I liked it. I could hardly speak. My hair was cut so short that it looked straight, and my whole face was changed. I didn't mind that I looked like a boy. It suited me, I thought, and I didn't have those greasy sausage curls slapping about my head and shoulders.

Friday afternoon arrived, and off I went in the back seat of the black car. Next to me was my carrier bag with my newest clothes and underwear, a pair of everyday shoes, a book, and under my clothes in the carrier bag, a story I'd written. It was only four pages long, but I was anxious to hear what someone else thought. I'd mentioned to my mother that I'd written a story, but she'd not asked me about it. Except for little granny, on whom I tested all my theories, my story-writing activity was strictly secret.

Sitting in the back seat, looking at the trees and fields and vineyards zoom by, I listened to the conversation going on in the front. I was happy to be going to the farm, but also a little afraid of what lay ahead. I was going to the home of strange people, to sleep there, to eat there. They were Christian, maybe they ate pork. We were never *ever* allowed to eat in Christian people's homes. And they were play-whites. Play-whites were the worst, my mother said. Real whites could almost be forgiven for believing they're better than other people, since they'd had it drummed into their heads since birth. But where did a play-white come from? No matter how I tried to convince myself, I couldn't think of them as my family.

The conversation in front was about harvests, grapes, soil conditions and labourers. I realised that little granny had knowledge of things my mother didn't. Her son was part of another world, a farmer's world. She'd said he wasn't white, but he looked it, and there were only white farmers by law. How would I manage four days in their company? What if I said the wrong thing? What if they ignored me? As if sensing my concerns, little granny turned in her seat. "We're almost there," she said. "Are you excited?"

If excited meant my heart beating a little too quickly in my chest, then I was excited. "Yes, Granny."

We arrived at an entrance with a board proclaiming "Groenkloof" nailed to a tree. I couldn't see the house, only a carpet of green vines with curly leaves stretching all the way up the hill. The car turned into a drive and rumbled past a row of trees, and came to stop at a cluster of barns and outbuildings a few hundred feet from a whitewashed house with a gable. Here, barefooted, brown-skinned children played with an old wagon wheel. A woman bent over a barrel washing clothes stopped briefly to look up, and called out to one of the boys.

"Kleinjan!"

A boy of about nine or ten with a crusty nose rose out of the group and came to stand at the side of the car. He waited for us to get out, then took our bags and carried them up to the house. I was sure this was the boy Joachim had told me about. He looked a bit young to be given the job of cutting off the head of a turkey, I thought. I looked at the other children, four girls and a boy, all younger than Kleinjan. Some of them recognised little granny and greeted her. But it was me they stared at, my clothes and hair they examined with their watchful eyes. I saw a fair-skinned little girl with a cute button nose and blue eyes. It was the dress that made me notice her, a lemon cotton one with smocking, too big for her tiny little frame, and out of place in the dusty yard. Except for the clumpy hair, she didn't look like the others. I smiled at her. Her little toes curled like cashew nuts into the ground as she blushed and turned her head the other way. I looked around for another face, one with short spiky hair, but there was no sign of Joachim.

I followed little granny and her son to the stoep, glancing back at the dusty faces. At the back door, the women had come out and stood waiting for us. I watched carefully for any change of expression. Helga looked her usual stiff self. Liesl smiled. Had they expected me, I wondered? Was the older woman with the shawl oupa Solly's wife? She came forward and kissed little granny on the cheek. "Hello, Ouma. It's been a long time, Ouma looks well," she said in Afrikaans.

"Hello, Olive," little granny responded in Afrikaans. "You look well too. Solly says your arthritis has been acting up."

"It's the change in weather, but I'm all right now."

"This is Khadidja." Little granny pointed to me. "Very clever. She likes books, and can tell quite a good story."

The last thing I wanted was to be singled out. I stood on the stoep, not knowing what to do.

"What a name," she said. "How do you say it?"

"Khadidja," little granny said. "It's a very special name, but we call her Titch. Soen vir ouma," she prodded me.

I looked at the shawled woman. She smiled, but there was nothing welcoming in her eyes. Did she want to be kissed? I moved forward and she leaned over me. I smelled her eau de cologne, and waited for her to look away so that I could wipe my cheek where her lips had been.

We went into the kitchen, a big room almost the size of our whole house. A long table of heavy wood was set for seven people with white plates and forks and a beaker of water. Along the wall was an oak dresser with cups and saucers and plates and a tin of freshly baked biscuits. I could smell them. A coal stove with gleaming kettles and pots burned quietly with low orange flames in a corner and gave off wonderful aromas. A young woman with a doek wrapped around her head was in front of it, turning meat in a pan.

"Sit down, Ouma," Olive said. "We're just waiting for the potatoes to be cooked, then we'll eat." Then, looking towards the stove, she said, "Frances, show the girl where to put her things."

I was the girl. She couldn't say my name. I watched Frances put a lid on the pan and trailed after her along a polished hallway to one of the front rooms. I wondered if Frances was the mother of the blue-eyed girl. She wasn't blue-eyed or fair, but there was a resemblance about the forehead and mouth, and just something about her manner when the shawled woman spoke to her that made me think it might be so. In the room there was a high double bed, a cupboard with an oval glass in the door, a rocking chair, a wooden chest under the window with a bowl of daisies, and a marble-covered stand holding a porcelain basin and jug. The room was cool, sweet-smelling and spacious.

"Put your bag in the cupboard," Frances said. "And keep your clothes in there when you take them off. She doesn't like anything lying around." I knew who the "she" was. And the way Frances said it made me think she didn't like the woman she worked for.

"Will I sleep in here by myself?" I asked.

"No. This was Ouma's room when she stayed here. You will share it with her. It's the boy's room now."

"You mean Joachim?" I asked eagerly. "Where's he?"

"At the Mostert farm."

I hid my disappointment. I didn't know whether being at the Mostert farm meant he was there for a day or a week, but didn't ask. I washed my hands in the bathroom that Frances showed me, and at supper was on my best behaviour. Little granny's son said a prayer during which even little granny bowed her head. I listened to the words. He was thanking God for the food we were about to eat. I compared this with our one word, *Bismillah*. The Christian prayer was like a conversation. I liked it. Then came the part I dreaded. I wasn't used to eating with a knife and fork, and watched how other people ate, how they behaved, what was allowed. People talked and discussed things. At our table you couldn't enter into grown-ups' conversations, and you ate to get your food finished. We also didn't eat extravagantly like this. We had meat in our food, but ate mostly breyani and mutton curry and bredies and bobotie, and roast meat on Sundays. I battled with the big chop on my plate, and in the end ate only the vegetables and rice around it.

131

I had questions when I climbed into bed, but little granny was exhausted, and was gone the minute her head touched the pillow. I couldn't sleep. The bed wasn't mine, the room was unfamiliar. It had different smells from the one I was used to. It had shadows on the walls, and hard polished floors that creaked as the night cooled. It had strange people down the hall. And I'd never slept away from home before.

The next morning at breakfast, sitting between little granny and Liesl and wondering what I was going to do that day, little granny asked when Joachim was coming home.

"He's at the Mostert farm, Ouma," Helga said.

"Didn't he know I was coming?"

Helga glanced at her mother. "He knew, but they'd invited him for the weekend. He's staying there until after Neville's birthday party tomorrow afternoon."

Little granny ate a little bit of her porridge. "Well, get him back," she said. "It's not every day I come to visit. And he's got a guest."

I didn't look at anyone. It was on my account she was ordering him home. Oupa Solly started to talk about a neighbour who was blinded in one eye after a welding accident, and said that he would drive over to the Mosterts later and pick up his grandson. I forced myself to sit still and listen. Liesl asked if I wanted another slice of bread. I said no. I didn't want to eat more, or listen to any more. I wanted to be excused, and didn't know if I could get up, or if I had to wait for someone to tell me. Finally, little granny noticed my fidgeting. "Why don't you go outside to play?"

I didn't want to leave her, but at the same time wanted to be with other children. I pushed back my chair and smoothed my dress. The weather was starting to get cold, but I had on the sleeveless dress with the satin ribbon in the waist. My mother didn't see me pack it in. She had packed mostly corduroy pants and jerseys and the two woollen dresses she'd made.

I left the kitchen and went to stand on the stoep. I saw the workers' children at the far end of the yard in front of the barn playing with a skipping rope. One of the boys wasn't tall enough to swing the rope and it kept getting caught around the shoulders of the girl who was jumping. I found myself going down the steps and walking towards them. They stopped playing when they saw me approach.

"Kleinnooi," one of them said.

"I'm not kleinnooi. I'm Titch."

They looked at one another.

"Can I play with you?" I asked.

Two of the girls giggled.

I decided that it would be easier to speak to them in Afrikaans. "What're your names?"

"These are Sofie and Triena, my sisters." Kleinjan pointed to the girls wearing dresses so short that you could see the perished elastic of their underwear. He turned towards the boy still holding one end of the rope. "This is Pietie. His father looks after the horses. And Uintjie," he nodded towards the blue-eyed girl. "She can't speak."

Uintjie, I thought. Wasn't that the name of a small onion? I looked at her. She stood on one foot and touched the heel with the toes of the other. She was like a doll, and so pretty, I wanted to pick her up.

"Who's her mother?" I found myself asking.

"Frances. She works in the kitchen. My mother's over there." He pointed to the same woman who'd called to him the day before when we arrived by car.

So I was right about the mother, I thought. I knew somehow that I mustn't ask about the father. I picked up the free end of the skipping rope, feeling that it would be a good day. "Kom ons speel. Who wants to be first?"

We played with the skipping rope for most of the morning, then they showed me the tree house they'd made out of a Port Jackson tree near the apple orchard. Kleinjan's father had pulled down the branches and tied them together, and the house had a room that was quite gloomy inside, with a real mat on the sand floor. There was a crate turned upside down, and two cracked cups and saucers with which to play housie-housie. Pietie went to the vineyard to steal a bunch of grapes, and Triena fetched her mother's jug from the buitekamer and filled it with water. With six of us crammed together in the small space, there was no room to play.

"Would you like me to tell you a story?" I asked them.

"Does the kleinnooi *know* a story?" Triena asked.

"I know many stories. Stories from books. But I can also make one up."

"Make one up," Kleinjan said.

"Okay." I'd given up getting them to call me by my name. "Once upon a time," I started, focusing on a chink of light in a narrow opening between the branches, "there was this little girl who lived with her father in a shed in the forest. She didn't have a mother, and lived there alone with him. It was just a little house deep in the forest, with two beds, and a table where her father liked to sit and read, and a big box of books. Then one day this boy appeared and said he'd come to fetch her. The girl didn't know what to do. She wanted to go with the boy, but didn't want to leave her father. The boy stood at the door, saying, 'Come with me, it's only for the summer, we'll come back.' The girl looked at her father sitting at the table. Her father didn't say anything, he didn't even look up. She left with the boy, and they walked through the forest. The forest was dark and gloomy with fat tree trunks and heavy branches and mossy paths. Occasionally the girl looked behind her, but the house was swallowed up by the trees, and she couldn't see it anymore. Finally they came to a road. It was a lonely road, there were no cars on it, no people, no life, just a tar strip cutting through the forest and leading up into the sky. The girl stopped. The boy was holding her hand and he waited for her to step onto the road with him. She looked sadly behind her, then dropped his hand, and walked back the way she had come."

They looked at me with anxious expressions.

"That's the end of the story, Kleinnooi?" Sofie asked.

"Yes."

"Why did the girl not go with the boy?"

"I don't know."

"Did she love her father more than the boy?"

"Uintjie's crying, Kleinnooi," someone else said.

I looked at the pretty little face, the stiff hair flaring out of her head. "Wat's verkeerd, Uintjie?" I leaned forward and touched her.

"She cries a lot, Kleinnooi," Triena said.

"Didn't you like the story?" I asked.

She nodded her head.

"Is that yes or no?"

"It's yes, Kleinnooi, when she moves her head up and down. Left and right means no."

"Then why're you crying? It's only a story. I can change the ending. Must I change the ending, or do you want to hear a different one from a story book?"

Uintjie shook her head left and right.

"All right. I'll change the ending. When they came out of the forest and reached the road, the boy took the girl's hand and said they must go down this road. At the end of this road was a house with a meadow and some chickens and cows. They would live in this house and be very happy. When the rain started in May, they would come back to the forest to visit her father. The girl looked at him. The boy gripped her hand more tightly. The girl stepped onto the tar. Holding hands, they walked together until they disappeared over the horizon."

We didn't return to the tree house after lunch. Instead we played kennetjie in the yard with a small piece of wood, which we flipped with a stick, and struck into the air. Joachim arrived home with oupa Solly, saw the game we were playing, and asked if he could have a turn. He said hello, but didn't seem at all surprised to see me there.

"Did you know I was coming?" I asked.

"Yes. My grandfather told me."

"I'm sorry they forced you to come back."

"They didn't force me, and anyway I'm going back there tomorrow afternoon for the party. My friend Neville will be eight years old. I asked them if I could bring you along."

My heart slammed in my chest. "What did they say?"

"They said yes."

I didn't show my excitement. I wanted to know more, but didn't want to spoil the moment. We played kennetjie and hide 'n seek for the rest of the afternoon, and ran around and laughed so much that I didn't even notice the drizzle that started to fall. When I did notice, my hands went immediately to my hair, but I had nothing to worry about. My hair felt springy and damp, but was still in place. At sunset, Frances called us to come in and wash our hands for supper. I had to leave Kleinjan and the others at the back door, but was happy that Joachim was there. It was easier that night at supper. His table manners, I noticed, were not much better than mine. We were served stewed meat with vegetables and potatoes that night, and both of us dipped our bread in the sauce and picked out the meat with our fingers.

At bedtime I was so tired, I could hardly remember the question I'd saved up all day. "Granny, what's a kleinnooi?"

"Why do you ask?"

"The children called me kleinnooi. I told them I'm not kleinnooi, I'm Titch."

She looked down at me at her feet, pulling off her socks. "It's just a word of respect, for a young girl."

"For a farmer's daughter, Granny?"

"Yes."

"But I've never heard this word before."

"You wouldn't hear it in Bo-Kaap."

I looked in her eyes. "Is it only for white people, Granny?"

She took a moment with her reply. "Yes."

"But I'm not a white person."

"No, but you're family. The children respect you." Her eyes crinkled into a smile. "And you're granny's little kleinnooi."

I fell asleep within minutes, and woke up shortly after dawn, anxious for the next day to begin. I looked at little granny, still fast asleep. I was sure that Joachim would be up, but I had to help little granny get dressed. It was too early to wake her. It felt cold that morning, and I put on the green corduroy pants my mother had made for me. I promised myself that I would go to the kitchen and come straight back. When I got there, Joachim was at the table talking to Frances who at that hour of the morning was already taking bread out of the oven.

"Can we have coffee, Frances, and some eggs?" Joachim asked.

Frances smiled at him, and said yes. The bread was hot, but she cut several slices, and we started to eat them with butter while we waited for the eggs. I was shocked when I saw Frances crack four eggs into the pan. I had never had two eggs at one time in my life.

"Do you read books?" I asked.

"Only school books. Do you?"

"Yes. I like to read. My mother buys us *School Friend* and *Girl's Crystal* every Friday. I also write."

His eyes widened. "Write? Stories, you mean?"

"Yes. I brought one. Would you like to see it? It's not long. It's a mystery."

"What's a mystery?"

"It's like when there's been a crime and you have to figure out who did it. Usually there's a detective or a policeman. It's the first time I tried a story like this."

"You mean you've written other stories?"

"Yes, but they're not very good. I haven't shown them to anyone."

"Then how do you know they're not good?"

"When I write them, they sound good. The next day, I can't believe I wrote them. When I like a story after a week, I know it's not bad."

He looked at me in amazement. "Really? I never met anyone who likes to write. Maybe you'll write for the newspaper one day."

"I don't think so. I don't like to write about things that have happened. I like to make things up."

Frances came with two plates and set them before us. "Kleinbaas se eiers," she said. "Soos kleinbaas dit lyk." She was calling him little master, telling him his eggs were just as he liked them. I liked that, and I liked it that there were no adults around. I saw again how big the kitchen was, the jars of jam and konfyt on the oak dresser. They were rich people, I thought. There were a lot of things to eat. An open tin of biscuits wouldn't last long at our house. A jar of apricot jam was gone in a week. At the Gamieldiens' house, it was gone in two days. Joachim and I ate and talked. He told me about his friend Neville. Neville didn't know it yet, but he was getting a bike for his birthday. When we were finished eating, he stood at the sink, with his eyes half closed, and waited for Frances to wipe his hands. Oh my goodness, I thought. He was letting Frances wipe his mouth. But I liked it. It showed that he liked Frances, and I could see that Frances liked him. Suddenly I wished that we had a Frances, and that I would be spoiled like this. I waited to see if Frances would wipe my hands too. She rinsed out the cloth in a basin of water, and turned to me. "Kleinnooi?"

My heart warmed. I held out my hands for her to wipe, and felt the hot cloth on my skin.

"Let's go get your story," Joachim said.

I'd thought he'd forgotten about it. "Okay, but we have to be quiet."

In the room, little granny hadn't moved, and I left him standing at the door while I tiptoed across to the cupboard and quietly brought out the carrier bag. I dipped my hand in under my clean clothes and took out the book with the handwritten sheets tucked between the pages. I left the bag on the floor, and walked on the tips of my toes to the door. "Here it is." I handed the pages to him out in the passage.

"Let's go sit on the stoep," he said.

We walked past Frances in the kitchen, and sat outside on the step where he started to read. I tried not to appear anxious. My story was about a girl who'd solved the mystery of the stolen crayons. I'd know soon what he thought. A story wasn't good if someone else wasn't interested in it. He read slowly, frowning once on the first page, and giving a little giggle on the last where he was supposed to find it funny. Finally, he gave it back to me.

"I like it, especially how the person who stole the crayons was the one who reported them missing. You don't know that till the end."

He couldn't know how his words thrilled me. "That's why it's a mystery. But is the girl too ugly, do you think?"

"No. I like it that she's ugly. You couldn't make her pretty and clever. Unless you gave her a limp or something."

I had many things I wanted to ask, especially whether he thought I was a good writer, but didn't want to go on and on about my story and bore him. "Do you want to go out and play?"

"It's Sunday," he said. "Church. But maybe they'll let me stay at home seeing as you're here."

138

"You go to church on Sundays?"

"Yes."

"Oupa also?"

"He drives us. He doesn't go in."

We were hardly finished talking when Liesl came out and said that little granny was asking for me. She had to get dressed and have breakfast. In an hour the family was going to church. I went inside to help little granny, but couldn't believe that she would go to church considering what she'd told my mother. I'd never been in a church; I was scared that I might get punished for being in a place with a man hanging on a cross. I changed out of my pants into one of my new dresses.

"Let her wear a hat," Olive said to Helga.

Little granny seemed ready to say something, but then changed her mind and watched Helga put a little black box thing on my head which kept sliding down on my forehead. Helga and Liesl had on smart dresses, white hats and gloves.

In the church I sat between little granny and Joachim, and watched the family as they listened with upturned faces to the sermon. The dominee had on a black cloak, open in front, with tassles, and preached in Afrikaans, in a voice that got louder as he became excited, *"En ek sê vir julle, broers en susters, slaan julle oë op na die Hemel …"* And I say to you, brothers and sisters, raise your eyes to the heavens.

Little granny sat with her hands in her lap, intent on his words. The people sitting on either side of us looked frequently in our direction. They were looking at me. They were all white. Mine was the only dark face in the church. I couldn't wait for the service to be over. Finally, the last hymn was sung and people gathered outside around the dominee and his wife, talking and shaking hands. I was standing with Joachim at the car, waiting for the family, when I noticed him suddenly turn to face the other way and mutter something under his breath. I looked to see what had disturbed him. It was a man and a woman with a baby in her arms coming out of the church. The man was staring at him, then started to walk towards us.

"Who's that?" I asked.

He looked at me, not sure if he should tell me. "My father."

It took me a moment to realise what he'd said. "Your father?" I stared at the couple, then saw Helga break away from her mother and sister and little granny, and come rushing over. The man took the woman by the elbow and left.

"Get in the car, you two," Helga said crossly.

We got in, not knowing what we'd done wrong. Helga stood outside like a guard.

"Why'd she do that?" I asked when we were in the car.

"I'm not supposed to know he's my father."

"You're not?"

"She gets money from him, but he's not to come near me. He didn't marry her. Ouma said she's to have nothing to do with him. I'm not an optelkind."

"What's an optelkind?"

"They didn't pick me up in the street. I *have* a mother."

As he said that, I felt a little pain in my heart, and wanted to touch him. "Do you want to speak to him?"

He looked at me, then turned his head to gaze out the window. I knew what that look meant, but he was a boy, he would never say it. I couldn't think of anything clever to say, and was glad when the door next to me opened, and little granny got in. We arrived home at lunch-time. Joachim said he wasn't hungry, he would save his appetite for the party later on. I wasn't hungry myself, but knew that there would be talk at the table, and so I asked little granny to put something on my plate. And there *was* talk, although Helga spoke in riddles as our "small ears" were also there. I didn't mind. I was an expert at puzzles and word games and converting grown-ups' conversations. Die hond – the dog – referred to Joachim's father. I learned that his name was Adriaan, and that he'd had the nerve to come to church and try to make contact. There were also things said about the woman, and I was surprised to hear little granny put her sixpence in the plate too. But I didn't hear the stuff I really wanted to know, like why he didn't marry Helga, and why Joachim couldn't know his father.

"What time are you taking us to Neville's party, Oupa?" Joachim asked, moving his chair back to get up.

"You're not going," Helga answered.

Joachim frowned at his mother. "We're not going? Why not?"

"The party's cancelled."

"Cancelled? But it can't be. I was there yesterday. I saw the stuff they –"

"Hush! Didn't you hear what I said?"

He sat down and looked at his grandfather for help. Oupa Solly patted him on the head, and said that there would be a next time. I looked at Olive and Helga. They didn't seem sorry that the party had been cancelled. But it was little granny's expression that puzzled me, the way she picked at the last few peas on her plate, the way her head bobbed as she came to some deep conclusions of her own.

I felt bad for Joachim. Parents had no respect for your feelings. They didn't care if you were with a friend, they just opened their mouths and embarrassed you. And they were often angry about things that had nothing to do with the thing they were scolding you for.

Liesl got up and gave us a toffee apple each. "Don't make yourselves sticky," she said. "You can go outside and play now."

Joachim was upset for a while, then forgot all about it. My last afternoon was spent with him and Kleinjan and the other children in the kraal with the horses and the new pony. My holiday ended in the morning when oupa Solly piled us into his car, and returned us to Sachs Street.

It was a weekend I would never forget. For a few days I'd lived in a magical world. I'd run around and played. I'd laughed, I'd told stories. My hands and face were wiped for me. There was no madressah. I didn't have to make my bed. It took me days to get used to my routine in Bo-Kaap again. As for Joachim, I saw him one more time, but that was a sad occasion, and we were big already and found it awkward to talk.

I had a good time at the farm. I must tell Alison about Uintjie and Yagiem and Helga and about the party I never went to. I think Uintjie's father is a white man, but I don't know who.

Khadidja arrived at her mother's house shortly before noon. Kulsum brought her up to date on family news and told her of yet another worthy project she was busy with. Khadidja had heard rumours about Gabieba's marriage, but didn't ask. Some things she wouldn't ask in front of her mother. She saw Kulsum seldom even though Kulsum lived less than a kilometre away from her mother's house, up the hill in Bloem Street. They had a relationship that stretched back many years, albeit of a different kind to the one she enjoyed with Alison. Kulsum had been with one man only. She was the kind of girl who wouldn't even hold her husband's hand in public. But with Kulsum, Khadidja could discuss God in a way she couldn't with Alison.

Ateeka sat in their company for a bit, then got up from the table to go to her room to perform salaah. "What do you think about sin and forgiveness?" Khadidja asked her old friend.

"A sin against God or a sin against someone else?"

Khadidja studied her. Kulsum was covered from head to foot in black robes. Not even sies Moena was bundled up to this degree. Because they were all women in the house, Kulsum had flipped back the flap covering her eyes, nose and mouth, revealing a surprising youthfulness. "A sin against God."

Kulsum took a sip of her tea. "A sin against God is easy. Make two rak'ahs, and ask God's forgiveness. God can forgive you anything. A sin against someone else is different. *That* person has to forgive you first."

"What if it's a sin against God that you know you might commit again?"

Kulsum looked skeptical. "Well, if you do wrong repeatedly, and just keep getting on and off your muslah saying sorry and not really meaning it ..."

"You'd be a hypocrite," Khadidja finished for her.

"And you know what God says about hypocrites. Can't you make sunnah salaah – extra prayers – and fight this sin? Thik'r also, remembrance of God's name. I have a good thik'r written down, I can let you have it. I'll leave it with your mother. It will help you."

"I'm actually ashamed to make salaah. I knew it was wrong before I did it, yet I did it anyway."

"You're human," Kulsum said sympathetically. "It's now, when you know you've done something wrong, that you mustn't forget God. We're all sinners. Fix that thing you're feeling otherwise it will be easy for you to do again. And try that thik'r. I find the best time to do it is after isha'i prayers, before I go to bed. You'll feel good, Khadidja. Try it."

Khadidja left with her mother for the hospital where they found Maan and Murida's mother-in-law and teenage children, Faried and Riana, taking up almost the whole room. The baby was in a bassinet next to the bed. Khadidja kissed her sister and leaned over the tiny infant who was swathed in a white shawl.

"He's beautiful," she said. "And so big."

"Almost four kilos," Maan said proudly.

"Pick him up," Ateeka said. "It's good luck."

Khadidja glanced at her mother and wondered what she would say if she knew what had happened between her and Storm the previous night. He'd pumped her guts out. A thousand Callaghans swam in her still. Just as well there was something wrong with her tubes or ovaries or whatever the doctors couldn't find.

"What long lashes," she said, picking the baby up. "And look at his little mouth." She put her index finger into the tiny hand, and it was immediately clutched by five little pink fingers. The child looked like her sister, she thought, another heartbreaker. The feeling rising up in her was to squeeze him tight and possess him utterly as her own.

Riana came to stand next to her. "Cute hey, Aunty? He looks like Mom. Can I hold him for a bit?"

"Sure." Khadidja gave a final little squeeze and a hug, then handed the fleecy white bundle to Riana, and went to sit next to her sister on the bed. Maan was on the other side with a box of Black Magic chocolates, his arm loosely around Murida's shoulder. Maan's mother, Rugaya, stood next to him with a plate of roast chicken and potatoes she'd brought from her own kitchen. "Hospital food is horrible," she said. "Who can eat it?"

"Thanks, Ma," Murida said.

"Have you thought of a name for the baby yet?" Ateeka asked.

Murida glanced at her son standing near the doorway. "Faried says he likes Isa. He says Muslims don't give their children that name. They don't want the child with the name Jesus, it's too holy."

"Then why's every other name you hear today Mohamed? Isn't that holy? I like Isa."

"I like Mustakim," Riana said. "Kim for short."

"All these fancy names," Khadidja smiled. "And Maan? What does he want?"

Murida looked sideways at her husband and squeezed his hand. "Maan wanted Ebrahim, after his late father, but he's happy to let them decide."

Khadidja watched the interplay between Murida and her husband. Her sister had adapted completely to a life of shopping, cooking, car pools, and a man who was generous and kind, but could also be bull-headed and hard to please. She knew from her mother about the incident with the girl at the Portuguese café. Her mother and Murida had visited the girl, and Murida had smacked the girl right in the shop, then gone to the girl's mother and told her what they'd done.

Khadidja was disturbed by the story, and angry with her mother for persuading Murida to stay on in the marriage. Ateeka had her own explanations. "There isn't a man alive who's free from temptation," she said. "You don't pick up a man like him on every street corner. He's a good man; he had a moment of weakness. Now you leave him, and you get someone who beats you, or doesn't care for you. Give him a chance. I'm telling you, he won't do it again." Murida followed her mother's advice. There never was another incident of infidelity.

Visiting hours ended. Khadidja dropped off her mother in Sachs Street, and took the highway to Woodstock where she exited at Roodebloem Road and went to visit Alison. She'd called Alison from the hospital to tell her about the baby and to say she was dropping by. Alison was in the front garden pruning the apricot tree when she pulled up. They sat outside and talked about Murida and the new baby and Kulsum's new venture.

"Has that girl not got enough to do with four children?" Alison asked.

"You know her. Miss Florence Nightingale since we were kids. But she's happy, and a bereavement counsellor's a good idea. We've never had such a thing in the Muslim community. People come to your funeral, to the seven nights, then disappear into a black hole, and it's just you and the boebe dishes. You need to talk about death, come to terms with the loss. We're very cut and dried sometimes. *Allah knows what's best. Get on with your life.* It's not that easy. A bereavement counsellor's long overdue."

"And she'll be good at it too. Did she say anything about Bieba?"

"No, but I know from my mother that Zane left. Gabieba's very secretive. She's the kind who has the baby first, then tells you she's pregnant. She's getting a job for the first time in her life."

"As what? Gabieba spent her whole life in the kitchen." She remembered Gabieba giving up her schooling to help her mother with the housework and forfeiting her chance to become a teacher.

"She did home baking for customers. Maybe she'll expand her business. But sies Moena told my mother that Gabieba wants to go out and work. She doesn't want to be in the house any more. I don't blame her. Cleaning and cooking for people her whole life."

"Do you know why they split?"

"No, but I think she has a spending problem. According to sies Moena, Gabieba had got so used to all those outfits she got from her father, that when she married, she couldn't stop shopping. She has over fifty pairs of shoes and two cupboards with clothes. Zane closed her Stuttafords account. Let's go in. I'm getting cold."

Inside the house they headed for the living room, and sat down.

"Where's Leila?" Khadidja asked.

Alison's expression changed. "She's in her room. She's grounded. No phone calls. No movies. No going out for a week. No pocket money."

"It sounds serious." She saw the pained look on Alison's face. "Don't tell me if it's too hard."

Alison leaned back on the couch and half closed her eyes. "I was out last night at my mother's. Leila has this friend, Nadeem, in the same class as her. They go out to movies sometimes. He comes and goes. Decent boy, from a good family. Last night when I arrived home, she wasn't here yet. I didn't think too much of it. Around midnight I went outside on the stoep. You know how it is. You become agitated. You think going outside to look makes them come back faster. I saw the car outside. He drives his father's Honda Ballade. I saw a movement in the car, like someone ducking. I don't know what made me do it, but I went down and opened the door. I saw my child naked, sitting on top of him."

"Oh my God."

"I freaked out," Alison's shoulders started to shake. "I mean we all did things when we were younger, but not at fifteen, not like this. Naked in the car with a boy, outside the door. Fucking him!"

Khadidja didn't know what to say. She watched Alison take a tissue out of her sleeve and blow her nose. She went to sit next to Alison, and put her arm round her shoulder.

"I'm ashamed, Titch."

"Don't be ashamed. I'm your friend."

Alison wiped her eyes with her moist fingers. "I told her to get out of the car and get into the house. She pulled her dress over her head, and came inside with her panties in her hand. I hit her, Titch. I'm not one of those mothers who can control themselves when their kids do something like this. I hit her with the first thing I could grab, and the first thing I grabbed was the dog leash you'd left here last time. I hit her and hit her, around the table, into her room. I never heard her scream like that."

Khadidja looked in the direction of Leila's room. She could hear faint noises of a television set, but was sure Leila knew she was there. "I don't know what to say, Alison. I'm sorry this happened."

"I threatened to tell her father."

"Don't. He'll make a party out of this. Besides, it's your girl."

Alison gave a wry smile through her tears. "She *is* my girl, and today I have a different feeling about it. I'm very disappointed, but I could've handled it differently. I'm not good at these things."

"You're a mother. You were in the moment. Don't beat yourself up about it. I probably would've done the same thing."

Alison was quiet for a moment, nodding her head. "When she comes out of that room, I have the job of bringing it up, discussing it. I'm damned, Titch, if I'm going to give my blessing for her to have sex."

Khadidja listened. At least four or five times a year she approved an article or filler for the magazine on the risks of indiscriminate sex.

"I mean, how do I tell her about God on the one hand and safe sex on the other? I'd be a hypocrite."

"You have to opt for the lesser of two evils. You *have* to talk to her about protection. Our mothers wouldn't agree, but we can't take a chance with our children's lives. They're going to do it anyway. You've got to get that message across. I know it's easy for me to talk, but if I had a daughter, I would talk to her about no sex. Leave the God angle. The God angle closes up their ears. The health angle has life implications. Emotional health, physical health. That's my opinion."

Alison nodded. "That's the job I have ahead of me." She got up. "Come, let's go and have something to drink." In the kitchen, she switched on the kettle, took out mugs, opened the fridge, and brought out half a chocolate cake. "She made this yesterday afternoon."

Khadidja poked her finger into the thick chocolate cream, and tasted it. "Nice. That girl can make a good chocolate cake. Have you gone for those classes yet at the imam's house?"

"No, but I was in CNA and bought one of those books on bad relationships. I saw myself in every third paragraph. It says in there that women spend all their time analysing men in an effort to avoid their own issues. It's easier to find something wrong with the men than with themselves."

"Probably," Khadidja chuckled. She sat down, kicked off her shoes and rested her feet on a stool. "The fireman came to fix my fence yesterday."

Alison looked up from cutting the cake. "Did he? How did it go?"

"Give me a cigarette."

"Oh dear. The green or the brown?"

"The brown."

Alison reached into her shirt pocket and handed her a packet of Stuyvesants.

"I didn't expect him," Khadidja started. "After that walk with him last week, I thought he'd got the message that I didn't want to see him again. Yesterday morning he rocks up at my house, and I let him in. He fixes my fence, he has lunch, he goes out to buy a bottle of champagne, and comes over for supper at seven." She paused for a light, and continued. Alison sat on the opposite stool and listened. "I didn't want it, Alison. I had no such intentions. It wasn't on my mind. I was just going to have a pleasant evening with food and conversation, and there I was in bed with him on top of me, tossing back and forth like an Easter bunny. It was horrible. Not only was I unprepared for it, there was no emotion, no feeling. It was disconnected and mechanical. He didn't look at me, touch me, his eyes were shut tight as if he was suffering."

"Good grief." Alison seemed outraged that Khadidja could be so calm about it, her own problems momentarily forgotten. "Do you think it was rape?"

"I wondered about that. I don't know. I said no, but I didn't kick him out. I could've if I'd wanted to. If it was rape, I allowed it."

"Not necessarily. It was a date, you knew him, you let him in, he took advantage. You'd said no. More than once." Alison looked at her, convinced that she was right. "You're not going to see him after this, are you?"

Khadidja couldn't look her in the eye.

In the middle of winter, with me sitting between Alison and Cecil with my knees pressed together and my hands shivering in my blazer pockets, Miss Jenkins stood in front of the blackboard and told us that Sybil Cloete had died the night before during an asthma attack. It was as if a hand reached into my chest and stole my breath. The class dimmed. I felt faint. I heard no other words after that. Just the day before Sybil skipped rope with us, and now she was dead. Stilled into silence, I stood with Alison and the other children in the playground during break listening to all the good things said about Sybil. She'd been shooter for the netball team.

She was the fourth cleverest girl in the class. Glenn Peters had liked her. I was too disturbed to say or do anything. I couldn't eat my sandwich. I felt cold even though I had a jersey on under my blazer and was standing in the sun. All I could think of was that Sybil was dead. I'd never seen a dead person. Her face kept coming before me – the two navy-blue ribbons at the end of her plaits, her dilly eyes with the thick glasses, the missing tooth.

The morning of the funeral Miss Jenkins lined us up, checked our noses, our hands, our hair, and told us how she expected us to behave. We were going to pay our respects to the family, and would visit the chapel where Sybil's body was lying. We were not to talk, we were to file by the coffin slowly. We were to shake the hands of the family and say how sorry we were.

Alison and I brought up the rear of the line. We were always first for everything, but not for this. I wanted to delay setting foot inside the chapel for as long as I could. The first thing I noticed when we arrived was the blue and red stained glass windows, giving everything a dark, purply look. They made me think of cemeteries and avenging angels.

Like a school of sardines all swimming together, the Standard Two class entered the chapel. Sybil's mother was red-eyed and sorrowful in a black dress and a small hat, and stood surrounded by people just inside the door.

Miss Jenkins turned to us. This was our cue. One by one, we shook Sybil's mother's hand and mumbled our sympathies.

"That's the father," Alison whispered about the man standing further along.

"How do you know?"

"Look at the hair. It's the same as Sybil's."

I was afraid to step into the chapel where the coffin was, but looked at the man Alison had pointed out with the blond hair. Hair this straight and this colour, we knew, came from white people, and he was very fair-skinned.

"Will the coffin be open?" I asked, beginning to feel hot in my neck. For two days I'd tried to forget about Sybil, but it was impossible. The atmosphere in the class was dark and sad. Sybil's seat was empty. Other children kept talking about her. Some of them couldn't wait for the funeral so they could see the body. I'd begged my mother to let me stay home, saying it was a Christian funeral, that I'd be the only Moslem there, hoping that religion would get me out of attending. It had no effect. "It's with the class," she said. "It's good for you to see."

When we had all expressed our sympathies to the family, Miss Jenkins led us down the aisle, and I saw it, a long white box on a stand. Even from where I stood behind the others I could see that it was open, I could see the nose and forehead of the girl whose crunchy peanut butter and apricot jam sandwiches I'd happily traded my meat sandwiches for.

"I don't want to go up," I whispered. I'd noticed a sickly sweet smell.

"Don't look," Alison said.

Miss Jenkins turned and gave us a glare. We kept our eyes down and shuffled forward. Then we were in front of it. Roses and death. This was what the smell made me think of. *Roses and death. Death and roses.* The words went round and round in my head. I looked at Alison's hemline. To look higher was to look smack into the coffin. Standing two feet away from it was chilling enough. Alison stood and stood, and I wondered why she was taking so long. I wanted her to move so I could also move and get away, but she took her time, and then I made a big mistake and looked. The picture was scratched forever in my mind: Sybil lying like a doll with her soft curls on a satin cushion. They had taken off her glasses and done her hair, and put her in a white dress as if she was going to a birthday party. The stillness of her face frightened me. I knew her skin would be cold. And I knew that before the day was over, the lid would close on her face and Sybil would be in darkness. It didn't matter that she was pretty or clever or good. God had taken a nine-year-old child.

At home I sat at the supper table with my food untouched before me. I couldn't eat. I wasn't listening. I had to pee, but was afraid to leave my spot near the stove where my mother was stirring custard in a pot.

"You can have my meat if you go with me to the toilet," I said to Murida.

"The toilet's right outside the door," she said in an irritated voice. "Put on the light."

I wanted to kick her, but had no energy for it. My mother took my plate away and gave me a glass of sugar water. "Drink this," she said. She put on the yard light and waited at the back door. When I returned, little granny was spooning custard into four bowls. She put the biggest bowl before me. "You like custard."

But I had no desire for custard. I was shivering, and couldn't explain the tightness in my chest. Alison had come home with me after school, and we'd sat on my bed talking about angels and worms and Jesus and hell, and I kept thinking of Sybil in her coffin in the ground. What really happened when people died? What happened to the body? Did it rot? Did worms come out of it? Would they wriggle out of her nostrils? What if the Moslems were wrong, and there really was a Jesus waiting at the other end?

All night I groaned behind little granny's back. I listened to her snore. I listened to the creaks in the floorboards. I listened to a car grunting up the hill. The night was full of strange noises – the patter of small feet in the passage, children's voices. I imagined the devil's breath oozing out of the walls, curling down towards me. I saw Sybil screaming with unmoving lips, *I'm alive!*

"Granny ..."

She was fast asleep, her lips vibrating in a soft snore.

"Granny ..." I rocked her with my hand. "Granny ... wake up ..."

She stopped snoring and turned her head. "What is it?"

"I'm feeling sick, Granny. I can't breathe."

She reached for the light switch dangling above the headboard at the end of a cord, and squinted her eyes at the clock on the dressing table. "It's three o'clock," she said, scowling at me. "What's wrong?"

"I'm scared, Granny."

"What're you scared of?"

"I don't want to die."

"Who said you're going to die?"

"Sybil was only nine. *She* died. I think she's in the room."

"In the room?" she frowned. She looked around the small room, blinking her eyes. The bed was against the wall. I was lying safe and secure between the wall and her left shoulder. The only other furniture in the room was a Dolly Varden dresser with a pink frill and a chair. "Sybil's not here," she said. "She's dead."

"Her spirit, Granny. Oemie told us once of this girl who died in an accident on a mountain road in Ceres, and that whenever cars came to the spot where it happened, a girl with a red jersey stopped them for a lift. They would tell her to get into the car, and when they got to the spot where she wanted to go and they looked in the back of the car, she wasn't there."

Little granny sighed. "Sybil didn't die in a car accident. Her soul isn't restless. It doesn't want to come back."

"Why did God take her? She was only nine."

"God didn't give her the asthma attack."

"Oemie says everything's put out. If it's put out, doesn't it mean God put it out? That Sybil would die when she was nine years old? Isn't it God? Even if He didn't give her the asthma attack?"

She rearranged the pillow under her head. "You will ask your granny now, in the middle of the night, about God's plans?"

"I'm scared, Granny. I'm scared God will take me."

"God won't take you. Not for a long time. Granny can see far."

"Granny has powers?" I asked.

"Powers?" The word was a strange one, and she frowned. "No, I don't have powers, but some people know things. That isn't the same as having brains, though. A person with brains might be able to run a bank, but it doesn't mean he sees. Seeing comes to those who allow themselves to feel." She turned to look at me. "It's hard to lose someone. Even for old people who know their time's near. But it's not something to fear. Before you were born, would you have believed that there was this world?"

"No, Granny."

"So, too, there's this other world waiting for us. We can't imagine it, our brains can't conceive it, but when we leave here, we'll go there. And if we live right in this world, we'll be happy in that one."

"But what about our bodies, Granny? Will we wake up in the grave when we're dead? I keep thinking of Sybil."

"The body's only the case that the soul comes in. You mustn't spend too much time thinking about it. Think of the soul. Do you know what's a soul?"

"No, Granny."

"The soul's the breath the angels breathe into you when you're just a thread in your mother's belly. If you hurt your body, you can always find some medicine to mend it. If you hurt your soul, you'll have a pain such as nothing can fix. God knows this, and everything he tells us to do is to take care we don't hurt this soul."

"Will Sybil go to hell because she's Christian?"

"People don't go to hell because of their faith. Sinners go to hell, Moslems as well as anyone. God wouldn't have sent down a Book if he thought we didn't need it."

I could see she was ready to go back to sleep but had one more thing to ask. "Has Granny seen a picture of Jesus?"

"I've seen pictures, yes."

"Is he a white man, Granny?"

Her eyes crinkled into a tired smile. "Jesus was a Jew. I don't know if that's white."

"But did he look like that, Granny? Sad with blue eyes?"

"Who can say what he looked like? People paint pictures. They go by other pictures they've seen."

"At school they say he's God."

"We can't see God, we only see God in his signs. That's why it takes faith to believe. It's God's first requirement of us, to believe in something we can't see."

"But why does God need us to believe in him? If he owns all the worlds, why does he need us? Moslems have to do such a lot of things. Christians only go to church once a week, and whatever sins they have, they're forgiven."

"Who told you this?"

"Alison. She said Jesus died on the cross for her sins."

"Alison will pay for her own sins, don't you worry. We'll all take our own packet to the market. How's your chest?"

"My chest, Granny?"

"Yes. Can you breathe?"

"Yes, Granny."

"All right. Close your eyes then, and go to sleep."

"Pick up the phone if you're there, Riempie. I know you're there. Answer. I want to talk to you."

Khadidja stared at the answering machine, waiting for the message to end. Eventually it was quiet. She realised that anyone looking out from the top floor of the fire station could see her house. She turned off the lights and lay on her bed in the dark watching the ten o'clock bulletin. Nightly scenes of unrest on American television had prompted Democratic Party calls for sanctions which banned new investments and loans to South Africa, withdrew landing rights for South African Airways, and banned imports of uranium and other products, but it was the leader of the coloured Labour Party, the Reverend Allan Hendrickse's swim on a whites-only beach near his home in the Eastern Cape which made the headlines that night. It rammed home the question of colour and she thought of her own involvement with a white man. Where could it possibly go?

For a few days she kept the lights off in the house and went out after work in case Storm turned up unexpectedly. On Thursday she found a letter in the postbox from the publisher. The publishing manager liked the strong women's perspective in *First Wife*, and was interested. Could she give her a call to set up an appointment? Khadidja ran inside with the letter and sat with it on her bed, reading it over and over again. She called Alison. "Alison, you won't believe my good news. *First Wife* has been accepted!"

"Congratulations! When will it come out?"

"I don't know. I have to call to set up an appointment. I don't know how long the process takes. There'll be editing. This is four hundred pages. My first book, Alison!"

Alison laughed. "I'm happy for you, Titch. But I'm not at all surprised. We'll go out tomorrow night and celebrate. Dinner anywhere you want."

The doorbell sounded. "Hold on a minute. There's someone at the door." She switched on the stoep light and looked out the window. It was Storm, dressed in a suit and tie. She went back to the telephone. "It's Storm."

"What does he want?"

"God knows. I'll call you back." She said goodbye and went out.

"I've been calling you, Riempie, leaving messages." He leaned with his hands on the gate, waiting to see if she would open it. "We broke bread at the house of one of the sisters. I thought I'd drop by and see if you were home."

"You broke bread?"

"We talk about the scriptures, sort of questions and answers. Everyone puts his opinion on the table. We partake of spiritual food. We take turns at each other's houses. The sister we saw tonight, her husband left her two months ago. We went to offer our support. She has three children."

Partake of spiritual food. She was surprised by his choice of words. They weren't his words, she knew. "You gave money to this sister who has three children?"

"Money doesn't solve everything. And we don't give things. We offer advice. Prayer."

"Do they accept that at the grocery store?"

"Don't be nasty, Riempie." He gave a wicked smile. "Aren't you going to invite me in?"

She was again surprised by how different he could be. One moment a skunk, the next a clean-hearted devotee who couldn't do anything wrong. "Come in for a minute." She unlocked the gate. "I have something to show you."

He followed her into the living room, sat on the couch and read the letter. His face broke into a smile. "They're going to publish your book?"

"Yes."

"You're too clever for me, Riempie," he said in wonder, turning the letter over and reading the last part again. "You'll be rich."

"Rich?" She laughed. "Writers don't do it for the dough. It's a fix. Just like cigarettes. There's something that happens to you with a piece of chocolate and an empty page. It's also an ego thing. Immortality."

"This all sounds very complicated. I'm a simple boy. I don't have your visions and dreams. What do you see in me, Riempie?"

"Am I seeing something in you? You're the one coming over here."

"You want me to. You're upset with me, but you wait. I know women. They play the hard-to-get thing, but wait for the phone to ring. Come sit here," he patted the seat next to him. "I'm sorry I messed up the other night. I shouldn't have forced you."

"You shouldn't have brought champagne into my house. The rest wouldn't have happened."

"I know. Come and sit here, and tell me about these books. We didn't really talk about them the last time."

She went to sit next to him. He relaxed back into the cushions. "I like this room, Riempie." He looked about. "Don't ever throw me out."

There were many things she could've said to him then, but she kept silent, surprised by how quickly she'd forgiven him.

"I like you, Riempie. I don't ever want to hurt you. I can't promise that I won't, but I don't want to. Do you know what our subject was tonight? Predestination and free will."

"And you're a simple boy?"

"I'm simple about some things – well, all things." He smiled shyly. "But these things I've learned. I've been with the church a long time. My pastor, Mr Bennett, tried to explain predestination and free will, but it's complicated. I don't understand it. If God's the planner of all things, and knows what you're doing before you've even thought it, you're doomed at the starting line. How do you have a chance?"

"It *is* complicated. We believe that actions are judged according to intentions – the intentions which immediately precede and accompany an action, not those which have been abandoned or changed at the moment of action."

She waited for him to think it through. "Go on."

"Intentions are an expression of the soul. The soul stands in a direct relation to the Divine Will. It's with our souls alone that we can comprehend and feel the existence of God. Because of this intimate relation to God, the soul partakes in the Divine prerogative of freedom –"

"Riempie, you're losing me. I'm entry level. The disks are full. Go slow."

"Do you understand what I've said so far?"

"I think so."

"So, if we're unfree, and therefore, in a higher sense, not responsible for –"

He lowered his head into his hands as if to shut out anything else she might say. "Too much, Riempie, too much. You're confusing me."

"Didn't you understand?"

"The soul part, yes. Not the rest. I'll talk to my leader."

She was irritated. "Do you ever arrive at any conclusions by yourself?"

"Our leaders are prophets and apostles, they know the truth."

"Prophets and apostles? Like in the Bible?"

"That's right. They have dreams and visions, and God sends warnings and messages through them. Remember the girl who didn't want to switch to my church? I asked my leader for advice. I didn't know what to do. She was already complaining about my going to church so many times a week. He said I would have a dream, and that he would come the following night to interpret it."

"He told you you would have a dream, and you had one?"

"Yes. And the next night at seven-thirty, he came, and I told him. It was a strange dream, not really about anything. He told me that he'd had a vision. In it he saw this girl taking me away from my church."

Khadidja waited expectantly.

"We broke up the same weekend," he said.

She got up. "Listen, I haven't eaten yet." Her manner indicated that she had things to do.

"Can I have some tea with you?"

Just open the door and say goodnight. She walked to the door. "Another time, maybe. Not tonight."

The call came before she left for work the next morning. "How're you, Riempie? I know you're getting ready for work. I just wanted to ask if I upset you last night."

There was something reassuring about his persistence. "No."

"You've never been to the fire station. Do you want to come and visit me?"

"Listen, I have two appointments this morning, I'm running late. I can't find my shoes. I'm leaving the office early today to go to a colleague's funeral, then to the gym. I'll talk to you when I get back."

"Have a nice day, Riempie. I hope I see you."

She went to the funeral, but came straight home. She changed out of her business suit into jeans, left the house, crossed the road and walked into the parking area of the fire station. Her pulse quickened when she saw the red truck with its shiny chrome equipment, and four men in blue shirts and navy pants hovering nearby.

"Hey, Storm!" one of them called as she approached.

She was wearing jeans and a white shirt tucked in at the waist. Her long hair, wild with corkscrew curls, bounced away from her shoulders as she walked towards them. Pietie Adams was right, she thought. They were all white. And obviously knew she was coming there for Storm. How did they know? And what were they thinking? It was still apartheid South Africa. The one who'd spoken seemed friendly enough, almost flirtatious.

"Riempie ..." He appeared through the wide doors in his work pants and boots, a mop in his hands. His back and chest glistened with sweat.

"I didn't know firemen did their own cleaning and cooking," she teased. He wasn't tall, but he was neatly packaged, very sensual, his navy-blue fireman pants unbuttoned at the top exposing a faint strip of reddish brown hair. She had a sudden impulse to possess him.

"This is Riempie," he said to the men on his right. "Riem, this is Dwayne, Darryl, Mikey, and –" He didn't get a chance to introduce the fourth man, who walked off with a grunt of disgust. Khadidja thought she heard the words *coloured slut*.

"I hear you're a writer," Mikey said.

Khadidja appreciated the effort to make her feel at ease. And Storm *had* talked to them about her, she thought. What exactly had he told them? Asking her to come and see him at the fire station obviously meant that he didn't care about what others thought. She glanced at the men leaning against the truck grinning at her –

tall, high-testosterone types, all with crew cuts. From their manner it seemed that they too had no difficulty with it.

"Yes."

Storm put down the mop and pulled on a shirt he lifted from the metal railing leading up a flight of cement stairs. "Come. I'll show you around."

Dwayne whistled after them as they left. They crossed the indoor garage, went down a passage, up the stairs, to a sparse little room at the end of another long corridor. The room had two single beds, lock-up cupboards, and a metal table between the beds. A reading lamp, the Bible, and a pair of glasses stood on his side of the table.

"This is it?" she asked. "I've always wondered what it looked like in here. It's paltry."

"Don't use all these big words on me, Riempie. What's paltry?"

"Insignificant, sparse. It's like a jail cell."

"I come here to sleep. What more do I need? We have a TV room downstairs, a ping-pong table. I don't watch a lot of TV."

She sat on the edge of the bed. He sat down next to her. "Why're you so pretty, Riempie?" His mouth was close, she was greedy to feel it on hers.

She handed him a yoghurt container. "Some fruit salad. Pawpaw and mango."

"For me?" He leaned back against the wall and opened it. "It looks good." He picked out a sliver of mango with his fingers and put it in his mouth. "You should become a Christian, Riempie."

"If you talk about religion, I'm going."

"If we can't talk about religion, what will we talk about?"

"Anything. The flowers in Kirstenbosch. How to make cheesecake."

"Are you scared to come to my church?"

"I'm not threatened by other people's beliefs."

"Come with me, then, on Sunday."

She got up. "I've got shopping to do. My mother and my friend Alison are coming tomorrow for lunch. Give me a quick little tour. I want to see the pole where you guys slide down. There *is* a pole, isn't there?"

159

He smiled. "Everybody always wants to see the pole. Let's go to the showers first. It's right here." He took her four doors down the passage and went into the men's room to check that it was empty. "Here it is. Stalls. No doors for a quick getaway. There's an order in which you wash in case the alarm goes. Your boots are already prepared with the pants' legs tucked into them, ready for you to step into. When the alarm goes, every second counts."

"What if you're halfway through shaving?"

"You don't shave in the shower. But whatever it is you're doing, you get out."

They left and walked down the same passage to the other end of the corridor. "This room here is a tuck shop. Chocolates, cool drinks, chips. It's locked now." He opened another door. "This is what you wanted to see." He showed her the pole leading to the big red truck on the floor below where fireproof jackets and helmets were lined up on hooks against the wall. "I'll show you how it's done." He sailed down the pole and disappeared from sight. She met him downstairs where he explained the dials and hoses on the truck, and showed her the jackets and oxygen tanks hanging in place behind the seats for the men to slip into when they hopped on.

"Nothing's left to chance. When the call comes in, we have to be ready to go."

She had to get away from him, she thought. She could smell his sweat; his half-naked body was distracting. In a minute she was going to touch him. They walked through the kitchen where a tall, lanky, blond male called Stretch was bent over the sink, peeling potatoes. It was his turn to make supper.

Some of the men who'd met her outside came in and stood around talking, drinking coffee, making fun of Stretch's tallness. Stretch laughed without taking his eyes off the potatoes. He seemed used to the jibes.

"Storm says you're Muslim," Mikey said.

"Yes."

"A Muslim and a born-again. What a combination."

"Who's a born-again?" she asked.

"Storm. He's Apostolic, but he's also born-again."

"You're a born-again, Storm?" Khadidja frowned. "Why didn't you tell me?"

Storm smiled sheepishly. "What's a born-again, Riempie? Just someone who's had an awakening. Don't people have awakenings all the time?"

"All the time, but don't born-agains get baptised again? A friend of mine at the office is a born-again Christian. At forty, he was baptised in his own pool."

"I don't think it took when they dipped Stormy in," Mikey laughed. "He's still deurmekaar, and now that he's met you, he's even more confused. Reading books by the Muslims, talking all day long about the things they do."

"The other Christians are lost souls," Storm said. "They believe Jesus will come down on a cloud, that he's sitting up there. What's he doing up there? Playing cards? Watching the rugby?"

"Hear that?" Mikey said. "Not even with the Christians can he agree. He doesn't agree with the Baptists, the Methodists or the Anglicans, and he hates the Roman Catholics."

Dwayne entered the conversation. "How many people have you brought into the church, Storm? That church had twenty people when he first joined. See all the sisters there now."

Khadidja couldn't resist. "Conversion by fornication, Storm?"

The kitchen exploded with laughter.

"You're nasty, Riempie. I didn't know you could be so nasty."

Alison and Ateeka arrived together in Alison's car and sat with Khadidja on the stoep admiring the garden while they waited for the chicken to brown in the oven. It was a different garden from the one Khadidja had inherited when she first moved in. She'd had the old lawn lifted and had laid down a dark green buffalo grass, which was neatly trimmed, with a row of hydrangeas leading up to the stoep. A covey of blackbirds chattered in the branches of a big tree, at the base of which several pots of pink and orange impatiens grew brightly in the shade.

"I'm watching you, Sief," Khadidja said in a reprimanding tone to her dog who had his nose in one of the pots. "He's pulled the plants out of that pot twice already."

"Well, you're the one who wants a dog," Ateeka said. "Just keep him away from my legs." She turned to Alison. "This girl never put a seed in the ground when she lived on Sachs Street. I didn't think she knew anything about plants. Did she tell you about the letter she got?"

"Don't brag, Ma."

"What mother can't brag a little about her child?" Ateeka asked.

Alison laughed and took out her cigarettes. "I was the first one she called, Ma." It was disrespectful to smoke in front of your mother or your friend's mother, but Alison had always been completely at ease in Ateeka's company. "Did Ma read her book?"

"My mother never reads any of my stories. Only those I wrote for the paper."

"I want to read Khadidja's book when it's published. You never told me what they said when you went to see them."

Khadidja sighed. "I got the manuscript back. They want me to rework a chapter. The editor's started to edit the manuscript. It's all scratched up with comments."

Alison blew a circle of smoke over their heads. "Did they say anything about the younger man?"

"They have no say over my characters. They can only say whether or not it works. And it does. But the book still needs fixing. They want an extra scene before the ending."

"That's the only thing in the book I didn't like. After she finds love, she lets it go."

"I know. I wanted it to happen between them also, but she would be a weak, pathetic character then."

Ateeka got up from her chair. "I don't know what you're all talking about. Let me go and check on the chicken in the oven."

A cyclist rode up and stopped at the gate.

"Hell. I told him I was busy."

"That's Storm?" Alison asked. "My goodness. He *does* look like Mick Jagger."

Khadidja got up and went to the gate.

Storm leaned over the handlebars, one foot on the gate. "I've just popped by. I know you have visitors. Who's the girl?"

Always when she saw him, something about his eyes or his hair or his mouth made her pulse race. "My friend Alison." She looked back towards the stoep and waved. Alison came down. Khadidja introduced them.

Storm extended his hand through the grille of the gate.

Alison shook it. "I've heard lots about you."

"You have? All good things, I hope. I haven't heard anything about you. What church are you with?"

"For God's sake, ask something about her – what star sign she is – before you jump right in," Khadidja said.

Alison threw her cigarette to the ground and stepped on it. "I don't belong to any church."

"You don't believe in God?"

"I believe in God very much. I'm Muslim. I converted. Maybe you're confused by my name."

"Why did you convert?"

"It's a long story. I grew up around Muslims. I liked the culture."

"You couldn't have understood your own religion then. Maybe it was all a fad when you grew up, and you did it without thinking. I know people who think it's fashionable to become Hare Krishnas or Buddhists. They're attracted by the beads and the chanting, and all that stuff they stick on their foreheads. You can change back. It's not too late."

"Aren't they waiting for you at work, Storm?" Khadidja asked.

"I'm off today, I told you."

Ateeka appeared on the stoep. "Lunch is ready!"

"Bye, Storm," Khadidja said.

"I'll call you later, Riempie. And I'll talk to you again, Alison. We have to continue this conversation."

"Is he for real?" Alison asked when they were alone. "He's a hunk, but he's got a stunning lack of respect."

He called early the next morning. "Wake up, Riempie. Get Sief's leash on. We're going to Muizenberg with the dogs."

Khadidja looked at the clock on the bedside table. It was six-thirty. Usually she was up at six, but she'd gone to bed late the previous night after watching a movie with her mother.

"Do you know what time it is?"

"I know. Get up. I'll pick you up in ten minutes."

"My mother's here, she slept over. We're going to my sister's house at one for the doopmaal, the christening."

"You'll be back in plenty of time. Just get up. I want to be back here myself by eight-thirty to get ready for church."

Khadidja replaced the receiver. A few minutes later she heard the hooter and got into the car with Sief. She had given up trying to understand her responses to him. She couldn't deny him. She was hopelessly attracted. Was it because to be with him was testing the boundaries? Was she simply looking for excitement? A rush? They took the M5 and Storm put his foot to the old Ford. She looked at the dogs in the back seat hanging their heads like dehydrated sunflowers as they sat patiently with a new black-haired bully in their midst. She started to laugh.

He took his eyes off the road for a moment. "What's so funny, Riempie?"

"This whole scene. Me sitting here with four dogs in the back. Look at them. They're like little kids going on a picnic, all anxious and excited. You've got some ugly dogs, Storm."

"Don't be nasty, Riempie. They're not ugly."

"They are. Look at this one," she pointed to a brown miniature with doleful eyes, "I bet he thinks he's a Labrador."

Storm laughed. "That's Misty, my pavement special."

"They're all pavement specials. Do you ever give them a wash?"

He looked hurt. "I look after my dogs, Riempie. They mean the world to me."

They arrived in Muizenberg, parked the car at Sunrise Beach, and let the dogs out. Storm's dogs charged straight for the dunes. Sief remained loyal to his owner and bobbed along at their ankles as they paddled through the waves, fascinated by the living waters under his feet.

"Look at the shore, Riem. You can see all the way to Strandfontein it's so clear. No wind and no seaweed."

She didn't have to speak. A cool winter morning, a deserted beach, the sun rising pale gold out of the sky. It reminded her of a time long ago when she was a child and the family made the annual visit to Kalk Bay on New Year's Day. They would arrive early in boeta Tapie's car to get the best spot. Boeta Tapie would help them spread out their blankets, leave to go home, and pick them up again before sunset. Muizenberg wasn't the same as Kalk Bay. Kalk Bay was a small beach with a fishing harbour. Muizenberg had white sands and dunes, and stretched on forever. She'd forgotten how wonderful it could be at this time of the day.

"People think because the water's warm here, it's the Indian Ocean. It's not, you know, Riem. The Benguela Current pushes the warm waters down here. It's still the Atlantic."

"Really? I thought Muizenberg was the Indian, that the Indian and Atlantic met at Cape Point."

"The Indian Ocean's further up. But it sounds good for the tourists. They can return to their countries and say they've stood under the spray of the two great oceans at the tip of the African continent. Anything with the word Africa in it. I read this opening in a story once: 'The African moon shone down on the homestead.' Have you ever heard of an American moon? Or a Scandinavian moon?"

She laughed. "I didn't know you read books other than the Bible."

"You don't know everything, Riem." He took her hand. She let him hold it. Then he let go and bounded off towards the dunes. "Misty! Lisa!"

She continued walking. A few minutes later he reappeared with the dogs. "The water's nice and warm, Riempie. Let's sit down in it, right here on the edge."

Her tracksuit pants were wet already, and the water *was* warm even though it was the beginning of winter. They sat down in the rushing waters, shouting as the waves crashed over them. The waters retreated, leaving indentations around their feet in the sand. Khadidja wanted to cry with the pleasure of sitting there with him.

"Riempie?"

"Yes, Storm?"

"Do you think your bum's nicer than mine?"

"You *do* have a nice bum. I think yours."

The water swept over them again and they howled with laughter.

"You think we're just two kids who haven't grown up?" he asked.

"I think so."

"How old?"

"Nine and eleven."

"Who's nine?"

"You."

"Do you think maybe our souls met in the past?"

The water rushed up and she shut her eyes against the spray. "Maybe. If I believed in reincarnation."

He looked at the outline of her body under the wet clothes. "Riempie? When're you going to give me your koekie again?"

She laughed. "I can't."

"Why not, baby?"

She watched the swirling water drag through her toes as it drummed along the ocean floor into the sea. "I'll hurt myself."

"*How*, Riempie? I don't understand."

She turned to face him. "When two people have a relationship and it breaks up, it's always one person who ended it, and one person who didn't want it to end. I might be the one who won't want it to end."

"We won't break up, Riempie. I can't be without you. Your spirit fills me." He put his wet face next to hers, whispering into her ear. "You mustn't talk about us not being together, Riempie. Promise me."

Her eyes stung. When the current rushed up, she dove into the waves. *Please, God, don't let this be a dream.* When she surfaced, he was next to her. He circled his legs about her waist in the deep water. "Riempie?"

They were bobbing in the waves. She could feel his hardness.

"Are you my Muslim baby, Riempie?"

She laughed.

"Yes or no?"

"Yes." Her mouth was inches from his. "I want to kiss your lips."

"Kiss them, baby."

She ran the tip of her tongue along the rim of his bottom lip. She started to laugh.

"What's so funny?"

"A white boy with fat lips. You have a Daffy Duck mouth."

"Don't be such a worm, Riempie."

"Open your mouth."

He pushed out his lips. She laughed harder, putting both arms around him. "You're not at the dentist, Storm, open up."

"We're going to drown, Riempie."

"We won't drown. Open your mouth, let me show you how to kiss."

"Riempie, no …" They popped in and out of the surf as she tried to pry his mouth open, first with her tongue, then with her fingers.

"My pants, Storm – they're at my knees."

He slipped underwater and dragged them off. It wasn't until he was up against her again that she realised he'd also pulled off her panties. But it was too late. Her legs went about him. He gasped. "Riempie …" His mouth was in her wet hair, the tangles washing over his shoulders in great blobs of foam. "I fucking love you."

Ateeka was in the front garden when they returned.

Khadidja watched her mother staring curiously at the two of them, and knew how she must appear in sopping pants getting out of the car. And with a white boy too. "I can't ask you in."

"Too bad, Riempie," he switched off the car and opened the door.

"Storm, no …"

He got out and reshaped his clinging wet pants about his legs to make himself look more presentable.

"Get back in the flippin' car. You can't meet my mother like this."

Ateeka came to the gate, her scarf wrapped tight about her head, the way she had it after she'd performed her prayers.

"This is Storm, Ma," Khadidja said. "The fireman I told you about. We took the dogs to the beach."

Her mother greeted Storm with a nod of the head, but didn't take his hand as he was busy handling dogs.

Khadidja opened the gate and held it open for Storm. "Go inside, Ma, before Sief shakes himself."

Ateeka walked quickly away in her flip-flops, turning to look at the dogs in the car. They had their wet noses pressed to the window, slobbering all over it.

"You shouldn't have come now," Khadidja whispered to Storm. And turning to her mother on the stoep: "Mummy, can you give me my black tracksuit pants in the bathroom, please?"

Ateeka seemed perplexed, but went to fetch them. Khadidja handed them to Storm. He went behind the tree and changed. They came into the kitchen where Ateeka had the pan on the stove with a big blob of butter starting to sizzle. Half a dozen eggs stood ready in a bowl.

"Set out another plate," Ateeka said.

Khadidja complied. Her mother was usually friendlier to her friends.

"Storm lives nearby, Mummy. Just up the road, in Kenilworth."

"Is that so?" Ateeka started to crack the eggs into the pan. "With your parents?"

"No, Aunty," he said. "They live in Claremont."

"Do you see them often?"

Storm sipped the coffee Khadidja had placed before him. "My mother comes to my house sometimes to tidy up. I tell her she doesn't have to but she likes to do it. She also takes my messages when I'm on duty at the fire station. People call when they want rubble removed. She sets up my appointments."

"You are close, then? As a family?"

He hesitated for a moment, looking first at Khadidja. "I'm close to the people at my church. My parents don't go to church. So we have little to say to each other. You can't go through life without God. My father says he believes in something, but can't say what it is. My mother goes to church once a year at Christmas. They've closed their ears to the truth."

Ateeka dished the eggs onto three plates. There was an efficiency and authority in the way she handled the pan. "The church is important to you?"

Khadidja watched her mother sit down. She could tell by the little frown on her forehead that she would want to know more.

"It's very important. When I was nineteen, I was looking for a church to belong to. My father took me to ten churches before I found the Apostolic Church I'm with now. I joined. My father didn't."

Ateeka didn't know the difference between one church and another. "What made you pick it?"

"Their philosophy. The leaders didn't drive big cars, the church was a humble little building. I signed a form promising to abide by the rules. Khadidja doesn't understand."

"Tell my mother the rules," Khadidja prompted.

"It's not a big deal, Khadidja."

It was unusual for him to call her Khadidja, but she liked the way it sounded. "Tell her," Khadidja prompted.

Storm turned to look at Ateeka. "Not to lend money, not to stand surety, to give ten per cent of my earnings to the church, to attend church six nights a week. I can't remember the other one. Khadidja doesn't understand the 'not to lend money' part. Borrowing and lending creates problems between people. Even family."

"What if your mother comes to you for fifty rand?" Ateeka asked.

"My mother won't ask. She knows the rules of my church. That's why the rules are there, so you won't ask."

"But what if she did come to you?"

"If she comes to my church, yes. I'll break that rule."

"She must come to your church before you'll help her?"

"That's right."

Khadidja saw her mother's look of concern. "Storm can't see the selfishness in it. It's religious blackmail."

"Call it what you like, Riempie. It's how it is."

"But your Book says to be charitable," Ateeka said.

"Charity starts at home. The church is my home."

They ate for several minutes in silence. "You're an interesting person, Storm," Ateeka said. "I haven't met anyone quite so, so … I don't know what the word is."

"So religious?"

"I don't know if it's religious."

"Spiritual? That's one of Khadidja's favourite words."

"I don't know if it's that either."

"Confused," Khadidja offered. "Fanatic."

Storm smiled. "It's all right, be nasty. I've heard worse. Tell me, Aunty, would you disown her if she becomes an Apostolic?"

Ateeka laughed suddenly. He had taken her by surprise.

"I'm serious, Aunty. Would you disown her?"

"My boy, she would never do such a thing. And mothers don't disown children."

"But what if she did? The Muslims turn their backs on those who turn Christian. I know that about them."

Ateeka's smile was sympathetic. "I can see you don't know Khadidja. You mustn't waste your time waiting for such a thing to happen. But what would your church say if you became Muslim?"

"Me? Never! I'm a Christian, and I'll die that way."

"I thought you said you were Apostolic, not Christian," Khadidja reminded him.

"You don't listen to what I say. I didn't say I wasn't Christian. I said we're not like other Christians."

"What's the difference?"

Storm moved his chair back a little and got up. "There *is* a difference." But he didn't say what it was. "The eggs were good, Aunty. Thank you. I know you're going out soon. I also have to be at church in half an hour."

Khadidja walked him to the door.

"What time will you be home, Riem?"

"I don't know. And tomorrow night I'm going to my mother's for supper. It's her sixtieth birthday. My sister and her brood will also be there."

He smiled boyishly, reaching out a hand to touch the tips of her wet hair. "You like all this family stuff, don't you, Riempie?"

That's it! It's the Mick Jagger look. The eyes, the wicked smile. "I do."

"What will they think if you bring an Apostolic?"

"They'll spray the house."

"Stop it, Riempie. You can be a real worm."

"Do you want to come?" She didn't know why she was asking him. Her nephew, Faried, was even more religious than his father, Maan.

"I'd have to skip church. I can't skip church for you, Riempie." He paused again, patting the dogs through the car window. "Pick me up. What time? The other thing I wanted to ask you – can I bring one of my leaders around next week? I've read a bit about your Qur'an. I'd like you to know more about us."

He was waiting at the gate when she arrived at his house at five-thirty the following evening. She noted the black pants and maroon shirt, the cinnamon-coloured hair darkened with gel. "Where're you going, all shined up like a new sixpence?" she teased him.

"I did it for you, Riempie. I can't wear jeans all the time."

She drove up Kenilworth Road to the Main Road, and turned right. Further along she would make a left turn to pick up the highway.

"Take a right here, Riem," he said suddenly.

She was almost past the street and took a sharp turn. "Where are we going?"

"We'll pop in quickly at my mother's."

"Your mother's? I don't know if I'm ready for your mother. It's five-forty. My family's waiting for us." She hadn't given any thought to his parents as yet, and whether or not they might be racist.

"We'll be two minutes. Just a quick hello."

They stopped in front of an old Victorian home with a broekie-lace verandah and a small, manicured garden. On the verandah was a cast-iron table and chairs, at which a handsome couple in their late fifties sat reading a newspaper. The woman was dressed in jeans and a white shirt. Her face lit up when she saw them.

"Storm." She came forward. "Who's this?"

"This is Riempie, Mom." He took Khadidja's hand into his. "My future partner."

The mother's eyes twinkled. She was as surprised as Khadidja by these words.

"Riempie," she said as she extended her hand. "What an unusual name. I'm Veronica."

"Actually, my name's Khadidja. Titch for short."

"Khadidja? That's also an unusual name. What is it? Spanish?"

"Arabic. I'm Muslim."

"My word. A Muslim friend? How did this happen?"

"She lives across the road from the fire station," Storm said. "Her dog escaped. I fixed her fence."

Veronica looked amused. "Did you hear that, dear?" She turned to the man behind her. "This is Khadidja, Storm's new friend."

"Hello, Khadidja. I'm Charles."

Khadidja took his hand and shook it.

"Muslim," Veronica added.

"I heard," Charles said. "A good little religion."

Khadidja studied the two people before her for clues to their son. A strong mother, she thought. Talkative, open. The father was friendly, but reserved. Mother's eyes, hair, spirit, full mouth. Father's physique. Instinct told her that Veronica had no qualms about her son befriending a Muslim woman. She wasn't sure yet about Charles.

"Charles reads quite a lot about the different religions," Veronica offered. "I think he's read the Muslim holy book also. Haven't you, dear?"

"I've read a bit about the Qur'an, yes. There're some fine things in it."

"Are you doing research, Charles? Working on something?" Khadidja asked.

"Oh no," he smiled. "I just like to read, and I like to know what other people believe. I believe all religions can offer you something. I find the past interesting."

"The past can confuse you," Storm said. "You can't follow ten different paths. There's only one way."

Charles gave a weary little smile. "That's true, Storm, the way of right living, and that includes respecting other people's beliefs."

"You can't make up your own rules for what's right, Dad. Come to church and you'll know what I mean."

Veronica flashed him a look. "I guess by now you know all about Storm and his church, Khadidja."

"I do."

"It gets unbearable at times. You can't force your beliefs onto others." She took Khadidja's elbow and led her to the verandah. "I don't know if it's him or that church, but he's been like this since he joined them. He has no time for anyone. His brother hasn't seen him in months. Storm says anyone who wants to see him can come to his church. I've gone there once or twice, but he wants me to join. I don't want to. I have my own church." Veronica laughed like a little girl. "So this is a complete surprise, Khadidja. You, a Muslim girl. I can't get over it."

172

Khadidja liked Veronica. "Storm knows my beliefs, Veronica. He knows not to trample on them."

"Oh, I'm so glad you're firm with him. Has he tried to get you to go to his church?"

"Yes, and I will go. I'd actually like to see what they're all about."

"Maybe I'm wrong about them. Go, and tell me what you think. Oh, I wish I could be a fly on the wall. This has been our biggest problem in the family."

Storm broke away from his conversation with his father. "Come, Riempie. Don't get too friendly with my mother. It's six o'clock."

Veronica walked them out to the car. "Khadidja, I'm very pleased to have met you. Something tells me I'll be seeing more of you. Come again, even without Storm. You know where we live now. I'd like to talk to you."

"This is the house where you were born? My goodness, it *is* high up." They had just arrived in Sachs Street, and stood for a moment on the pavement looking at the cream house with the green windows and stoep with the three-foot wall. Storm had lived in Cape Town all his life, but had never been up in the old Malay Quarter.

"See this field? We used to play here, search for snakes under the stones, sit high up there with our blankets and jam sandwiches, looking at the boats in the harbour. We grew up with this view."

He looked around, taken by the spectacular sight of the city spread out at his feet. "Jeez, you can't imagine that the sea's this close. I never knew it looked like this from up here. This is a short little street."

"It's an afterthought. Five houses when I was born, and still only five today. All on the same side, facing the hill. The Christians have moved out. The Gamieldiens are still here, and the people in the double storey. The council called it Sachs Street after a Jewish man who used to live in that corner house." She pointed to a pink, box-like dwelling at the other end. "It's changed owners a few times. Black people lived in it when I was little. An imam and his wife live there now."

"The whole of Bo-Kaap is Muslim?"

"Not every household, but Muslims have occupied the area since the slave days. People don't move out. Houses are passed down from family to family. I mean, who would want to leave? You have the mountains, the sea, the city, this spectacular vista, and mosques on every corner."

They went inside and found her mother and Murida's family in the front room. On the coffee table were several gift-wrapped parcels and a vase with a dozen red roses. Khadidja hugged her mother and wished her a happy birthday, and handed her a narrow little box in silver wrapping. "A little something for you, Ma. To keep the time."

"Thank you, my girl. We wondered what had happened to you. Hello, Storm." Ateeka showed no surprise at seeing the fireman in her house.

Khadidja greeted the rest of the family, and introduced Storm. "The fireman?" Murida asked, unable to contain her curiosity.

"Yes," Khadidja said. "The fence fixer." She noted Maan's quiet amusement and winked at him. Ateeka shepherded them into the dining room where the table was set. Khadidja took the baby from her sister, and held him out to Storm. "Isn't he beautiful? His name's Mustakim. Kim for short."

Storm's mouth curled into a smile. "He looks like a chortler, Riempie."

"A chortler? What's a chortler?"

"One who chortles. A chuckler. You're the writer, don't you know?"

"That's what I thought you meant. You mean he's a little laugher."

"Laugher's a word? You make up all these words. If I remember them, and use them, someone will laugh at me. The other day I used 'paltry' on the fire marshal, and he didn't know what I was talking about."

Khadidja laughed and squeezed his hand. "That's because they're all dof in die kop. Too much smoke inhalation."

Maan was in the seat across from them, watching. He glanced at his son, Faried, a third-year theology student at university. Faried was exceptionally bright, and Khadidja knew that if she had questions regarding the scriptures that she couldn't find answers to, Faried would be a reliable source.

Her mother and sister brought in the food and set it on the table: roast leg of lamb with potatoes, yellow rice with raisins, butternut squash, corned tongue – and a pot of tomato trotters, a dish wholly out of place for a birthday treat, but something which Maan always asked for when Ateeka cooked. When everyone was seated, Maan made a doa'h – said a short prayer – in honour of his mother-in-law's sixtieth birthday, and supper got under way.

"This is very good food, Ma, this tomato stuff," Storm said after a few mouthfuls. "What is it?"

Khadidja noticed that he had gone from aunty to ma.

"It's walk-aways," Riana laughed. "Trotters. Granny and my father are the only ones who eat them." She was the youngest and the less serious of Murida's two teenagers, seventeen and nineteen respectively. She behaved with Storm as if he was family.

Storm licked his fingers. He had picked up the bone with his thumb and index finger, unconcerned that he was in someone else's home. "It's sticky, but tasty. Can you make this, Riempie?"

"Riempie?" Murida asked. "What's Riempie?"

"Tell her, Storm. Even I don't know why you call me that."

"I read this book once," Storm said, giving his boyish smile. "It had two little dogs in it, Ratel and Riempie. She reminds me of a little doggy. Always scrambling around, a little Miss Nosy Parker."

"Ah, that's so cute," Murida said, smiling approvingly.

"Can you make this food, Riempie?" he asked again.

"No. And I don't want to know how. I don't eat it."

"See, Ma?" he said. "Won't do anything for anyone else. Won't even become an Apostolic."

Everyone laughed.

He looked around the table. "What would you say if she became an Apostolic?"

"Why would she do that?" Faried asked.

"She says we can't stay like this if we marry. We have to be of the same religion or it won't work."

"Storm ..." Khadidja tried to get him to stop. She caught the look on her mother's face.

"And I agree with her," he pushed on. "I mean, how can it work if one goes to church and the other to mosque? We'll fight. And you people will disown her if she marries a Christian. Won't you?"

They knew now that he was serious. Still, they were amused. "We won't," Murida said. "How can we do that? Besides, my sister will never convert."

"You don't know. She might. I mean, what if there's a kiddie?"

"A kiddie!" Khadidja stiffened. "Storm, what're you talking about?"

"I mean, if there's a kiddie, will it be raised Christian or Muslim?"

"Muslim," Faried said.

"Why can't it be Christian? Why do the Muslims always force you to change to their religion? Or why can't it be both, if you also believe in Jesus as you claim?"

Faried glanced at his father. He was no longer laughing. "Because that's just how it is. You can't be a little of this and a little of that, and a lot of nothing. What direction should the child follow? It would be confusing. And we don't believe Jesus is God. We believe in him as a prophet. We don't worship human beings. The early Christians, the Unitarians, they believed in the one God. She can marry one of those Christians." The statement was made with such finality, such an air of calmness, that no one said anything in response.

Storm picked up his serviette and wiped his mouth. "He's right, Riempie. We live in different worlds. I like the way your nephew put it – a little of this, a little of that, and a lot of nothing. We have to walk the same path or it won't work. One of us *has* to convert."

Khadidja's nostrils flared. "I don't know what you're talking about, Storm, but maybe you should talk about these things with me first before you bring it up in company." She was furious. A lot had been said and presumed, making her look irresponsible in front of her family. And he was using her own argument against her, as if it hadn't been her concern first.

They drove to her house in silence. He opened the gate for her. In her anger she'd forgotten that she'd picked him up at his house and that he had to be taken home.

"Can I come in for a few minutes?"

"No."

"You're angry, Riempie. I only said what I felt."

"You involved my family. They have lots to talk about now. We've never talked about kiddies and marriage. You just threw it out into the open without any warning."

She unlocked the door. He took her in his arms and buried his head in her hair. "I love you, Riempie. It's driving me crazy. We want to be together. But I don't see how we're going to do it."

She responded against her will. It was the second time he'd said that he loved her. He'd also said that he didn't know what love was.

"You can't just spit out the first thing that comes into your head. It's my family, for God's sake. Do you know how what you said makes me look?"

He moved her away from the door, to the couch. She straddled his lap and put her arms around his neck. "What're we going to do, Riempie? It doesn't look like you're going to convert."

"Why do you want me to convert?"

"If we want to get married. You say it'll hurt you to do it if you're not married. I don't want to hurt you."

"Are you asking me to marry you? One day you talk about wanting to be free, the next you hit me with something like this. What is it that you really want? Sex? You don't have to get married for sex. There're plenty of women out there who'll have it with you. You're very confusing."

He took his hands out of her hair. "I *am* confused. I'm confused around you. I can't think when I'm here. I'm very involved with my church, Riempie. You want to take me away from my church. And I want to be a preacher. The preacher sits in the front pew with his wife." His eyes took on a faraway look as he talked. "I can see you sitting there next to me. I can even see you up there preaching. You could influence a lot of people. But how, Riempie, how, if you don't become an Apostolic?"

"Will you stop?"

"I can't. This thing's getting worse between us. Will you change for me, Riempie?"

She got off his lap. "For God's sake, you're acting like a child. Weren't you listening to my nephew?"

"Your nephew's a poep."

"Oh, now he's a poep. First you agreed with him."

He closed his eyes and rested his head on the back of the couch. "This is eating me up. Have patience with me, Riempie. Can I stay with you tonight? We won't do anything, I promise. I just want to hold you. Please. Let's work it out."

JUNE 14

Took Storm with to Mummy's sixtieth birthday celebration. Murida and the family there. Storm spoke out of turn. Faried set him straight on a few things. Very impressed with Faried. Will have to speak to him about some other questions I have. Also met Storm's parents. I like Veronica.

∼

On the morning of my tenth birthday, I received a present I would never forget. I came into the kitchen already dressed in my school uniform, fully expecting my mother and little granny to wish me a long and happy life and the promise of chocolate cake in the afternoon, only to find the two of them whispering over their coffee. I knew they were talking about my father when I heard my mother switch suddenly to Afrikaans.

"… die slang was al in die bos …" The snake was already in the bush.

It was a new expression to my ears, but somehow I knew it had something to do with the s-word.

"I want you to come straight home after school. Your father's getting married tonight," she said to me. "You and Murida are going there for supper. He's sending a car for you at four-thirty."

I dropped the spoon in my porridge. "Daddy's getting married?" Not happy birthday, not how does it feel to be ten, not I'm having a party for you, but this horrible, ugly news. "To whom?" I asked.

"To Salieyah," my mother said, almost chucking her cup in the sink.

"Salieyah? Why does he want to marry her? She's not even pretty."

178

"They don't have to be pretty," she snarled.

I looked at little granny. Little granny fiddled with the spoon in her saucer. "Eat your porridge, my girl," she said.

"I'm not hungry. I thought I would get an egg on my birthday."

It must've struck my mother then that she'd forgotten about her younger child's birthday for her face lit up, and she came over to me with open arms, and hugged and kissed me. "Oh, Ma se skattebol ... how can I forget to say happy birthday? Happy birthday, my girl. May Allah grant you lots and lots of happy years and make you a good girl, Insch Allah." She looked at my great-grandmother. "Little granny and I didn't forget. Go look in my room."

I put my porridge bowl in the sink and went quickly to her room. There, next to the bed, stood a small bookcase that I hadn't seen before with two books on the top shelf. I picked up the books and looked at them. Both had pictures on the cover of a girl·in old-fashioned clothes. One was *My Cousin Rachel*, the other was *Emma*. I'd never heard of the writers Daphne du Maurier and Jane Austen before. I opened the first book and read the first sentence, *They used to hang men at Four Turnings in the old days ...* The opening thrilled me. And it was about murder. Murder mysteries were my favourite. I looked at the second book. It started with a description of Emma Woodhouse, handsome, clever and rich. I liked stories of girls who were clever and pretty, although I'd never heard a girl described as handsome before. I was excited about receiving the books. My sister got gifts like records – she had one of Elvis and one of Cliff Richard – but I always got books. And these were fat ones, a whole week's reading.

"Titch! It's three minutes to eight! You'll be late for school!"

I ran out to the kitchen. "Thanks, Mummy. Thanks, Granny. I love the books!" I kissed them hurriedly on the cheek.

"The bookcase is from little granny," my mother said.

"The bookcase is mine? For my books?" I couldn't believe it. I didn't think little granny had money.

"It's yours. Now hurry up. Here's your lunch." My mother handed me a wrapped sandwich. I could see through the waxy paper that there were two biscuits in the package as well. "And hurry home," she reminded me.

I thanked my great-grandmother with several more kisses, and ran out. Alison was waiting for me at the top of the steps leading down to the street below. She was moving from one foot to the other, as if holding in a pee. "You're late," she said. "They'll make us stand outside."

"They can't. It's my birthday."

She forgave me immediately. "Oh yes. I forgot. Happy birthday. Did you get anything?"

"Yes. My own bookcase. And two books."

"What kind of books?"

"Two fat ones. Not modern stories."

"I don't think I'd like books for my birthday."

"What do you get?"

"Toys. This year I'm getting a doll that cries when you turn it over."

"My mother never buys dolls. Last year I didn't even get books, just socks and underwear. Oh yes, and a ping-pong bat with a ball on an elastic."

"My brother Mark has one of those. The elastic is always breaking."

We were running and were almost at the school gates. I noticed that the bell hadn't rung yet and that the children were still outside. "I've got something to tell you, but you can't tell anyone."

She kissed two fingers and touched it to her forehead. "I promise."

"My father's getting married tonight."

Her eyes opened wide. "He is? To whom?"

"To a girl called Salieyah. I met her once when he came to pick us up."

"Is she ugly?"

"No. But I didn't think he would do such a thing. He told us he would never marry again. We would be his only children."

"My mother's sister's husband said the same thing to his children."

"Aunty Mavis's sister is also divorced?" I'd thought my mother was the only divorced person in Bo-Kaap. We reached the school gate and slowed down.

"Yes. He told my cousins when he left and married this other

180

woman that they mustn't worry, there wouldn't be babies. They were worried that if there were other children, he would forget all about them. His wife sommer had three babies in a row. In December, my cousins got shoes for Christmas. The new children got toys. It's all the stepmother's fault, they hate her. But maybe you will like this stepmother you're getting."

"I won't. How can I?"

When I arrived home from school that afternoon, our outfits were laid out on the bed. My mother made all our clothes, even crocheted our socks. The weather was starting to get cool – I was a March-born child – and I wasn't happy to see the pleated tartan skirt and cream blouse I'd have to wear, and the cream ankle socks and patent leather shoes. These were winter clothes, and it wasn't winter yet. Even though Murida was older, she had to wear an identical outfit, but with stockings instead of socks.

"I don't want to go," I said.

My mother was looking for my red silk ribbon in my drawer. "Why not?"

"I don't like it there."

I wanted to add that I didn't like Oemie, but quickly changed my tune. "And I have cramps."

"Cramps?" I often had cramps, but hadn't complained of them in a long time. Usually, I got a hot bandage wrapped around my stomach, and a half glass of hot water with Jamaican Ginger in it.

My mother looked at me suspiciously. "You have to go. Don't let it be said that I turn my children against their own father. You'll feel better when you get there."

"I won't," I said. "I hate him."

She sat down on the edge of the bed. "You hate your father?"

"Yes."

"Hate's a strong word. We don't allow that word in this house." She went out of the room and reappeared with little granny. I was surprised. What had I done? I'd noticed with my mother that little granny was usually brought in to come and talk to me on particular subjects. Little granny came and sat on the edge of the bed. She didn't bring up the subject of hate. Instead, she asked the stupidest thing. "How do you feel about having a new brother or sister, Khadidja?"

It took me a moment to realise what she was saying. "What, Granny?"

"A new brother or sister."

"I don't want a new brother or sister!" How could she ask me such a thing? I ran from the room in my underwear, into the shed outside in the yard, and slammed the door.

"Titch!" my mother called.

I sat in the dark, hugging my arms about me. The door jerked open. My mother stood there with the feather duster. "Come in right now before I give you a hiding!"

I looked at her. "It's all your fault Daddy left!" I shouted.

The feather duster dropped from her hand.

I realised I'd done a terrible thing. "I'm sorry, Mummy … I'm sorry."

She gave me a look that said she didn't like me very much, then turned and left me there. I went inside and got dressed. Murida's face told me I was in big trouble. My hair had grown almost to my shoulders since my visit to Groenkloof, and my mother arranged my curls and put in my ribbon without talking to me. When the car hooted outside the door, I stood coated and puffed up in my patent leather shoes at the window in the front room. My father didn't come himself, which was just as well as I would've been rude, and had sent his brother, uncle Mietjie, to pick us up.

Murida got into the car in front, and I sat in the back. Uncle Mietjie tried to make conversation. "We're having early rain this year," he said. "How are you girls doing in school?"

I didn't care about the weather or my studies, and neither did Murida from what I could tell. She wasn't outspoken like me, but gave a clue to her feelings when she asked, "Uncle Mietjie, does my father like Salieyah?"

Uncle Mietjie hadn't expected the question and took his eyes off his driving for a moment to look at her. "Your father's a lonely man," he mumbled. "He's entitled to some happiness."

The words hurt my ears. Lonely? My father was lonely? What a nerve. I forced myself to remain quiet.

The drive wasn't long, and I arrived at the house on Duke Street with a Table Mountain fog in my head. I was sure my face was enough to warn my father. Still, he put on a show for the people, holding out his arms for me like Father Christmas. I let him kiss me, but kept my arms stiff at my sides. Murida let herself be squeezed and kissed by everyone.

"At which table do you girls want to sit?" oemie Jaweier asked. Tables had been set up in three of the rooms. The main table in the dining room was where my father would be with Salieyah. "I want you to sit at your father's table, but if you want to be with your cousins in the other room, it's all right." I knew where I wanted to sit, but let Murida make the decision. "We'll sit with Daddy," she said, which was the thing I'd expected her to say.

But I didn't get to sit next to my father. That was Salieyah's place. And on the other side of my father were oemie Jaweier and oupa Braima, and uncle Mietjie and his wife. Next to Salieyah was her mother and father. It was an oval-shaped table, and Murida and I ended up next to them.

I studied Salieyah from where I sat. She was dressed in a cream woollen dress with a black chiffon scarf on her head. There was red lipstick on her lips, a mole on her cheek, and black stuff under her eyes. She wasn't half as pretty as my mother, but she was young, and was allowed to say and do things none of us would've been allowed to get away with. Right in the middle of oemie Jaweier's conversation with uncle Mietjie she showed her ill-breeding by interrupting them. There was nothing worse in oemie Jaweier's eyes than one who didn't have manners.

The humiliation for the family came during the serving of the tea when my father wanted to brag. "Murida's going to high school next year. Where did you come in class, Murida?" he asked, knowing the answer full well.

Murida tried not to sound too smart. "Second, Daddy."

"Second?" he faked surprise. "How many students are there?"

"Forty-two."

My father turned his attention to me. I who could sit all day looking at numbers and never figure out those trick maths questions that start out with the words, *if a car is travelling at twenty miles an hour,* and you had to come up with speed and time or the cost of petrol. My brain could never work those things out. But I was the cleverest in the class when it came to spelling and composition, and had a gift for language, Miss Jenkins said.

"And you, Khadidja? Where did you come?"

I stabbed my fork into my pudding. "First."

"First out of the whole class?"

I glared at him. "My mother helps me with my homework."

"Really?" Salieyah's mother said. "You have homework already, at your age?"

"I'm ten," I said. "It's my birthday today." I didn't look at my father who hadn't even wished me happy birthday. "We have lots of homework. My mother pays someone to help me with my sums. She pays for lots of things. No one else supports us."

The room went silent. When I looked up, I saw shame and disappointment on my father's face. I pushed back my chair and left the table. As I walked down the passage, I heard oemie Jaweier try to make light of my behaviour. "Children, hey …"

I felt awful. I hated my father, hated my grandmother, and hated what I'd done. As I sat with my cousins in the back room hearing their small talk but not really paying attention, I wished I'd been allowed to stay behind in Sachs Street.

My father drove us home himself and didn't say a word to me about my bad manners. At the front door, he gave both of us a kiss. "Happy birthday, Khadidja. I ask Allah to make you a happy little girl, and give you everything you want."

"Thank you for the present, Daddy."

He looked at me, confused. I could see that I'd hurt him. He slid his hand into his trouser pocket, took out a handful of silver, and put five shillings into my hand. "Buy yourself anything you want," he said.

I looked at the money and imagined the chocolates and toffee rolls I could buy. Then I threw it to the pavement with such force, it bounced off the ground and rolled into the sluit. I didn't wait for his reaction. I opened the door and went inside without saying goodbye.

My father would never know how I felt. I myself didn't know

184

what that thing was that gripped me. I wanted to cry, run outside and say I was sorry, but couldn't get myself to do it. Murida came in and laid out my crimes like an old tablecloth for everyone to see my flaws. She told my mother that I'd embarrassed my father at the bride's table, adding that I had pushed back my chair so roughly that it had almost fallen over, which it hadn't, and that I had stormed out of the room, which I really, really hadn't. On top of it, she said, I was so ungrateful that I had thrown the five shillings he gave me for my birthday on the pavement, and she and my father had had to search around in the dark for it. My poor father had had tears in his eyes.

My mother listened as Murida rattled off my sins. She hadn't forgiven me yet for what I'd said to her that afternoon, and I knew I was in for a good dose of the silent treatment. But then she glanced at little granny, and I could tell from that glance what she thought. I wasn't her best behaved child but she was secretly pleased with what I'd said at the supper table. That night I wrote out my feelings to God. *Dear God. It doesn't matter if one obeys all your rules. I hate my father.*

I burned the paper immediately afterwards, and whether God knew what I wrote or how I felt, I didn't care.

I noticed my mother become slim and quiet over the next few months. She started to wear lipstick on her shopping walks into town. I worried that there might be a special admirer, but my mother's admirers were out in the open – a little tea on the stoep or in the front room – nothing serious. I was just getting used to the idea that my father had remarried when I heard the dreaded, dreaded news. Kulsum from next door was the bearer of this news. She'd heard her mother tell her father that Salieyah had given birth to a son. I smacked her when she told me. How would her mother know, I charged; what rumours was she spreading? But of course it was my mother who'd told sies Moena, not having told her own children first, and I knew that Kulsum was speaking the truth even before my mother confirmed it at supper that night. "Your father bought a cottage in Wynberg. You have a half-brother, Ismail."

I had had two months to get used to this new development when my father arrived at the door to pick us up to come and spend the

185

Easter weekend with him. I sat in the back of the car although he said both of us could sit with him in the front. It was easier in the back. You didn't have to talk. You could listen and watch. The thing I was thinking as he drove past the racecourse to get to his house was that he didn't look like the happiest man in the world.

At the cottage I noticed that some preparation had been made for us. There was a bed with a pretty bedspread on it in the back room, and we were told that we could put our things in there. That would be our room. I liked that. But the thing I liked best was the baby in the soft white shawl in the bassinet in my father's room.

"You can pick him up," Salieyah said.

I looked at Salieyah. She was fat now, fatter than my mother who was very trim with her new figure, and had this sweet-smelling, cuddly baby she'd grown in her stomach and given birth to. I'd wondered what I was going to do at my father's house for three whole days, but there was a baby to hold, and Salieyah seemed anxious for company. From the very first night, I noticed that things weren't right in the house. My father seemed irritable, and after supper, put Brylcreem on his hair and went out. I knew that he wasn't just going down the street or to a friend. I'd seen that look on his face when he still lived with us, and got a horrible feeling in my stomach. Salieyah didn't know what to do with us when he was gone, and pretended everything was okay.

On our first morning in the house, my father got up early and went out. Salieyah had made fried eggs for his breakfast, and the pan was still warm on the back of the stove when we got up. She asked if we wanted eggs or porridge. Both of us said eggs. She used butter in the pan, lots of it, and gave us two eggs each, with several slices of bread. I was reminded of my breakfast with Joachim at Groenkloof, and the way Frances had fussed over us. There were two kinds of jam – fig and watermelon – and our coffee was strong with condensed milk and sugar. When we'd washed the dishes and packed them away, Salieyah almost made our hearts stop when she went around the house searching for a cigarette. The only women we knew who smoked were the daring ones in American magazines and hairdressing salons, and to see our father's wife with a cigarette stuck between her lips greatly impressed us.

After the cigarette, Salieyah went on a shilling search, and found some change in the pockets of a pair of our father's trousers hanging behind the bedroom door. She sat in her petticoat on the edge of the bed and counted it out.

"Can you girls go to the shop?"

"Yes, Aunty."

I'd been holding Ismail throughout breakfast, and now she took him from me. "You don't have to call me aunty. Call me Salieyah. I'm only nineteen." She handed us the change. "Buy four cigarettes. You can spend the rest."

We couldn't believe her generosity. There was enough for a chocolate, a toffee roll and pink Stars. Murida and I shared everything, down to the last Star which we cut in half with a knife when we reached home. It was one of the few times when there were no disagreements between us. Back home, she had her own friends, her own interests. At my father's house, she had only me. Our three days together with the baby, and with Salieyah, made us almost friends.

My mother didn't say anything when we told her of our visit. She'd expected to hear bad things, but there were no bad things to report. We didn't tell of Salieyah's smoking, but did mention that our father went out every night. She listened and glanced at little granny. Little granny nodded her head in that bobbing way she had when she had nothing to add. We went to my father's house several more times during school holidays, and as we reported on the comings and goings at my father's house, my mother softened towards the girl who'd taken her place. By the time Salieyah had four sons and my father was wearing out the tyres on his Peugeot driving to Athlone after someone else, my mother and Salieyah had met a number of times at family functions and had become friends.

∽

For one week Storm came to Khadidja's house every night on the days he was off duty, with a small leather bag slung over his shoulder. In it was a gun, a battered copy of the King James Bible, and a toothbrush. He would shower, she would iron his shirt for church, they would sit on the couch and discuss the day and many other things when he returned. Later he would go outside to relieve himself under the tree, open the bedroom curtains wide, and put the gun on the floor on his side of the bed.

"Why do you keep a gun, Storm? And what if I get out on this side of the bed and step on it accidentally?"

He pushed the holster under the bed. "You won't step on it, just be careful. I don't take chances with my life. I know how to handle a gun, I've been in the army. You should also have one because you live alone."

You live alone. Always there was that reminder. "I don't think so. Anyway, it's a safe neighbourhood."

He got under the covers. "Nowhere's safe, Riempie. People watch your place, you can't take things for granted. Come here, and lie next to me."

It was a confusing time for Khadidja. She was happy that he was there, yet at odds with herself. Her balance was out; she felt restless. How could she go on her knees and pray, then overturn God's commandments?

One night, lying at opposite ends of the couch, he had her foot in his hand, massaging her toes. "You have nice feet, Riempie. Maybe I should call you Pretty Toes."

Khadidja loved it when he kneaded her ankles and feet, taking each little toe between two fingers, loosening the joints, unlocking the tension. He would caress the sole of her foot, press his thumb into her heel, roll it between his palms for extra friction. She had never thought that foot stroking could be such a sensuous thing. "Did you always have sex the same way, Storm?"

"The same way?"

"Well, you know, no preliminaries. You don't like to do all that stuff women want before the main event."

He looked a little crestfallen. "Don't you like it when I do this, Riempie? Rubbing your footie? Doesn't this count?"

"I love it, and you know what I mean. No one's ever played with my footie. But we're not in bed now."

"Do you have to be in bed to do these things to someone you like?"

She had to agree that he was right. Her husband had done his act in the bedroom and, for the rest of the time, had been a cold fish. Storm was always touching her, holding her hand, playing with her hair. "It's just that sometimes I wonder if you have an aversion to touching a woman, you know, intimately."

His face reddened.

"Did I say the wrong thing?"

"No." He looked at her over the foot in his hand. "Did I tell you about this incident with my mother's friend when I was eleven?"

"No."

"My mother had this friend who lived on the street behind us. One day she saw me at the shop after school and asked if I would help carry her groceries. Her house was only around the corner and I said fine. I walked home with her and when we got to her house, she told me to wait in the lounge. I thought she was going to give me a tip. She came out with no clothes on, took my hand and put it on her bush. It looked like a spider, Riempie. I got such a fright, I dropped my books and ran from the house."

"Oh my word. Did you tell your mother?"

"I didn't know how I could tell her. What would I say? It was her friend, maybe she wouldn't believe me. And I got a blooming hiding for losing my books." He pressed two thumbs into the ball of her foot. "How does this feel, Riempie?"

She didn't bring up the question of sex again. It was important, but not the high point of the relationship, and they would work it out in time. It was how he spoke to her, the silly little games they played, the laughter, the spontaneity. He was a curious man, and there was something comforting about his persistence to be with her. When he slept, she studied the outline of his face for clues to her future. At dawn he would wake suddenly, bring coffee to bed, and she would read to him from Al-Bhukhari's *The Early Years of Islam*, and travel back fourteen hundred years. He would listen in earnest to the stories and practices of the Holy Prophet, his lids drawing closed as he tried to imagine the past. Afterwards, he would have questions. It was the time she liked best, when he leaned back in the pillow, an eager listener, when he was calm and vexation hadn't started up in him yet.

189

One morning he asked if she would read something else. She gave him three choices: poetry by Rumi; *The Complete Fairy Tales by the Brothers Grimm*, which she still had in her collection; or a short story by either Alice Munro or Mark Twain.

"Mark Twain, Riempie. That name sounds familiar. I don't like poetry."

"Mark Twain's very good," she said. "I think you'll like 'The Mysterious Stranger'." She opened the book to page 55.

"*It was in 1590 – winter. Austria was far away from the world, and asleep; it was still the Middle Ages in Austria, and promised to remain so forever.*" Storm closed his eyes and immersed himself in the tale.

A half hour passed, another half hour, and another. She reached the last page. "*For as much as a year Satan continued these visits, but at last he came less often, and then for a long time he did not come at all. This always made me lonely and melancholy. I felt that he was losing interest in our tiny world and might at any time abandon his visits entirely. When one day he finally came to me I was overjoyed, but only for a little while. He had come to say goodbye, he told me, and for the last time. He had investigations and undertakings in other corners of the universe, he said, that would keep him busy for a longer period than I could wait for his return …*"

She glanced at Storm over the book. His eyes had opened a little and had a faraway expression. Light was starting to seep into the room.

"*… strange indeed that you should not have suspected that your universe and its contents were only dreams, visions, fiction! Strange, because they are so frankly and hysterically insane – like all dreams: a God who could make good children as easily as bad, yet preferred to make bad ones …*" She noted the frown on his brow as she read this. "*… who could have made everyone happy, yet never made a single happy one; who made them prize their bitter life, yet stingily cut it short; who gave his angels eternal happiness unearned, yet required his other children to earn it; who gave his angels painless lives, yet cursed his other children with biting miseries and maladies of mind and body … who created man without invitation, then tries to shuffle the responsibility for man's acts upon man, instead of honourably placing it where it belongs, upon himself; and finally, with altogether divine obtuseness, invites this poor, abused slave to worship him!*"

"Riempie …"

"*You perceive now,*" she continued in a voice that said it was the end, "*that these things are all impossible except in a dream. You perceive that they are pure and puerile insanities, the silly creations of an imagination that is not conscious of its freaks – in a word, that they are a dream, and you the maker of it … It is true, that which I have revealed to you; there is no God, no universe, no human race, no earthly life, no heaven, no hell. It is all a dream – a grotesque and foolish dream. Nothing exists but you. And you are but a thought – a vagrant thought, a useless thought, a homeless thought, wandering forlorn among the empty eternities!*"

She closed the book slowly on the last line: "*He vanished, and left me appalled; for I knew, and realised, that all he had said was true.*"

"Riempie … what a story. Wow."

"It's my favourite. I read it first when I was a teenager, at the height of my nonsense. It's well written, isn't it?"

"I don't know anything about stories, but I liked it. I didn't know short stories could be so long. If that's a short story, what do you call *Little Red Riding Hood*? A snapshot?"

"Just about," she laughed, thinking how he could sometimes surprise her. "Short stories aren't usually fifty pages long. I think it's the best story I've read about Satan."

He smiled to himself. "I think so. I liked him. But it's not true that stuff he said about God. You know God's real, and the devil's real too. It's all a ruse, to make you lose your footing." He got out of bed, picked up the gun and put it in his knapsack. "It's late, I have to get going. I like our mornings together, Riempie. Will you always read to me?"

After a week of staying with her, he returned home from church one night, and sat with his head lowered in his hands.

"Riempie, I miss my cats."

"Your cats?"

"Yes, Riempie. They sleep with me. Four of them sleep on the couch, the rest snuggle up with me on my bed. And I can't trust that boarder alone in my house. I want to go home."

Khadidja didn't show how his words shocked her. Hearing that he wanted to go home, when he'd toyed with the idea only two days earlier of renting out his house and coming to live with her, passed through her, swift and painful, like an electric bolt. "You must go, then," she said.

"When are you coming to sleep at my house, Riempie? You haven't stayed at my place yet."

"I can't sleep in a strange bed. And I can't take all those cats." She got up from the couch and lifted their tea things from the coffee table. "There's a documentary coming on at ten. I have some things to do before I watch it. Are you leaving?" She was ready to see him off, to reclaim her space.

"Maybe I'll stay to watch it with you. I'm not in a hurry."

He looked relieved now that he'd told her, she thought. Probably he'd thought she would make a fuss. "I'd actually like to be alone for a bit. I haven't done my prayers yet."

"All right, Riem. You want to be rid of me. Don't forget our meeting at the leader's house on Thursday."

"I won't."

When he was gone, she turned out the lights, went to her bedroom and dialled Alison's number. "Alison, is that you? It's Titch. You sound terrible. Do you have a cold?"

"I'm not well. How're you?"

"I'm okay, but I've been so busy, I haven't had a chance to call you. What's going on? Something happened?"

"It's my own fault. Farouk was here Tuesday night. I'm too out of it to talk about it now."

Khadidja glanced at the clock on the bedside table. Nine-thirty. "Do you want me to come over?"

"I'll only depress you."

"Put on the Milo. I'll be there in fifteen minutes."

Leila opened the door when she arrived. Khadidja hadn't seen her for some time, and noted the new hairstyle, the school book in her hand.

"You're studying?"

"We have exams coming up."

Khadidja's nose twitched. She could smell the slightly sweet aroma of dagga, and was surprised that Alison would smoke while Leila was in the house. "Where's your mother?"

"In her room." Leila cast her eyes down the passage. "Where the smell's coming from. Aunty must tell her she's not fooling anyone with that stuff she sprays around the house. She must stop smoking."

"What're you talking about?"

"Aunty knows."

Khadidja touched the blunt edges of the girl's hair. "I like the cut. A bob suits you." She walked down the passage and knocked on Alison's door. She found Alison red-eyed and bleary, lying on top of the bed in tracksuit pants and bra, with an ashtray overflowing with cigarette filters. The room reeked of stale smoke and misery. A plastic bag with dagga was next to her on the bedside table. Khadidja threw her a pyjama top she found on the chair. "I can smell the stuff from the front door. Leila knows."

Alison reached for her Stuyvesants. "She knows too much."

"Did you eat?"

"No."

Khadidja went out to the kitchen and put on the kettle for tea. Minutes later she carried in a tray with a teapot and cups, and a plate with crackers and cheese.

Alison blew her nose and sat up. "This is it, Titch. This was the last time. I'm giving up cigarettes, dagga *and* men."

Khadidja had heard that before. "What happened?"

"I mean it. I have to make a change in my life. I keep saying it and never do it. Farouk came over here Tuesday night. Alison, listen, I want to talk to you, he said. Why're we going through with all this? We have thirteen years together, that woman means nothing to me. I made a mistake, it's not too late. So we have tea together and Leila goes to study at a friend's house. One thing leads to another, and we end up on the floor. He wants to stay the night, he wants to come back, we can start again. I say I want to talk to Leila first. I just don't want her to wake up in the morning and see him there. He agrees, and leaves before she comes home. I have hope. This is the first time he's admitted the affair. On Wednesday I don't hear from him. I thought, okay, he's thinking also. That's good, we're not rushing into anything. On Thursday I still don't hear from him and decide to drive past the place where the bitch works. Something just told me. Guess what I saw there: his white BMW."

"Shit."

Alison dragged on her cigarette until the stub glowed red between her fingers. "I won't say anything when I see him. I got played. It's all right. It's what we've been talking about, you and me. This is my last little binge. Next week's going to see a different Alison. I'm starting classes at the imam's house. I don't know what else I can do."

Khadidja studied her for a moment. "A psychologist?"

Alison ground out the cigarette in the ashtray. "No. I thought of it when that thing happened with Leila, but no. You're always telling me I must feel this pain of separation. Well, I'm going to. Without painkillers." She pushed herself up on the bed and made a valiant effort to look more presentable. "How about you? I haven't heard from you since your visit to your mother's house when your fireman talked out of turn. Any repercussions from the family?"

"My family's smart enough to know not to interfere. I was surprised by how much faith they had in me though, especially my sister. But something else has happened. Storm spent a week at my house."

"What?"

"You can say we lived together in inharmonious sin. I had patches of ecstatic happiness, and moments of deep depression. At night I looked forward to him coming home to me. In the morning I was riddled with guilt." She told Alison about their readings in the mornings – the story of Satan, the mysterious stranger, also the history and traditions of the Holy Prophet. "Then just like that, tonight he comes home after church and tells me he misses his cats."

"His cats?"

"I couldn't believe it. During the week he was talking about renting out his house and moving in with me permanently, and tonight he tells me he misses his cats. And asks when I am coming to sleep at his house."

"What did you say?"

"Nothing. You know my twenty-five per cent in reserve rule. I didn't question his leaving. I didn't want to know. I didn't want to hear things that would upset me. But I was also relieved. I'd been living in a dwaal, feeling guilty, questioning my own motives, waiting for something to go wrong. And here it was, the agonising was over. Under the best conditions, he couldn't be happy."

Alison swung her legs over the bed, and sat for a moment. "He's strange, Titch. I know you like him, but –" She shook her head and didn't complete her sentence.

"C'mon, we've been friends forever. What?"

Alison looked up at her, undecided. "I should be the last one to give advice, but the way I see it with Storm, he's fun, he's a turn-on, he's interesting in a weird kind of way, but he's not at your level, Titch. You're a heavyweight next to his little brain. I'm just wondering if you're not going to get bored with him after a while."

Alison's words hurt Khadidja more than she knew. Yet it was what the boys at the fire station had alluded to, what Storm himself had been saying. "He *is* a lamebrain, but even lamebrains are entitled to some happiness." She realised she was being defensive. "Ah hell, I know all this, Alison. I don't know what it is that keeps me there. I don't even get any joy in bed. And he's so stupid sometimes, so gullible and naïve, I feel like shaking sense into him. Yet, I can't let go. On top of it, I'm allowing his leader to come to my house."

"A church leader? Why?"

"Storm wants me to know more about his church. I don't know what good it will do, but as a last resort … Maybe it's not even them, Alison. Maybe it's just him. I'll soon know. We were going to go there, but I decided to invite someone on my side as well, and told Storm that they could come to me." She got up. "Call me tomorrow and tell me again what you've just told me."

Alison picked up the dagga pouch from the bedside table. "I don't have to call you. You know better than me what you have to do. Come. Before you go, I want you to see this."

Khadidja followed her past Leila's room to the bathroom. Alison held the pouch over the open bowl, and flushed. "Say goodbye to the bad guys," she said.

Khadidja watched in disbelief as the weed slid out into the rushing waters and disappeared in a brown froth.

On Thursday evening, Storm arrived promptly at seven in his church suit, with Underdeacon Bennett, the Bible and several books on Christian theology. Storm's hair was gelled back; he looked pious and sombre. The underdeacon was a tall man with very short hair and questioning eyes, dressed in a dark suit, with a Rolex on his left wrist, and reminded Khadidja more of an army lieutenant than a man of the cloth. She knew from his bearing and the way he shook hands that he would be a strong adversary. Next to her on the couch was the slight Bashier Salie, a young Sufi. She had picked Bashier for his great knowledge and reserve.

"You've come armed," she said jokingly. "This is just a chat, Mr Bennett. An exchange of ideas."

Underdeacon Bennett pulled himself up straight, and made an attempt at a smile. "Well, in an exchange of ideas about two such divergent religions, I think one should be prepared, and I hope I can enlighten you." He looked at his disciple to begin the proceedings. "Storm?"

Storm took this as his cue, and sat forward a little. "Riempie and I asked you here because we have a problem, Underdeacon. We want to be together and don't know how we can do this. I can't become a Muslim and she won't turn Apostolic. I feel if she knows more about us, she may change her mind."

Bennett looked at Bashier to see who would speak first. Bashier nodded that he could go ahead. "Well, Storm, we can't change a mind that doesn't want to be changed. You know the way the Lord works. Perhaps I should ask Khadidja. Is there something you would like to know about the Apostolics?"

"Not really, Mr Bennett. We have this problem, as Storm says. I agreed to the meeting as a last resort. I can't see what you can tell me that would make me change my mind about my faith. I wish he would believe that."

"They believe the Bible's been tampered with," Storm said. "They believe in Jesus, but don't believe he's God. They believe what suits them."

Khadidja flashed him a look. "You're getting away from the point, Storm. I'm not sitting here to debate our different faiths. When I was young, Mr Bennett, I was very arrogant about the whole notion of God. I didn't believe in this unseen, missing God who'd never been around to answer any of my prayers, and had little regard for his commandments. Then one day my friend's five-year-old twin daughter died in a car crash in which I was the driver. It was my fault. I was high on stimulants, and had run a stop sign. There was nothing I could say to myself after that to feel better, and what made it worse, my friend couldn't talk about it. It was a Jewish friend who told me that my behaviour was a cry to get closer to God. I laughed at him, but wondered whether he might be right. And that's when it happened, when I opened God's Book it spoke to me." She looked at the faces in the room staring intently at her. "I quit smoking. I quit playing poker for money. I decided to pray, took a few minutes each day and tried to make contact with God. It was difficult, the estrangement had been long, and at first there was silence. But slowly things started to change. I was calming down. I wasn't so angry. I saw that I didn't have to prove anything to anyone. I agree with Storm that we're all sinners, and I'm the first to admit that I have a problem with the ego, but my life is different to before." She looked at Bennett directly, lowering her voice. "I found the recipe, Underdeacon. Why change the ingredients?"

"How do you know it's the right recipe?" Storm asked. "Unless you're saved by Jesus, you're not a believer."

"I'm sorry you don't understand."

Storm turned to his underdeacon for support. "Tell her the penalties, Mr Bennett."

Underdeacon Bennett lavished a kind smile on his congregant. "She has her own faith, Storm. We have to respect that."

"But we haven't solved anything. What will we do?"

"If there's no compromise, there's only one thing you can do. You must go your separate ways."

"But I love her."

"You haven't known each other that long, Storm. How do you know it's love? You can't let love come between you and the Lord. The love in this world is fleeting. The love of the Lord is forever."

"Why does he have to choose between God and a woman?" Khadidja asked.

The underdeacon turned to look at her. "Love for the wrong woman may take him out of his faith. I don't mean a bad person, but a wrong choice. Ask your leader or imam." He looked to Bashier. "I'm sure he'll agree."

Bashier directed his response to Khadidja. "You asked me to consider your problem and to see if there was a way to accommodate both of you, Khadidja. I've thought about it for a long time. God prefers people to marry rather than live in sin. Marriage, after all, is just a contract between a couple who have decided to stay together. Only two witnesses are needed and I can easily marry you. But is that what you want?" He cupped his head in his hands, deep in thought, forcing the others to wait for him. "Marriage is about compatibility. There's no compatibility when there's disagreement about God, when you argue about how children will be raised, whether you go to mosque or to church. In the Bible it says, *be ye not unequally yoked.* In the Qur'an, *do not associate with a disbeliever.* Those words aren't there for nothing. They're meant to protect us. And so in a way Mr Bennett is right, although I don't know that I agree with everything he says. He is right, of course, that love for God is eternal, but loving your God and loving a woman are two separate things and can't be spoken of in the same breath. God very much wants us to be happy in this life too. The question I want to ask you to think really hard about, is whether you think the two of you are compatible."

Khadidja had no answer to give him.

"I'm not talking about whether you like the same bread or the same movies or the same jokes, but whether there is a fellowship of the soul. Think of marriage as a slow trek across the desert. Rising temperatures, changing conditions, danger when you least expect it. It's easier if both people drink from the same well."

"You're saying there's no hope for us?"

"There's no hope when there's disrespect about the other's views. How long can it last with two people trying to change each other's point of view about God? Storm could become Muslim, of course, and that would solve everything. Have you asked him?"

"He could never become Muslim," Underdeacon Bennett said flatly. "The church won't allow it."

"The church?" Khadidja asked. "Isn't it up to him?"

"Storm doesn't always know what's good for him. The way of the flesh isn't the way of the Lord. The church will fight for his soul."

"That's the most arrogant thing I've heard, Mr Bennett," Khadidja laughed. "Storm has given you power of attorney over his soul?"

"We don't lose congregants to other faiths."

Khadidja glanced at Storm, who'd engineered the meeting and was now letting someone else speak for him. "I hope you're enjoying this, Storm. You bring your leader here, then sit with your mouth full of teeth. *Say* something."

Storm gathered himself up in his seat. "I don't believe in some of the things you people do, Riempie. I mean, why must you go to Mecca? Why must you fast? Why must you pray five times a day?"

"And why must you be so intolerant? Did I ask you to become Muslim? You read a few pages of the Qur'an, and think you can comment. Did you make any effort to find out about my religion?"

"He doesn't have to," the underdeacon answered. "He has a Way. But show us a better way, and we'll follow."

Khadidja smiled. "That's the party line, Mr Bennett. You don't mean it. Your ears are as shut to my way as mine are to yours. Anyway, you mustn't worry about Storm. He told me the other day he wanted to buy himself a big-screen TV, but had to give his money to the church. If he doesn't give money or he doesn't give enough, his trucks get punctures, he can't sleep, things go wrong in his life. So there's no chance he'll convert, and I don't want him to. The money he must give to the church every month will continue to test his selfishness. The brainwashing will keep him locked in."

The meeting ended. It was only when they were out on the stoep saying goodbye that she realised she hadn't offered them tea. She thanked Bashier for his time and promised to call him soon. It was not yet nine o'clock, but she went to bed. The night passed slowly as she battled to fall asleep. She turned on the television and found Larry King on CNN. On the show was the replay of a Reverend Billy Graham rally at the beginning of the preacher's career in 1949. His fiery delivery made her watch.

… You *can* find an answer to the dilemmas and perplexities of life. Your life *can* be changed. It *can* be transformed. You can become a new person from this moment on – by surrendering your life to Jesus Christ …

She listened. What were the chances that on such a night, weighed down and miserable, these words should come to her through television? *The Larry King Show* came on late. His subjects ranged from Hollywood scandals to American politics. Was it an omen?

In the morning, edgy and unhappy, she unplugged the telephone and left the curtains drawn. She didn't want to attract anyone to her house. Three days later, she had a dream about Storm. They were nine years old, on a bed, talking. He was lying back with his long hair spread out across the pillow, his tan skin glistening in the candlelight. There was nothing sexual about the scene. They were children, best friends. She was telling him something funny, he was laughing. She touched him. He bit her on the arm. They rolled around on the bed.

The next morning she went out into the garden to hose the lawn.

"Riempie …"

Her heart fluttered. He'd come up silently on his bike. "You're avoiding me, Riempie. I've called you. The phone just rings and rings. I miss you."

She didn't say anything.

"Are you coming to see me at the fire station later on?"

"What for? We can't talk. We don't do anything. There's no intellectual life. I can't take your intolerance." She couldn't say that the real reason for the break-up was his leaving.

"What about if we don't talk about religion?"

"We tried that. It lasted a week."

He looked at her with pleading eyes. "What if we give it another try? Just one more time?"

She turned off the hose, stamped her feet a few times on the ground to rid them of dirt, and glanced at him. "I'll see how I feel this afternoon." She went inside and sat for a few minutes on the couch. She'd gone out to hose the lawn with the express purpose of seeing him. She'd put out the bait, and predictably, the honey badger had come. By evening she had convinced herself. The thing would sort itself out. Church leaders and doctrine couldn't stop two people who wanted to be together.

Stretch and Dwayne were outside smoking and saw her cross the yard. "I don't know what you've done," Stretch teased her when she drew up, "but he's been really miserable these last few days. Have you two had a fight?"

"My God, you guys really know everything." They walked with her up to Storm's room. "Did he tell you about the underdeacon he brought to my house?"

"Yes," Dwayne laughed. "He said your guy didn't have a chance against Mr Bennett. Bennett finished your guy off."

"Is that what he said?"

"Yes. Your own guy said it was better for him to stay Christian."

Storm was on his bed reading a book, and smiled like a school-boy when he saw her. The other two stood for a moment in the doorway. "Come in," Storm invited them in. A third fireman she hadn't seen before came in behind them. He was introduced as the paramedic, and he looked in Storm's cupboard.

"Looking for booze," Dwayne said. "Trevor checks everyone's rooms to make sure there's no liquor on the premises."

"Surely no one drinks while they're on duty?"

"No," Dwayne said, glancing at Storm. "But they check anyway. It's routine. No one's upset about it. Tell her how you used to smoke and drink, Stretch, how your wife almost left you. Stretch is an al-coholic, but he's been good for four years."

Khadidja watched to see if Stretch was upset by these revela-tions about his personal life, but he only grinned. "I still go to the meetings. I still have to stand up in front of everyone and say, my name's Stretch, I'm an alcoholic. Storm's also an alcoholic. He won't admit it, but he is. He doesn't drink regularly, but when he does, oh boy. He goes on a three- or four-day binge, and has the shakes for a week afterwards."

Khadidja was surprised to hear this, then remembered that first night at her house when he'd brought the champagne. He'd fin-ished the whole bottle over supper. She'd thought of all kinds of addictions, but not this.

"I'm not an alcoholic." Storm sat up suddenly from where he'd been slumping with his back against the wall. "I can go without it for months. How does that make me an alcoholic? It's only beer, anyway. What's wrong with a beer? Only sometimes I have wine."

Stretch smiled. "See there? I told you."

"Some people can't even have one drink, Storm," Dwayne said. "You know what happens to you. There're consequences. And you don't stop after one." He turned to Khadidja. "He's had two warnings already. One more and he's out."

"I've had lots of warnings. I'm still here."

"What's a warning?" Khadidja asked.

"An official warning. You get three, and you're gone. You have to let us know if you're sick and not coming in. There're three platoons. We work twenty-four-hour shifts. You have to make arrangements for someone from a different platoon if you know you're going to be off. When something's bitten his arse and he's drinking, he doesn't even call. But the officers know about him. He only ever stays away when he's on a binge. Ask him. They've talked to him at the church too, several times."

"They make it sound worse than it is, Riempie. I have a little glass of wine now and again, or a beer. I know when to stop."

"He's like the gambler," Stretch smiled, "who sets out to prove he's not compulsive and that he can abstain from gambling for a whole month, then on the thirtieth celebrates his success and blows it all in one day."

For a week or more, Storm kept his promise and didn't talk about religion. He went home after church in the evenings to change, then returned to her house for tea and a snack. One night she asked about his mother, Veronica.

"She smothered me, Riempie." He pulled his face in distaste. "I was the first child. My father was away a lot of the time in Jo'burg on business. He would take the train there and be gone for weeks. She looked to me for love, and smothered me with affection. I was three or four, just a child. How could I make up for that loneliness in her life? And my father was strict. I remember when I was eleven. There was this girl on my street. I wanted to go home with her after school. He came to her gate and made the biggest racket. I was forced to go home. He was a real disciplinarian and would thrash us in front of our friends. When I was sixteen he caught me and this other girl smoking dagga out of the neck of a broken bottle. He went berserk and kicked both of us out of the house. I ended up with this bergie with six cats in a hokkie in Kalk Bay harbour for six months."

"What?"

"Yes," Storm laughed, remembering. "He was this thin, scruffy thing with a beard and a missing front tooth, but he knew his Bible. I met him because of a sign on the door that said, *Jesus is Here*. I didn't know if the 'Here' meant on earth or in the hokkie. The bergie was sitting outside on a milk crate, handing out pamphlets he'd written himself. I asked him about the sign. He's the one who really tuned me in to Jesus."

"Did your parents come and look for you?"

"They did, but I didn't make it easy for them. I let my brother Archie know where I was, and found a job at the post office, and moved into a room with a friend in Muizenberg. I was hardly there when I was called up for the army. I went home for one weekend, then left on the train for Pretoria. You don't want to know about my army days, Riem."

Khadidja had little knowledge of what happened to white boys in the army. Coloureds, blacks and Indians were not called up for duty. "Why? Were you a corporal? A lieutenant?"

"I was a dog handler."

"Did any of those boys try to pull off your pants?"

The dimple in his left cheek deepened. "No, but there were some pretty boys there, Riempie. It was tempting."

"Have you been with a boy, Storm?"

Storm was lying on his side on the couch, a naughty smile on his lips. His arm reached out for her, pulling her close. "No. I like girls. Girls are my weakness. Even that horrible thing that lives in my house. I took her in because she was ugly. I can't have pretty girls living with me. I'd be all over them."

"Something happened with you and the boarder?"

His eyes looked at her, then away.

"Come on, tell me." She knew him. He would rather not say than tell a lie.

"She was seven months pregnant when she saw the ad and came to look at the room. I thought that here was someone I could have in the house without trouble. She was pregnant, ugly, and it would be good to have a baby in the house. But the flesh is weak, Riempie. A few weeks after she was there, it was raining and we were watching television in the lounge. She said to me, 'Storm, I need to get fucked'."

"What? She said it?"

"Yes."

"Were you so familiar with each other that she could talk to you like that?"

"No."

"What did you do?"

"I didn't know what to do. I asked her if I should take her down to the boys at the fire station."

"The boys? You were going to let the firemen do her?"

"She said yes, she was desperate. She was groaning and said she'd never been randy like that, it must be the pregnancy. It was raining, Riempie. I was tired. I didn't want to get in the car and drive down there in the rain, so Stormy did the job himself."

She stared at him, nodding her head, not knowing whether to laugh or cry.

"It was crude and ugly, not like what we do. There was no feeling to it. I just got on and did it."

"What did you do about her face?"

"I closed my eyes, Riempie. I always close my eyes. Anyway, how did we get onto this?"

"We were talking about mothers and fathers and pretty boys and ugly girls."

"Oh yes. It's hard to be a kid sometimes, Riem, it's hard to please parents. They're easily disappointed. They don't realise that you can be just as disappointed in them."

"I know," she said, remembering when her father had told her and her sister about marrying Salieyah, about not having more children, then having four in a row. And all the times he'd called with promises to take them to bioscope, then had shown up late and just driven them to the Rhodes Memorial Zoo for a little walk-around, with some girl waiting in the front seat of the car, then had driven them home again. "As a child, I remember, I was always lonely around my father. I think I knew before he left my mother that he was going to leave. You sense it. And then you live in fear, waiting for it to happen."

"Are you close to him?"

"No." She looked at the clock. It was almost eleven. They'd been talking for two hours. "Why don't we go to a movie tomorrow night? We haven't been to see a movie together yet."

For a moment he looked interested. "I go to church, Riempie. Have you forgotten?"

"Can't you skip a night?"

"I'd have to ask."

She looked at him, not saying anything.

"The leaders depend on me, Riempie." He seemed to feel the need to explain. "And I haven't been to a movie in ten years. You sit there in the dark with a bunch of strangers and breathe in dirty air and look at a screen, trapped for two hours. I'd rather go for a walk. How much does a movie cost these days?"

"Not much. It's my treat."

"It's not the money. It interferes with my church time. Maybe the late show."

"I don't like to go to movies at ten o'clock. Never mind. I'll go with Alison."

"Yes. Why don't you do that on a night I'm on duty at the station? You don't have to do everything with me, Riempie. Go out with your friends. When we're together, I like to talk."

The next morning he called to say he'd changed his mind. On Saturday night they went out, first for coffee, then to the cinema. There were stares in the coffee shop and in the queue waiting to buy tickets. Storm seemed unaware. She knew already that he didn't have the slightest concern about the colour of her skin. He had taken her to his parents' house. Nothing could be a greater test than that. Sitting in the back row and watching the previews before the main show, he squeezed her hand. She turned to look at him in the dark.

"I'm glad I came, Riempie."

"Me too. Maybe we can do this once a week," she whispered back.

"Maybe." He had a box of popcorn on his lap, his eyes riveted to the screen.

The movie was a Meryl Streep tear-jerker, which produced huge sighs of satisfaction at the end.

"That was a good movie, Riem. I liked it. I can't watch violence and killing. I think the last movie I saw was *Scarface*. I had to go lie in a bath afterwards. Did you see it?"

"Hey, djou," she imitated Al Pacino's Puerto Rican accent. "Come here mang, gimme kiss."

He laughed. "You're so funny, Riempie. Stop it." He pinched her affectionately on the bum.

"You know, a movie critic actually counted how many times they said the f-word in that movie – a hundred and forty-four times."

He laughed again, holding her hand. "You're too much, Riempie. The boys at the fire station said to me, 'Stormy, you can throw away all your dictionaries and encyclopaedias with that girl.' They were right." He kissed her on the cheek. "Thanks, Riempie, for bringing me. Do you want to do this again next Saturday night?"

On Veronica's birthday, Storm presented his mother with a miniature orange tree with shiny green leaves Khadidja had picked out at the nursery and dressed up with a red satin bow and a card. It was the second time she would be visiting the Callaghans.

Veronica was surprised. "Oh, this is beautiful, Storm. Oh my." She looked at Khadidja as if to say, I know you had something to do with it. "Did you see this, Charles? It's lovely. Just what this living room needs. Where shall we put it?"

Khadidja suggested a spot next to the fireplace. "What about here? There's enough light, and it's out of the way. This tree's going to need space."

Everyone agreed that it was the right place for it. Veronica fussed about with the tree a bit, then came to sit opposite them on the couch. Her husband was in a wing chair by himself with the *Argus*.

"I had a feeling you might come today," she said. "I said to Charles, 'Storm's coming, I must bake a cake.' I've noticed a change in him these last weeks." She looked at Khadidja. "He's less rest-less. Not as cranky."

"I'm happy, Mom. Riempie's my partner."

The word partner interested Khadidja, and she wondered in what context he was using it.

Veronica rattled on as if hearing her son talk about a partner was no surprise. "I'm so glad, Storm. I'm so glad you've met Khadidja. Aren't we, dear?"

Charles smiled. "Just don't do anything rash," he said.

Khadidja watched him from under her lashes. She wasn't sure she knew what he meant. "Like what?" she asked.

"Well – think this thing through thoroughly. Don't go rushing off to get married or anything like that."

"Why not?" Veronica asked. "If that's what they want? Storm needs someone who's strong, a girl who doesn't put up with his nonsense."

Charles looked up briefly from his evening paper. "Storm's brought many girls here before, you know. We get attached to them, then we never see them again."

Khadidja was sure that that wasn't the reason. Charles Callaghan might be interested in various philosophies, but wasn't too pleased that his son was mixed up with a girl of mixed race. "We're not going to do anything foolish," she said. "It's all been decided by church leaders and clerics. Storm and I have an agreement."

"You met the church leaders?" Veronica asked. "When?"

"I met Mr Bennett. About two weeks ago."

"What did you think?"

Khadidja gave a rueful smile. "Storm's his property. The church will fight for his soul, Bennett says."

"My goodness," Veronica exclaimed. "What were you talking about that he would say that? C'mon, you've got to tell me."

Khadidja looked over at Storm. Storm had the sports section on his lap. "Maybe Storm wants to tell you."

"I don't want to talk about it," Storm said.

"Mr Bennett was here once," Veronica continued. "Storm brought him to come and talk to us without first checking if it was all right with us. Charles got up and went to watch cricket in the other room. I didn't know what to do. That Bennett's a nice man, but as a group they're very persistent. I blame them for what's happened to Storm. Storm has no time for his family now. Every person he meets he wants to convert and bring to his church. He says the church is his family, he doesn't need us. He never spoke like that before he joined them. He's only here today because of you. That's why I'm glad he's met you. Maybe you can talk some sense into him."

Khadidja watched Storm. His mother had just made a serious charge. She waited for him to deny it, or to say something in defence of the church or its leaders, but he turned the page and said nothing.

"He heard me," Veronica said to Khadidja. "He knows what I'm saying is the truth."

"Storm gets something out of his church," Charles said without looking up from his paper. "He's happy with them."

"That's not what you say when Storm doesn't visit us and stays away. Then they're stealing your son and you're upset with them. Are you saying Storm's better off with them than with Khadidja?"

"Don't put words in my mouth, Vee. He's been there a long time, you don't want to disturb that. The church keeps him stable. And he's still Christian. You don't want him turning Muslim, do you?"

On Sunday morning Storm arrived at her house at eight-thirty. Khadidja had agreed to go to his church, and wore dark pants with a cream silk shirt. She drove with him in the Ford Sierra to a modest little church with a fenced parking lot. She had expected a flock of congregants, but there were just three cars and a handful of people standing about. There was nothing grand about either the building or its onlookers. All eyes turned to the Ford when it cranked through the gate and stopped at the end of the lot.

Storm switched off the ignition. "It's not nine-thirty yet, we can sit for a few minutes."

Khadidja looked at the women in their pleated skirts and blouses and hats. She could tell from their glances – she'd had these glances before, with Saville, long ago – that they were surprised to see her with Storm, and remembered suddenly the time as a little girl in Paarl when she'd had to go to church and had a hat plunked on her head. She wasn't into hats, but perhaps she could've tied her hair back to make it a little less noticeable, she thought.

"Are they racist here?" she asked.

He seemed surprised by the question. "No. We have all kinds. You'll see."

"There're not many people."

"We're not big. I've been to big churches before. It doesn't mean anything. Jesus hung out with the poor and the needy. We're just poor people here."

They got out and walked up to the entrance. She noticed Mr Bennett in a splendiferous silver suit coming out of an inner doorway. "Brother Storm. Khadidja. How nice." He seemed genuinely happy to see them. "Come inside." He led them in personally, and talked with them for a few minutes until another congregant claimed his attention.

The church had twelve pews on either side of a narrow aisle, and a small stage with a pulpit and a chair. A short, squat man with glasses was behind the pulpit riffling through papers, which she imagined was that morning's sermon. No more than thirty people made up the congregation. Khadidja compared the building with that other church. The other one had been an old structure with high ceilings. The pews had a little door that closed behind you, and the dominee had to go up a few steps to reach the pulpit. The church had been chock-full of people.

"Brother Storm," a voice said behind them.

It was the leader who'd been up on stage. He smiled, his glasses touching his round cheeks. In his right hand was a pen and a scrap of paper.

"This is Mr van der Spuy," Storm introduced her. "This is Khadidja Daniels."

"Khadidja?" He pronounced the name with a slight guttural accent. "How do you spell that?"

"Why?" she asked.

"Mr van der Spuy wants to welcome you properly," Storm explained.

"Please," she whispered. "I'm just a visitor."

"It's just a formality, Riem. We welcome everyone that comes to the church."

"I don't want my name mentioned, please. I just came to observe."

The church leader slid silently down the length of the bench. Minutes later, he was back up on stage.

"Beloved," he started, "another week has gone by. We have to give thanks to the Lord for our bounty, and to say thank you to a few people for their dedication and hard work during the week. There's also a birthday and an anniversary. But first, we must welcome a new member to our church. A friend of brother Storm, Katia."

Khadidja kicked Storm in the ankle. "I told him," she hissed. "And I'm not a member."

Storm looked straight ahead and said nothing.

Khadidja listened to the greetings and celebratory messages, and happy birthday being sung to a fifteen-year-old youth who stood awkwardly in front of the congregation with a lopsided smile. When it was over, a girl wearing a hat with flowers got up and came to stand with a group of children in the front row. She gave the cue and they started to sing.

"That's Melissa," Storm whispered.

Khadidja looked at the girl in the straight skirt and blazer who was the second-best sister in the love triangle, who'd been touched and not loved. She had stiff, curly black hair, a thin, droopy nose, and puffy eyes that slanted upwards like a cat's. Her mouth matched the puffiness of her eyes and reminded Khadidja of someone who'd just been to the dentist.

"Beloved … we must heed the Word. The world is in turmoil. Look at what is happening in our country today. We live in a world of capitalism and greed …"

Khadidja tried to concentrate. Next to Van der Spuy, on a chair to one side, was Underdeacon Bennett sitting upright. Every so often Bennett looked up at the speaker, nodding his head sagaciously as if to confirm the veracity of his words. Khadidja looked around at the other faces. They seemed mesmerised by the monotonous drone. She listened to the words, waiting for the gold nugget or two which would confirm the philosophy of the church for her.

"… only the Apostolics, beloved …"

Van der Spuy seemed uncomfortable in the role of speaker, she thought. His sentences were short and choppy, as if he threw things in as he went along; the sermon had no real point and jumped all over the place. His constant use of the word beloved seemed foreign to his tongue and came out sounding flat and insincere. But most disturbing to Khadidja was the recurring reminder that only a handful of people, a small group of believers, would be saved. Everyone else was slated for hell.

"I don't believe this," she muttered.

Storm stirred out of his stupor momentarily to look at her, and sighed blissfully. She couldn't believe the effect on the congregation. Van der Spuy could've told them that Jesus was stopping by Newlands Stadium, and they all would've bought tickets.

"Beloved, don't forget. On Monday night, testifying. Tuesday night is bread-breaking. Wednesday night is finance night. On Thursday, testifying again. On Friday, choir practice. On Sunday, the play. The people who will take part in the play must all confirm the arrangements with Melissa. Rehearsals are at her house on Saturday afternoon."

Khadidja glanced at Storm. His legs were crossed at the knees, he was lost in his own world. She looked behind her. In the back row was a pretty girl with smoky looks, who held a toddler on her lap. Khadidja caught the girl looking at the back of her head.

Storm saw her look behind her and turned also. "That's my baby," he smiled. "Sandy."

Khadidja knew he meant the girl, not the child. She took another look. The girl was still looking at her. No malice, no emotion. Just soft, pretty eyes gazing at them from a distance.

"You didn't tell me about her." She wondered if there were still more Sandys or Melissas she didn't know about.

"I only saw her three times," he whispered.

"Why? She's prettier than Melissa. I would've gone for her rather than for that froggy pond in the front."

He glanced at her briefly to show he didn't like that last remark. "Don't be nasty, Riempie. Melissa's nice. Sandy wanted me to take her out. I didn't want to get involved with someone who had a kid."

The service ended after eleven. Khadidja watched the leaders and their wives position themselves near the door.

"I'm not shaking hands again, Storm. I'll wait for you in the car." She smiled at a few faces, made a detour around the group and escaped.

The car was unlocked and she got in. From the window she watched Storm talk to Underdeacon Bennett at the door. "It looked serious, that conversation you had there," she said when he got into the car.

Stormed eased the Ford out of the parking lot. "Mr Bennett said you're from the natural world. I must be patient with you."

"The natural world? Is that right? Natural as opposed to what?"

"Don't start, Riempie. What did you think of the service?"

"It was everything I expected."

"Good or bad?"

"We agreed not to discuss one another's beliefs, didn't we? I promised to come, and I did. I'm glad I did. I understand things a little better now."

He stopped at a red light and turned to look at her. "We have to do something about our situation, Riempie. You can see my people. We're just humble people. We're not about big buildings and fancy cars. All I want is to be with them, and for you to be with me. Are we still going to my mother's for lunch? Maybe we can talk to them, maybe they have an opinion."

"I already know their opinion. Your mother doesn't care what religion you follow as long as you're happy. Your father doesn't want you with a Muslim." She watched him change into first gear and pull away. "We'll go, but let's not stay too long. Let's go see a movie tonight."

"It's church, Riempie."

"You just came from church."

He glanced at her, heavy and broody. "You promised not to nag me about the church."

"I'm not nagging."

"You're trying to get me away from my church."

She looked out the window. The morning had started bright and hopeful. In her heart she knew they could never be together. "It's not going to work, Storm."

"I know."

"Take me home. I don't want to go to your mother's."

They drove in silence the rest of the way. He stopped at her gate and she got out. "I'm not seeing you any more, Storm. I'm making an appointment tomorrow with a psychologist. If you really want to be my friend, please don't call or come to my gate. We can't be together. Only parts of us fit."

JULY 12

July's wetter than last year. Cold and drizzly. Dark. No silver linings. Why do I like toys so much that I'll destroy myself for them?

～

Kulsum, Fatima and I were playing hopscotch on the pavement when we saw the midwife with her black bag turning the corner into our street. "Daar's die vroedvrou!" Fatima said excitedly. Moosa had been dispatched by Gabieba more than an hour ago to Dorp Street to get her.

I was excited for the Gamieldiens although my mother said it was ridiculous for sies Moena to be having another baby. Sies Moena was old already for all these babies, she told little granny, and how sies Moena was going to manage with another one, she didn't know. I was less concerned with sies Moena's state of mind than with little granny who'd had a stroke and changed right under our eyes. The doctor had given her pills and said she would come right, but it was two months already and she still hadn't regained her spark. She had lost her memory, sometimes asking where her food was when she'd just eaten, and saying she'd eaten when in fact she hadn't. There were also spells when she spoke out of turn and once had to be stopped from exposing family secrets – that my mother had a secret admirer who visited on Tuesday afternoons – in front of Vuyo's mother who'd come to borrow a cup of flour. She could recall things from eighty years ago, like the pink and white pansies in her grandfather's garden, but couldn't tell you what she'd had for breakfast. Once when her son Solly visited, she told my mother there was a stranger in the house. When she started to wet the bed, it was decided that I would sleep on a cot in the room.

The previous evening at the supper table her voice had started suddenly to slur and she slumped in her chair, her head dropping sideways. My mother thought she was fading into a coma and told Murida to phone the doctor. The doctor, who came immediately, gave her two glucose injections in the arm. Almost at once little granny opened her eyes and started to speak.

"Her sugar levels were low," the doctor explained. "But she might've had another episode. I'll stop by tomorrow afternoon after surgery."

My mother tried not to look worried. Murida returned to her school work. I went to lie on the cot with a book, one eye on little granny, the other trying to concentrate. When she fell asleep, I stood over her with my palm over her nostrils to feel whether her breath was fast or slow. My mother came in and saw what I was doing, and reassured me that little granny was all right. She had just eaten the wrong thing.

The midwife was a short, stout woman in a white uniform called Mrs Vermaak. When Riaz and Vuyo saw her from where they were up on the hill, they came running down. We watched as she knocked on the door and Gabieba let her in. We all knew Mrs Vermaak. She was the same midwife who'd delivered me and Murida and seven of sies Moena's children. Sies Moena had told my mother that when Seraj, the second son, was born, Mrs Vermaak didn't register him, and waited for another child to be born before she made the trip to the government office. Seraj and Ebrahim were registered at the same time, and to this day, sies Moena wasn't sure whether Seraj was born on the 5th or 6th of July, and whether it was 1941 or 1942.

Moosa came round the corner. We knew he'd been to motjie Janie's café for Stars when we saw his shocking pink tongue. He sat down with us in front of the gate, and put two Stars down on the pavement. "You can all have a piece," he said. There were six of us. A Star was no bigger than a toffee. To split it fairly, we needed a knife. The Gamieldien children couldn't go in the house while the vroedvrou was there. Vuyo offered to get one from his house. While he was gone, Riaz said we couldn't eat anything cut with a Christian knife as Christians cut pork with it. Fatima said that when her mother bought cheese from Mr Levine, Mr Levine also cut the cheese with a Christian knife. Kulsum said Mr Levine wasn't Christian, he was Jewish, and Jewish was almost the same as us.

"Sshh," Moosa stilled all of us. "We'll just say *bismillah* when we cut it, it'll make it all right. Just don't let Vuyo hear."

The knife came. Moosa cut the Stars six ways, whispering under his breath. The Stars were hard and cracked in all directions. I'd picked my piece to be on the inside, and got a few slivers. But it wasn't the smallness of the piece or that I could hardly taste it. What counted was that Moosa had shared his sweets with us girls.

We started to discuss what was happening in the house.

"It's in the black bag," Riaz said.

"It isn't," Moosa corrected.

"It is. It's a monkey. Mrs Vermaak chops off the tail and it becomes a baby."

We all laughed. Riaz was the youngest and didn't know anything. We'd all heard the monkey story before from our mothers, but knew that the baby was inside the stomach. We just didn't know how it came out.

"I can tell you," Vuyo said. "My brother Sipho was born in the same bed where I slept."

"What?" We all knew Sipho. He was two, and was still being carried around on his mother's back in a red striped blanket.

"It's true. I woke up in the middle of the night from her screams. I saw my father standing with a woman at the side of the bed. When I realised what was happening, I pretended to be asleep."

"Did you see anything?" I asked.

"A little. The head comes out first."

"Where does it come out?" I thought I knew, but wanted him to confirm it.

"There."

"Where there?"

"You know where," he said, becoming embarrassed by the whole thing.

"Was there blood?" Kulsum asked.

"Yes. I couldn't watch. My mother was rolling and groaning and screaming at my father. I turned around."

We were still talking when an ambulance came charging round the corner and stopped right in front of us. Two men jumped out and opened the doors at the back, and brought out a narrow little bed. They wheeled it into the Gamieldien house, and minutes later emerged with sies Moena on it. I could tell from the bump under the white sheet that the baby was still in her stomach. Mrs Vermaak got into the ambulance with her in the back, dabbing her face with a cloth. Boeta Amien got into his own car and followed the ambulance with its flashing lights and screaming siren. Gabieba stood at the gate, a frightened look on her face.

"What happened?" we asked.

Gabieba was the eldest sister, but looked as scared as us. "It wouldn't come out."

"What do you mean?" Kulsum asked.

"The feet were coming first."

"The feet? Isn't it supposed to be the head?" I asked.

"Mrs Vermaak couldn't turn it around."

"How do you turn a baby around?"

"With your hand." She saw our faces and stopped talking.

"What about Mama?" Riaz asked.

"Mama's strong. They'll take the baby out at the hospital."

We looked at one another. I don't know what the others were thinking, but I was thinking that if you put the women of Sachs Street all in a row, sies Moena was the thinnest, the most tired-looking, and with all her teeth out of her mouth, looked older than Mrs Benjamin who was almost a pensioner.

We followed Gabieba into the house. She was wearing a full apron over a house dress. I wondered what kind of outfit she would be wearing on her next outing to town. She had regular outings now on Saturday afternoons, with her friend Reedie and with other friends too. And they didn't always go to bioscope, Kulsum said. They ducked and sometimes met boys in front of Movie Snaps in Darling Street, or in the Gardens. Imam Bassadien's son, Zane, had once come to visit, but boeta Amien had quickly put an end to it.

"He mustn't come here and sit the seats warm. Bieba's too young."

"Can we see the room?" Kulsum asked.

"No, wait in the kitchen," Gabieba said. She went to clean up, then came out and made apricot jam sandwiches. Moosa pumped up the primus stove and boiled tea in a pot. The Gamieldiens had so many children, there were no rules about what you could eat and when you could eat it and who could eat with you. Children were in and out all day long with sandwiches, a piece of cake, a samoosa, a leftover frikkadel. Even Riaz could go to the bread bin and make himself a peanut butter sandwich without asking.

After the sandwiches and tea, we went back outside, but didn't play far from the front door. When we heard the telephone ring, we ran inside to see if Gabieba had news from the hospital. But it was a call from one of boeta Amien's customers asking when his suit would be ready. We sat on the pavement and waited. When we saw boeta Amien's car come round the corner, we jumped up. I knew from the way he got out that something terrible had happened. His eyes looked troubled, and his mouth did a funny thing when he spoke. "You had a sister," he said to his children. "She didn't live."

They looked at one another. "She's dead, Booia?"

I couldn't listen to more, and stole away silently up the hill. How could a baby die before it was born? It wasn't even a day old.

I sat on the grass high up on the hill and watched what was going on down below. Hardly fifteen minutes later, I saw a malboet with several children trailing behind him. Malboets were those men asked by imams or the family to spread the news of death in the community. "Mense, mense, kom hoor. Daar's kifayit ten o'clock môreoggend." People, people, come hear. There's a funeral tomorrow morning at ten o'clock.

Galiema received the news of the death with her Christian husband on the stoep. I saw neighbours enter the Gamieldien house. I saw the doctor arrive to come and check on little granny. I recognised him from the short white coat he wore over his suit. My thoughts were not with little granny now, but with this tiny face I hadn't yet seen. I saw my sister come out and call me. I saw a green van deliver benches. Cars started to fill both sides of the street. I watched boeta Amien's car leave, and return a short time later. Seraj and Ebrahim got out. Seraj carried a white bundle in his arms. The sun was going down when I finally decided it was time to go home.

Murida had been looking for me. "Where were you all afternoon?" she asked irritably. "The baby next door died, there's a kifayit. And it's maghrib. You know you have to be in the house maghrib time."

"Where's Mummy?"

"Next door." She lifted the lid on a pot and dished up a bowl of soup. This was a new thing now, to dish up my supper when my mother wasn't around to do it. "Mummy said you must come next door when you're finished eating."

"What about granny?"

She looked at my great-grandmother sitting all propped up with cushions in a wheelchair in front of the coal stove. "Granny can stay here. Nothing will happen."

"We can't leave her alone. Wasn't the doctor here? I saw him."

"He was. He said that we have to be careful what we give her to eat. He took her blood. She's fine."

I looked at little granny, birdlike in her wheelchair. "I'm not going."

Murida pushed the soup bowl towards me. "You have to. And wash your hands, they're dirty."

Murida's scarf was wrapped around her head in the same way as my mother wrapped hers. The good thing that I will say about my sister is that she put on her scarf at maghrib without being told. I noticed, though, that when it was wrapped around her head tight like my mother's, she liked to give orders.

"You're only fifteen. I don't have to take orders from you."

"I'm going to tell Mummy how cheeky you are." She closed her school books on the table, and left to return to the Gamieldiens.

I poured the soup back in the pot. My mother knew I didn't like soup, and that I didn't eat anything with beans in it. I wanted bread, sweetmilk cheese and some of that honey she kept in a jar on the top shelf of the dresser. In front of little granny, I brought these items to the table, took a spoon and dipped it deep into the condensed milk, which was already there, and let the toffee-like mixture trickle-drip onto my tongue.

Little granny watched me. She didn't know what year it was, or the colour of her own underwear, but something in her expression spurred me on.

"Does Granny want a piece of cheese?"

She looked at me, not understanding.

I cut off a thin piece of cheese and put it in her hand. "Come, Granny, eat." I took her hand and moved it to her mouth. Slowly she ate the cheese. Something disturbed her throat and she coughed. She wouldn't stop coughing, then she started to turn a funny colour. I tapped her back and rocked the wheelchair, panicking that perhaps I'd choked her, but after a while she settled down. My afternoon on the hill had made me hungry. I cut two slices of bread and spread butter on them, piled them up with cheese and a tablespoon of honey, making my fingers all sticky. To wash it down, I poured the last of the milk from the bottle in the fridge. We had a pint a day. When we ran out, we used condensed milk. I knew these last drops were for my mother's tea.

The evening passed slowly. I was scared to be alone in the house with little granny, but refused to go next door. Outside, the cars took up both sides of the street. I could hear voices drifting in from the Gamieldien stoep.

My mother popped in briefly around ten to put little granny to bed. "You're still up?" she asked.

"I'm not sleeping on the cot tonight. I'm sleeping with Granny."

She looked at me. "Did you eat?"

"I had bread and cheese. And milk. I didn't want soup."

She kissed me on the forehead, and helped me in next to little granny.

"When's Murida coming home?" I asked, building up to the next question.

"Soon."

"And Mummy?"

She pulled the blanket over me. "Sies Moena's only coming home in the morning. I have to be next door."

I didn't sleep, and suffered the same fear as when Sybil Cloete had died, that something terrible would happen to me. Only this time I had no one to talk to. I couldn't get the picture out of my head of a baby alone in the ground. God's victims were getting younger. Who was next?

At breakfast the next morning, Murida told me what had happened. I listened with my hands over my ears.

"The doctor couldn't turn it around quickly enough. The cord caught around the neck and strangled it."

I lifted my hands a little. "What cord?"

"The cord that connects the mother to the baby."

"Oh." I still didn't understand.

"Gabieba helped with the washing," she continued.

"What do you mean?"

"She was in the room with the toekamandies, the people who wash the body. One of the family has to help. They start with the head, I think."

I plugged up my ears and didn't want to hear more.

"Gabieba cried when she came out, but wouldn't tell us anything. She said the head toekamandie said you mustn't talk about what you see in there."

"Why not?"

"I thought you weren't listening?"

"I'm not."

My mother came in from next door and went straight to the bedroom to see to little granny. When she came out, she was all businesslike and in a hurry. "Murida, sponge Granny down, and put the sheets in the bucket to soak. Later, you'll have to wash them and hang them up. I have no time to do it." And looking at me, she said, "Granny looks a little better today. She can sit outside on the stoep."

Murida didn't want to have anything to do with pee sheets and wet nighties. "Granny's heavy," she said.

My mother hadn't had any sleep and wasn't in the mood to be argued with. "Granny's light, and you know how to lift her. Wheel her into the bathroom and do it there, or bring the water into the room. And you, you haven't been next door yet. Murida can stay here for a few minutes with Granny. Go next door and greet."

"Yes, Mummy." She knew I wasn't going to go.

At ten I stood at the front window and watched. I wouldn't go out on the stoep where people could see me. If I could stay where it was safe and pretend that nothing had happened, nothing would happen to me. I didn't want to be around a lot of sad people, and didn't want to hear any stories about the Angel of Death the old people were fond of telling to frighten you into being a good Muslim child. I was angry with God.

From where I stood behind the curtain, I saw a strange car stop. Sies Moena and her son Seraj got out. Several women rushed forward to get her. Sies Moena almost collapsed in their arms. A few minutes later, there were men in the garden and in the street, and I could tell from a sudden tension that things were about to start. I heard a voice reciting Arabic. I pressed my face flat into the window, and saw the imam I'd seen once visiting next door, with his hands before him, saying a prayer. Moments later, boeta Amien passed through the gate into the street carrying a white bundle in his arms. Behind him were his sons. Right behind them, a troop of men in red fezzes, and boys. One of the sons took the bundle from his father and continued walking. Then another took it, and another. I lost sight of them before they reached Pepper Street.

I watched the women on the stoep. Some had handkerchiefs in their hands and stood with sad faces surrounding sies Moena. I couldn't see my mother, but spotted Murida with Kulsum and Fatima and Gabieba with their girl cousins near the loquat tree.

"Why didn't you go next door?" a voice said suddenly behind me.

I turned in surprise. It was my great-grandmother sitting in her chair next to the window. Her eyes sparkled like old times and she appeared completely normal.

"Does Granny know what's happening next door?"

She leaned forward slightly to peer through the lace sheers. "The baby died."

"Yes, Granny. In the hospital."

She nodded wisely. "She's better off, my girl. You mustn't be sad and you mustn't be afraid. Where she's gone now, she's safe from everything."

I wanted to know more, but she had slipped out of the present and was back dreaming about her childhood or her gardens or whatever it was that kept her nodding quietly to herself.

I went to the telephone in the hall and called Alison. Alison lived on Pepper Street. "We stood outside," Alison said. "We saw them. I'll come right away. I have this week's *Beano* and *Dandy*. And guess what? I got my period!"

Not two months after the Gamieldien baby had died, the principal came into our science class and spoke to Miss Jephta who was at her table marking papers. Miss Jephta called me up to the front when he left.

"There's been an accident," she said. "You have to go home."

A heat rose up in me. I knew something serious must have happened for this message to come to the school. "Can Alison come with me, Miss?" Somehow I knew I didn't have to explain. Everyone knew Alison was fasting with me, and that we were best friends.

She looked at me, then glanced at Alison over my shoulder. "Alison, go home with Khadidja."

"Is it my granny, Miss?" I asked.

From the long time she took to say she didn't know, I knew that it was.

Out on the street, we ran as fast as our feet could take us. Alison was talking, but I wasn't listening. Little granny had had another stroke. That was all I could think about. She'd fallen out of her chair and broken something.

We were up the steps already, on Sachs Street, a few feet from my front door. I saw three cars and a green van. The van was the same one that had come to the house next door delivering benches the day the baby had died.

"You look sick," Alison observed.

"That van delivers benches for people at funerals."

Alison looked at the van. "Maybe it's someone visiting."

"It's not. I know it's not. Let's go to your house."

"My house?" She frowned. "But your mother. Maybe it's not your granny, maybe it's her. Don't you want to go and see first?"

"It's my granny. I know it."

"Granny May will ask why we're home early."

"Let's go somewhere else then. The Gardens. I have change. We can buy chips and feed the squirrels."

Alison caught her breath. "You're going to break your fast?"

"Yes."

Alison said nothing. It wasn't every day I shocked her. *She* was the shocker – I was only the follower, according to Kulsum and Fatima. According to them, Alison was a rough girl, not up to our standards. What they meant was that Alison had taai hair and was Christian. "Why's she fasting with you anyway? She's not Moslem. Does she want to get off on labarang?" They couldn't believe that Alison was doing it just because she wanted to. Like I sometimes looked in the Bible and read some of the stories there.

"Do you want to go?" I asked. "I'll go by myself if you don't want to."

"Don't you want to go and see first?"

"No."

Alison nodded her head towards the stoep where sies Moena had just come out of the house. "We'd better go before she sees us and tells your mother."

We took the steps two at a time into the street below. We turned left on Bryant, and ran until we got to Leeuwen Street where we turned again and hastened our steps to the Gardens on Wale Street. We only relaxed once we were safely under a tree with a steaming parcel of salt and vinegar chips on our laps. I felt bad. I'd never cheated during the holy month, but the more I thought of little granny and what was happening at my house, the more I stuffed the hot chips into my mouth.

We wandered over to the museum, then left for the Grand Parade. Alison took money out of her blazer and asked a man at one of the stalls if he sold loose cigarettes. The man looked at us. I could see he was Moslem by his fez, and wondered if he could tell if I was one too.

"It's for my mother over there," Alison pointed to a woman waiting at a bus stop with OK Bazaars packages at her feet.

"Only Cavalla," the man said.

Alison bought two. "You didn't tell me you smoked."

"I only did it once. Have you tried?"

"No. Doesn't it burn?" I was talking and acting normally, but there was a tight feeling in my chest which made me feel as though I would stop breathing at any time.

"No. You feel lekker." She headed towards three boys playing dice. I followed. There were times when I trailed after Alison without question.

We reached the boys. Alison put the cigarette to her mouth. "Have you got a light?"

A boy tossed her a box of matches. Alison lit the cigarette and handed it back. "Where are you girls going?" he asked.

I didn't like this forwardness when he didn't know us, and walked away. Alison talked for a minute, then caught up with me and held out the cigarette. "Here, like this." She made a sucking noise with her mouth. "Not too hard or you'll get dizzy."

I took the cigarette and brought it to my lips. Immediately I coughed. "Not like that," Alison laughed. "Like this." She dragged on the cigarette, her eyes tearing as she inhaled. I tried again, and this time managed to keep the smoke in my lungs. After a few puffs, I felt my shoulders relax. It was a strange feeling, making me almost a little lightheaded. Then little granny's face appeared before me, and dark feelings rose up in me again. I took a few rapid puffs and pushed all thoughts of death out of my mind.

We finished the cigarette standing behind a stall watching the people on the Parade go about their business. Alison lit the second cigarette with the stub of the first, and we finished that also. My head was feeling strange.

"School's out," Alison said. "I think we should go now. Your house or mine?"

I knew I was in serious trouble, but wasn't ready yet to go home. "Yours. Let's buy some peanuts."

"We're going to eat in the street? What if someone sees us?"

I realised how bad it would look for a Moslem girl to be seen eating during the month of Ramadan, and didn't like it that Alison, who wasn't even a Moslem, had to remind me of this. "Okay, we'll take them with us."

224

Granny May opened the door when we arrived. "Oh Titch," she said, putting her fat arms about me. "I heard the news about your granny. I'm so sorry."

So my great-grandmother really was dead, I thought, hoping Granny May wouldn't sniff the cigarette smoke on us. She was dead, in the house where I had to go. In the room where I had to sleep. Probably she was lying in my bed. Little granny with her red hair and flower petticoats. Little granny who'd told me stories of her mother and father and grandfather, and who'd listened to all my complaints. She was gone. Forever. Would oupa Solly come to the funeral? Would the Paarl family? Where did my mother think I would sleep when I went home?

Granny May made peanut butter sandwiches and tea, and then remembered it was the Moslem holy month. "Aren't you fasting?" she asked.

"She has her period," Alison lied. "Girls don't fast when they have it."

Granny May let us eat our sandwiches in the lounge where Alison turned on the gramophone softly and put on *Jailhouse Rock*. I was happy to listen to this music. It took my mind off angels and graves and rotting bodies. Granny May popped her head in briefly to tell us she had to go to the next-door neighbour, and Alison turned the music up loud. We sang and danced and swivelled our hips just like we'd seen Elvis do in the bioscope until the front door opened and Alison's brother Mark came in. Her brother Willie had had a must-marriage, and wasn't living with them anymore.

"You didn't open my cupboard, did you?" Mark asked.

I knew about this cupboard. Alison had told me about the record by Paul Anka, *Diana*, he kept in there. There were other records also, but this one was special because he liked a girl called Diana at the fish shop. He'd never spoken to the girl, but was building up his courage. In the meantime, he played the record to death, and no one was to go near it. "No, Mark. We won't touch your *Diana*."

"Good." He claimed the lounge and the gramophone for himself, and allowed us to listen to a new record he'd bought. We didn't much like Frank Sinatra, and went to Alison's room where we played cards. At six o'clock Alison's mother, aunty Mavis, arrived from work and started supper in her high-heel shoes, a cigarette wedged between her lips. Aunty Mavis was a thin woman with hard hair flattened back with coconut oil, ending in a stiff little stub held by an elastic band at the back of her head.

"Does your mother know you're here, Titch?" she asked. "Granny May told me what happened."

"I don't think so."

She stirred the onions in the pot, squinting over her cigarette. "Don't you want to call her? She'll worry." Aunty Mavis was struggling just like us, but had a telephone and didn't mind if you used it.

The telephone rang. Mark answered it. "For you, Ma."

"Who's it?"

"I don't know."

Aunty Mavis took the receiver from him. "Hello?" A short pause. "She's here, yes. No, no, I understand. She's all right. I'll get her." Aunty Mavis held out the receiver. "Your mother wants to talk to you."

I took the receiver and braced myself. "Hello?"

"Titch? What're you doing there? Didn't the principal tell you to come home?"

I didn't answer.

"We've been looking for you everywhere. It's after maghrib. Come home right away."

"Can't I stay with Alison tonight?"

She was silent so long, I thought she'd gone off the line. "Didn't you hear what I said?"

"Yes."

"It's Ramadan. There's a death in the family. You can't sleep out."

"I don't want to come home," I pleaded. "I'm scared."

"Why're you scared?" I heard the exasperation in her voice, then I heard her talking to someone else. "Hassiem, here, talk to her."

My father was there, I thought. She was putting my father on the phone.

"Khadidja?"

"Yes, Daddy?"

226

"I want you to come home. Your mother was worried about you. People are asking where you are. Do you want me to come and fetch you?"

My father had never fetched me from anywhere – I was tempted. But I knew also that his stay would be short and that after the funeral, he'd be gone.

In aunty Mavis's kitchen, life was going on normally. Aunty Mavis was slicing potatoes and setting out plates. Granny May was pressing school clothes on an ironing board. Alison was mashing up strawberry ice blocks. Springbok Radio was playing in the background. There would be no radio on at my house. Only crying and praying and long faces.

"I want to stay here."

"Your mother wants you to come home."

"I don't want to."

My mother came back on the line. "Titch?"

"Yes, Mummy?"

"Call aunty Mavis there."

I held out the telephone. "Aunty Mavis, my mother wants to talk to you."

Aunty Mavis knocked her cigarette ash into the sink, and came forward like a ballerina, almost on the points of her shoes. She took the receiver from me and spoke into it. I watched her face. She kept nodding. "Yes. Yes, yes. Oh no. Oh yes. We have extra blankets. It's quite all right. I'll see to it. Alison will come with her first thing in the morning. Don't worry about anything."

Yesterday morning my great-grandmother had a third stroke and died. They called me at school. I didn't go home and slept at Alison's house and stayed with Alison until almost lunch-time, when I knew everything was over. I knew it was over because I stood on Alison's stoep with her and watched. Granny May stood with us also, and all the neighbours stood on their own stoeps. We watched the men carry the bier on their shoulders. As they passed by us, walking quickly, mumbling, the drumming of their footsteps getting fainter as they went round the corner, I felt something come over me that I'd not felt even when the baby next door or Sybil Cloete had died. It made me almost burst out, but I didn't. Alison

was holding my hand. Granny May was crossing herself. Bye, Granny,
I said in my heart. I'm going to miss you.

∼

Khadidja was at the living-room table reading short story entries
for the magazine when the doorbell rang. She wondered who it
could be at that time on a Saturday morning. She had run a competition in *Lifestyle* for the best true story on women's obsessions,
and had received over two hundred entries. Together with an assis-
tant editor, they cut the entries down to two, and now she couldn't
decide whether to publish the one by the thirty-year-old stewardess
obsessed with a gambler who asked for money and who'd pawned
her movie camera, or the one by the secretary who got herself pregnant on purpose so her boss would be forced into a decision to marry her. She put this last entry down on top of the others, and went
to the front door.

"Veronica …" Khadidja couldn't hide her surprise. "How are
you?"

Veronica waited for her to unlock the gate, then hugged her. "I'm
fine. Well, not really. I just came from Storm's house, and I thought –
well, I didn't even know where you lived, but I remembered him
telling me some time ago that it was right across from the fire station, a house with a big tree. And here I am." She looked up at the
house. "I'm glad I found you."

Khadidja thought her a little out of breath. "Come in. You look
flustered. Is something wrong?"

"Yes. Do you have a few minutes?"

"Of course."

Veronica stopped for a moment on the stoep and admired the
blooming impatiens in the clay pots. "Lovely flowers. They really
do well in the shade. You know, I said to Charles the other day, that
beautiful orange tree Storm gave me for my birthday, he never
would've done that on his own. We know that you had something
to do with it."

"Actually, Veronica, he did do it on his own," Khadidja lied. "We went shopping for seeds, and he said he thought you might like a plant."

Veronica followed her into the house. Khadidja set out two cups and put on the kettle. "What happened, Veronica?"

Veronica became solemn. "I need your help, Khadidja. I know it's an imposition, but you're the only one who can help. Storm doesn't listen to any of us." She clasped her hands together in front of her face. "I don't know if you know he's got a drinking problem."

"The boys at the fire station told me. And he came here once with a bottle of champagne, but I haven't seen him drink since. I've not seen him drunk."

"He's a secret drinker. He can go months without drinking, and then something happens, and he's off to the liquor store. When you don't hear from him, that's when you know. Did the two of you break up?"

"Last Sunday. When we didn't come to your house for lunch. I'm sorry about that."

"He came on his own, but didn't say anything. He's not one for talking. Yesterday his brother called to say he went round to Storm's place for a gate he'd promised him, and found Storm drinking at eleven o'clock in the morning. Storm hadn't been to the fire station in three days. I have a key to his house and went there this morning. Oh God!" Veronica wrung her hands in despair. "I couldn't believe what I saw. He was in the kitchen cleaning carrots with a big butcher's knife. His hair was wild, his eyes were bloodshot, he had on a crumpled T-shirt and tracksuit pants, and looked like he hadn't slept in a week. I asked what was wrong. 'Bugger off,' he said. I tried to reason with him, but he wouldn't give me a chance. I asked if it was about you. He got really mad then. 'Bugger off out of my life,' he said, waving the knife in the air. 'I don't want to hear her name. Don't come here and mention her name. I want to hear nothing about her.' I said, 'Put down the knife, Storm.' He wouldn't. He chased me out of the house. I came here to ask whether you could go over there and talk to him."

"Me? I can't."

"Just go and talk to him. I know it's because you broke up that he's drinking. He can't handle it."

"You're not blaming me, Veronica, are you?"

"Of course not. I told Charles that you were the best thing that's ever happened to Storm. I've never seen Storm act with another woman the way he acts around you. He listens to you, he respects you. Just go and talk to him. Maybe you can persuade him to see a doctor. Just go there and be his friend."

"I can't be his friend. If I go there, I'll undo all my best efforts of the past week."

Veronica looked tortured. "I know how you feel, Khadidja. Storm's difficult, he has problems, but I know he loves you."

The kettle boiled. Khadidja switched it off and made a pot of tea.

"Why don't you go over there, and talk to him?" Veronica persisted. "I'll drive behind you. You won't have to go there alone. I'll wait outside."

Khadidja fiddled with the pot, stirring a spoon into the brew to help it along. It would be easy to justify doing such a thing to herself, she thought. She would be stopping him from harming himself. "Please, you don't know how hard this is."

Veronica sensed a weakening. "Come, my girl. I know you can help. Here, let's drink our tea and go over there. Weekends are bad for him. There's no church on Saturday, so he'll drink the whole weekend."

Ten minutes later Khadidja was in her car in front of his gate looking up at the house. She got out. Immediately the dogs started barking. She approached the gate. There was no doorbell. She looked back at Veronica who was in her own car parked behind the Honda. Veronica made a sign for her to knock on the window. Khadidja hesitated. *Get in the car and go home. You know you're doomed if you see him.* She reached up on her toes and rapped on the window. "It's me! Open up!"

"Coming ..." a voice said from somewhere inside the house. He opened the gate. She had prepared herself, but was still shocked when she saw him in faded red tracksuit pants torn at the knee, a grimy sweater that had food stains on it, and hair stiff with dirt and sleep. He looked like something fished out of a junk pile.

"Riempie ... what're you doing here?" His eyes were moody and red, his voice squeaky like a child's.

She walked past him into the house. "Good grief, look at this place!"

"My ears, Riempie ..." He held his hands to his head. "Don't shout."

"Been having a little drinking party, have you? This is what you do with your life when you can't get what you want?"

He closed the door behind them. "You told me to bugger off. You didn't want to see me. Who told you to come here? My mother?"

"Your mother should stop caring about you, you're not worth it." She looked around at the bottles and cartons and dirty ashtrays. "Where's Mr Bennett now? Why are the brothers and sisters not here saving your sorry arse? Look at you!" She poked him with the tips of her fingers on his chest, pushing him backwards. "Why aren't they?"

"It's not their business."

"You made our business their business." She prodded him, pushing him into the back of the couch. "And your drinking *should* be their business. Where's the father of the house now?"

He was backed up against the couch, shielding his face with his hand. "You're nasty, Riempie. I don't like you like this."

She poked him harder. "Not turning up for work, drinking yourself to a standstill. A full-blown alcoholic!"

"You told me to get lost. What did you expect me to do?"

"Drinking's the answer? Not turning up for work? Stop feeling sorry for yourself. Look at this place. It's a flippin' pigsty. Where's your boarder?"

His eyes became furtive.

"Where?" she asked again, and pushed past him and went down the hall to the boarder's room.

"Don't be such a bully, Riempie. No one's there." He rushed up ahead and placed himself in front of the door. Khadidja plucked him away by the front of his sweater, surprised by her own strength. The boarder sat on the edge of the bed, clutching the baby, frightened by the commotion.

"Were you in here with her?"

"No."

"Tell me the truth!"

"You know I don't lie to you. I wasn't."

Seeing the girl's frightened expression, Khadidja realised that she was out of control. Angry. Both at herself and at Veronica. She returned to the living room and sat down on the couch. It was the first interval of silence.

"Riempie?"

She didn't look up.

"Riempie, can't we try again? I'll go see a psychologist. I love you too much to let go. Let's give it another try."

She sat with her head in her hands and refused to speak.

"Riempie?"

"This is too hard for me."

"Give me a chance, Riempie. I don't want to lose you."

"A psychologist can't change your beliefs. It's your beliefs that are driving you."

"Maybe there's still a way. I'm willing to give it a try. A month ago I wouldn't have said this."

She wanted desperately to believe that he was right, but somehow didn't believe that a psychologist could help. "What about your drinking?"

"I promise I won't have another drink."

"You'll go to AA?"

"I'm not an alcoholic, but I'll go."

She got up. Her body felt as if she'd been lying down for a week. "I want to hear nothing about your church. Not a word."

"No church."

"And nothing about your leaders."

"No leaders."

"And nothing about the natural world, the spirit world, or any world with apostles and disciples in it."

"I promise."

She walked slowly towards the door. "I'm going home. I'm exhausted. If it wasn't for your mother, I would never have come."

His features softened and he looked almost normal again. "Can I come to your house and have a bath, Riempie? We can go to a movie tonight if you like. I promise you, I'll be good."

She turned to look at him, at the state of his house. She knew as she stood there that she should get out and never see him again.

"Don't make promises you can't keep. You're not in charge of your own promises. I want to go home and think."

When she got home, she found Veronica waiting outside the gate.

"What happened?" Veronica asked anxiously. "I didn't want to wait in case he came out and saw me."

Khadidja opened the gate. "He's going to see a psychologist."

Veronica gripped her hands together in delight. "I don't believe it. I told you. He'll only listen to you. Did he say when?"

"One thing at a time, Veronica."

"And the two of you? You've made up?"

"I wouldn't call it that."

Veronica followed her through the gate. "Things will work out, you'll see. You know how to handle him."

"If I was smart, I wouldn't have gone there."

Veronica looked disappointed. "Don't you love him? You do unbelievable things when you love someone. And things don't always come right the first time. Charles was my first love, but I didn't get him that easily. I waited three years while he went overseas and did all the things he wanted to do, even going out with other girls. I was patient. Not like the girls today who want everything right away, and end up separated and divorced. I made the right decision, and I'm happy today. I've known love. I've always known love. I know you can have it with Storm."

Khadidja didn't doubt Veronica's sincerity, but didn't delude herself about her motives either. Veronica knew that with Khadidja, her son had a chance. "Would you like a sandwich?"

"Yes, please. All this drama's made me hungry. Was he rude to you?"

"No. It was the other way around. I was angry. I pushed him around a bit."

"It's enough to be angry. And the boarder? She was there?"

"She was in her room with the baby. I wouldn't be surprised if Storm had been with her. They both looked guilty. Storm didn't want me to go in."

Veronica looked shocked that she could suggest such a thing. "He wouldn't do that. Not while he's interested in you."

"You don't know, Veronica. He's been with her already."

"How do you know?"

"He told me. She was seven months pregnant when he had sex with her." Khadidja told her the story.

Veronica looked crestfallen. "Oh my." She took the plate offered by Khadidja and buttered a slice of brown bread. "His problem is that he's too honest sometimes, and doesn't realise that he hurts people."

"Maybe he should keep his pants on, then he wouldn't have a problem about being honest."

"He's not a bad person, though. He has problems, but he's not evil. I should tell you some things about him if he's going to see a psychologist. They ask things about the past, don't they? I don't know if this has any relevance, but he was a clingy child when he was young. I remember his first year in school. I had to go there during school breaks and hold his hand through the fence until the bell rang."

"He says you smothered him when he was young."

"Of course. He wanted it."

"He says his father was away, and you looked to him for love. You sucked him dry with your neediness."

Veronica laughed. "Is that what he said? Oh my. Maybe he's angry with me for that then, because he's angry with me for something. He's not angry with his father, just with me. And Charles and I can't understand why he prefers the people at the church to his own family. We don't know what we've done wrong. We've tried to recall incidents from the past. I don't know if this means anything, but there was this time when we went camping at a river up north when Storm was about ten years old. Storm grew up around boats and the sea, and he and three friends went off in a boat in the early afternoon, but by sunset they still weren't back. We were very worried and went looking for them, calling their names, thinking that the boat had capsized and that they'd drowned. It was dark when the coastguard found them – they'd lost one of the oars. They were cold and scared, and the parents of the other boys were so happy to see them, that they hugged and kissed them and took them straight home. But Charles was very upset and gave

234

Storm a heck of a hiding. Storm cried all night. In the morning his eyes were all swollen and his face was still wet. He couldn't understand why the other boys had got love, and he had got a hiding." Veronica took a bite of her bread and chewed on it, thinking. "Sometimes we talk about it. Charles feels that maybe that incident hurt Storm. If you ever get the chance, Khadidja, tell him about it. Tell him his father only did what he thought was right. It's not like today when you can't hit your own children and there're all these books telling you how to raise kids. Bring it up with him. Maybe there're other things we don't know about. We're not afraid to talk about them with him if it'll help."

For her fortieth birthday, Alison invited a group of women who recited at birthdays and anniversaries, known as moerieks, to come to her house for a religious get-together with family and friends. "I want blessings, Titch. I'm through with parties."

Khadidja wasn't surprised that she'd opted for something spiritual, but was surprised by the changes in Alison since her decision to turn over a new leaf. Alison had made a list of don'ts, stuck it on the fridge door where she couldn't miss it, threw out her tights, her tube tops, her cigarettes, and started to attend classes on Wednesday nights at Imam Adams's house in Walmer Estate. The turnaround was so complete, Khadidja marvelled at the changes in her friend.

Seated next to Leila and Alison's mother, aunty Mavis, on a bench listening to the women recite in the front room, Khadidja watched Alison through the doorway in the kitchen getting the tea things ready. Alison looked up from the pies and tarts she was busy arranging on plates, and waved for her to come to the kitchen. Khadidja got up quietly and tiptoed past the guests.

"They're reaching the end," Alison said. "The cups are ready. I need help with these last barakats – there're twenty-nine people." A barakat was a plate of cakes wrapped with cellophane for the guests to take home.

"Do you want me to pour the tea?" Khadidja took a custard tart from one of the plates and bit into it.

There was a sound behind them. A tall, good-looking man with a white robe over blue jeans and a pair of leather sandals entered the kitchen.

Khadidja wondered at the familiarity of this man coming into the house through the back door. No men had been invited.

"This is Imran," Alison whispered. "Imran, this is Titch."

"I've heard a lot about you," he said. "Alia says you're an editor."

It was strange for Khadidja to hear Alison called by that name. She smiled at Imran, taking his hand. "I must say I've not heard about you."

"Imam Adams's son," Alison said. "Where I go on Wednesday nights."

"I see," Khadidja said, suddenly understanding. Alison had never mentioned him. She heard the reciting in the next room come to an end, and picked up the teapot. "Where's the sugar for the tea? They're finished inside."

She and Alison had never had secrets from one another. Even chance encounters were discussed. And Imran dropping in like this wasn't a chance visit. She thought back to how many times she'd called Alison over the past month. Two or three times, not a lot. Alison had called at least once a week. Still, Alison hadn't mentioned him. Was this a new man in her life? She had a chance that evening to ask when the guests had left and Leila had gone to bed, and it was only her and Alison washing the dishes.

"So … I turn my back for five minutes, and there's an imam's son."

Alison smiled. "I wanted to be sure before I said anything."

"To be sure? There's something serious, then? You're having an affair?"

"No, no," Alison said quickly. "It's not like that at all. We're just seeing each other. He won't have sex without marriage."

"You're talking about marriage? I wasn't even aware of the dating part yet."

"Calm down. We've just talked about it. He can't come here night after night and sit my seats warm, and pretend there's nothing."

Khadidja put down the dishcloth and sat down at the table. Alison joined her. "My goodness. How? And so quickly? Talk to me."

"It never entered my mind that I would meet anyone when I

started classes. It's for women only. The second Wednesday I was there, the imam had to leave for PE and Imran filled in. He basically just met us and said that his father had to leave urgently. One of the women asked about second and third talaqs. He said he wasn't an imam, but told us what he believed was the right answer. After that we left. I'd left my car keys on the coffee table, and went back for them."

"You'd left them behind on purpose?"

Alison's dimples deepened into a mischievous smile. "Yes. I went back up the steps and he was still there. I followed up on that question about divorce – let him know that I was going through something similar. I asked if he could ask his father to check out something for me. I left my number."

Khadidja smiled. "I was never as smooth."

"I had nothing to lose. Two days later he called. The rest is history. It's only been steady now for about two weeks. I didn't want to say anything in case it was dust in the wind."

"And it's not?"

"No."

"What does he do?"

"He's an accountant." She waited a moment before continuing. "He wants a short courtship, and if things work out between us, he wants a wife."

"What?" Khadidja couldn't believe what she was hearing. "A month ago you were lying on your bed like a sack of potatoes feeling sorry for yourself."

"He's nice, Titch. He's attractive, he makes me laugh, and while I still have it, why not? Men don't marry you for your brains. They want to look at you and get stiff. Whether you can cook and raise children, those things they think about afterwards. It's the same for us. We want brains and a sense of humour, but we also want chemistry. He's younger than me, and that's the way I like it."

"Not just a boyfriend. A husband! Alison!" Khadidja was stunned by the news. "Was he married before?"

"Yes, for seven years. There's a son, Ebrahim, about eight. He's been divorced for two years already. He didn't say much about his ex-wife, but there was this thing that happened at a friend's house when they took Ebrahim to a pool party for six-year-olds. She got in the pool, too, wearing a bathing suit. There were men present."

"That's why the marriage ended?"

"There was a man there she got involved with, and there were other incidents. She also smoked dagga."

"Oh my word. Does he know about you?"

"Of course not."

"And don't tell him. Men can't know everything. You've stopped, anyway." Khadidja smiled at her friend in wonder. "Well, Alison, I must say I didn't expect this. I came here for your fortieth birthday, and it looks like I'm coming back for wedding cake. I can't get over it. What does Leila say? Does she know?"

"She knows there's something going on, but nothing else. I'll tell her when there's something to tell her. She asked him last week if he knew the ayah in the Qur'an where it says that a woman must wear a scarf. It says a woman must be veiled, but it doesn't say the scarf must be on her head. She had a whole discussion with him about it."

Khadidja smiled. "Testing him."

"Oh yes. She said in her opinion it made a lot of sense to be veiled in those days because of the heat, but this wasn't the desert and people had it all wrong about the purpose of the scarf."

"I bet his father would've had some good answers for that."

"I'm sure he would have, but of course, Imran knew it had nothing to do with scarves or religion. It was just letting him know who she was. Anyway, enough about this. What about you? The last time we talked, Storm was going to see a psychologist."

Khadidja's smile faded. "He went for two sessions and cancelled the rest. He said the psychologist was a poep. He wasn't going to let anyone talk to him about his church, or change his opinions. It's tormenting him, this relationship. You can see it in his eyes, in his body. He went to his leader the other night and told him that it didn't look like I was going to convert. The leader told him not to underestimate the power of the Lord, to have patience. Storm said it was taking too long, and before he gave up faith in his God, maybe it was better to end it. He said he felt so hopeless sometimes, he felt like putting a gun to his head."

"Oh no."

"I told him I couldn't be responsible if he did anything stupid to himself. I have an appointment with a psychologist myself. I want to move on with my life."

"Honestly, Titch," Alison shook her head, "you have to."

"I'm thinking of going away for a few weeks. To Europe somewhere. I have to be physically far away to get back my sanity."

"Let's say he asked you tonight to marry him. Would you, the way things are? He stays a Christian and you a Muslim?"

"Don't ask me that. It's too tempting."

Anna Birnbaum's office was on a cobblestoned street on Greenmarket Square, two streets away from the magazine where Khadidja worked. The room was friendly, with love seats, a wing chair, patchwork dolls, pictures of grown-up children on a side table, and crayon drawings of what appeared to be stick-like figures of mothers and fathers holding hands with young children on the wall.

Anna was in her forties, dressed in a long rustic skirt and brown ankle boots, with eyes that looked at you from under raised eyebrows. She listened to Khadidja explain why she was there.

"That's quite a list," she said when Khadidja had finished talking. She turned to Storm. "And you, Storm?"

Storm had sat quietly throughout Khadidja's opening comments about their relationship.

"I just came with. Riempie said maybe you could help us."

Anna smiled at the use of the name Riempie. "You've heard Khadidja talk about your church, that you're trying to convert her. What do you feel about what she's saying?"

"I can't change to another religion. I told her. There's only one way for me. I can't think like the Muslims. They're too strange. Five times a day they have to pray. They can't eat this, they can't eat that. And what do they go to mosque for? They don't *do* anything. We do things at our church. We go out and save people."

Anna glanced at Khadidja. "Yet you're with her."

"I'm with her because I want her to be happy."

"Not because you want to be happy also?"

"Of course, otherwise I wouldn't be here. But I can't take her nonsense, the things she believes in."

"You have difficulty with her beliefs?"

"They don't make sense to me. How can you be together and have two sets of beliefs? Who will follow who?"

Anna sat back slightly and surveyed him. "I'm listening to you, Storm, and I'm wondering. I think you're fascinated by her religion."

Storm almost rose out of his chair. "Fascinated? I hate it! I hate her religion! Do you know the things they do? I could never do them!"

Khadidja was shocked by the extent of his loathing. She'd never heard him use the word hate before.

"I didn't say you understood it," Anna said. "I said, I think you're fascinated by it. I think she feeds you. Spiritually. Do you love her?"

He frowned, as if it was a stupid question to ask. "I get along with her. She understands me. I can talk to her. She knows things."

"Things about God?"

"Sometimes. I don't believe all of it. I don't understand why they go to Mecca and do all those things. What's the point of seeing where a prophet lived thousands of years ago? How does it help you?"

"Belief is a very personal thing. Are you happy with her?"

"Happy?" His face darkened. "I've never been so unhappy." He started to count on his fingers the many things he was unhappy about. "She doesn't believe everything in the Bible. She moans when I have to leave in the evenings for church. She doesn't understand anything about the Apostolics, and doesn't want to. I can't see why she can't change to my faith. I want her to be saved."

Anna glanced again at Khadidja. "What do you mean by saved?"

"Only through the Lord Jesus Christ can she be saved." He looked directly at her. He was angry. "Look, I didn't come here to hurt anyone, but it says clearly that only through Jesus will you come to the Lord. Everyone else will burn in the hellfire."

Anna turned to Khadidja. Khadidja nodded her head slowly. She had learned more about his feelings in the last few minutes than during the past month. "I'm tired, Anna, of the argument. He can't see how selfish and manipulative he is, and I can't be with someone who's so downright disrespectful. My faith's not negotiable, and that's never going to change. And just for the record," she turned to face him, "let me say that I would never be part of any one elitist group making themselves more special than another – whether that be Jewish, Christian *or* Muslim. There wasn't only one prophet and one message. There were many warners, and many books, but there's only one God, and that God, fuckface, " she said angrily, "doesn't belong to the Christians alone. Now I'm sick of you and I'm sick of myself. Do you want to wait outside while I finish my business?"

On the trip home no one spoke. Khadidja drove. Storm looked out the window. A block away from his house, he turned to her. "You were nasty in there. I didn't deserve it."

She kept her eyes on the road. On Kenilworth Road, she stopped at his gate without turning off the ignition. He got out and leaned his head through the window. "And now, Riempie?"

She moved the gear into first. "And now we go our separate ways. Call your leader. Ask him if you should have a dream tonight." She released her foot on the clutch, and drove off.

A week later in the psychologist's office she sat with her head in her hands, blaming herself for the mess she was in.

"Tell me about your mother."

"My mother?" She was surprised. She wanted to talk about Storm. "I grew up in Bo-Kaap, in a little road high up on the hill. Just my mother, my sister and my great-grandmother. Well, my great-grandmother only came when I was eight. We were alone already by that time."

Anna nodded for her to continue.

"My mother sewed clothes for people. When I was twelve, she got a job in a factory. She didn't want to do it, but she only had a Standard Six education, and had no choice. Things were expensive. My sister had finished high school and wanted to study further – not that she did anything with that extra education. She got married and had two babies in quick succession. Anyway, my mother wasn't happy working in a factory, and when her friend Moena got her an order for thirty outfits for the minstrels for New Year's Eve, she quit. But the factory had given her an idea. She saw that there was a market for home baking, and made pies and roetie and mince curry, and twice a week went to the factory to sell them. It was a hard time for her. My father gave us no money. The only money that came in was the money she generated. But hard as things were, we always had our toffee rolls and comic books on Friday nights, we had the best outfits at Eid, and we always had three pairs of shoes: one for school, one for the house, and a special pair for when we went out."

"She looked after you girls."

"Yes."

"Did she marry again?"

"No. We were quite selfish, my sister and I. We wanted her all to ourselves. But she didn't want to marry anyway. No one was going to make fish of her children, she said. If he'd been married before and had children of his own, he would make meat of them, and fish of us. She wasn't going to let another man make us feel second best."

Anna closed the folder on her lap. "When you come next time, we must talk about your father."

"We're not going to talk about Storm?"

"We will, but the problem's not Storm. You must understand your past to know why you're with a man like Storm."

AUGUST 24

Rainy and wet. Must make a fire tonight. I like Anna. It's a pity this boundary thing with psychologists and their patients. I could learn a lot. I miss Storm.

⁓

It happened when I was six, an argument over a woman in a shop who'd not charged my father for cigarettes. The arguments over women weren't new – my mother's tears and accusations were familiar – but it was the first time I saw her lose control. I remember it clearly. My father in grey pants and a navy-blue blazer, standing at the kitchen table, listening to my mother scream at the top of her lungs. My mother was at the stove, her foot on a carrier bag stuffed with his clothes.

"Get out!" she screamed, kicking the bag viciously out the back door, "and don't put your foot back here!"

My father stood with the car keys in his hand and watched the bag fly across the floor, vests and shirts and underpants tumbling out into the yard. He looked at us children watching him. He was ashamed of my mother's actions, but guilty also. "You like to believe nonsense," he said. "This thing's all in your head."

"In my head? Do you think I'm bedonderd? Get out!" she screamed, grabbing the pan with the frikkadels from the stove and throwing it at him. The pan missed his head and thunked against the wall – hot oil and meatballs, and fat drops spattering on the points of his shiny black shoes. My father took his handkerchief, wiped the grease from the tips, turned on his heel and left, the tread of his step on the linoleum passage so soft, it made his departure all the more final. He paid no attention to me trailing behind him. At the front door he noticed me with an expression that said, your mother's crazy, but I didn't seem to register as his child, or anyone who belonged to him. I was just a silent bystander watching the last ugly moments of a man leaving his wife and children.

I stood on the step and watched him get into the car. I watched his face as the engine turned. I waited for him to roll down the window to say something to me. The car moved away slowly, the taillights glowing red as it turned right into Pepper Street. *I hate you, God*, I said. *I hate you*. I can still feel the coldness creeping into me. It's not a coldness of the arms or the legs or the body. Even now I can't explain it.

My mother didn't do her usual fussing over our brushing our teeth and saying our *Shahadaah* with us that night. She picked up the frikkadels, cleaned the floor, went to her room and forgot to give us supper. Murida and I stood in the empty kitchen. We'd never dished up our own food before. Outside, we could hear children playing and laughing. Inside the house, we were choked up with our mother's grief.

Murida lifted the lid of the glass dish on the table. "Maybe we should eat," she said.

"I'm not hungry. Is he coming back?"

"I don't know."

My mother's eyes were puffy the next morning. She gave us a stiff porridge for breakfast, and said that there was no need for us to go repeating to friends what had happened.

By the third day of my father's absence, my mother was going to the front window to look out whenever she heard a car, and I heard her tell sies Moena that perhaps she'd been wrong to throw the pan at him. Sies Moena first said that he deserved it, then suggested several ways to get him back, one of them being that my mother should go round to his work and tell him to come home. "I don't beg," my mother said. "He must come on his own." There was hope a week later when oemie Jaweier arrived with uncle Mietjie, my father's brother. They talked in the dining room with the door closed. When they left, there was a pocket of oranges on the table and an envelope with money in it. The envelope told me my father wasn't coming back.

A week or so later, I was playing with my doll on the stoep when I saw the Packard turn the corner into our street. I was so excited that I almost ran up to him, but he wasn't the kind of father with whom you could do this. He got out of the car and stood on the pavement, looking up at the house as if seeing it for the first time. His clothes were bright and airy, as if he was going on a holiday, and looked quite the opposite to the scarf wrapped tight like a bandage around my mother's head to hold in all her troubles.

"Where's Mummy?" he asked. He apparently remembered I was his child, but didn't kiss me or touch me. I didn't answer. He made some impatient sound with his tongue, and walked past me into the house.

I stayed on the stoep. I knew why he was there. It's funny how sometimes you know these things without anyone telling you. I slipped into my mother's room, found her bag on the dressing table, and took out a shilling. I left the house quietly, and walked towards

Pepper Street. I wasn't allowed to go to the shop, but I'd been to the café on Long Street with my sister and remembered big glass jars filled with Stars and toffee rolls and gum balls and bull's eyes. I had money to spend, and didn't want to go to motjie Janie's where someone was sure to see me.

I reached the corner and looked down the road. The weather had changed; I could feel the mist through the thinness of my dress, and couldn't see all the way into town. I walked down Pepper Street and reached a group of boys playing kennetjie. There was an argument going on with a girl who had woolly hair and a pair of black walkers without laces, and who was sitting in a very unladylike way on the pavement. "Why can't I play?" she asked. "I can play!"

"We don't play with girls," one of them said. I didn't know her then, but she was to become my best friend when I went to school for the first time a few months later. Alison.

I looked behind me to see if anyone was coming, and quickened my step. On Long Street, a long, long way down the hill for a six-year-old to go by herself, I entered the Portuguese café and waited for Mr da Costa to serve the people ahead of me. I had a chance to look at the covers of the comics and magazines hanging from an overhead line, and to decide which sweets I would buy. I didn't know how much I could get for a shilling, but imagined at least four toffee rolls. Toffee rolls were my favourite, and one toffee roll could last almost a whole afternoon if I wasn't greedy.

Finally there was just Mr da Costa with the thick eyebrows looking down at me from behind the counter. I felt he could see by my face that I'd stolen the money. I asked for the chocolate with the red wrapper. "The small one or the big one?" he asked. I placed the shilling on the counter to test its value. He placed the big bar in front of me. "What else?" I pointed to the stars, gum balls and prize packets. To my astonishment he placed all of these sweets in a brown paper bag together with the chocolate. I left the shop realising that I'd stolen a lot of money. I took the chocolate out of the bag and stood in front of a small furniture shop, pretending to be interested in the items in the window while I ate my stolen goods. The first few bites sent pleasure waves to my brain. After the sixth row of chocolate, I couldn't eat anymore.

My walk back up Pepper Street was filled with dread. The mist had got thick, my curls felt heavier, and I hardly noticed the girl playing kennetjie with the boys in the street. When I turned into Sachs Street, I looked to see whether the car was still there, but it wasn't. My worst fears were confirmed. My father hadn't come home. He'd come to our house for something, then left again. I didn't know what mood my mother would be in. I saw Kulsum and Fatima at their gate and talked to them.

"What's in the bag?" Kulsum asked. "Nothing," I replied. After a few minutes I went in. My half-eaten chocolate was in the bag with the other sweets. I flattened it against my side as I walked normally up the steps to the front door. The house was quiet except for the wireless playing in the kitchen. I passed my mother's room and stepped into the one I shared with my sister Murida. She was lying reading a comic book on the bed.

"Where were you? Mummy was looking for you."

"Where's Daddy?"

"He fetched his clothes. He's not coming back."

My heart squeezed at these words. I sat down on the bed, the brown bag crunching under my leg.

"What's that?" she asked.

"Sweets."

She put down her book and sat up. "Where'd you get them?"

"Daddy gave them to me." The hurt look on her face gave me pleasure. "He told me to share them with you."

She leaned forward to see what was in the bag. "You ate the chocolate," she said in an accusing tone.

"Not all of it. I kept half for you."

She tried to snatch away the bag. "Give it here."

I held on to it. "The chocolate's yours. The rest we have to share. There's only one prize packet."

"How do I know you haven't had one already?"

"Because I haven't, and I didn't even have to tell you I had it."

She grabbed the bag and it split in half, spilling gum balls and Stars on the floor.

My mother came in, a cross look on her face. "What's this?" she asked. "Your dress is all wet, and look at your hair. Where were you?"

I didn't have to look at my hair. It felt like a dragon on my head. "I was at the shop."

"The shop? Didn't I tell you that you mustn't go to the shop by yourself? And who gave you money for sweets?"

I couldn't bear to tell one more lie. All the way up Pepper Street I'd been worried that she'd know how much money was in her bag.

"Where did you get the money?" she asked again.

"Daddy gave her money," Murida said.

My mother waited for me to confirm it. I looked down at my feet hanging over the side of the bed. My black patent leather slip-ons – last year's labarang shoes, and now my everyday ones – had fallen to the floor. I noticed dirt under one of my toenails.

"Look at me!" she ordered. "Where did you get it?"

"I stole it. From Mummy's bag."

She raised herself up and stood so straight, her skirt corrected itself about her waist. "You took money from my bag?" The look on her face said she couldn't believe her child was a thief. "How much did you take?"

"A shilling."

"A shilling! Didn't I tell you what happens to children who steal?"

"Yes, Mummy."

"Then why did you do it?"

"I don't know." My heart thumped in my ears. I expected at any minute to feel my ear pulled or my bum whacked. But she didn't do anything.

"Pick up the sweets," she said. "Give them to the children out-side."

I stared at her. She surely couldn't mean it.

"What're you waiting for?" she asked. "Next time you steal, there'll be consequences. You didn't get a hiding because you told the truth. Next time even the truth won't save you."

My father came to the house today for his clothes. I went to the shop on Long Street. I was forced to give away my sweets. I told Kulsum to keep them for me.

~

Six weeks after her fortieth birthday, Alison got married for the second time. The nikkah was a small ceremony after sunset prayers with only the immediate family in attendance. Alison wore a cream sari and the ceremony started with a poem written and read by Leila, followed by a short khutbah.

Sitting on a couch next to aunty Mavis at the back of the room, Khadidja listened to the imam's words of advice to the new couple.

"Women are a garment unto men, and men are a garment unto women," he said. "In a sense you have to think of marriage as a mutual relationship, a mutual obligation. But marriage is something that needs to be worked on. It's not something that falls from heaven. Marriage is something that needs to be worked on on earth. A marriage is a structure that must be rebuilt every day. Perhaps somewhat of a daunting task, but it's true, otherwise we take each other for granted. So while I want to wish you happiness and love throughout, perhaps I should say also that if you do disagree with each other, may you also have a good disagreement. With these few words, I want to make a final do'ah."

Khadidja bowed her head in prayer, and nudged aunty Mavis to do the same. Out of respect for the occasion, aunty Mavis had on a scarf, and kept her cigarettes in her bag. The ceremony ended. They watched as the imam wished the couple good luck, and people started to go up to the front. Leila came towards them.

"Hello, Granny." She kissed aunty Mavis on the cheek. "My mother's done it again. Doesn't she look beautiful?"

"She looks lovely. That was a wonderful poem you wrote. Such wonderful things you said. I didn't even know you could write poetry. Are you happy that your mother's married again?" Her eyes squeezed tight as she coughed into a wad of tissues.

"I'm happy if she's happy." Leila leaned over and kissed Khadidja on the cheek. "She could've waited a few more months, perhaps, but at least she picked one with a brain. He's not bad. How's Aunty?"

"I'm fine, thanks. Mubarak," Khadidja wished her. "I think she and Imran look good together." She saw a boy come up behind Leila and wondered if this was the one Alison had caught her with in the car.

"This is the boyfriend," aunty Mavis said.

Khadidja shook his hand and listened to the exchange.

"Nadeem and I have a science project to complete, Granny. We're doing it at his house, it's too busy here."

"You must do your homework, but don't come home late. It's still your mother's big day." She turned to Alison when they were gone. "That child's the smartest of all my grandchildren."

Aunty Mavis obviously didn't know anything about the car episode, Khadidja thought. She would've bust a heel knowing what her grandchild had been up to in the back of a Honda. Still, Khadidja marvelled at the way Leila had blossomed so suddenly over the past months. Her understated manner with Nadeem showed that there was something between them. "Alison's masterpiece. I think she'll be accepted in the States. Alison said she wants to go to university there."

"I hope her father doesn't put up a fuss. I want her to go. I have some money saved, but don't tell the others. They already say I play favourites."

"What does aunty Mavis think about Imran?"

Aunty Mavis looked over at the man who'd just married her daughter. "Well, I never thought my Alison would end up with an imam's son, but when she brought him to my house the first time, I liked him. You know, some Muslims can be funny to Christians. They're nice to you, respectful and everything, but you know they don't really want to be your friend. I didn't feel that with him. He ate the sandwich I made him, he was friendly, and when he laughed, I saw his back teeth. He wasn't fake."

"Aunty Mavis likes him," Khadidja smiled, enjoying her philosophy.

"Yes. Good men are scarcer than fresh bread on Sundays, and when you're lucky enough to find one, you mustn't let anything mess it up. You and Alison think you know all the answers, you don't listen to your mothers, but your mothers know better than you. Alison listened to me this time. I said, don't play games with this man. Don't always be right. My Alison wasn't born Muslim, and she's a divorced woman with a child. How many men want that? They want eighteen and nineteen. And someone like him, so refined, an imam's son, and so good-looking – I could turn Muslim myself."

Khadidja laughed heartily.

"Anyway," aunty Mavis patted her arm, "you're next. Alison says you were dating this nice-looking boy, but it didn't work out."

"You can't eat looks, aunty Mavis. Looks can't pull a cover over you at night. He was hellbent on turning me into an Apostolic."

"An Apostolic?" Aunty Mavis started to cough again. "He's mad. Doesn't he know about the Muslims? They'll keep their foreskins before they change."

"What about your sister? Do you think there was any jealousy?"

"Well, sometimes I thought she was jealous of me, but I think I was more jealous of her. I hated it that I had this hair, and that people always made a big fuss of her just because of her looks."

"There was some sibling rivalry."

"Some. She wasn't everyone's favourite, though. She wasn't my great-grandmother's. And she wasn't smarter, although she did better than me in science and maths."

"And now?"

"Now we're adults," Khadidja laughed. "We're friends. Sometimes I still wish I could be a little like her, a bit more pliable, fit in more. I don't have her patience. She enjoys being a wife. Sometimes, though, she ticks me off. The other day she told my mother that Storm would never marry me. Why tell my mother? Is she God that she can make these predictions?"

"Maybe she doesn't want you to get hurt."

"I'm sure she doesn't."

"Do you think there's some rivalry now?"

"There is nothing for her to be envious about. She has a husband, she's happily married."

"You're a journalist, you'll soon be a published writer."

"Those things have never meant anything to her. And honestly, no one's impressed by them. Well, not family and friends anyway.

Muslims don't raise their children to be in the arts, not in this community anyway, and I've always been a bit of an outsider. They don't see me as creative – just odd."

"Do you think you liked Storm because he gave you back the missing years – your childhood? I mean, look at the things you did together. Reading to him in the morning. Playing with your foot. Splashing about in the ocean. And look how you met him. What was it he said to you at the gate?" She looked down at her notes. "*Just love, and a cup of coffee.* I don't hear these things every day. You come in here, and take me along on this journey, and it's such an adventure that I almost want to say, forget about the therapy, and go with the romance. Do you think you're only attracted to men who give you a rush?"

"I was married to Rudy. I was attracted at first. The one before him, though, Saville Eisenberg, had me by the short hairs. I think I married Rudy to get over him."

"Why?"

"Saville and I were too much the same. He was Jewish. We never spoke about it, but it was always there, between us. Then of course, the whole colour thing. He didn't have any hang-ups about it, but maybe his colleagues did. I went with him to restaurants and movies, but never to office functions. When his mother got ill in Israel, I was glad he went."

"So, two men out of the faith."

"There was also one in high school, and another one when I was a reporter, before I met Saville. The one in high school was Alison's brother, Mark. For a few months I was attracted to boys who had a record collection. High school stuff, nothing serious. The one when I was a reporter didn't care if he became a Hare Krishna. Religion wasn't an issue. I got bored."

"Have you dated any Muslim men?"

Khadidja's eyes narrowed as she tried to remember. "Oh sure. Bioscope, New Year's Eve parties, but no one I brought home to Mom."

"Except Rudy."

"Yes. And that happened so quickly. I was standing in a wedding dress before Saville could tear up his return ticket."

"You keep in touch with Saville?"

"Telephonically. I asked him to help Alison with her divorce."

Anna smiled. "Did you take him home with you?"

"Oh yes. My mother liked him. She liked to call him her Jewish son."

"Would you have taken him home if your father had been there?"

Khadidja's face darkened. "I don't know. I don't think so."

Two weeks after Alison's wedding, Khadidja boarded a plane with a group of tourists and went on a ten-day visit to Italy. At the airport, waiting for the connecting flight to Florence, she called Alison.

Alison had seen her off just thirteen hours previously, and was surprised to hear from her so soon. "How was your flight?"

"I'm not there yet. I'm at De Gaulle Airport. I sat next to this girl, Jennifer, who's also doing the tour. It passed the time a bit. I think this trip's going to be good for me, Alison. I should've done it a long time ago."

"I'm glad to hear it. You won't believe who called me at the office this morning. He said he'd been calling you at the house. When there was no answer and the answering machine didn't come on, he thought something had happened to you. He went over there, jumped the fence and looked in all the windows. He couldn't see anything. The bed was made up, everything looked tidy. And Sief wasn't there. So he called your office and they told him you'd gone overseas. I told him you did go, and that Sief was at my house for the time being. Your neighbour was keeping an eye on the place. He said he was with you the other day at the psychologist's office, and that you'd said nothing to him. He asked for your number overseas. I said I didn't have it; you were going to a hotel with a group of tourists. He wanted to know which hotel. I said I didn't know. He said, give me the number. I said even if I had it, I couldn't. He said, give me the flippin' number. What do you want me to tell him? I know he's going to call again."

Khadidja didn't have time to analyse this new development on an international line, but her heart pumped like a nervous puppy. "Nothing."

She boarded the plane for the short flight to Florence, and sat with Jennifer, thinking about Alison's conversation. The group consisted of twelve people in their thirties and forties. Overnight flights cut through layers of protocol and people found themselves familiar comrades or bitter enemies in the morning. After a long flight, and the stopover in France, the group had made friends, greatly aided by their tour guide, a tall Norwegian called Ulf with ice-blue eyes and silver locks.

"He keeps looking at you," Jennifer murmured.

"Looking's free," Khadidja said, not turning to look at the seat on the other side of the aisle. But she'd noticed his glances already at Cape Town airport. "He doesn't look the type to be escorting people around. I picture him more as a mountain climber, dangling from a cliff somewhere in the Himalayas."

Jennifer laughed. "True. And such a strange name. Ulf."

"Arnulf, it says on the card. Ulf. Ulfie wolfie."

"A gentle wolf," Jennifer giggled. "Cute."

Khadidja realised that Jennifer liked him. "We'll be together for almost two weeks. Maybe something will happen."

"I don't think so. He's not interested in me."

They arrived in Florence. Ulf organised transporation to the hotel. The trip had been a long one, but it was early afternoon, and they wouldn't waste it. They checked in, freshened up, and trooped off. In front of Palazzo Vecchio, Ulf gathered the group about him. It was June, the beginning of the Italian summer, and the square was full, the afternoon hot.

"In 1929 the foundations were laid for a palace which was to be the seat of the Priors of the Guilds and of the Gonfaloniere of Justice, the major governing bodies of Florence ..."

Khadidja was fascinated. She'd heard much about Italy's art and architecture and cathedrals and palaces, but hadn't imagined that they would be quite like this. And she changed her mind about Ulf. Ulf had a strange accent, but knew his history.

"... the site which was chosen was near the river and next to the old church of San Piero Scheraggio, and the land was bought from some private citizens. The space which was to form the square in front of the palace had once been the site of the houses of the Uberti family, rebels and Ghibellines. This space was therefore damned and never to be built on again. Because of this the building had to be built slightly irregularly and too close to the church …"

Like anxious children, they followed Ulf to the entrance, and waited in a long line to get into the palace.

"… bloody events continued to plague the building. In 1461, the brave captain of the Florentine army was thrown out of a window and decapitated on orders from the Gonfaloniere. In 1478, after the failure of the Pazzi conspiracy against the Medici, the conspirators, including the Archbishop of Pisa, were hanged from the windows of the palace."

The afternoon sped by in a whirl. Khadidja couldn't take it all in. A quick espresso in the square, and they proceeded to the Uffizi Gallery. The highlight for her that first day, however, wasn't the palace or the gallery or the cathedral with the high ceilings where you inserted lire into a machine and the history of the cathedral was cranked out in a monotone voice, but a modest building with a gold letterplate in downtown Florence.

"Dostoevsky really lived here?" she asked. "The author of *Crime and Punishment*?" Some of the others in the group were snapping pictures. She and Jennifer stood with Ulf on the other side of the road where they could admire the building from a distance.

"It is the house, yes. Dante's house is also in Florence. The building has been heavily restored, but it stands on the spot where Dante's family owned some buildings. And of course, you know, the prince of darkness – Machiavelli's grave is here too."

"Of course. He's Italian. I'd forgotten that."

"And in Tellaro, a few hours' drive from here, DH Lawrence had a cottage. It is there still. He came to Italy to write. We'll go to Lerici and Tellaro in the next few days – but Shelley and Lord Byron were also here. There's a bay named after Byron, Byron's Bay. You have an interest in these people? You are a writer?"

"Yes."

"What do you write?"

"I'm the editor of a women's magazine. I have a book coming out."

"It is on history or art?"

Khadidja laughed. "No, nothing so impressive. I make up stories.

People like to peer into other people's lives. Do you know a lot about art?"

"A little. Do you know a lot about tragedy?"

"No. But I have an imagination."

"I see. I have an imagination also, but not in the same way. I don't write books or anything like that – well, not works of fiction. You will not believe my real profession."

"This isn't what you do for a living?"

"No."

"Let me guess," Jennifer said. "You're really an undercover curator for a museum."

Ulf laughed. "I'm a lecturer in Historical Archaeology at Oslo University. Occasionally I get bored with the academic world and take on small adventures. This is one of them."

"But you came with us from South Africa."

"I have a guest room in Camps Bay. I work at the university only for six months of the year. I do not do this tour-guide thing for money. I do it for the experience and, of course, to meet people."

"Is it true that Europe is a land of atheists?"

He laughed heartily. "I don't know about the rest of Europe, but people in Norway – academics anyway – do not care much about religion. The church is run by the state. And of course there are religious people there, but I'm not one of them. Why? You're an atheist?"

"No, no. I would be too afraid to be an atheist."

Returning from their excursions in the evening, Khadidja would check with the hotel concierge to see if she'd received any calls. There were no messages. On their fifth evening in Florence, after a particularly exhausting train trip to Venice at seven in the morning, gondola rides, shopping, and arriving back after eleven, the concierge handed her a white piece of paper. At last, she thought. She went straight to her room to make the call to Alison.

"He called me at six o'clock the next morning," Alison said. "He sounded awful, like he hadn't slept, and at first I couldn't make out what he was saying. He said I mustn't tell you that he'd called and asked about you, and I wasn't to tell you that he'd asked for the number."

"What did you say?"

"I said I hadn't spoken to you."

Khadidja lost all enthusiasm for the trip after that, and couldn't wait for it to be over. To know that he had begged Alison for her telephone number, and then changed his mind the following morning. He was moving on. He was getting over her. She woke up in the morning feeling headachy and grumpy, and at night excused herself early from the group to lie on her bed.

The day before their return to Cape Town, Ulf suggested supper at Montepiano. "There is a wonderful restaurant in the mountains. The drive there is very scenic. We can spend our last evening in an old-fashioned, very fine family restaurant, sampling the finest green ravioli stuffed with walnuts, and the best mascarpone."

Khadidja was almost cheered, so happy was she to be going home the following day. In her own environment, she would know immediately if Storm had moved on. There would be no drive-bys, no messages on the answering machine. It would be better for her, and even better if he had found someone else. That way she would *have* to desist.

The restaurant in Montepiano was a large room in an old building set with round tables, white tablecloths and bowls of fresh flowers.

"What will you have, Khadidja?" Ulf asked after he'd obtained everyone else's order. She was seated next to him.

"Pick for me," she said. "I feel reckless."

"If you are feeling reckless, you will have a little Bacardi, then?"

"No," she laughed. "Not that reckless."

He turned to the waiter and spoke in Italian. The waiter was an older man in black pants and a white starched shirt. He listened to the order with hooded eyes, as if the godfather himself had just whispered into his ear. He made no notes, and returned twenty minutes later with everything.

Dinner took three hours. First, the antipasto arrived in small bowls kept warm by candles with low flames, served with fancy breads. Half an hour later, the ravioli, linguini, fettucini. Then the main course, veal cutlets and grilled steak. Khadidja had stopped eating after the ravioli.

"I am hoping that everyone has had a good time in Italy, and that you have all seen something to remember," Ulf said over cappuccino and dessert.

"I've enjoyed it immensely," a woman called Muriel said. "I've been on tours before, but have never had such an informed guide."

Compliments were hard for Ulf. "Italy has a lot to offer. I couldn't run out of things to show you."

"Will you do this tour again?" Jennifer asked.

"No, no. I will return to Norway in a few weeks. I'm doing an Atlantic crossing with a friend. Maybe in a few years' time, when I'm bored." He turned to Khadidja. "I hope you have enjoyed this trip, Khadidja."

"I have, very much. I'll recommend Italy. And you too, if you're still available."

His blue eyes warmed. "Tell me, do you live far from the Camps Bay mountains?"

She chuckled. She'd never heard them referred to as the Camps Bay mountains before. "I used to be quite near Camps Bay actually, when I lived in Bo-Kaap. Now I'm in Wynberg. Why?"

"There's a good opera coming up at the Nico. *Madama Butterfly*. I thought maybe – do you like operas?"

"I can't sit through all that corseted singing."

He laughed. "What about the ballet?"

"Same thing. I can only watch for a few minutes."

He looked disappointed. "That is a shame. I have these tickets, and now I don't know what I will do with them."

"Well, if you already have them, and you can't find anyone else, of course I'll go with you."

"I believe that you are a Muslim?"

"Yes."

"In Norway we do not know much about Muslims except what we see on the television and read about in the newspaper. I have met some Muslims in Cape Town and found them not to be terroristic at all. This man at the UCT, this professor, he has told me quite a few interesting things. I would like to know more about this religion. Does a Muslim man pray with his wife, is it allowed?"

The question was a new one. "He prays with his wife, yes, but they can also pray on their own. I can recommend a shop in Athlone if you would like some good books. Do you know Klipfontein Road at all?"

"Yes, but I cannot take in these details now. Can I call for directions when we're back in Cape Town? You have a telephone?"

On her first night home Khadidja drew all the curtains and kept the house in darkness except for the bedroom where she unpacked her suitcase. She had bought espresso coffee-makers for her mother and Alison, and a leather change purse for Leila for looking after Sief. She walked with these items in the dark to the living room where she put them on the couch to remind her to take them with her the next day.

The phone rang while she was in the bath. It was a cold winter's night. She was neck-high in foam, twitching her toes, feeling the heat radiate up her thighs, listening to the answering machine take the call. *This is Khadidja Daniels. I'm not able to take your call right now. You know what to do.*

"Titch, it's me. Mummy says you're back from your trip. Come by tomorrow afternoon for tea. It's Maan's birthday."

Khadidja thought about her sister and her family. How uncomplicated her sister's life seemed, she thought. Babies and birthdays and teas, and deciding what material to buy for the next couch she wanted recovered. Why hadn't she bought her sister a gift? Murida was thoughtful when it came to birthdays and anniversaries, and always managed to find interesting little things. Even when it was no special occasion, she would buy something that she thought someone might like – like the unusual silver bookmarker she'd seen at an antique book shop, and bought for Khadidja. She closed her eyes, luxuriating in the scented foam. Her body felt relaxed. The nausea had left. She felt almost hungry.

She stopped by Alison's house first the next day. Alison noticed immediately that she didn't look well. "There's no food in Italy? You look like you've lost weight."

"There's plenty of food. And good food too."

Leila was cutting a chocolate cake she'd baked. "You do look a bit pale, Aunty."

"It's a long trip, I'm tired. But I know how that sounds after just coming back from a holiday." She turned to Alison who was busy setting out cups and making tea. "How's the honeymoon going? Where's Imran?"

"Imran's got cricket at three. He went to pick up his son to take him with to the game."

"I didn't know he played cricket. Maybe he knows Rudy."

"He does. They're in different teams, but play against each other from time to time." She looked up curiously at Khadidja, and smiled. "I can see it in your eyes. You want to know if she's pregnant yet. No sign."

Khadidja watched Leila cut the cake and took the slice offered to her. "So Imran's met the wife, or seen her at least."

"She came to the game. A short little thing. I met her also."

"You did? You never told me. When?"

"While you were away. I was going to tell you. Big breasts, no spark. Plein soos môre die heel dag."

Khadidja forked a piece of cake into her mouth, and felt suddenly nauseous.

"Is something wrong?" Alison asked, seeing the expression on her face.

"It's not the cake," Khadidja said, getting up and walking quickly to the toilet.

Alison went after her and waited outside the door. "Are you all right?" She could hear vomiting, then the tap running. A few minutes later Khadidja emerged in somewhat of a daze. "It must be that pineapple I had this morning."

"You look green. Make an appointment with Marwaan. You should have a check-up. Maybe you caught something over there."

At Murida's house everything was laid out when Khadidja and Ateeka arrived. Thin porcelain plates with gold-leaf edging, crystal glasses, silver dessert forks and spoons. There were bowls of cashew nuts and nutty chocolates, baked chocolate eclairs with rich cream in the centre, a strawberry cheesecake, and delicate cheese and broccoli quiches.

"You must try the quiche," Ateeka said when they were all seated at the table. "It's one of Murida's new recipes. She uses butter-milk instead of cream."

"I'm tired of coconut tarts and chocolate cake," Murida said. She was always with her head in some new recipe book trying to get away from the old style of cooking so Maan could lose weight. Maan still ate his curries and bredies during the week, and doubled up on the light stuff over the weekend. The new diet had had the op-posite effect.

"I just had chocolate cake at Alison's." Khadidja lifted the baby from Riana's lap onto hers. "Can Kimmy have some?"

"Just a spoonful," Murida answered. "He hasn't eaten his lunch. See if he'll eat the quiche. This child just wants to eat sweets all day."

"Who gives them to him?" Faried asked.

"Not me," Murida said. "Your father. Look at him already, those fat cheeks."

It was an invitation for Khadidja to bite into them. Mustakim was ticklish, and squirmed with delight.

"How was Italy?" Murida asked.

"Italy was great. I have never seen so many castles and palaces and galleries before. We also had a fun group, and a great guide. A Norwegian."

"Did you meet any exciting men over there?"

"Only dead ones. I stood right in front of the house where Dos-toevsky once lived. You go to Italy and you realise this place has no history. This one place we were in, Tellaro, an old section, we walked in the shadows between these looming dark houses along narrow, winding alleyways. It had such an atmosphere, you could almost hear the grinding of carriage wheels on the cobblestones and expect a charioteer to come charging around the bend with plumed horses and whips."

Maan smiled. "Sounds like you had a great time. She's lucky to go to all these places, hey Ma? While we're stuck here working like slaves."

"And buying a new Mercedes Benz every year," Khadidja teased him. "You can go anywhere you want, with your whole family."

"What about Mecca?" Ateeka asked. "You mustn't wait till you're old." She turned to her eldest daughter. "You were going to tell her about Abdul."

"Oh yes, " Murida said. "Maan brought home this friend for supper the other night. He'd just lost his wife. No children. I said to Maan, now here's someone Titch might be interested in."

"All these men who've just lost their wives," Khadidja said. "What is it with them? They lose a woman and they have to have a replacement right away?"

Murida looked crestfallen. At forty-four, with her three-times-a-week-at-the-gym figure, she was still the better-looking sister with her dead straight hair now held back in a sleek ponytail touching the small of her back. Her earrings were black onyx and gold. Her outfit was a loose, aubergine Indian thing with pants, highlighting her rich creamy skin and the green in her eyes. "I haven't mentioned anything to him yet. I just thought, here's a nice man, very eligible, you might find him interesting. He's a dentist."

"Is it because he's a dentist or because he's interesting? You're assuming it's over with Storm."

"Isn't it?" Murida glanced at her mother. "It was just an idea – forget it."

"And telling Mummy that Storm wasn't going to marry me. Are you such an expert now, that you know this? And don't look at me like that, Ma. I don't care that she knows you told me. If you want to say something about the men I date, come to me. Don't go to Ma."

"You're out of turn," Ateeka said. "Your sister never meant anything."

"She never means anything, but she says a mouthful."

"Stop it now. It's Maan's birthday. What's wrong with you?"

Khadidja got up. "What's wrong with me is that I'm sick of everyone discussing me behind my back. Storm's my affair." She turned to her brother-in-law. "I'm sorry for spoiling your birthday, Maan."

"Don't worry about it. Sit down." He got up and put his arm around her. "I don't know anything about this business with Storm. I liked him when I met him. Murida just thought it might be nice if you met Abdul. She only wants you to be happy."

"I'm not upset about that, it's that she went to talk to my mother about it. What does she know about Storm? What's her real reason for going to my mother? Is she looking to score points? My whole life she's done that, squealing behind my back."

Murida turned red. She glanced at her children. It was clear from her expression that she was shocked by her sister's outburst.

"You're blowing this thing out of proportion and behaving badly," Ateeka said. "Not everything's a dark mystery, and that skepsel's no mystery at all. We can all see plain as day that he's not interested at all in Islam, only in changing you. That first day I saw him get out of the car with those wet clothes, I thought, here's someone who can take care of my child. He has good manners, he's a hard worker, he knows how to speak to people, and I see how he is with you. But it can't work. It'll never work. He has no respect for other people's beliefs, and he'll grind away at you until there's nothing left. Even if you were to marry him, you won't be happy for long."

Khadidja watched her nephew and niece looking down at their plates. She'd embarrassed their mother and spoiled the birthday party. She wanted to say she was sorry, but couldn't bring herself to do it. And what her mother had just said – what was the point of trying to explain that she'd said this herself?

She picked up her bag from the couch, leaving behind the red shawl she'd bought for herself in Florence and giftwrapped for her sister. "Thanks for that wonderful do'ah, Ma."

Her first week back after the trip was quiet. There were no phone calls, no surprise visits. She had told him to buzz off, yet couldn't understand why she was depressed. He had never stayed away from her before. Even if it was just a drive by the house on his bike or in his rubble truck, he'd always made contact. But there was no contact now, and she found herself looking longingly towards the fire station to see if she could catch a glimpse of him in the yard. Every time she heard the truck arrive, she ran to the window and looked out. But it was as if he had disappeared.

Then there was her rude behaviour at her sister's house, which still plagued her. She didn't call anyone to apologise, but sent a fancy fruit basket with biscuits and jams to her sister with the note, *Hope all is forgiven. Come for lunch on Sunday. One o'clock.*

Her mother called to say Murida was pleased with the offering, and thrilled with the red cashmere shawl Khadidja had bought for her in Italy. Khadidja wasn't to let on that she knew, but Murida had already gone out to a safari shop for two cream cushions with tigers she thought would look good on Khadidja's green couch. "She's a good sister," Ateeka ended. "You mustn't be so nasty to her."

"She always goes behind my back to you, Ma. Khadidja spoke to a Christian boy on the phone. Khadidja took a frikkadel out of the pan. Khadidja was rude to Daddy. My whole life."

"Those things were when you were children. She's grown-up now and cares about you very much. She's happy, she wants you to be happy. Is there something so wrong with that?"

"Well, I'm glad she's happy. I'm not like her, Ma. I've never been like her. But I'm sorry I was rude. Especially in front of the children. I'll make it up to them on Sunday."

A few evenings later Khadidja was in her garden with a spade and a rake scooping up dog mess when she heard the bike at the gate.

"Riempie ... you're back ..."

She turned slowly at the sound of his voice.

"You're a worm, Riempie. You left without telling me anything, and went to Italy."

She came to stand at the gate, hoping he couldn't hear the thump in her chest. "How're you?"

"I missed you like hell these past few weeks." His eyes had a desperate look in them, like one who'd not slept for days.

She felt like touching him, biting his mouth. All her most carefully rehearsed rebuffs and retorts, all Anna's advice, counted for nothing. "I missed you too."

A smile curled the corner of his mouth. "Open up, Riempie." He rattled the gate slightly. "Let me in."

She took out the key and unlocked it. He leaned his bike against the post and circled his arms about her. "Oh, God," he sighed, "I can't believe I'm here again." He walked her into the house and held her away from him to look at her. "I can't be without you, Riempie. I thought I could when you went away, but I can't." He moved her towards the couch and sat her down on his lap. "Promise me you won't do this again. You won't go away anywhere without telling me."

She put her arms around his neck. "I promise." Her mother's words popped briefly into her head. *He'll grind away at you until there's nothing left.* Her mother was wrong, she thought. She didn't understand. She didn't know the gravity of the feelings that existed between them. It wasn't a passing fancy. It was something deep and connected, beyond her control. She touched her finger to his mouth, along his bottom lip, peering into his eyes – like an inquisitive child.

"What did you do in Italy, Riempie? Did you go by yourself?"

"I went with a group, and a tour guide. We were based in Florence and went every day to a different place. I saw the Leaning Tower of Pisa. We had gondola rides in Venice. Venice is beautiful, in a seedy kind of way. We saw Byron's Bay, Tellaro, Lucca, and of course all the palaces, galleries, cathedrals and castles you can wish for."

He smiled, happy to listen to her. She told him about Ulf and the other people in the group, and the places they'd visited, ending with their last evening in the mountains in Montepiano. "I had a great time," she concluded, "but home is home. I'm happy to be back."

He sat for a moment holding her close to him again. "Riempie? When're you going to give me your koekie again? I haven't had sex for a while."

"For a while? What do you mean, for a while?"

He looked sullen.

"What do you mean, for a while, Storm? You didn't say six weeks ago, or since we broke up, or since the last time. You said for a while."

"You told me to bugger off, Riempie. You told me you didn't want me anymore. You went away and left me here all by myself."

"Were you with someone?"

He didn't answer.

"Were you with a woman, Storm?"

He looked at her with hooded eyes. "There's this neighbour across the street. He invited me to coffee one morning."

"Yes?"

"His daughter was visiting from Jo'burg. She'd left her husband and was looking for a place to stay. I told her my boarder had moved out, I had a room for rent."

"Go on."

"She came to look at it. She wore shorts."

"I'm listening. Go on."

"She had these tight little titties, Riempie ..."

For a moment she couldn't say anything.

"You told me to bugger off. I tried to forget you. You can't get mad at me now. I'm being honest."

She got off his lap. "Get out of my house."

"Riempie ..."

"Get out!" She pulled him up by his jacket, and shoved him towards the front door.

"Don't be so violent, Riempie, you're scaring me. What did you want me to do?"

"Get out!" she screamed, opening the door, and walking ahead of him to unlock the gate. "And don't come here again!"

In Anna's office the next day Khadidja poured out the whole story. Anna listened to her describe her behaviour at her sister's house, her feelings of remorse, the willingness with which she opened the gate to Storm a few days later and again invited misery into her life.

"I can't behave myself at a birthday party, and I can't say no to a man. I mean, I told him to bugger off, yet I was outraged that he went with someone else. What did I expect? I'm stupid, and juvenile, and weak. That's the real Khadidja. The selfish Khadidja, the jealous Khadidja, the needy and desperate Khadidja, who wants love so desperately that she's willing to sell her soul."

"Will that Khadidja compromise her faith for a man?"

"Never."

"Then don't be so hard on yourself. Tell me how you feel right at this moment."

"Like a rodent with no hole to slip into. I don't know if it's rage, disappointment, disgust. I'm angry."

"Anger is a seductive negative emotion, but it can help you. Right now you need to be angry."

"I feel so betrayed, and yet I don't know who betrayed me. If I betrayed myself. I'm upset with my family, yet they're all right. And it's that they're right, and that I know they are, that gets me. I don't know what I'm feeling, honestly."

"You're experiencing the same feelings now as when you were a child. Remember what you told me about standing on the stoep when your father's car left? This is the same – what I call the small little abandonments. We all have them from time to time, but for some of us, they're triggered by painful childhood memories."

Khadidja closed her eyes and listened.

"The relationship with Storm is an attempt to correct the past. There's this theory of the baby who gurgles happily when his mother comes into the room, and becomes apprehensive when she leaves. He's not sure that she's coming back, so he tests it. Every time she leaves, he reels out the yo-yo, and when she returns, draws it back in. In and out, in and out, until he feels safe. Your father left when you were very young. You never felt safe after that. Storm doesn't want to leave you, or so it appears. So you reel out the yo-yo to test it. Will he leave his church for you? Will he quit his leaders? No matter how the two of you fight, he always comes back. There's safety in that. Unfortunately, it's all an illusion. The safety's not real, or not lasting. Just like your father, he's unattainable."

"Are you're saying that I picked him deliberately?"

Anna nodded. "We know the psychological make-up of someone when we first meet them. You recreated your childhood with Storm, and that part's wonderful and healthy, but you're also looking to fix the past. We do that when we've been hurt. Children blame themselves for their parents' break-up. They think it's their fault. If only they'd done this or that. But it has nothing to do with them." She paused to see if Khadidja understood. "So you stay in the relationship so you can reject him over and over again. You also stay because to leave would mean that you've failed again."

"I won't be predictable. I won't stay."

"Good. This isn't about Storm, Khadidja, it's about you. I can help you to reach the place you need to be to get over him, but you have to work with me. It's the pain we try to avoid that keeps us trapped. Forget about what he did. It's not helping you. You're here for you, not for him. He's also trying to break away."

"He's the one calling and coming around."

"Eventually he'll stay away. But you must also want him to stay away. Next week I want to try a bit of hypnosis to relax you. I want to know more about when you were a child."

Khadidja went home, fed the dog, and got straight into bed. In the morning she counted five calls from Storm on the answering machine. She had decided to let the answering machine take all her calls. She made coffee and buttered two slices of toast. The smell of the coffee nauseated her, and she poured it down the sink. She left for work without eating anything.

For a week she kept the curtains drawn all day. After work, she went to visit Alison, her mother, went to movies with Riana and Faried, and adhered closely to Anna's advice. *Give up the need to know why things happen the way they do, Khadidja. The wound's not the problem. It's the power of the wound. We don't want to give up the language of wounds. Storm's a victim. Give up your victim consciousness. Don't be a victim too.*

Storm started to appear at the gate. When she came out to feed the dog, or to water the lawn in the evening, or to get the post, there he was, on his bike or in his truck. "All I want to be is your friend, Riempie. Why can't we be friends?" Friends now, she thought, after everything? Friends? What kind of friends could they be?

Sometimes she continued with what she was doing, sometimes she asked how he was. A week later, she was desperate for his company. Why couldn't she be his friend? She didn't have to let him into the house; they could talk about ordinary things. She turned off the answering machine. The phone rang and she was talking to him.

"Can I see you for half an hour, Riempie? I miss you and I know you miss me."

"How do you know I miss you?"

"I can smell it from here."

"You can smell that I miss you?"

"We're animals, Riempie. We have senses. I just want to see you, for half an hour. I miss the living room, your books, your nonsense. Just half an hour."

"No."

"Then talk to me for a few minutes."

So you reel out the yo-yo and test it. "What do you want to talk about?"

"Tell me about the book. I don't know what's happening."

"It's coming out in six months."

"You'll be a real writer, Riempie, an author. I don't think working for a magazine is the same thing."

"The reviews will tell. Listen, I have a pot on the stove, I must go."

By Friday of the following week, she'd got used to his calls, and was back talking to him like old times. At the end of their conversation there was the same question – could he come and see her for half an hour – with the same reply. On Friday evening, she was tired and cranky. It had been a day of deadlines and catastrophes. She'd also contracted a bad cold. Her plan was to have the chicken soup her mother had made, and go straight to bed. When the telephone rang, she walked with the tissue box in her hand to answer it.

"Riempie ... how're you?"

"I'm sick."

"What's wrong?"

"I don't know. A sore throat, I think. And a headache."

"Do you have lemons?"

She thought about it. "I have a lemon tree at the back of the property."

"Go out and pick some. I'll make you a drink."

"You can't come here, Storm."

"Just half an hour, Riempie. I'll make you a hot lemon drink, and then leave. You're sick. Just let me come for an hour."

"An hour? I say no to half an hour, and you ask for an hour?"

"Just for an hour, Riempie. I'll make the drink, talk to you for a bit, then leave."

She looked at the clock. It was ten to eight. Her body ached for her bed. "Half an hour. That's it."

Ten minutes later she went out to unlock the gate. He broke his first promise at the front door when he took her in his arms, and refused to let go.

"You have to go to bed, Riempie," he steered her towards the bedroom. Khadidja watched him pull back the covers on the bed, draw back the curtains, and open all the windows. "We need air in this room. You need lots of fresh air."

She let him go about fussing and fiddling. His strangeness was a drug. He was taking charge. Taking off her clothes, helping her into bed. Slipping in beside her. Holding her. Kissing the top of her head like a dear, dear friend.

"Where's my lemon drink, Storm?"

He went out to the yard. A few minutes later she heard him rattle around in the kitchen. He came in with a mug of steaming lemon.

"Drink this, Riempie. I put in three sugars."

She sat up and tried to sip the hot liquid. "It's too hot."

"Take off your nightie, you don't need it."

"I'm cold. The windows are open."

"I'm here. I'll hold you."

She slipped the nightie over her head. *He makes you feel safe. You never felt safe as a child.*

"The hour's almost up, Storm."

"Stop it, Riempie. I'm staying. Drink up."

When she was done, he put out the light and held her. She curled up under his arm. Her nose was blocked, but she could smell him. A lick under his armpit, and she balled up into herself like a contented kitten. *Please, God … this is all I want … let this be a new beginning.*

In the middle of the night, she woke up. His arm was circled around her waist, his ankle hooked around hers, his mouth in her hair. She moved against him. He stirred. She turned around.

" … like this, Riempie …?" he touched her.

She was soaked in their juices. "Yes, Storm …"

All night he loved her, stroking her, kissing her, taking nothing for himself. She was delirious – sick with flu, but happy to be so greedily loved. Close to dawn she woke up with a tight throat. The sheets had come off and she was shivering. She sat up, watching his sleeping face in the dark. He woke up.

"What's wrong, Riempie?"

"My throat's sore, I can't swallow. I feel really bad. I should've slept in my nightie."

He looked about in the dark. "I'll make you something to drink."

"Thanks." She heard the back door open. He was going out to pick more lemons. She dozed off, shivering under the sheets, which felt cold to her now. She wanted to put on her nightie, but knew he wouldn't want it. Minutes later, he appeared with the drink, and sat on her side of the bed.

"Drink this, you'll feel better. When the chemist opens at nine, I'll get you some medicine."

She snuggled back under his arm and fell instantly asleep. Some time later she was woken up by a sound. She opened her eyes. It was daylight. He was standing in front of the window with a mug of coffee, looking out, agitated.

"What's wrong?"

"I can't lie in this bed all day. I have to see what's going on at home. I'll come back at nine when the chemist opens."

Her throat felt raw, her head ached. The smell of the coffee nauseated her, and she raced out of bed to the toilet.

He sat on the bed listening to her throw up down the hall. A few minutes later she emerged, looking worse than before. "Riempie, you look awful. You're really sick. Go back to bed. Can I get you something?"

"No. Just some flu pills when the chemist opens." She pulled the nightie over her head and got back under the covers. "Take the key and let yourself out."

When she heard the door close behind him, she succumbed to her illness and drifted off. Almost immediately, it seemed, the telephone rang.

"Riempie, it's nine. How're you now? Do you still want the medicine?"

She struggled to wake up completely. "Yes," she croaked. "I need Corenza and something for my throat. Come here first, I'll give you the money."

Ten minutes later, he rang the bell. He had the key, but didn't want to enter the house without knocking.

She got out of bed and glanced at herself in the hallway mirror. Her eyes were sunken in her head, her face puffy. But it was nothing like the wretchedness she saw when she opened the door and found him standing there with a scowl on his face. She was too ill to ask what was wrong.

"Come in. I'll get the money."

He followed her into the bedroom and leaned against the bedpost while she searched through her handbag for money. She counted out sixty rand and gave it to him. "That should be enough."

He took the money, but the Storm of the previous night was a different one from the one who stood in front of her now, pinched and uncomfortable, a dark look on his face.

"I'm not going to see you today. I'm going to watch the rugby," he said suddenly.

She looked at him, confused. She never asked him about his plans.

"I want to be by myself. I want to drink beer and champagne whenever I want. You don't allow me to drink. You don't want to become an Apostolic. I can't love you. I *can't* be your partner. You mustn't think of me as someone in your life. Do you understand? I shouldn't have come here last night."

A pee drop escaped and rolled down her leg. "What're you talking about?" She was shivering, frightened. Somewhere deep inside her an old pain returned.

"I'm not for you, Riempie. I can't love you. You must forget about me. Find yourself a Muslim man and go on with your life."

The words spread like a cold tide over her sick body. She put her hands to her face and lay down on the bed, turning away from him.

"Did you think me coming here and staying with you meant we're together again? It was a mistake."

She heard nothing more. Not the money he put back down on

the table, and not the door as it closed behind him. She lay in bed like a wounded animal. Mercifully, she fell asleep. At some point the telephone rang. She surfaced to darkness. She'd slept away the whole day. Her hand reached for the receiver.

"Khadidja? It's me, Storm."

She held the phone to her ear, hearing only some of the words. "I'm very sorry. I know I hurt you. I can't be what you want me to be, but I want to be your best friend, and your lover."

She put the phone down. It rang again. "Don't hang up. It's me, Riempie. I'm so sorry. If you believe in God at all, you *have* to forgive me."

She reached down and pulled the extension out of the wall.

Close to midnight she got up and sat on the side of the bed with her feet touching the cold floor. Her head felt like a bag of marbles, her ears hurt when she swallowed. There was no medicine. The house felt cold and unfriendly. She sat shivering in the cold air wafting in from the window. Her eyes adjusted to the dark and she found her tracksuit pants and sweater where he'd tossed them onto a chair. She put on her shoes, threw a toothbrush into a bag, and got in her car.

The house on Sachs Street was in darkness when she arrived. After a second ring, her mother opened the door.

"Tell me about the pain you're feeling. Where do you feel it?"

Khadidja sat in a crumpled heap in the corner of Anna's couch. There were circles under her eyes, a cold sore on her lip. A box of tissues was beside her.

"I feel it like a wound. A physical pain, almost like pleasure. You can't see it, but you become aware of it, like a second skin. You challenge it. You tell it to hurt you, to rip your guts out so you never forget how it feels."

"What did you say to him?"

"Nothing. I stood there. I didn't know him. *I can't love you. Get yourself a Muslim man and go on with your life.* I can't tell you how I felt." She closed her eyes, and opened them again slowly. "I trusted this thing between us. How someone can swear that he can't be without you, how he can go to church six times a week, then do these horrible things."

272

"That's the contradiction."

"I didn't want to see him. He insisted. *Half an hour, Riempie*. The whole night he holds me and loves me and looks after me. The next morning he throws me to the dogs."

"He has no impulse control. He didn't plan to stay the night when he called. Remember what he did with the boarder? Impulse. The first night at your house when he got into your bed after drinking champagne? Impulse. The neighbour's daughter? Impulse. The black girl he stopped in the street and asked to come and work for him, then had sex with her, and the next morning, fired her? Impulse. A study was done in the sixties in America with four-year-olds to test the struggle between impulse and restraint. The kids were told they could have two marshmallows if they could wait for the experimenter to run an errand first, or one marshmallow immediately if they didn't want to wait. Some of the children took the one marshmallow immediately. Some of them were able to wait the ten or fifteen minutes, and got two. A decade or so later these same children were tracked down to see how they'd fared. Those who had resisted temptation were more socially competent, trustworthy, dependable, better able to cope with the frustrations of life, and had no fear of entering projects and sticking with them. The ones who'd grabbed the marshmallow tended to have fewer of these qualities and were more likely to shy away from social contact. They were stubborn and indecisive, easily frustrated, thought of themselves as bad or unworthy, and were still unable to delay gratification. Storm has difficulty with his emotions. He acts, then regrets. It's a constant pattern in his life. He doesn't know emotional wrongs. The church is the glue that keeps him from blowing his brains out. I don't think he set out deliberately to hurt you, Khadidja, he's not nasty like that. He struggles with his evil ways, as he puts it. The reality is that he'll continue to hurt you."

Khadidja looked down at her hands. "I should've listened to my mother."

Anna smiled understandingly. "There are a lot of should'ves and could'ves, it's all part of the fight with yourself. But it's a process, Khadidja. It took months to get into this, it's going to take time to get out. Sometimes we have to revisit the scene to see what we've left behind. Storm had to come back to convince himself that he couldn't continue. You too had to go back. Maybe you'll go back again, and again. Maybe you'll even decide to stay. That, too, is your choice."

"Did I imagine that he loved me? Was it all in my head?"

"He loved you, and he still loves you. But he doesn't need you the way he needs the church. There's less pain giving you up."

He doesn't need you the way he needs the church. The words buzzed in her ears. She walked down the flight of stairs, and came onto the square, a busy marketplace in the centre of town. A man standing at one of the stalls examining a wooden African mask caught her attention. What made her give him a second glance were the sunglasses, the dark hair, the suit. He wasn't a banker or a lawyer, or even a South African; he was a foreigner. She could tell that from the way he stood. As if aware of her watching him, he looked up. His stance changed, his look singled her out and became that of an old bull, watching, awaiting the next move. She held his gaze and continued in his direction, slowly, aware of the picture she cut in her fitting canary-yellow dress, her wild hair flowing out behind her. She glided towards him, watched him put down the mask. His chin lifted slightly. He stepped into her path.

"I'm at the Cape Sun," he said, depositing a card in her hand. She looked at the card, then at him. Her mouth curved up on the right, hardly a smile.

"I'll wait. Until six o'clock."

She sailed past him. Her office was on the other side of the square. She looked back at him briefly and continued to walk on. From her window on the fifth floor, she looked out. He was gone. She'd dreamt it, she thought. But the card was still in her hand. At her desk, she couldn't concentrate on her work. She kept looking at the clock. At twenty past four, she left the office. It was a five-minute walk to the Cape Sun Hotel. She asked for the room number. When she knocked on the door, it was opened immediately. The sunglasses were off and she could see the cold, blue, arrogant eyes of a man she knew had seen and done things she would be afraid to write of.

"You are the most beautiful woman I have seen in South Africa. Won't you come in?"

She arrived home after eight and listened to the messages from Storm and her mother on the answering machine. She felt numb. The scene in the hotel room played over and over in her head. The Rocky Whore Show. It even had music from *The Bold and the Beautiful*.

The phone jarred next to her. She stared at it dumbly.

"Titch, it's me, Alison. If you're there, pick up."

She stepped out of her dress and walked to the bathroom to run water into the tub. When it was filled, she sank into it. With her chin above the steaming foam, she closed her eyes and listened to Albinoni's organ and violin composition of grief drifting in from the living room. She'd discovered the healing properties of Albinoni when she'd left Rudy. In no time she was crying. Gently at first, then loud, wracking sobs. How long she stayed in the bath, she didn't know. The music had stopped, the water was cold. She heard the doorbell, then banging on the door. Dripping water onto the floor, she walked naked to the living room and peeped out behind the curtains. It was Alison. She opened the door. Alison followed her back to the bathroom where she lowered herself into the tepid water.

"Titch, my goodness." Alison sat down on the edge of the tub. "I've been calling for days. I've left messages. Where've you been?"

Khadidja shivered under the water. "Do you know what I did today?"

"What?"

"I picked up a stranger in Greenmarket Square. He told me to come to his hotel room. I drank champagne. I let him fuck me."

Alison stared at her with an open mouth.

Khadidja covered her face with her wet hands, her body shaking under the water.

"Come on, you have to get out." Alison dipped her hand in, pulled out the plug, and turned on the hand spray. Khadidja allowed her to run the hot spray over her, washing the soap out of her hair. Alison wrapped the towel around her shivering body and helped her

out of the tub. "You can tell me now. Let's first get you into bed."
She walked Khadidja to her room, pulled back the bed covers, and
tucked her in.

"What happened? Tell me everything."

Khadidja took a tissue from the box on the bedside table and
blew her nose. "It started on Friday night. He wanted to see me, just
for half an hour."

"Who? Storm?" She lay back against the headboard listening, re-
arranging a pillow under her head. Khadidja neared the end of the
story.

"It was our best night together. I was sick with flu, but so happy.
And just like that the next morning, he tells me: *I want to be alone. I
can't love you. I don't want to love you. Don't think of me as a husband
for you.*"

"Fucker."

"Right after he'd spent the night. Then he had the nerve to call
and say he was sorry, and could he be my best friend and my lover.
After all he'd just done. He had to be forgiven so he could have a
normal day while I lay in bed, gorging on my grief. I don't know
what time I got up, somewhere in the middle of the night, and
went to my mother. I stayed there until the next night. I only went
home for Sief. He had water but no food."

"You told your mother what happened?"

"Everything. She slept next to me and held me, and didn't say
once that she'd told me so."

"And the psychologist?"

Khadidja closed her eyes for a moment. "She said he has no impulse control. His neural circuitry's fucked. He still loves me, but
doesn't need me the way he needs the church. It was after I heard
that, leaving her office, that I saw the man in the square. I can't explain it. It was like I'd stepped out of myself – I was drawn to him.
It was out of my control. He handed me a card, I went to his room.
We didn't talk. I was aware of everything. Taking off my clothes,
drinking champagne. It was animal-like and visceral. Afterwards,
he put two hundred Deutsche Marks next to my bag. I took it. I
was a slut, why not go the whole way? It added to my disgust. I got
in the car and drove home. I can still smell the stink of my crime."

Alison looked at her for a long time before she spoke. "You know, you have to forgive yourself. You were in a lot of pain."

"I was aware of everything playing out before me. I did it knowing it was wrong. I wanted to do it. Like the night of the accident. I knew I'd smoked too much dagga, I knew I shouldn't have taken that drink from Claude, yet I did, and I got in the car and drove. I was breaking the rules, Alison, like I always did, and your kid died."

Alison closed her eyes.

Khadidja continued. "You tell me I have to forgive myself. Are *you* going to forgive me? You never talk about that night. Every year, on Nazli's anniversary, I feel the pain with you. You don't share it with me."

Alison looked at the drawn curtains in the room, a faraway look in her eyes. "It was long ago, Titch. I've forgiven both of us for that night. If I was angry with you, I was angrier with myself."

"*Were* you angry with me?"

"Yes."

The telephone rang. They listened to Khadidja's recorded message on the answering machine. They could hear breathing. The person calling didn't leave a message.

"That's probably Storm," Alison said.

"Probably. Do you want to talk about that night?"

"We just have. It's over, Titch, in the past. I think of her still, but it gets easier. That's why I'm so paranoid sometimes over Leila. I would go mad if something happened to her." Alison turned to look at her. "What're you going to do now?"

Khadidja sighed. "Start again."

"I know what that feels like. You don't think you'll ever come out of it, but you do."

"Did you really move on, Alison? Are you really over Farouk, or was Imran your drug to buffer the pain?"

"He was, in a way, and I knew it when I met him, but so what? It wasn't a fling, and I know I have work still to do. I have my days when I still hurt when I think of how Farouk betrayed me, but I don't want him back, and every day I think of him less and less." She put her feet under the blankets. "Imran's easy. He's the same every day. Did I tell you he's a hiker? He goes away for a week once a year with four guys, and they do a long hike. He wants me to go with them next month on a two-day hike in the Drakensberg. He bought me a pair of hiking boots."

Despite her misery Khadidja managed a smile. "The imam's son. A hiker."

"Yes."

Khadidja sank deeper under the blankets. Her body felt warm, the pain had gone away. She could close her eyes and fall asleep. "I'm glad you got the right man, Alison, and I'm glad we're friends. Men can't have friendships like women. If they could, they'd be honest with one another. Honest like *we* mean honest, with the heart. We fight, we disagree, but we're not mean. They're mean. They tell you they don't want to hurt you, then twist the knife in till it bleeds. I'm glad Imran's different. At least one of us got it right. When I first met him that night at your house, I thought, what's this girl up to? She's on the rebound, she's just lonely. Well, it proves something. With some people, it's the right thing right away and it works."

> *Dear Storm*
>
> I've decided not to return your calls, but I want you to know what you've done, and how it all started. Remember that first day you brought that champagne into my house? I begged you not to do it, and told you it would bring bad luck. And look what happened. Your insistence, your need to get your own way, and everything flows in a different direction. It's not my plot anymore. You're doing the directing, I'm acting out the scenes. Little by little, a piece of me comes away …

"Did you send it?"

"I never send any of my letters."

"Why'd you write it?"

"It stops me from calling."

"Are you weakening?"

"I've never been strong."

"He hurt you."

"I know."

"He'll continue to hurt you."

"He came by my gate this week."

"What did you do?"

"I didn't go out. I know what he wants. He wants me to forgive him."

"Are you going to?"

"I don't know. I prepare all these things in my head that I'll say to him, and I don't."

"What kind of things?"

"To fuck off, to stand on the white line on the M3."

"Why don't you?"

"I won't mean it."

"What does this mean?"

"You're the psychologist. It means I sit by myself on the couch at nights and don't flippin' understand why I can't have him."

"It's good to be angry, but you're not angry enough. Do you like writing the letters?"

"They help me cry. That, and Albinoni's Adagio in G Minor. Afterwards, I put the letters in a drawer. I read them until I grow bored with my own anger."

"Have you made the sign?"

"Yes. HE DUMPED YOU. I like that better than BE NICE TO YOUR-SELF. It's taped to the kitchen cupboard and the bathroom mirror."

"Anything that will help you stay focused. You must conjure him up as the devil. Think of him with horns sprouting out of his head, boogers in his nose, anything. Get yourself to a place where if you think about him, you feel nauseated."

"I don't have to do that to feel nauseated. I'm throwing up practically every day. I have a doctor's appointment on Friday to see why I feel so bilious all the time. I'm not getting enough sleep."

"When do you think you started to write?"

"When I was a child. Even when I couldn't spell properly, I liked to put down my thoughts. Some of those thoughts got me into trouble when they were discovered. I was truthful on the page, especially the letters. The stories were where I could be a liar, a creator, a doodmaker, without guilt."

"Did you have evil thoughts as a child?"

"Oh yes. The biggest one was that I wished for my father to die."

Khadidja arrived at Marwaan Hendricks's surgery in Walmer Estate just as the last patient was leaving.

"It must be a year since you've been here, Titch," he said, removing his stethoscope from around his neck, sitting down with the air of someone who was glad the day was over. They had gone to high school together and were old chums.

She looked around the surgery with its bottles and ointments and medical supplies. "You don't look like you've missed me," she laughed. "Look how busy you are. How's the family?"

"The family's okay. How's your mother?"

"Good. Mouthy as ever. Cheats on the diet. So have I been eating a lot of wrong things. I've been feeling crappy lately. Listless and nauseous. It started during my trip to Italy. The throwing up's not so bad now, but my breasts are sore, my pee smells different, I'm eating a lot of junk. Unless I go to my mother or sister, I seldom get out the pots to cook."

He led her to the examining table. "Let me take a look." He peered down her throat, listened to her heart, took her blood pressure, checked her breasts, pressed her abdomen in a few places, then handed her a small plastic container to take with her to the toilet.

She came back and handed him the urine sample. He tested it at a side table, then returned to his desk.

"What is it?" she asked.

"You're pregnant."

"Pregnant?" She stared at him. "How can I be pregnant? You know how I've struggled to fall pregnant. How many times haven't you taken my urine, and given me pills, and done tests? I'm no ways pregnant. It can't be."

Dear Storm

I don't get it. You give me up for the church, yet you can't stay away from my house. I could understand if we had different Gods, if I worshipped idols, but not even for God did you dump me, but for a handful of men. Men you call apostles and prophets, men you believe have been selected by God to save the world. Six times a week you go to church. What for? You go to the Bible for guidance, then use it to back up your promiscuity. The flesh is weak, Riempie, I get a sniff, and I want it. Men can't be without it. It's not wrong if she wants it and I want it also. Where does it say it's wrong? It doesn't say anywhere in the Bible that if she's not forced, and she likes it, that it's a sin.

Wrong, Storm. It *is* a sin. To the person who's left hurting. It's easy to say the flesh is weak. You have no control, no limits. You don't respect boundaries. The church is an addiction. Like your drinking, your sexual exploits. You're this frightened little boy with a swollen prick who needs a preacher to put in a good word so you don't get sent to the principal. It doesn't work that way. The preachers and apostles can't help you. God doesn't have third party arrangements. You fuck up, you foot your own bill ...

Driving home along Rosmead Avenue, she saw the bike first. She noticed it because of the handlebars, flaring out sideways like the horns of a Cape buffalo. He'd put it together from other people's junk. Just like the car, the contents of his house, he was a mish-mash of odd bits and pieces. She stopped the car in front of the gate and got out.

"Riempie."

She glanced at him. It was their first face-to-face meeting. He looked even younger, she thought. His hair was cropped short, she could see his skull. Her face felt warm all of a sudden. She was aware of the life she carried within her.

"I miss you," he said.

She opened the boot of the car and started to take out the grocery bags. *Don't hang out with victims. Give up your victim consciousness.*

"Aren't you going to talk to me? Can't you forgive?"

"You're forgiven."

"I know I hurt you, I'm sorry." He got off his bike and came to stand in front of her. "I can't love you, Riempie. If you were a Christian, things would be different."

She felt the pain of that morning all over again. "Why do you come here? You're over me, but you're not letting me get on with my life."

"Get over me, Riempie. Get over me so we can get back to being friends. This is messing us up. I miss you. I miss coming to the house. I don't understand why I can't be your friend. Why can't I be your friend? We won't have sex, I promise, and I won't come often. You can have a boyfriend. I won't interfere."

She unlocked the gate and walked up the path.

"Riempie, listen, Melissa's got this book on co-dependency," he called after her. "She says I'm addicted to you. You should read it, it's really good. It will help you get over me. Riempie!"

Dear Ulf

Thanks for the flowers and the lovely note. It's nice to be pampered at a time when things look so bleak. And thanks again for dinner the other night. I'm sorry if I talked your ear off, but you shouldn't have asked what was wrong. I've promised myself that by January I'll be over the fireman. I'll also be seven months pregnant. I can't tell you how I'm looking forward to this baby. It's the one thing right now that makes me get up in the mornings. At least I have stopped listening to Albinoni. But I cannot lie and say I'm not thinking of Storm. I think of him all the time. Sometimes I smile at the good things that happened between us, and sometimes I feel pain, like something hot's touched me. It happens so fast, I can't say where it hurts. But it's getting easier. I'll write a book one day about the virtues of therapy. Anyway, I'm rambling on. When you return from Oslo I'll invite you over for supper, and you'll meet my friend Alison and her new husband.

Take care of yourself, Ulf. Don't climb too many mountains, and I hope you find what you're looking for. Fondest, fondest regards.

"I'm going to have a baby, Ma."

Ateeka was in her kitchen rolling out pastry. Khadidja had come after work to have supper and spend the evening with her, also to break the news. Ateeka heard the words, but they didn't really seem to register. She glanced at her daughter sitting at the table paging through a magazine. "What was that?"

"In March, Ma. I'm going to have a baby." She stood up and lifted up her blouse. "I'm pregnant."

The light faded slowly out of Ateeka's eyes. "A baby?" She stopped rolling and looked at Khadidja from the neck down. Her eyes settled on Khadidja's belly, then travelled up to her face again. "It's true."

Khadidja nodded.

"But I thought –" She put down the rolling pin and sat down. "I thought you – the doctor said – you and Rudy –"

"Rudy wasn't tested, only me. The tests didn't really show anything, but we just assumed I was the one who had problems."

Ateeka sat still in her chair. It was too much for her to absorb all at once. The evidence was before her, yet she couldn't fully grasp what her daughter was telling her. "So you mean, all this time …" Her eyes burned with the next question. "It's Storm's?"

"Yes, Ma," Khadidja gave a wistful smile. It was the worst kind of news for a mother. "I've always wanted a baby, Ma. Over the years I watched Murida and my friends have them, and I would just be the aunty or the godmother coming with the baby seat, attending the shower, always a bridesmaid, never a bride, longing for that same cuddly feeling of motherhood. And now, this wonderful, wonderful gift. Everything I've gone through has been worth it. I might never have known I could have a child, and when I think I might have stayed with Rudy and always have blamed myself for not giving him children. Things happen for the best."

Ateeka picked at a flake of skin on her left hand. "I don't know what to say."

Khadidja took her mother's hand into hers. "This is the best thing that's happened to me, Ma. Don't be disappointed. It happened with someone I loved. I can't have him, but I'll have a part of him."

Khadidja left her mother's house and drove to Kloof Street. Alison's car was at the garage for repairs, and she needed a lift home with a friend. Alison got into the car with a steaming packet of chips. "They make the best chips on Long Street."

"I shouldn't really be eating these," Khadidja said, putting the car into first gear and driving off. "I've already put on seven kilograms. I don't want to battle afterwards. Murida took a year to lose the weight after Faried."

"How was your visit to your mother?" Alison asked, opening the packet, making it easy for Khadidja to slip her hand into them. "Did you tell her?"

"I had to. Look how big I'm getting. She took it well, but you know how it is. She'll worry about what people will say about her unmarried daughter. She wanted to know if Storm knew. I said no."

"I'm glad, Titch. I know it's better if a child grows up with a father, but Storm isn't the father you want. He'll be damaging to you both. It's not a big thing bringing up children alone today. Mary did it. With no manual."

Khadidja smiled. "Mary was a virgin. She had divine help."

"You have us. Your baby's my baby. Your mother will spoil the child rotten. You have a built-in babysitter. Kimmy will have someone his own age to play with. Maybe I'll get lucky also, and we can enrol all the monkeys in one school. A baby will be good for you. When you first told me you were pregnant, I thought, please God, don't let her consider an abortion."

They took the turn into Rhodes Avenue and saw a group of people in the road. "That's my house," Alison said as they got closer. "My mother's sisters. What're they doing here? Oh my God. Something's happened to my mother."

Khadidja stopped the car, and they jumped out. "Aunty Dorothy …"

A woman in a flowered pants suit, a fuller version of aunty Mavis, stepped forward, and clutched Alison. "Oh, Alison, we didn't know where you were. Thank God you're here. There's been an accident."

"An accident? What kind of accident? Is my mother all right?"

Aunty Dorothy looked at her sister, Charmaine. Charmaine put her arms around Alison. "You must be strong now, Alison. Prepare yourself. Your mother was standing on a drum in the yard trying to pick lemons from the tree, and fell. She was unconscious when

Margie here," she pointed to a young woman in jeans smoking a cigarette, "found her in the yard. Margie called Mark immediately, and the ambulance. Mark and Willie are at Groote Schuur with her now. We didn't know where you were."

"It's those fucking high heels," Alison said. "How can you go stand on a drum with high-heel shoes? What if she doesn't come out of it? I kept talking to her about those shoes."

Charmaine seemed to be the pacifier in the family. "There," she soothed, patting Alison on the shoulder. "We don't know if she was wearing high heels. It doesn't matter. Your mother's going to need you. You must be strong for her now."

Alison disentangled herself from her aunts. She looked disoriented. "Where's Leila?"

"We don't know," Charmaine said. "Margie knew where Mark worked and called him there. If I were you, I'd get to the hospital."

Aunty Mavis was brain dead. After three days in a coma, Alison, Mark and Willie gave their consent for her to be taken off life support. Alison took it hard, and stayed in the room even after the doctors confirmed that it was all over. With Khadidja, she watched the body being wheeled down the corridor to the lift.

"Did you see what they did? They wrap you in white plastic. Oh God, Titch, I'm going to miss her."

Hello Khadidja

Always I am smiling when I read your letters. I miss the Table Mountain and the good food of the Cape. It is a good place to live, and you are happy there. You need support, I can see, from good friends. And perhaps a good Norwegian man in your life. But you are not interested in Vikings with long hair who eat stuffed boar and maize. I don't blame you. Norwegians can be boring, and the men can make only pancakes. They are a bunch of atheists also which you don't like. But I must evaluate all what you have said. Why don't you come to Norway, and spend a month or two at my house in Trondheim? You are a talented writer, born with some gifts. You can succeed with the beginning of a new book in these blue-green forests. Perhaps the story of a Viking who is turning up all the stones for the right maiden. It will help you at least to be away from the people who put out fires ...

The doorbell rang. She put down the letter and went to answer it. Her heart lurched when she saw Storm at the gate.

"Riempie ..."

She stood for a moment not knowing what to do, then walked out to him.

"I just wanted to say hello. I'm filled with the spirit this morning."

She smiled at the innocence with which he said it. He'd gone to church on his bike, and had clothes pegs on the cuffs of his suit pants to keep them from flapping into the spokes of the wheel.

"It's a beautiful day, Riempie, isn't it?" His face turned upward as he breathed in the scents of her garden. "All this," he waved his hand at the trees and the flowers, "it's the natural world. We had a good service this morning. Underdeacon Bennett talked about how fleeting life is, how arrogant we are to think we can last forever. Really, Riempie, there's nothing here for me."

"What do you mean?"

"I mean if the Lord takes my hand now, I'm ready. I've had enough of this life. It's an empty life, Riempie. My life will start when I leave here."

She felt saddened by these words. "You're still in this world, Storm. The Lord would want you to be happy here also."

"You can't be happy. Look around you. Lost souls everywhere. People don't want to listen. They shut the door in your face. They don't want to hear anything. They don't want to know the way. We're sinners, Riempie. Only through Jesus can we be saved." He saw her look of disappointment and smiled suddenly. "You're putting on a little weight, Riempie."

"Am I?" she looked down at herself, holding in her stomach.

"Yes. But it looks good. Your face was a little too thin. You look different. Your cheeks are rosy." He smiled, a naughty, innocent smile. "You are beautiful, Riempie. Do you know that?"

Her heart warmed. "Thanks."

"What's happening with your book?"

"It's coming out in two months' time. I've got the proofs. I have to read them as a final check for the printers, and send them back. Do you want to see what it looks like before it becomes a book?" She didn't know what had made her ask him that.

"You'll let me into the house?" he asked, surprised.

"Yes."

His eyes searched hers, not quite believing his good fortune. "When?"

"This afternoon. I have to go to town first, to my mother. I'll be back at three."

"You'll make me coffee and everything, like before?"

"Yes."

"And we'll sit on the couch and talk?"

"Yes."

He got back on his bike, smiling. "I'll see you at three, Riempie."

She went inside and read the rest of Ulf's letter, but was still reeling from seeing Storm so suddenly again. He would be back in her house. Sitting on her couch, laughing, talking nonsense. She would show him the proofs, see how things went. Maybe there was a change of heart, a change of attitude, perspective. Maybe they could have dinner. Maybe they could start again. But as she fantasised and imagined them together again, her mood started slowly to change. By the time she was in the car going to her mother's house, she regretted that she'd invited him.

"Is something wrong?" Ateeka asked after she'd been there for an hour. "You've hardly said a word."

"Storm came to my gate this morning. I was happy to see him and invited him to come and look at the proofs of my book this afternoon. I don't know why I did it. I make all these promises to myself and can't keep them."

"You don't want him to come? I thought that was what you wanted."

"It can't work, Ma. He won't change. The psychologist told me that I blamed myself for Daddy leaving, and that I'm attracted to men who hurt me, and get into these relationships so that I can have a chance to fix the past. I don't want men who treat me well, I want the bastards because I have something to prove to myself."

"Oh, Titch. You mustn't believe everything these people say. What do they know?"

"They know, Ma, they see ten people like me every day. It makes sense. Look at my relationship with Daddy. I've been angry with him my whole life."

Ateeka put her arms around Khadidja. "I know, and there's many a day I asked myself when you girls were younger, if I'd done the right thing. But I did. If I hadn't left your father, I might not have lasted this long. I couldn't live with a man who ran after other women. There's a child you don't know about, a daughter. She was born at almost the same time as Murida."

"We have a sister?"

"Yes. A Christian mother. There's no contact with the girl, but I believe from an old friend of your father's that she's married with children and living in Jo'burg. My problems with your father didn't start when you were five or six. I suspected things before we were even married. I waited years before I actually asked him to leave. I wanted to be sure I could be enough for you children."

"You were always enough, Ma."

Ateeka's eyes became misty. "It's not like today, when people have babysitters and you can go out to work. I didn't have my mother, and there were days I had no money for meat, and would give you girls porridge for supper. But we ate. You had shoes on your feet. No one could say anything about my children. I never reported him for not paying child support. I didn't want anyone to say, *daar gaan Ateeka se kinders, hulle pa's in die tronk.*" There goes Ateeka's children, their father's in jail. She wiped her face with the corner of her scarf. "And look at you girls now. Murida's happily married and you're a writer. Now your father wants to be proud of you. Now he *can* be proud. Let me tell you, my girl, to have a baby is a blessing from God. If you don't want Storm to come, call him. Don't let him carry on coming to the house."

On the drive home, Khadidja thought carefully about what she would do. It wasn't a catastrophe that she'd invited him. She didn't have to be nasty. All she had to do was act normally, show him the proofs, then say she was going out. The sooner he left, the sooner she could forget he had been there.

She arrived home at twenty to three, and changed into a loose pair of pants and a denim shirt. She looked at herself in the mirror and realised that the clothes made her look even more pregnant. She took them off and pulled on her jeans. She glanced at her watch. Two minutes after three. She went into the kitchen and switched on the kettle. Everything was ready for a quick tea and dismissal. At ten past three he still hadn't arrived. Had he forgotten, she wondered? She tried to read a book, and read the same words over and over again. At three-thirty, she started to get angry. She went to the window to look out. There was no sign of him. The telephone rang. She stared at it for a moment, then picked up the receiver.

"Riempie, listen, I'm in the yard here with all my tools, working on the brakes of one of my trucks."

The receiver was pressed into her ear.

"My hands are all dirty. I haven't had a shower. I'm busy, Riempie. I'm wondering if you'll let me continue with my work."

It was like a little electric shock to her heart. "Of course."

"Thanks, Riempie."

"Not a problem."

"How's your mother?"

"She's fine."

"Okay, Riem. Take care."

"You are looking splendid, Khadidja. This pregnancy suits you," Ulf said. They were having lunch at the Kirstenbosch Gardens, after which they would look at a few houses in Newlands to give Ulf an idea of what it would cost to set up a permanent residence in South Africa.

"Nice and fat, you mean."

"No, no, not fat." His blue eyes twinkled. "You will never be fat. You do not have the structure for it. I know about the body, the different types. But I don't think you will put on too much weight, and if you do, you are a high-energy person, your metabolism will eat it up."

Khadidja studied his face as he talked. She liked to listen to Ulf, his way of speaking, pronouncing words. He had difficulty picking the right ones sometimes, and she laughed at him, but knew exactly what he wanted to say. "I think also this baby will be good for you. Yes, it will remind you of the fireman, but that might be good also. The baby will keep your hands busy. Your brain is too occupied, Khadidja, you think too much. Always you are thinking, and thinking up the stories. My brain can't keep up sometimes. I am thinking a woman like you was too much for that poor fireman."

"He wasn't an idiot, Ulf."

"Oh no," Ulf said in an apologetic tone, "I am not saying that. From what you have said about him, I think that he is a very creative person also. That story you have told me about him switching the battery from one truck to another, and the licence in the windscreen so that he does not have to pay for two vehicles to be on the road, that is quite creative. And of course, to know so much about the Bible, even with his own interpretations, I think that he would make, actually, a very good preacher. But there would be no business for him in Norway," Ulf concluded with a laugh.

Khadidja finished her lemon drink. "Ulf, why are we talking about him?"

"Because you want to, Khadidja. You like it when you can talk about him. I am talking about him with you these days while I'm here so that when I come back to Cape Town in two months, I hope you will be talking about something else. Perhaps about me. Today you love the fireman. Perhaps in six months you will love Ulf."

Khadidja laughed heartily. "You're funny, Ulf. You have no problems. How could I be interested in a man who had nothing for me to agonise about?"

Ulf smiled. "You are an interesting woman, Khadidja, and very clever. I will not become a Muslim for I do not have a feeling for it, but I have a feeling for you and whatever you believe. That is perhaps a solution for you with a man outside of your faith. You must have made the discovery by now that you will not marry a Muslim. You will put a man to the ultimate test. How much does he want you? Will he give up queen and country to have you as his wife? You have made it so difficult, that it will be almost impossible for anyone to get it right. I have no God to give up, Khadidja, and don't believe in the rules made by men thousands of years ago, but I think you can be happy with an old Viking like me."

She was comforted by these words despite an impulse to resist him. "You're not old, Ulf. We're the same age."

"I know," Ulf smiled, "but you have said that I'm too old for you. You like the boys with the fat lips and the hard bums, Khadidja. I do not have the fat lips," he pushed out his bottom lip, "or the bum. But it is easy to grow this hair and buy a Harley Davidson. I will have the twenty-year-olds after me then."

Khadidja looked at his mop of curls, almost platinum in the sun. He was good-looking, she thought, in a Scandinavian kind of way. Also generous and kind and very funny. Laughing had always been important to her. Why couldn't she feel something for him? "It's almost two, Ulf. Let's start. Did you want to see the houses in Newlands first, or the two in Claremont?"

Ulf took his glasses out of his shirt pocket and opened the real estate section of the Saturday paper he'd brought along. "This one here," he said, pointing to a listing of a house situated on a mountain stream. "It says a rock star owns it, it has many unique features. I have a feeling about it."

Khadidja had looked at all the houses he'd marked, but looked at the listing again, noticing the asking price for the first time.

"It's one point two million, Ulf. That's a lotta smack. Are you sure? You will only be living here for six or eight months of the year."

"I am sure. I am not worried about the money if I like the house." He closed the paper suddenly and frowned. "You are in need of some money for the baby?"

"Oh no," she said quickly. "And I would never take it from you. I wouldn't even ask my mother."

"Who would you ask?"

"No one. Maybe Alison. But I have money. Not a lot, but enough. I am going to live with my mother when my house is sold, and invest the proceeds until I decide what to do. Come, we'd better go. We have six houses to look at. I don't want to be in the sun all afternoon. I'm ready for ice-cream. Have you had those nice fat ones on a stick with the thick chocolate? God, Ulf, you haven't lived until you've tried one of those. I'm eating too much. Stop me."

Ulf smiled. He paid the waitress and followed Khadidja to the ice-cream vendor.

The real estate agent beamed as he entered the dining room and sat down at the table with Khadidja. "It's all in here," he waved a leather-bound folder.

Khadidja felt buoyed by his enthusiasm. One of her half-brothers was a real estate agent, but she'd given the listing to a stranger so she didn't have to explain why she was selling the house. Her choice of realtor had been a good one. He'd had one show house the previous Sunday and had an offer to show her.

"Am I going to scream when I see it? Am I going to lose money?"

"I think you're going to be pleased."

She watched him open the folder and set it in front of her.

"Oh my God!" she exclaimed. "It's almost our asking price."

"And we have room yet for negotiation if you give them immediate occupation, which will work out for you as you're anxious to move. We can use it as a bargaining point. They want occupation in two weeks. We can up the price by maybe five thousand. Is two weeks too soon?"

Khadidja looked around the dining room. She'd already started to pack things in boxes. "It's not soon enough. If I get that extra five, it'll help offset my loss. I paid transfer taxes to get in here. Now there's commission." She signed the offer and saw him out. "Good luck. I hope we get it." When he was gone, she called Alison.

Alison was overjoyed. "Congratulations! That was quick. When do you move?"

"In two weeks. Hopefully. I just signed the offer. They want immediate occupation. I asked for five thousand more."

"They'll go for it. Properties are scarce in Wynberg, especially where you are, on Rosmead Avenue. It's all working out. Who's going to help you move?"

"Moosa and a friend of his."

"Leila and I will also help. Will all your things fit in at your mother's?"

"No. Ulf just bought a house. I'll keep some of the things at his place for the time being. He's only going to live there for six months of the year."

"And Storm? Have you run into him?"

"No. No phone calls, no trips to the gate, and not a word from his mother. I'm glad. I'm bursting out of my clothes. It's very noticeable now."

"Do you think he saw the sign on the lawn?"

"I didn't have a sign. He has no idea I'm moving."

Dear Storm
By the time you receive this letter, I would've left Wynberg ...

She crumpled up the page and started again. The letter had to be right. It was the one she would stick in an envelope and send to him.

Dear Storm
By the time you receive this letter I'll be gone. Women have this mistaken belief that they can save men, and in the process, they make complete fools of themselves. I thought we had a chance, I thought love would prevail over our differences. When it didn't, and you broke it off, you said, get over me, Riempie, so we can be friends. As if I could switch myself on and off like a reading lamp. What did you think we were? We *were* friends. We had a friendship of children who liked each other, who liked to play. We had a religious intimacy despite our differences. We loved God, we wanted to be good. What screwed us was your inability to accept me for who I was. So it's too late now. You can't pull a plant out of the ground, let it lie around in the sun, then stick it back in the ground ...

She looked at what she'd written. It was corny, but love letters were sentimental missives from the heart. The envelope was ready. All she had to do was seal it, get in her car and drop it into his post-box where he would find it in the morning. She glanced at her watch. In an hour Alison would come and they would load up the two cars with her clothes and drive to Sachs Street. Moosa and his friend would come in the morning with the truck for the rest.

It was a cool summer's night. She looked around the living room – the rolled-up carpets, stacked chairs, boxes, picture frames, buckets and brooms. The ghosts had gathered. The house was empty and hollow-sounding, except for a roaring fire in the grate. She picked up the letter, looked at it a last time, and tossed it into the fireplace where it was sucked up hungrily by hissing flames.

Hello Ulf
Thanks for your offer to come to Norway, but I cannot bear the thought of being in a country where the sun will shine twenty-four hours a day, and in winter you have to wear a hat with a lamp on your head so you don't get depressed. In any event, I can't stand being on a plane. I wasn't able to write to you before, as I have been busy moving. I am living with my mother now, and getting bigger as I write. I had an ultrasound last week; the doctor tells me it's a boy. Of course, I am very excited. I have three months to think of a name. Isn't it funny, Ulf, my whole life I have dreamed of being published, my book will come out next month and it's something of an anticlimax. I think this whole thing with the fireman has dented me. I am feeling a little sorry for myself, but will allow myself this small luxury. In any event, I am comforted that I have good friends, and thank you for your nice words. I'm sorry you can't be here for the launch. Keep warm.

Khadidja looked at the gold-plated sign at the front entrance of the cottage she entered – *Anna Birnbaum, Psychologist*. Had the sign always been there, she wondered? She hadn't noticed it on her visits on Wednesday afternoons.

Anna met her at the front desk as always. "You are in a good mood, Khadidja. You look well."

"Thanks. I'm filled with the spirit of the Lord, as the fireman would say. Full of God's sunshine." She followed Anna into the inner office and lowered herself onto the couch. "It's a big day for me. I've come for my graduation papers."

"Your graduation papers?"

"Yes. A therapist can also become an addiction. This is the last time I'm seeing you. I've enjoyed coming here, but it's time to let go of your hand."

Anna smiled appreciatively. "You've been a pleasure, Khadidja. I've learned so much from you too. I'm sad when my patients leave, but also glad when they're ready to go. What do you want to talk about?"

"I thought I would do something different. I want to tell you a story, and then I want you to tell me what you think of the ending."

"All right."

"Once upon a time there was this ugly little girl who didn't believe anyone could love her. She lived in a fantasy world, and all the boys she picked had to be the prince of all the stories she'd ever made up in her head, and all the girls had to want him. As she grew up, she met a few princes, a few knights, and even a king or two, but didn't love any of them. Then one day this ragpicker comes along in a rusty old bucket, and doesn't look like a prince, and doesn't even pretend to be one, but her heart does a somersault when she sees him. They play this game, *ringa ringa rosy* – a group of children in a circle – only it's the two of them holding hands, and they go round and round, singing and laughing. *Ringa ringa rosy, pocket fulla posy. Hush, hush, hush, we all fall down.* And the girl falls, and she cannot get up, and she looks at the ragpicker looking down at her, but he does nothing. He leaves her there crying. He tells her he can't play with her any more, and goes away. She cries and cries, and never forgets him. The years pass. One day, after a very long time, he returns to the neighbourhood to look for her, and finds her living by herself. He tells her he's been on this journey, over mountains and meadows, but wherever he walks, he keeps ending up at this log over a river, which brings him back to the same spot. He doesn't understand it. He has a compass, the compass works. He's made a terrible, terrible mistake."

Anna waited for her to continue.

"That's it. That's the ending."

"That's not an ending."

"All right. The girl invites him into her parlour. She wants to hear of his travels and what's happened to him."

"That's not it either."

"Okay. She sees him coming and shuts the door. She doesn't want to hear anything."

"*That's* the ending."

A week before her son's first birthday, Khadidja dialled the number of a house in Walmer Estate and waited for the telephone to be answered. When she heard the voice she wanted to hear, she replaced the receiver, put her son in his car seat, and drove off. Fifteen minutes later she pulled up in front of a whitewashed cottage in Duke Street. The windows were open and the smell of roast meat greeted her as she walked up the path. She rang the bell. She could hear the radio and voices at the back of the house. She looked about the polished stoep, the bench with the *Sunday Times* and a pair of reading glasses on it. A sound behind her made her turn. A heavy woman, dressed in black leotards with a dress over them and a scarf wrapped turban-fashion about her head, stood there with a wooden cooking spoon. Her eyes widened at the sight of the visitor.

"Khadidja!"

"Hello sies Hajiera. How're you?"

"I'm fine, Algamdu lilah. And you?"

"Very well, thank you. Is my father home?"

"Yes. Come in, please. My, look at the baby. Hassiem! Come see who's here!"

"I hope I didn't come at a bad time."

"Not at all. We take it easy on Sundays. The children visit in the afternoon." She reached out her arms to take the baby, but he had his hand in his mother's hair and refused to let go.

Hassiem appeared through the beaded curtain, dressed in green pants and a cream jersey.

"Khadidja …" He was shocked to see her. She'd never been to his house.

"Hello, Daddy." She came forward and kissed him on the cheek. "How's Daddy?"

"I'm fine," he said, trying to adjust to her sudden appearance.

"This is Luqman." She held out her son. "Luq for short."

"Marsha Allah," he said, acknowledging God's greatness. "Can I hold him?"

"Yes. Go to Grandpa, Luq. This is Grandpa. Say, hello Grandpa."

Luq looked at the face of the man before him – a stranger, but one with friendly eyes. He smiled suddenly. "Hiyo," he bubbled, and reached out his chubby arms.

Hassiem took his grandson and held him proudly. His gaze went from mother to son. "His hair," Hassiem said as he stroked the sleek copper strands.

"He looks like his father," Khadidja said.

Hassiem looked at her briefly, and for just an instant she saw the question there, the question no one asked. "He looks like you too. This little frown here, and the mouth. We saw his pictures at Murida's the other day."

"Daddy was there?"

"Yes. We went for supper last Sunday. We got all the news."

She felt guilty. Murida never forgot a birthday or anniversary, and it had been her father's sixty-sixth birthday on February 27th.

"Let me go and check on the chicken," Hajiera said, excusing herself. "You *must* stay for lunch."

"Thanks." Khadidja had never had a conversation with Hajiera except to greet her when they'd met at family functions, and felt a kindness towards this woman who'd lasted the longest in her father's life. There was someone to give him his tea, iron his shirts, and be a comfort to him in his twilight years. She followed him into the dining room.

"You were out this way?" he asked.

"No. I came specially to see Daddy." She looked at the photographs on the sideboard – pictures of Murida and her family, the baby Mustakim, the other grandchildren – and took a chair opposite him. "Luq's turning one next Sunday. We're having a little party for him at the house. Just the family. We'll have a clown for the children. Daddy remembers Alison? She has twin girls now, six months old. She'll be there also. Her daughter, Leila, is leaving for Washington. It's sort of a party for everyone. I would like Daddy to come."

~

On a hot day in March, a white van with the words 3-IN-1 GAR-DENING AND LAWN SERVICE painted in green letters on its side cruised along the mountainous M3, and came to a stop at Rhodes Avenue. The driver was nervous, he kept looking at a scrap of paper in his left hand with an address scribbled on it. A just-breaking news bulletin on the radio cut into his thoughts ... *the votes are in. The African National Congress is now the official government of South Africa!*

He listened to the news, then changed the station to one playing classical music. The lights changed. He turned left and travelled up a leafy avenue. Half a mile along he made a right turn off Rhodes, a left, drove all the way up to the top and stopped at a gate with the number 3 on it. There were no other gates, no houses. He resettled his sunglasses, got out and crossed the road. He stopped at the gate, undecided, then slipped his hand through the wooden slats. The latch clicked open. He followed the curve of the driveway, coming suddenly upon a biscuit-coloured house in a clearing of tall oaks and pine trees. He was in the middle of the forest, in a magical setting – chocolate brown and green, a stream running down alongside. He saw the woman under the tree near the front door picking fruit. She was dressed in jeans and a white T-shirt, with hair reaching into the small of her back.

"Mom!" he heard a voice above him. He looked up and saw a boy dangling from a tree.

The woman turned. The plums dropped from her hands.

"Riempie ..."

The woman stood mesmerised. The boy clambered down and came to stand next to her. "Mom, who's this?"

The man stared at the boy.

The woman watched him. She saw his eyes change. She watched him take a step back, turn, and walk slowly down the driveway. For a terrifying, heart-stopping moment, she wanted to run after him.

"Mom, what's wrong? Do you know that man? He called you Riempie."

She tousled his hair. "I don't know him. I think he had the wrong address."

I didn't sleep with Ulf that night, I stayed in the attic. Ulf didn't ask why. He never asks. I stay with Ulf because he makes me laugh, and keeps me interested with his knowledge of things, his wit, his vulnerabilities, the way he loves my son. Every day stands separate from the one before it and the one to come. We go to concerts and plays and to places far away. Our life is quiet. There're no witches, no wolves, no angry kings or lost little girls. Sometimes on Fridays he comes with me to mosque, and sits at the back against the wall listening to the imam deliver his message. He tells me that if he believed in God, he would be Muslim. I don't say anything. Ulf doesn't know it, but in his heart he is the best of believers.